A TRACE

Mary Minton has been ~~~~ ~~~~ ~~~~
Leicester Education Cen~~~~ ~~~~ ~~~~
include sailing and desi~~~~ ~~~~ ~~~~
been an avid reader. She has eight previous novels
published by Century. She now lives in Leicestershire with
her family.

A TRACING OF ANGELS

Mary Minton

ARROW

To Terence Cooper and Monica Delbridge
also Alex Patterson,
who talked to me about Ireland,
the Ireland that we all loved so much.

Published by Arrow Books in 1995

1   3   5   7   9   10   8   6   4   2

First published in the United Kingdom in 1994 by
Century, 20 Vauxhall Bridge Road, London SW1V 2SA

Random House Australia (Pty) Limited
20 Alfred Street, Milsons Point, Sydney,
New South Wales 2061, Australia

Random House New Zealand Limited
18 Poland Road, Glenfield
Auckland 10, New Zealand

Random House South Africa (Pty) Limited
PO Box 337, Bergvlei, South Africa

Random House UK Limited Reg. No. 954009

A CIP catalogue record for this book
is available from the British Library

Papers used by Random House UK Limited are natural, recyclable
products made from wood grown in sustainable forests. The
manufacturing processes conform to the environmental
regulations of the country of origin.

ISBN 0 09 921271 4

Printed and bound in Great Britain by
Cox & Wyman Ltd, Reading, Berks

1

When Ross Ferris set out on a visit to Ireland he had hoped in a vague way to recapture the summers of his childhood, which had been spent at the family's residence, Three Gables, on the east coast. It overlooked the bay at Killiney, which was spoken of as being as beautiful as the Bay of Naples.

Unfortunately, the house, which had been neglected during the past few years, brought unhappy memories of his father's behaviour, marring the happy times, and after two days he decided to leave early and visit his mother's sister and family.

His Aunt Eileen and his four cousins had shared his childhood summers and on the last week of the holidays had taken him to their home so he could go with them to the yearly Puck Fair.

It was the highlight of the holidays and he thought with nostalgia of those halcyon days when he and his cousin Brendan had been free to roam at will when they were ten or eleven years old. Oh the joy, the feeling of adventure in being able to do what they wanted without parental control.

Ross had not seen Brendan for two years, when they had both celebrated their twenty-fifth birthdays in London, which had happened to coincide with the Coronation of Edward the Seventh. It was certainly a day to be remembered. They had met up with some of the friends they had known at Eton and they had all ended up in a police cell. They had treated it as good fun.

Ross's father had thought differently and struck him across the face with his riding crop, calling him a stupid oaf. Bitterness soured Ross's tongue as he thought of his father's brutality, then he dismissed it. It was the present he had to deal with, and he hoped that Brendan would be able to lift him from the pit of boredom he had fallen into.

To his relief Brendan still had his boyish air of adventure and, slapping him on the back, said, 'Tomorrow, Ross boy, we'll be at the opening of the Puck Fair, livening things up.'

Brendan's three sisters were away visiting an aunt but there was a joyous meeting with Ross's Uncle Patrick and Aunt Eileen, and Ross felt renewed.

Unhappily, by the time he and his cousin were on their way to the fair the next morning the jaded feeling was back and he wished himself miles away. Not that he wanted to return to London. After spending a season of high living and going through a series of affairs which had gone sour on him, he had been glad to get away.

The fair was a big three-day event held every August to commemorate the day when, according to legend, a troop of Cromwellian soldiers routed a herd of goats, which obligingly stampeded in the direction of Killorglin, thus warning the inhabitants of the approaching army. Soon after, the grateful populace installed King Puck at the fair in honour of saving the town.

For weeks beforehand gypsy caravans lined the roads to the fair from all parts of Ireland. Ross had always thought it a lovely sight to see the barrel caravans, brightly painted, drawn mainly by piebald or skewbald horses, the gypsy women in their colourful clothes of red and green.

On the first day of the fair, called Gathering Day, the Puck goat was paraded through the town with great excitement before being installed on a lofty platform over the Market Square, where it stayed for the three days, looked after by caring attendants.

It was a part of the fun to be jostled about and Ross tried to show an interest as Brendan, who was well known and popular, was constantly hailed and stopped by friends. But in spite of being made welcome, too, Ross eventually excused himself, saying he had seen someone he knew and moved away, promising to meet up with Brendan later. He walked past stalls where vendors were shouting their wares. Those of dairy produce vied with farming tools, clothes, sweetmeats, fruit, toys and, of course, fortune-telling booths, and roundabouts for children. Then he came to pens where pigs were grunting, sheep bleating, cows lowing, and was wondering how he was going to endure staying on at the fair when he suddenly caught a glimpse of a gypsy girl through a gap in the crowd. The gap closed, but suddenly knowing he had to see her again he pushed his way among the people. When he did see her his heart began to pound. Maybe it was love at first sight for he had to admit that he was very much intrigued by this dainty creature, with her wild dark hair and raucous voice.

Yes, raucous, something he normally detested, so why should he find this voice attractive? A group of men had gathered around her and he edged his way among them. She had a tray of baubles, which hung from her neck by a velvet cord. On her right arm were looped fine silken scarves in rainbow colours. When she waved and called to people to come nearer, the scarves fluttered in the breeze. All who had stopped were men. She picked up a tortoiseshell comb with long prongs, the top cut into the shape of stars.

'A comb for your lady, sir?' In front of an older man she dangled a necklace of turquoise beads. 'A gift for your wife, sir?'

A man called to ask the price of the scarves and the gypsy spun around with the graceful movements of a ballet dancer. This was no ordinary pedlar girl. The man bought a scarf, grinned and reached out to touch her cheek. She drew back and, turning swiftly, held up another scarf and offered it to the watching people for a shilling. She sold seven or eight, and while this was taking place, Ross studied the girl. Although she exchanged pleasantries with the men there was nothing coy about her, yet she seemed to exude a sensuality that he was unable to define. Her features were neat, although in no way could she be called beautiful, but Ross thought she had the most interesting and appealing face he had ever seen. He decided at that moment he would get to know her. He stepped forward and fingered some of the items on the tray. Most of it was cheap jewellery but when he touched a bracelet in the form of a serpent he realized it was silver.

Stolen perhaps? When he asked the price she gave him her full attention.

'Now that, sir, is quality. I bought it from a titled lady, whose husband . . . ' she lowered her voice, 'does not think it necessary for a wife to have money of her own.'

'Neither do I,' he said.

She took the bracelet from him and put it back on the tray, saying in that case she had no wish to do business with him. Ross, realizing he was out of favour, smiled.

'I was teasing. I wanted to see your reaction.'

She held out the bracelet to him. 'You are forgiven, sir. Make me an offer.' Her impish smile was a delight.

As they began to bargain some of the other men joined in. When the bidding had reached ten shillings, Ross called, 'Two guineas!' which brought a gasp from the small crowd who had gathered to watch the proceedings.

'Done,' the girl announced. She held out her hand, palm upwards. Ross slapped it, as farmers did when making deals. He felt inordinately pleased with himself, even though he knew he had paid too much for the bracelet.

He found the girl watching him and suddenly she

said in a low voice, 'I must go, thanks,' and was away so quickly he had to barge through the crowd to reach her. He caught her by the arm.

'Please tell me where I can get in touch with you.'

'You can't.' She glanced at his hand on her arm and he released her. She hurried away and within seconds was lost in the crowd.

The next moment he heard Brendan calling his name. His cousin was breathless. 'A friend told me you needed rescuing. What's been happening?'

Ross looked at him in a slightly bemused state. 'Would you believe it if I told you that I had fallen in love since I left you a few minutes ago?'

'I would be surprised if you hadn't,' Brendan teased.

Ross shook his head. 'No, no, this is different. I've never felt this way about any female. She's a gypsy girl, selling jewellery.'

'That must be Rosin Dannet. I know of her but I've never met her. I would say she isn't a gypsy.'

When Ross asked why not, Brendan said, 'Gypsies have close family ties. She travels the countryside alone, never with the caravans. She has a pony and trap. She hasn't been around for ages.'

'Well, I want her and I'm going to have her.'

'I'm afraid you won't get her and don't think you'll win her with your looks and charm, old son. She's nobody's woman. I think you should forget her. After all, what is she, a pedlar girl?'

'I don't care what she is. I want her and I haven't failed to get a woman I want yet. What do you bet me I won't?'

'I'll lay a hundred pounds.'

'Aren't you being rather reckless, cousin?' Ross was smiling.

'No, because Uncle Edward, who has met her, said she was the first virgin he had known who was determined to remain one – and he should certainly know.'

The two men laughed, their uncle being one of the most likeable rogues where women were concerned.

Ross suddenly sobered. 'I'm serious about this girl. I must see her again. Where do you think I can find her?'

'I don't know and I do beg you to be sensible, Ross. According to Uncle, she's a will-o'-the-wisp, always moving from place to place. No one knows anything about her. She sells good jewellery from time to time, but where does she get it from?'

Ross touched his pocket where he had put the bracelet, feeling suddenly guilty. Had he been helping a thief to get rid of her spoils? She had hurried away after she had sold the bracelet. It did nothing, however, to change his mind. He promised himself, with a feeling of recklessness, that he would find her if he had to travel the whole of Ireland.

The following morning, Brendan told Ross he had several things to attend to but would be free during the afternoon. And so Ross had a leisurely breakfast with his Aunt Eileen, then the two of them walked in the garden talking about the family.

Ross said, 'The gardens at Three Gables are running wild. I didn't want to stay. For some reason, my father seemed to predominate. I know, of course, I'll have to go back and arrange for repairs to be done. I was treating the house like an enemy and it doesn't deserve it. We spent so many lovely summers there.'

Eileen sighed. 'Yes, before your father decided to *honour* us with his presence. Your mother would never have got into the state she did if he had stayed away.'

Yes, Ross thought grimly. His father was to blame for a lot.

Eileen and Ross's mother had both been born and bred in Ireland, both beautiful, but whereas his mother had been gentle, rather weak-willed and had used illness as an excuse in the years before she died to avoid his father's rages, Eileen was strong and had stood up to his father many times to protect his mother and himself.

His aunt said, 'Do you see your father at all, Ross? I didn't like to ask yesterday before you had had time to settle in.'

Ross was silent for a moment and in the stillness of the morning the humming of the honeybees sounded loud.

'Yes, but we are no more than civil to one another. I hate him, Aunt Eileen, and I would never visit him had it not been for the promise I made my mother to keep in touch. It's been the most difficult promise to keep. He refused to control his temper when he was with us, but I noticed he managed to control it all right when he was faced with someone who was stronger and more aggressive than himself.'

There was a silence and Ross, on impulse, told his aunt about Rosin, knowing she would understand. Eileen had once been crazily in love with a travelling salesman, who had turned out to be no more than a confidence trickster who relieved her of every piece of jewellery she possessed.

When Ross had finished telling his aunt of his feelings for the girl she said, 'I was much younger and less experienced than you, Ross, when I nearly died of longing for my vagabond lover, but I don't think that age or experience makes much difference when such a feeling possesses one's very soul. I do hesitate, however, in suggesting you find her. She is a gypsy.'

When Ross mentioned that Brendan had told him she was not a gypsy, Eileen said, 'But she is a pedlar girl, Ross.'

'I don't care, I want her.'

'Very well, find her, talk to her, see the type she is. Your ardour may cool. If it doesn't, heaven help you, because you'll go through the fires of hell if she won't have you. Even after all these years I have a longing to see Preston Rafferty.'

Ross stared at her. 'But I thought that you and Uncle Patrick were very much in love?'

'We are, but I know now there are two kinds of love, the kind where you live a comfortable, pleasant life, and the other kind where you exist in perpetual torment, not knowing if the man you worship will walk out on you at any time.'

'And if you had a choice now, which would you choose?'

'To live in torment, of course.'

Ross was so taken aback he could only stare at her.

Eileen said, 'Because, Ross, then I would be really living. Now I simply exist. I know exactly what your uncle will say when he wakes, when he leaves for work and when he returns. I know what he will say when he makes love to me at bedtime, and what he will say if he wakes up suddenly and wants me. I must sound brazen, but you are a man of the world, Ross, so I know you won't be embarrassed.'

He was not embarrassed, just extremely interested. He had never heard such comments from a woman before. 'What about the girls and Brendan – I thought your life was wrapped around them too?'

'Mother love is yet a different kind of emotion. When they were young I would have killed to protect them from harm. I probably would now but I am not so possessive of them as I was in the past. I accept their faults, their selfishness. I was looking forward to the girls coming home from school, but they wanted to spend two weeks at their aunt's house. Six cousins from various families have birthdays with the subsequent parties. Who could blame the girls? I would have been the same.' She suddenly laughed. 'I'm looking forward to seeing their faces when they know that you have been staying with us. They'll be furious not to have been here.'

'You didn't tell them?'

'No, why should I?' She gave a mischievous grin. 'We wouldn't have been able to have had the talk we've had now. There would have been a constant tug of war, each wanting to be alone with you. You are still their favourite. Now then, about this Rosin. Go and have a talk with her.'

'How can I until I can find out where she is?'

'Oh, I know where she is.'

Ross, stopped, feeling a restriction in his chest. 'You do? Where?'

'She's lodging with a woman called Queenie McKnott. If you come with me to the bottom of the garden I'll point out the cottage. It looks quite close, but actually it's about two miles away.'

Eileen pointed out a group of hills and gave him directions to get to Queenie McKnott's cottage by crossing fields and burns. 'It's no palace,' she said, 'but Queenie is a very generous, warm-hearted woman, who will give shelter to anyone who needs it.'

When Ross said he wouldn't mind if she lived in a dungeon, so long as he could see Rosin, Eileen teased, 'Oh, away with you, but don't come back roaring like a lion with a sore head if the girl has moved on.'

He grinned. 'You'll hear me if she has.'

Eileen watched him until he was out of sight, then walked slowly back up the garden path, hoping that Ross would not get hurt by his obsession with this will-o'-the-wisp girl. She loved him as dearly as she did her own son.

Memories of the day that she and her sister told each other they were pregnant came flooding back. How excited they had been, crying and laughing together. They shared morning sickness, quickened at the same time, went into labour together on the same day and, to their joy, they each had a son, born within two minutes of one another. It was their ultimate joy.

Their sons could be twins – not that they physically resembled one another, but they were so alike in many ways. They both had adventurous spirits. Although Ross had the stronger will he would listen to reason as Brendan would, and both were affectionate and generous.

Ross was a handsome man, well built, and had great charm. Brendan was much slimmer and although he was not attractive like Ross he had his own charm. Brendan had been engaged to be married when he was twenty-one, but the poor girl had developed a fever and died three weeks before their wedding day.

Ross had never once talked of marriage, but Eileen hoped he would not become so obsessed with this new girl in his life that he would want to marry her. She half regretted having told him where she was, yet knew he would have gone in search of her anyway.

Ross set out for the cottage. He vaulted gates and took burns in his stride, not caring if his feet slipped off stones and got wet. The grass and foliage were vivid green after a week of rain that had ended the day before he arrived. He revelled in the fresh morning air and in seeing the mountains already coloured with heather, the purple mingling with the remaining yellow furse, giving a golden touch to the scene.

He remembered when he was a boy walking with his Uncle Edward on just such a morning. His uncle had exclaimed, 'Mother of God, could heaven be better than this?' and after that, while Ross was young, he always thought of heaven as being like Ireland.

Queenie McKnott's small thatched cottage nestled at the foot of a hillside, her nearest neighbour being quite a distance away. A small herd of sheep, two cows and two goats grazed on the land in front while throaty hens rooted close by. A cockerel strode arrogantly among them.

It was Queenie who saw him first. She had happened to glance out the window as he was coming across the fields. She said to Rosin, a note of excitement in her voice, 'A man's coming this way and he's in a hurry, to be sure. He's rushing like a river through a gorge as though he's determined to push a mountain aside.'

Rosin, who was sitting at the table sorting out her jewellery, replied without interest, 'And who is he?'

'I know him now, but I can't remember his name. He takes after his uncle, who has the power to charm the very Divil himself. And a fine fellow he is, an' all. I wouldn't be a bit surprised if he's coming to call on you.'

At this Rosin got up and came to the window, then immediately withdrew. 'I don't want to see him, Queenie. I'll go out.'

'You will not, now. It's seldom I'm honoured with a visit from the gentry and I need your support. Open the door wider so he'll know there's a welcome for him. I'll just tidy myself a wee bit.'

Queenie, a big woman with a gaunt face, who wore men's boots with studded soles, thumped across the earthen floor to a press, took out a stiffly starched white pinafore, replaced her soiled one with it, then tidied strands of hair that had escaped. They were always escaping. She turned to speak to Rosin and found she had vanished.

Then a long shadow appeared on the earthen kitchen floor. Queenie smoothed her hands over her apron and went to greet the visitor.

Ross gave her a slight bow and said, 'Good morning, Mrs McKnott. I understand that Miss Dannet lodges with you. Is it possible to speak to her? My name is Ross Ferris.'

'So it is, sir, I had forgotten it for the moment. Would you step inside. I'll give her a call. She's just gone to see to her pony.'

Queenie went outside and called, 'Ro-shayne! You have a visitor.' When this brought no response, she cupped her hands to her mouth and yelled, 'Ro-shayne? Where in the Divil's name are you?'

11

'I'm here.' She came from the other side of the cottage, saying in a low voice, 'I don't want to see him.'

'Here she is now, Mr Ferris,' Queenie said cheerfully as she went in.

Rosin, her expression sombre, went forward. 'Good morning, sir. You wanted to see me?'

'Yes, Miss Dannet. I bought a bracelet from you yesterday and wondered if you had two more similar. I had intended to give it to a friend as a birthday gift, but as my three cousins will be home soon, and as I haven't seen them for some time, I thought it would be nice to give them a gift each.' The idea had occurred to him as he walked over the fields.

'I do have other bracelets in different designs I can show you.'

She went to the box on the table and began to sort through it. Queenie pulled out a chair for Ross. He sat down and thanked her but he was watching Rosin. She was wearing a simple pale blue cotton dress with a close-fitting bodice and full skirt. Although she was small she had a shapely figure. Her manner was different, subdued, a little aloof. Her dark lashes were long and thick and as her gaze was on the jewellery she was sorting through, he still had no idea of the colour of her eyes.

She laid out three packages wrapped in cotton and began to unroll the first one, saying as she did so, 'I'll give you the price of each one, Mr Ferris. I won't expect you to bargain for them.' Her manner was brisk. 'I did it yesterday to draw the crowd. Quite wrong of me, but I enjoyed it.'

'So did I. I'm a gambling man.'

She held up the first bracelet. 'This one is fifteen shillings.' The bracelet itself was plain, but it had an intricately shaped fastener, inset with a small ruby. The second one was a chain with several animal charms attached. She gave the price of this as ten shillings. The third piece was gold. 'Nine carats only,' she said. It was broad and embossed in flower patterns.

Ross studied each one, then turned to her. This time she was watching him and before she looked away he saw that her eyes were amber with gold flecks. They were beautiful eyes.

He pointed to the bracelets. 'I'm curious. It's not usual for a vendor to mix better goods with the cheaper quality. Am I allowed to ask the source?'

'I'm not a thief.' He tried to protest that he had not thought such a thing, but she interrupted him. 'I buy them from women in the bigger houses who sell for the same reason as I do. They need the money.' She began to roll up a bracelet in the cotton and he stayed her hand.

'I apologize if I have offended you, Miss Dannet. No innuendo was intended. I'll take the two silver ones and because they are all different I shall get the girls to draws lots for them, then there will be no grumbling.'

'They don't deserve them if they grumble over gifts,' she said, her voice sharp. 'And you obviously don't understand. I'll take the money for the bracelets, if you please. I have to leave now.'

He was suddenly incensed at the way he was being lectured by this slip of a girl. He said, 'And you don't deserve to trade, with your appalling manner.'

'Do you expect me to crawl for it?'

She picked up the bracelets, put them in the box and would have left had not Queenie barred her way, saying coaxingly, 'Apologize to the gentleman, why don't you, Rosin? Money doesn't grow on trees.'

'I do not grovel to man or woman because they have wealth,' she retorted.

'I mix with people from all walks of life,' Ross said, 'and I have not found anyone grovelling to me, nor do I want them to.'

'You obviously have never known what it is to be

13

poor or you would not be so condescending.' Her eyes blazed.

'I'll tell you one thing, Miss Dannet, I suggest you try to control your childish tantrums or you will end your days in misery.'

He saw her looking about her frantically as though seeking some item to throw at him when Queenie began to wail to Rosin that she had brought bad feelings into her home and that the evil ones would take some getting rid of.

Rosin was immediately contrite. She ran to Queenie and flung her arms around her. 'I'm sorry, Queenie, I truly am. I shall say five hundred Hail Marys and get rid of them.' She turned to Ross and begged to be forgiven 'for Mrs McKnott's sake'.

He said that for Mrs McKnott's sake they would forget it had ever happened. Queenie was satisfied. Ross felt quite pleased. Rosin was not only warm-hearted but she had spirit, which made an interesting combination. He would definitely not lose her.

2

When Ross returned he was smiling. His aunt inclined her head. 'So, all went well, I take it?'

'I would say so. Rosin Dannet is a firebrand but she is also affectionate. The ingredients suit me.'

Eileen McCoy frowned. 'I dislike the word "ingredients". It's cold-blooded. This is a flesh and blood girl. You speak like your father, who treats women either as cattle or objects.'

Ross became angry, 'Please, Aunt Eileen, don't ever compare me to my father. It's an insult.'

His aunt's head went up. 'And I think it's an insult to women to speak of their traits as "ingredients". There's something so clinical about it.'

'I'm in love with Rosin.'

'No, Ross, you might think you are, but this girl is just a challenge to you.' When he made to protest she raised her hand. 'Let me finish. When one speaks of love it should be softly, instead of which there was a hardness in your voice when you said she had the right "ingredients" to suit you.'

Ross groaned. 'When you describe it in that way you make me sound soulless. It's unkind.'

'Have I ever been unkind to you, Ross? I've loved you like my own son from the day you were both born.'

'I know, I know. I'm sorry, Aunt Eileen.' He took her by the hand. 'Come and sit down and I'll tell you about Rosin. I want you to see her as I saw her and I think you will understand my feelings.'

He told her about Rosin's anger when she thought he was hinting that the bracelets had been stolen and how she explained she bought them from women whose husbands did not allow them to have money of their own.

Eileen questioned that women in such a position would stoop to deal with a pedlar girl.

'Ah, but according to Mrs McKnott they do. She was in service when she was younger and according to her there were many lonely wives who longed for something to happen to lighten their lives. Many a woman, she said, would have a servant bring a gypsy fortune-teller to her in secret. Rosin apparently reads palms, cards and can read tea leaves, too, where the person is able to afford tea. She visits servants in kitchens, sells her wares and tells their fortunes. The mistress learns about it and Rosin is asked to visit the woman secretly.'

'It all seems very underhand and I must say I disapprove of –'

'She is a virgin.'

His aunt's eyebrows went up. 'She told you so?'

Ross grinned. 'No, the information came from Uncle Edward. He told Brendan that he had never met a virgin so determined to remain one.'

Eileen found it impossible not to smile. 'I must admire her for resisting not only his charm, but his wealth. He's very generous to his . . . lady friends.'

'After I had bought the bracelets, Rosin left. She had to meet someone. She travels by pony and trap. I'm going to try and find her tomorrow. I'll ride, if I can take one of the mares.'

'You can, but the girls are going to be disappointed.' Eileen drew an envelope from her skirt pocket. 'A letter came a few minutes after you left. They'll be home tomorrow, about midday. Your Uncle Patrick apparently wrote and told them you were coming.'

'Even if I do find Rosin I won't be away long. I'll go to the stables and see Paddy.'

'Ross, wait a moment. Don't you think it would be sensible to take more time to think it over? You have your own business, you are your father's heir and will be a very wealthy man one day. Your pedlar girl won't fit into your life, not even as a mistress.'

'Rosin would never be any man's mistress, I'm sure of that.'

'Surely you would never contemplate marrying her?'

'I might.' He moved away. 'I won't be long.'

Eileen stared after him, aghast. She knew he was strong-willed, but had never imagined he would go to such lengths. She was reminded of her eldest daughter Tara, who, when she was quite small, decided she was going to marry her cousin Ross. Eileen had teased her, told her it was manners to wait until she was asked and Tara had replied, without any arrogance, that she would decide when she wanted to marry him.

Tara was the beauty in the family, tall, willowy, with golden hair and deep blue eyes. Now, just turned eighteen, she was never happier than when she was socializing. She had had many offers of marriage but informed each man that she was spoken for, though she would never divulge the name of this secret suitor. It had been some time before Eileen realized that Ross was the chosen one.

Tara had a stubborn streak that could be infuriating at times and Ross was the only one who could bring her out of such a mood. In spite of this, Eileen knew that although she would welcome Ross as a son-in-law, it would not be as the husband of Tara, feeling they were wholly incompatible. Nor would Fiona be a suitable wife. At seventeen she, too, was attractive with her curling brown hair and green eyes but she was the studious one. She spoke French, Italian and Greek fluently and was determined to have a career. Ross did not approve of young ladies following a career.

Eileen often thought that Ashling, a year younger than Fiona, was his favourite. Although Fiona had told her when they were children that she was the ugly

17

duckling, the shy Ashling had a quality that the other two girls lacked. She had a warmth, a caring, not only for people, but animals.

It was strange that she had all the traits of Eileen's husband, Patrick, because she was not his child. It was Eileen's secret and no one would ever know.

Ashling had been conceived when Preston Rafferty had come back briefly into Eileen's life. Her husband had been away for several weeks at the time so she had known at once that it was Preston's child.

Eileen had christened her third daughter after Preston's mother and prayed the child would take after the gentle woman.

When Ross came back he said he had arranged to take Silver, the mare, and promised, whether he found Rosin or not, he would be back in time to greet the girls.

The weather had changed by the next morning, the sky was overcast and storm clouds were building up. Thunder was already rumbling in the distance. This pleased Ross. He had always found something exciting about riding in a storm and controlling a horse who was spooked, not only by the thunder but by the wind that had suddenly sprung up. The rain began with drops the size of pennies but within seconds it was a deluge.

Thunderclaps reverberated among the hills and sheet lightning flashed every few seconds. To Ross there was something primitive in the atmosphere and he experienced a wildness that he sensed was shared by the horse. As they approached a field gate he dug his heels in the animal's flanks, leaned forward and man and beast sailed over as one. He gave her a pat and they galloped on.

As quickly as the storm had started, it ended. The sun came out in all its glory, and steam from Ross's light jacket and shirt mingled with that from the horse.

18

He slowed the mare and, leaving the field, she settled down to a steady trot.

The scent of honeysuckle twined in the hedges was strong, and raindrops glistening among the foliage twinkled like diamonds. Ross felt that life was good.

With the end of the storm, Rosin was foremost in his mind again and he thought of his aunt's cautionary words. He would need to think things over very carefully before contemplating linking his life with a girl such as Rosin. He might lose the respect of people in business who mattered to him now he had branched out on his own.

His father, a merchant banker, had thrust the challenge on him. 'You have to prove yourself before I shall give you a position in my firm. Other people might be pleased with your report from Eton and your degree, but they do not impress me. I know of your childish escapades at college and I certainly do not want an imbecile working for me.'

Ross, although seething at the attack, forced himself to say calmly, 'There is a saying that all work and no play makes Jack a dull boy. I did play, but I also worked and got my degree.'

'No doubt by a fluke,' his father sneered. 'I need proof that you will be worthy enough to join my firm. I know you have money that your godfather left you. If you can increase it substantially within a year, without borrowing, I'll give you a position.'

With that he stalked out leaving Ross with murder in his heart.

Within minutes, however, he was planning his future. His mother had given him instructions before she died that if he needed help at any time he was to contact John Davies, an old friend of her family.

John Davies, a tall, quietly spoken man, whose dark hair was touched with grey, owned a large shipping agency. He invited Ross to sit down for a talk.

19

At the end of an hour he said, 'Well, we've covered a lot of ground and I must say I'm impressed by your interest and knowledge of finance.'

'And I am impressed, Mr Davies, by your success with investments. But wouldn't you say that it's mostly a question of luck?'

John Davies smiled wryly. 'There is always a certain amount of luck, of course, as there is in any business, but to invest one must have shrewdness and the ability to know when the time is right to buy and to sell. One must also have a gambling instinct, which I feel you have. There's a saying that before one enters the market it's wise to own one's house and to have a year's salary in the bank. You own Three Gables and you do have money behind you.'

There was more talk and, at the end, it was agreed that Ross would go to the office every day and that John Davies would help him with investments.

When Ross thanked him, John replied, 'You have your mother to thank, Ross. She was a far-sighted woman.' He paused then went on, 'We had been in love since we were young. Then your father came along with his smooth talk and stole her from me.' His expression became grim. 'Nothing would give me greater pleasure than to keep you from having to go into your father's business and having you under his thumb. It would be a small repayment for what he did to your mother. I could never forgive him for that.'

His handgrip was strong.

With a little luck, and with sound advice from John Davies, Ross had substantially increased the money by the end of the year. His father had had difficulty in suppressing his anger at his success but had offered him a position in the firm, as promised. When Ross informed him he did not need it, he had stormed out without another word.

Ross travelled several miles before he found anyone

who had seen Rosin. A farm worker told him she was up at the big house, telling fortunes.

'Good she is too. Saw a birth in the mistresses teacup last year before herself knew about it. Told her it would be a son and heir and, Mother of God, it was an' all.'

In the grounds, Ross saw Rosin's pony trap. He had a long wait and when Rosin came out of the house he stood watching her. She had two bundles and her box of wares, which she carried to the side of the house where the pony was grazing. When she was ready to leave Ross went to her. She eyed him with annoyance.

'I told you I wanted to travel alone.'

'And I told you I would find you wherever you went.'

'Don't you understand? I need to be alone because of my work.'

'Your fortune-telling, you mean?' He smiled. 'I'm afraid I am not so gullible as your customers.'

She looked at him with a penetrating gaze.

'If I tell you something about yourself would you leave me and let me go on my way?'

'Yes, if you tell me that one day I shall marry you.'

'You are connected in some way with money deals.' She was staring into space.

Ross smiled to himself. She probably knew that his father was a merchant banker.

Then she said, 'You have a hatred for a man. He's tall, well built like you. You have a resemblance to him. He's stern.'

This shook Ross for a moment, then he decided that it was possible she could have found out that there was enmity between his father and himself.

'The man I see with you has a small birthmark under his chin,' she went on, and then Ross was really shaken. The birthmark was hardly noticeable.

Rosin was still staring unseeing into the distance.

'You could not have known this by studying tea leaves,' he said. 'Where did you get this knowledge?'

21

She brought her gaze to him. 'It was the stones.'

'What stones?'

'They're called runes. A man who had lived out in India gave them to me. He told me I would be able to use them, that I had the power. He said they would bring me peace.'

'And did they?'

She shook her head. 'No, because when I looked at them I saw images of people. I was afraid and put them away. That was four years ago. Then last night something impelled me to look at the stones again.'

'And what happened?'

'I saw images of two men I don't know. This morning I saw you and felt afraid.'

Ross felt a coldness touch his spine. 'Why were you afraid? Am I doomed to die, or something?' He tried to speak lightly but failed.

'No. I could see myself involved with you and I don't want to be involved with anyone. I want to live my own life, be free.' She made to leave and he caught hold of the reins.

'If we are destined to be involved you can't escape it.'

She looked at him, her gaze steady. 'Yes, I can. I could die if I wanted to.'

He was shocked. 'Don't do anything foolish. I'll stay away from you if it means so much to you to be free.'

She suddenly gave her impish smile. 'Oh dear, you've misinterpreted my words. I have no intention of taking my own life. I simply wanted to point out to you I need not be bound to anyone. May I go now?'

'Yes, but I believe sufficiently in fate to know that we will meet again. Even the first three letters of our Christian names are the same.'

He released the reins. She gave them a gentle tug and the pony moved away. Rosin glanced back once and Ross was sure there was sadness in her eyes. When she had taken the bend in the road he started back on the return journey and, needing to think clearly, he kept the mare at walking pace. He had never believed in fortune-telling of any kind, but had to admit he was impressed by Rosin. He had heard of people having second sight, and knew of all the usual fortune-telling methods, but he had never heard of runes.

When he reached the open fields he set the mare at a gallop, and arrived back on the estate feeling dishevelled and ill-tempered.

Eileen, seeing his expression, said, 'So you were unable to find the girl?'

'Oh, I found her all right, but was thwarted by some stones called runes.'

'Runes? Well, would you believe it, I have some. My friend Maeve gave me them, she's an expert.' Eileen eyed him, puzzled. 'But I can't see how runes could thwart you in any way.'

After Ross had told her all that had happened, Eileen said, her tone teasing, 'I think you should forget your Rosin.' Then she added more soberly, 'I'm sorry, Ross, I'm being unkind. The girl must have been upset by her experience. Maeve made no mention of seeing any images. Nor did I see any. But then I didn't take to the stones. I'm too impatient to sit and study them.'

'Study them?'

'Oh, yes, that is the purpose of them. There is a spiritual aura to them. Before Maeve studied them she was highly strung, had awful nervous headaches, but when she came back from Mexico it was difficult to recognize her she was so calm, so serene. She said she felt this aura the first time she touched the stones. I didn't feel anything.'

'What sort of stones are they?'

'There are different kinds. Mine are the sort found on river beds. They're smallish, flat and are a soft black. They have a Celtic origin and go back thousands of years. White symbols have to be painted on them.'

'Such as?'

'There are so many different ones, and although each set of runes can vary, many of the basics are the same, a man, a woman, a child, the months of the year, a tree . . . I understand that the signs were used as an alphabet in days gone by. You can use your own symbols, too. Maeve first used hers as a therapy, but later she used them to help people with their problems. She is very experienced but it took years.'

'What kind of problems?'

'All sorts. You can ask various questions and get answers.'

'So it's really just another form of fortune-telling?'

'Not exactly, it's . . . well it's not like a gypsy reading tea leaves. This is a spiritual thing. It's more complicated than tea leaves. You have to spread a white cloth on the floor and cast the runes onto it. It's the position of them that's important and it takes a very long time to learn what the signs mean in relation to one another. I assure you, they do work.'

'But in what way?' Ross was beginning to sound a little impatient.

'Well . . . to give you an example, Maeve, who had been married for four years, wanted to know if she would have any children. From the way the stones lay she learned that she would have three and, as November was a month given she thought that she would have the first one that year. She had so much faith in the runes she started a layette, even though she was not then pregnant.' Eileen laughed. 'And guess what. In November she had triplets!'

'Oh, really, Aunt Eileen.' Ross was laughing. 'Do you mean to tell me that if I wanted to know if a girl I was in love with would agree to marry me I would get the answer?'

'Yes, if someone could read the runes for you. It's no good me trying, you need an expert. I'll get Maeve to show you. I'll try and find my set. I think they might be in the attic. I feel too lazy at the moment to go up and look for them. Meantime, I do think, in fairness to Rosin, you should forget her.'

His chin set in a stubborn line. 'I can't. Not yet, anyway.'

'You will when the girls are home,' Eileen said with a wry smile. 'They won't give you a chance to think about your pedlar girl. Go and freshen up, you'll feel better.'

When Ross came down, Brendan and his father were there. An argument was going on with Eileen accusing her husband of wasting money on a man who drank.

'No, Eileen,' Patrick protested in his gentle way. 'Danny MacMahon is a good worker, he cares for his family, but just once he got into debt and I gave him the amount to get him back on an even keel.'

'It was foolish,' his wife protested. 'He would simply go and spend it on drink.'

'He wouldn't. I know Danny. He gave me his word he would stop drinking for a while so he could pay me back and he will. He's an honourable man.'

Eileen sighed. 'Oh, Patrick, you'll always be a fool with money.'

Ross, who had stayed in the background not wanting to intrude, was not sure whose side he was on. His uncle was a caring man who looked after his tenants. He knew every family, the names of their children, and parents told him their problems. He kept the rents as low as possible, and was well respected and, in many cases, loved by the older people. There were always some people, however, who took advantage of his generosity. Some landowners disagreed with his methods, not realizing that Patrick's good will kept down a lot of tensions. When the argument seemed at an end Ross went forward.

Brendan got up, smiling. 'So what mischief did you get up to this morning?'

25

It was Eileen who replied. 'None. Ross and I have had a nice long chat and caught up on all the news of the family.'

Patrick said amiably, 'And what skeletons did you bring out of the cupboard?'

Ross, thinking of his aunt's secret, replied lightly, 'I should imagine they've all been dug up by now. Past generations took great pleasure in unearthing them.'

Brendan began, 'I remember my grandmother telling me —'

But his mother interrupted, 'Just look at the sky. I hope the girls won't arrive in a deluge.'

Dark clouds were rolling in and before long it looked as if night were approaching. There was no storm but when the girls did arrive it was a truly depressing day.

When they tumbled out of the carriage, however, they were so full of high spirits, their clothes so colourful, it was like a sunburst.

Eileen and Ross, who had been waiting for them on the terrace, ran down the steps to greet them. Tara, who was out of the carriage first, greeted her mother briefly, then flinging her arms around Ross she kissed him on the cheek and scolded him for not letting them know he was coming to stay.

'You are a dreadful man, cousin Ross. If Papa had not informed us of your visit we might have missed seeing you.'

He held her at arm's-length, smiling. 'I am here for another week and knew you would be home by then.'

Fiona drawled as she pulled Tara away, 'May we be allowed to greet our cousin?' She held her cheek for Ross to kiss then added, 'Dear Tara must always have the lion's share.' She stepped back and pulled Ashling forward, saying to Ross, 'And now greet your favourite cousin.'

Ross, aware of Eileen's startled look and Tara's annoyance, gave Ashling a big hug and held her close for a moment. Her cheeks were pink when he released her.

As they went up the steps, Tara linked her arm through Ross's in a more proprietary way than usual and he decided he would have to be careful not to encourage her at all.

Everyone sat down to lunch and there was a lovely convivial atmosphere as they ate in lamplight, all contributing to the talk, but with Tara and Fiona holding sway, telling them about the parties they had attended and giving them news of the relatives they had met and who had sent special messages. Although Tara had kept casting saucy glances at Ross during the meal she was on her best behaviour afterwards.

That is, until bedtime, when Ross, returning from the bathroom to his room, found her in his bed.

3

Ross, furious, went over to the bed and grabbed Tara by the shoulder. 'I'm going out of here and if you haven't gone by the time I return I swear I shall drag you –'

'Ooh, lovely.' She looked coyly at him. 'A caveman.'

'I hadn't finished. I shall drag to your parents' bedroom and tell them of your behaviour.'

Her expression changed. 'No, Ross, no. I'll go, I promise. It was Fiona's fault, she dared me to do it. It was just a silly jest.'

Tara made to get out of bed and he picked up her dressing gown and threw it at her. 'Then she's as big a fool as you. I'll talk to you both in the morning after breakfast. I'll be on the terrace.' He stormed out.

It was difficult to settle. Uppermost in his mind, of course, was the image of Rosin. When would he see her again? Perhaps if he called on Mrs McKnott he might learn more about her. Then he suddenly thought of his Uncle Edward, who had apparently met her. He was in Paris at the moment but was due back in a day or two. He would have a word with him when he returned.

Ross spent a terrible night, tossing and turning and was wide awake at six o'clock. He lay until nearly seven and was not in the best of moods when he went downstairs. To his surprise Tara and Fiona were out on the terrace. It was cool for August, with the sun constantly disappearing behind heavy clouds. Tara had a rather forlorn look and for a moment he felt sorry for the way he had treated her the night before. Then he noticed a look of defiance on Fiona's face and he greeted them coldly.

'I didn't expect to see you both up so early.'

'We couldn't sleep,' Tara replied in a low voice.

Fiona stared at Ross. 'I slept. Tara woke me.'

Ross squared his shoulders. 'I haven't much to say but I want you to get into your heads that if you still want to get up to silly pranks I am not going to be a part of them.' To Fiona he added, 'I've always thought of you as a sensible girl and I'm surprised that you would want to put me in such a compromising situation.'

Her head went up. 'Nothing happened.'

'No, but just think if your father had come to my room and Tara was in my bed . . . '

'But he didn't, did he? So why make such a fuss?'

'If you don't know I won't pursue it. But for heaven's sake take that hoity-toity look off your face. It doesn't become you.'

She flushed a deep red. 'Nor are you improved by making a fuss over a bit of fun.'

'If you call that fun I suggest you keep it for a boy your own age.' To Tara he added, 'And if you take my advice you'll keep to your own bed or you'll soon get yourself a bad name.'

With that he walked away, knowing at the same time it would have been foolish to have treated the incident as a prank. Tara was a born coquette and would have to be controlled.

He set off across the garden. Soon he heard someone call his name. He was not sure whether it was Tara or Fiona but, not being in the mood to talk to either, he kept on walking. Then the voice called, 'Ross, wait. *Please*,' and he realized it was Ashling. He stopped and turned.

When she reached him she paused to get her breath. 'Fiona sent me to ask if you would come back and talk to Tara. She's sobbing her heart out.' He made no reply and she pleaded with him. 'You are here for a holiday, Ross. We were looking forward to it. If there's an atmosphere it will be terrible for all of us.'

'Yes, of course. Come along.'

He went charging away and Ashling kept giving little running steps to keep up with him. Eventually she said, 'Fiona told me briefly what had happened. It was foolish of them but no harm has been done.' She paused, then went on, 'You never used to be bad-tempered, Ross. What's happened? Are you in love?'

It startled him. Well, well, discerning Ashling. He slowed. 'I don't want to discuss it.'

Ross felt annoyed with himself for giving way to temper, realizing now that because things had not gone the way he wanted the day before he had vented his anger on the girls.

Tara, who was sitting at one of the tables at the end of the terrace, looked up as they approached, her eyes swimming with tears. Fiona was standing behind her gripping her shoulder, looking as if she were ready to fight for her sister if need be. Ross sat on a chair beside Tara and took her hands in his.

'Oh, come on,' he coaxed. 'There's no need to weep.'

It was Fiona who replied, 'You were very hurtful.'

Ross wanted to point out that he was speaking to Tara, but said instead, with a grin, 'Judging by the quarrels I've heard between the two of *you* in the past, my comments were mild.'

Tara gave a brief smile, followed by a hiccupping sob. Fiona shrugged and appeared to relax a little, but she did say, 'I still feel you could have been less harsh.'

He kept smiling. 'If I had, the incident would soon have been forgotten.'

'I think you're right,' Tara said as she wiped her tears away. She gave a sudden little giggle. 'I was quite enjoying it.'

'You would, of course,' Fiona retorted. 'I must have

been mad to have given in to your pleading.' She turned to Ross. 'I'm sorry I behaved so stupidly. I shouldn't have listened to Tara's harebrained idea.'

Tara sat up. 'It wasn't my idea. You suggested it.'

'I did not. It was you who mentioned the bedroom scene. You said you thought it would be fun.'

'You're wrong. You first talked about it while you were getting dressed. I can remember you saying –'

Ross said, 'Let us forget it, shall we? I can hear voices. The family are coming down to breakfast. We must try and act normally.'

Eileen came out onto the terrace. 'I couldn't believe it when I saw you all. Have you been to bed?'

'Oh, yes,' Fiona said. 'We all just happened to wake early. We've been for a walk and, speaking for myself, I'm ready for breakfast.'

Eileen led the way into the breakfast room. After Ross had greeted his uncle and Brendan and they had all sat down at the table, Ross could not help putting his cousins into catagories: Tara the coquette, Fiona the schemer and Ashling the discerner. And where did he fit in? He decided there were a number of categories that could accommodate him. He was quick to anger. But then he was quick to get over his outbursts. When he had seen Tara so tearful he had wanted to take her in his arms. So, he had a soft spot he had not really been aware of. He was strongly attracted to women. He had had too many affairs. He had a bad habit of rushing into them without weighing up the women . . . and a big fault of tiring of them quickly. But, he had never been so obsessed with anyone before as he was with Rosin. Would he tire of her once he really got to know her? No, he was positive about that.

Ross came back to the present when Eileen said, 'Ladies and gentlemen, my nephew is in a trance. We must find out what he's dreaming of.'

'A princess and a fairy-godmother,' he replied

31

promptly, and tried not to smile as everyone stopped eating.

Patrick, who was as amiable at breakfast as he was at bedtime, said, 'I'm not sure where to find a princess but I can offer you a fairy-godmother.' He looked fondly at his wife. 'My dear Eileen can provide anything we need.'

Eileen pulled a face. 'I can produce a lost cuff link or a clean shirt on demand, but I do not possess any magic.'

'Oh, but you do, my love.' Patrick patted her hand, then he cut and speared a piece of bacon. 'You can take a load of worry off my shoulders with only a few gentle words.'

Brendan grinned. 'All we need now to make the fairy-tale complete is a golden carriage and four snow-white ponies . . . or is it six?'

Tara, who had never taken her gaze from Ross, said softly, 'Ross would carry his princess on a horse with him and they would gallop into the sunset.'

Fiona replied wryly, 'He would probably want to show her what a good rider he was and, in taking too high a fence, they would end up in the ditch.'

The men laughed; Tara wailed, 'That's a mean thing to say.'

Brendan teased her. 'Fiona wouldn't recognize a happy ending if she saw one. She always hated fairy-tales.'

Ashling, speaking for the first time since they had sat down to breakfast, said gently, 'She didn't really. It was just that she shone at school and talking about fairy-tales was thought to be for young children.'

'That's nonsense,' Eileen protested. 'Grown-ups enjoy them as much as children. Pantomimes are always sold out.'

'Because parents go to please their children,' declared Fiona.

'No,' said Ashling, 'we have gone with other people our own age, and although some of the men have derided pantomime, they too have been quiet at the romantic parts. Without the magic of fairy-tales we would miss a great deal in life.'

Brendan clapped. 'Hear, hear! Good old Ashling.' He looked round the table. 'Who started this anyway?'

Ross put up his hand. 'Guilty.'

'Case dismissed,' said Patrick as he laid down his knife and fork. 'So what plans have the prince, the princesses and the fairy-godmother for today?'

Ross said quickly, 'The prince has an appointmemnt this morning but is free this afternoon. Or he can switch if necessary.'

Eileen looked up. 'I thought we might call on Maeve. She can tell us about the runes, and the afternoon would suit her. She seldom gets up before eleven o'clock.'

Tara said, 'You had some of those stones, Mama. Fiona was getting to be quite good at them.'

Eileen said they were probably in the attic and Tara said happily, 'Then we'll find them.'

Ross, knowing that Brendan had a busy day ahead of him, had thought of trying to visit Queenie McKnott to find out more about Rosin, so was glad that the sisters were all friendly again and had something to occupy them.

Tara was the only one who wanted to know who he had an appointment with and when he made no attempt to enlighten her and she persisted, she was roundly scolded by her mother who told her it was none of her business, adding, 'I'm afraid you are getting a little out of hand, Tara. If you don't mend your ways, we'll have to see about sending you to Great-Aunt Henrietta.'

'No, Mama, please. I promise not to poke my nose into anyone's business from now on.' There was an imp of mischief in her eyes and Ross smiled to himself. Tara was Tara and he really didn't want her to change. She still hadn't quite grown up. He felt he had been an adult since he was twelve years old when his father had thrashed him soundly for taking a piece of cake from the pantry. Useless to explain that Cook had given him permission. Yes, that was definitely when he had grown up, realizing fully the inhumanity of man, the injustice of being punished for something for which he had not been guilty.

The day had brightened when he left the house to walk to Queenie McKnott's cottage. He prayed Rosin would be there and settle his restless urge to see her again.

Unfortunately she was not, and Queenie said she was not expecting her for two or three days. She pushed some strands of hair into her bun and apologized for not seeing him coming.

'I was busy knitting. I'm making Rosin a cardigan. Autumn will soon be here. Sit you down and I'll get you a cold drink.' Knowing she would take it as a slight if he refused the drink he sat down. She was back in seconds. 'There now, and good health to you, sir.'

Ross held up the mug. 'And to you, Mrs McKnott.' He pulled out a chair and asked if she would join him, there were one or two things he would like to ask her about Rosin.

She sat down but shook her head saying, 'Now then, that lovely girl's life is a closed book. I have no idea where her home is or if indeed she has a family. She never mentions her parents or any brothers or sisters. The only people she talks about are the ones she meets during her travels. Even then she never says much and certainly never says anything but good about them.'

Ross shook his head. 'It's not right that she travels alone. There are men of all kinds who roam the country-side who would think nothing of molesting a girl.'

Queenie chuckled. 'Oh, she has an answer for that sort. When I talked about such a thing she pulled out a knife from a sheath at her waist and said, "A small stab of this in a part they hold most dear soon cools

34

their ardour." Pardon the frankness of the words, sir, but I felt it would set your mind at rest.' She leaned forward in a confidential way and added, 'I knew when I saw you with her that you had a fondness for her.'

'Yes, I do, Mrs McKnott. I can't get her out of my mind. Just talking to you about her brings her closer.'

'Come any time, Mr Ferris, sir. I'll be glad to talk of Rosin. She's been good to me and I think of her as a daughter. Didn't have a daughter of my own and my two sons went to Australia to find jobs. They also found wives and settled there. My mother went to visit them and stayed there. She's dead now, God rest her soul. It was she who wanted me named after Queen Victoria and my father gave in to please her, but he never did like the name. Then my youngest brother started calling me Queenie and I've been Queenie to everybody ever since. But there, I'm rambling on about myself when you want to know about Rosin. Now what else can I tell you? She sells her goods but she never seems to have much money. Mind you,' she added quickly, 'she always insists on paying me for her keep.'

Ross said, 'She shouldn't really be short of money. She sells better-class jewellery, which she told me she bought from wives who wanted to have money of their own.'

Queenie nodded. 'She does so. I hear that she gives money to the poor.

'And I understand she makes money telling fortunes.'

'She's good. She looked into her crystal ball a while ago and told me that I would be seeing my sons and their families soon. And what happened? Less than a week later I had a letter from my elder son saying that very thing.'

'I only wish Rosin would stay in one place,' Ross said.

'She'll not do that. She's always talking about being free to go where she pleases. It's hard work travelling around. I assumed she's never had a proper home, that she comes from tinker parents. Mind you, I did think at one time she came from a better-class home, where maids did mending and so on, and that she had run away.'

When Ross asked what had made her settle for the tinkers, she said, 'Because she has such a wide knowledge of folklore. She knows many legends, knows birds, animals, trees, flowers.'

Ross hesitated a moment then asked Queenie a little tentatively if she thought that Rosin liked him.

'Oh, she does that, to be sure. I could tell by the way she looked at you. But, as my old grandmother used to say, "Love doesn't consist of looking at one another, it's wanting to be going in the same direction." And that, somehow, doesn't seem to be so in your case. I doubt whether you would want to go a-wandering across the country and Rosin, I feel sure, would not want to be mixing with wealthy folks in London. Marry into your own class is best.'

'I don't entirely agree with you, Mrs McKnott. A pauper has been known to marry a wealthy girl and a rich man a chorus girl.' He smiled, 'And, if we are to believe it, lived happily ever after.'

Queenie nodded. 'Yes, according to what we are told, but what is the truth?' She suddenly changed the subject and asked after his aunt and uncle and cousins, saying she had met them once and thought what a nice family they were.

Ross felt at ease with this gaunt-faced woman, and was surprised to find himself telling her about the girls and their little squabble.

'Ah, well,' said Queenie, 'they're all in love with you and you know what they say: it's because of men that women dislike one another.'

Ross chuckled. 'You're full of little philosophies, Mrs McKnott.'

36

'They came from my grandmother, God rest her soul. I lived with her, my mother and my five aunts and, as we lived and slept in one room, there was a lot of good things I heard and a lot that I ought not to have listened to.' Her face broke into a crooked grin. 'But I wouldn't have missed that life for anything. I never knew my grandfather nor father. It was my grandmother who got me into service, saying it might put a bit of polish on me.'

Some hens came in and began rooting about with their throaty clucking. She shooed them out saying, 'Sometimes I let them stay for company.'

Ross asked her gently if she had liked being in service.

'Oh, yes, indeed, I did. I had some education. The youngest daughter was my age and was very friendly. She asked if I could have lessons with her and because she was the only girl at home they gave in and so I had the use of books. Yes, I liked being there. Then she married young and I eventually married.' She paused then went on, 'Mr McKnott was much older than me and turned out to be not a very nice man.'

'In what way?'

'Well, you see, Mr Ferris, sir, I like to talk but Mr McKnott didn't. It got that he said to me one night, "Arrah, whisht, woman, get to your scratcher." It was early and I wasn't ready for bed, but having been told I was to do what my husband bid me, I went. This went on for a week then I rebelled.' Queenie sniffed. 'When he opened his mouth to shout at me I told him I was leaving. He could look after himself and the house and animals. I had my coat on when he told me to take it off and sit down. He never spoke to me for a month, so I talked to the animals. He died five years ago and I prayed he would go to heaven and that the people up there would make him a nicer man.'

There was such a simple faith in her that made Ross feel mean and undisciplined for having lost his temper with his cousins.

When he left the cottage it was with the promise to call again.

Before he reached his aunt's house he heard someone shouting, 'Cousin Ross is here!' Tara picked up the skirt of her dress and ran down the front steps with Fiona and Ashling closely following.

Tara, who reached him first, exclaimed, 'What do you think? Uncle Edward is home. He sent a messenger to say that he wants us all to go for lunch.'

'He's sending a carriage for us,' said Fiona.

Ashling contributed to the news by saying, 'There's to be no formality. We are to go as we are.'

All animosity between the girls had gone and they were children again, full of excitement for an unexpected treat.

Eileen was at the top of the steps, laughing at their antics. Tara was clinging to Ross's right arm, Fiona to his left, with Ashling walking backwards, all talking together.

'Isn't it just like being at Three Gables when Uncle Edward would arrive and take us for a picnic?' said Tara.

When they reached the terrace Eileen said with a grin, 'Thank heaven you came when you did, Ross, otherwise I would have had to send out a search party for you. We dare not have gone without you.'

Tara suddenly squealed, 'Oh, look!'

A beautiful carriage in a pale chocolate colour with a mirror shine was coming up the drive drawn by a spanking grey.

Fiona said, in reverent tones, 'Uncle must have won at the casinos.'

When they first drove away in the carriage the talk was all of the comfort, the lovely pale chocolate velvet

38

upholstery, but when Eileen mentioned to Ross that she had found the runes, the carriage was forgotten.

Eileen brought out a small black velvet purse. 'I brought them with me. I thought you would like to see them.' She pulled the drawstring and took out two stones. 'There, it will give an idea of the designs.'

Tara went one better. Taking the purse from her mother, she spread her legs and tipped the contents of the bag onto her skirt, saying it would make it easier to study them. She picked up a rune and held it out. 'How Fiona can make out that the sign on this one represents a man defeats me.'

Fiona explained it. 'The white stick represents the body, the parallel one across the top is the arms and the V above it is the man's head.' She laid that one down and picked up another stone. 'This one is the woman and, as you will see, the only difference in the head is that the V is inverted.'

Ross studied both, then looked up. 'I'm afraid I can't see why the position of the Vs made you decide on the sex.'

Before Fiona had a chance to reply, Ashling said in a droll way, 'I would say that the inverted V shows that the woman's brains are kept intact, and the open V lets the man's brains fly away.'

Eileen, Ross and Tara laughed. Fiona looked from one to the other in disgust. 'Really, I'm wasting my time. I found the runes really interesting but you three obviously haven't the brains to understand the first things about them. I'll put them away.'

Ross stayed her hand and said quietly, 'I'm sorry, it was probably very rude of us.'

Fiona said, with a rueful expression, 'I'm sorry, too, but I feel there's something spiritual about the runes and it seems wrong to mock them.'

Eileen gave a little shiver. 'If you feel there's something strange about them, we'll get rid of them.'

'No,' Fiona protested. 'I just feel it's as though they were trying to communicate with me. Believe me, they're interesting.'

It was agreed they would keep them and, with Fiona's prompting, they studied some of the strange signs, but left further discussion of them to when they had more space to spread them out.

Edward spent each year between his apartment in London, an hotel in Paris and a farmhouse that was midway between Killorglin and Killarney. He had spent a lot of money renovating the farmhouse, then extending it. It was now an L-shaped one-storey building with whitewashed stone walls. The front and back gardens were planted with shrubs only, Edward saying that he wanted to enjoy a simple life.

Although the furnishings in the house were simple, too, it had a homely air. In autumn, visitors enjoyed blazing log fires in the massive recessed fireplace, with stone benches on either side where one could sit. Edward, who was waiting at the door when the carriage started up the drive, came out and waved. He was a tall, slimly built man, his thick silver hair curling at the nape. He had clear-cut features and carried himself well. His eyes, which were dark grey, often held an impish glint. Ross had never once seen his uncle lose his temper. He was always immaculately dressed and at that moment was wearing cream trousers and a pale lemon silk shirt.

There was a joyous reunion, with Ross getting special attention from his uncle, who walked to the house with his arm around his shoulders, saying, 'It's good to see you, dear boy. The last time I was in London you were abroad. We must talk later.'

Over the meal Edward kept everyone entertained with talk of his travels. He had stayed in a château this time and gave such a graphic description of the architecture, the furniture and the art treasures that the girls

40

were begging their parents to take them to France for a holiday.

Eileen said wryly, 'When we are as wealthy as your uncle Edward then I think we might consider it.'

'I am not wealthy,' Edward protested, smiling. 'I would like to get married, but I simply can't afford it.'

The family laughed at this, but Edward said, 'That is how it is at the moment. I may not even own this house tomorrow, but by next week I might have bought a yacht or a palace in Venice, then you could come sailing with me and live in the palace.'

The girls, who were taken with the idea, were full of questions.

Then Tara said suddenly, 'Oh, we've forgotten the runes. We should cast them and see what happens. We might find out about the prospective rich husbands that Uncle Edward has chosen for us.'

Ross, who worried about his uncle's erratic finances, had wanted to talk over the situation but as it happened they did not even get down to studying the runes. A neighbour, a man with three attractive sons, called and the runes were temporarily forgotten.

4

It was evening before they got down to studying the stones.

A white cloth was spread on the floor of the sitting room and the runes were cast. Eileen started by saying that since finding them in the attic many things about the stones that her friend Maeve had told her had come to her mind. She pointed to the black stones, some with the white symbols uppermost, others on the reverse side.

'Maeve said that the symbols vary and that these here have been made by the person who gave them to me. You can make your own symbols, but the regular ones are more associated with an alphabet, such as the letters S, A, D, B, N, M. Others are near an F, the bars sloping downwards, a T with the top part sloping. There's a diamond shape, an R with a shortened right leg. I'll ask Maeve if she will bring her set one evening. The numbers of runes in a set can be anything from fourteen to thirty-one; this one is twenty-four. I'll give you a rough idea of what each sign stands for, but you must remember it all depends on what relation they are to one another when they fall. The ones that fall on the reverse side must be put back in the purse, shaken and cast again. This can be done several times. If you feel they are not working out, put them all back and try again another day. In my set everything revolves around the one that has a question mark on it. Any message received is a combination of all the symbols and what each one stands for. Maeve has a set where the central one means fate, and that speaks for itself. Now, shall we have a go at finding a message? Fiona has a very definite feeling for the runes. I find it a little uncanny. We shall try and work together. Maeve is always saying that it's an intuitive thing.'

Patrick said, 'I'm sure it's impossible to get a message for one person when so many people are sitting around,' and Eileen gave a 'Shush'.

After a while Fiona said in a low voice, 'I'm not really sure what I'm looking for.'

'You may not find anything,' Eileen whispered. 'Maeve studied them for months before she asked them any questions. She started by trying to sort out the signs and their meanings.'

Fiona said, 'When I first handled them I felt something spiritual about them. Now I'm not sure that I want to feel spiritual.'

'It won't do you any harm, sister, dear,' Brendan teased.

To which his mother replied drily, 'Nor would it to any harm to you, Brendan, *dear*.'

Ashling said, 'Please, be quiet. Fiona needs to concentrate.'

Another hush settled over the room and it was some time before anyone spoke. Then Eileen said, frowning, 'Nothing seems to make sense.'

Fiona pointed to a group of runes. 'This seems to indicate that a gentleman is suffering a money loss.'

Brendan chuckled. 'It could be me. I'm always overspending.'

Fiona made no reply to this, but a few moments later said, 'What do you think, Mama?'

Eileen said quietly, 'I don't really think that I'm qualified to work out anything sensible and I don't think we should continue.'

There was a wail from Tara at this. 'Oh, don't stop, it's fun.'

Patrick said in his gentle way, 'I still say there are too many people. If anyone were to go to a gypsy to have his or her fortune told it would be alone.'

'Perhaps so,' Edward replied, speaking lightly, 'but you must admit that studying the stones is most interesting. I vote with Tara that we go on. That is, of course, if Fiona is willing.'

It was some time before she continued and then asked her mother's help. 'This group indicates that two people are cheating. A man and a woman. Do you agree with this, Mama?'

Eileen had gone pale. She got up. 'I need some air. It's warm in here. Will you excuse me?'

Ross got up too, saying he would go with her. He presumed that the study of the stones would have ended there but it was voted by the others to carry on. There was a dampness in the air. The night sky had closed in and Eileen, who had walked ahead, was a wraith-like figure in the mist that was swirling over the land.

When Ross came up to her Eileen stopped. 'Oh, Ross, when Fiona talked about a man and a woman cheating I wished for a hole to form in the floor and swallow me up. I felt so guilty.'

'It could have meant anyone. Forget it.'

The next moment Patrick was there with a shawl, which he draped about his wife's shoulders. 'This dampness is penetrating, Eileen. You could catch a chill.'

'I'm all right,' she said. 'It was so hot in the room.'

Patrick agreed, then said, 'What did you think of a man having money troubles in the reading of the stones? Quite amusing, wasn't it? Maybe Fiona remembered what Edward said earlier about not being able to afford to marry. I had to smile at the coincidence.'

Eileen said, a bitter note in her voice, 'I wish I had never brought them with me. And I shall certainly see they disappear when we get home.'

'Why, my love?' Patrick asked mildly. 'The young ones were enjoying them and they do no harm. I don't think they should be denied this entertainment because we older ones are so sceptical about these things, although I was surprised that Edward wanted to continue.'

'Should we ever be surprised at your brother's behaviour?' Eileen snapped. 'I feel very cross with him. He flings his money away, not only on gambling but buying presents for all his fancy women. He's so wildly extravagant he doesn't seem to stop and think what he's doing.'

'Now be fair, Eileen, love.' Patrick spoke gently. 'He made it, he has a right to spend it and you must admit that he's never once asked us for money. In fact, when he did have big wins we all benefited – also the people who work for him.'

'I'm sorry,' Eileen said. 'It's just knowing that if he is in difficulties you will be the one to come to the rescue. You are always giving, Patrick, and we do have our own expenses, dowries to provide for the girls when they get married, the workers to help when necessary. The years seem to roll on so quickly.'

Ross, suddenly annoyed with himself for being so depressed, put an arm around her shoulders. 'I'll help. I'm getting on my feet.'

'Oh, Ross, I'm being mean, you have your own problems.' She pulled the shawl up to her throat. 'This mist is chilling. We'll go inside.'

The stones had been put away and Brendan and the girls were listenening to Edward describing a day at the races at Longchamp when he had been on a winning streak. 'Seven winners in a row! Then I lost every penny at the casino that same evening.'

'How could you bear it?' Tara wailed.

'It's all a part of gambling. If there had been no losing there would have been no excitement in winning.'

Tara said, 'Will you tell us, Uncle, why you never married?'

'Of course, my sweet, it will add to your education. It was because I was afraid to,' Edward was smiling.

'It's a terrible risk, you know. Having had quite a lot of lady friends I have found that after knowing them a while they are not the same charming people they were when we first met.'

'The ladies didn't change, Uncle,' Ashling said quietly. 'It was you who didn't want them to have any faults.'

'Ah, sensible Ashling,' he said. 'I put them all on a pedestal. No person should be put on a pedestal. Remember that, girls. Every man, every woman has faults and no man is honest.'

Ashling's head went up. 'My father is an honest man. He would never lie to anyone.'

Eileen felt a constriction in her throat as she thought of how she had deceived her husband and of the irony that it was Ashling who was praising him. She said, 'It's a chilly evening with a November-like mist. I think we ought to be going.'

Later, when Eileen was in bed with Patrick, she said, 'Isn't it strange that Ross and Edward are both educated, intelligent men, yet Edward hasn't the willpower to give up gambling, nor Ross the pedlar girl he's in love with?'

'Eileen, my dear, from time immemorial intelligent men, and women, have gambled and they have loved someone of the opposite sex to distraction. Some have taken their own lives, unable to bear being parted. I don't think that we have the power to change anything.'

Eileen felt her cheeks go hot. Although she and her lover had taken care to try to keep their affair secret, someone could have become aware of it and told Patrick. Ashling was a small baby and he had accepted that she was born early ... or had appeared to accept it.

*

The girls slept together in a bed large enough for six. At first when they got into bed they had talked of the exciting life Edward must lead, having travelled to so many countries.

Tara said dreamily, 'How wonderful to stay in that beautiful château. Do you think we can persuade Mama and Papa to take us to France for a holiday?'

Fiona was doubtful. Ashling said she would rather go to Three Gables for a holiday, reminding them of the summers they had spent there when they were younger.

'Yes,' Tara said, and thought there were times in those days when Ross would take her for walks on her own. That was when she had fallen in love him. If she could get him alone again how wonderful it would be. She could show him that she could behave differently, after that awful fiasco of getting into his bed – which was all Fiona's fault for suggesting it. Sometimes she had wondered if Fiona was in love with Ross. She had said she wasn't in love with anyone, she was not going to get married for a long time. She wanted a career. But she did have a lot of admirers and played up to them. It was very difficult to understand her sister at times.

Tara decided that when Ross was ready to go to Three Gables she would try to persuade her mother to take them there for a time. She might then get the chance to be alone with him.

Fiona regretted having suggested that Tara get into Ross's bed. She had wanted him to get the impression that she would slip into bed with any man, instead of which she had blabbed that she had not been responsible for the idea. Ross was no fool, he would have it all worked out that she was jealous of her sister. She had loved her cousin since she was a child, but had never had as much attention from him as Tara had.

She would have to try to get into his good books again. If they went to Killiney with him there might be a chance . . .

Ashling had been aware of undercurrents between her sisters from being very young, but had not realized until recently how antagonistic Fiona was towards Tara. Tara could be very silly at times, but there was no badness in her – not like Fiona, who would make very unpleasant remarks at times. She was obviously jealous of her elder sister, but why? She was very attractive and had as many young men as Tara claiming her attention.

Ashling was very fond of Ross. She would not be so presumptive as to call it love. She had had no experience. Young men were pleasant to her, but no one had attempted to kiss her. Ross had always been so kind to her, so gentle, possibly because she was the youngest and the plainest. She thought he would make a lovely husband.

Ashling's last thought before she drifted off to sleep was to wish she had been a little better looking.

The next morning, Tara said eagerly, 'Mama, can we all go for a holiday to France? Uncle Edward was telling us yesterday about the beautiful château. It all sounded so wonderful.'

Eileen was silent for a moment then she shook her head. 'I'm afraid that would be impossible.'

When Tara asked why, her father answered, 'Because it would cost too much, Tara. We just can't afford it. We have, shall we say, certain unexpected commitments.'

Then Eileen, changing the subject, asked Ross brightly what he was planning for the day.

Ross, who had been stirring his coffee for some time, his mind on other things, looked up. 'Do? Actually, I was thinking I must spend a few days at Killiney, arrange for some repairs to be done to the house and for the garden to be tidied.

Tara immediately pounced on this. 'Can we come with you, Ross? We can work on the garden. We used to help the gardener the summers we stayed there. He never failed to tell us we were good workers.'

Ross gave a faint smile. 'The gardens were well kept then. They were like a wilderness when I called on my way here.'

Patrick said, 'Now then, Ross, I've just been thinking, it might do them a world of good to put in a few days of hard labour. Keep them out of mischief.' He turned to his wife. 'What do you think, Eileen. It would not be costly like going to France.' When she hesitated he went on, 'You were saying a while ago you would like to go back to the house sometime.'

'I did, but Ross wants to see about repairs. We don't want to be in his way.'

Although Ross had wanted to be alone to do some thinking, he felt unable to say so. 'How could I refuse the help of three energetic young ladies?'

Brendan then asked his father a little tentatively if he could be spared for a few days to accompany them to Killiney and after some discussion his father agreed.

By this time Ross had abandoned all thought of having time for contemplation and decided to send a telegram to John Davies to see that all was well business wise in London.

To this Ross had a reply saying, 'Everything running smoothly.'

Eileen said, 'Well, that's good news.'

'I'm not sure. John always sends odd replies if everything is all right when I'm away.'

'Such as?'

'The answer to the last telegram I sent was, "Flowers blooming everywhere". The previous one said "There's a glut of diamonds". The one before that mentioned a choir. Oh, yes, "The choir is in fine voice". It's a little whim John has.' Ross folded the telegram and tapped it against his chin. 'I wonder . . .'

'If there was anything wrong,' Eileen said, 'John would have said so.'

Ross, feeling a little more settled, sent a telegram to his steward who looked after Three Gables, asking for rooms to be prepared and beds made up for two days hence.

Later, however, he decided he would travel early the next morning. The sooner he arranged about the repairs the sooner he could get back to London.

When he told his aunt of his decision she said, 'Don't worry about us, we've done the journey often enough and Brendan will be with us. But I think you are being foolish to worry about the business.'

'If I'm satisfied that I don't need to return to London I shall stay on at Three Gables.'

Although he had made up his mind to put Rosin from his thoughts Ross had a sudden urge late that evening to know if Queenie had heard any more about her. Once he had left Killorglin it was going to be a long time before he would get any news. He decided he would get up early and walk to Queenie Mcknott's cottage. She had told him that she started milking the cows at six o'clock. If he did not stay too long talking he would have plenty of time to have breakfast and get to the station in time to catch the nine o'clock train.

The morning was warm and sunny with not a cloud in the sky. Ross set out at a steady pace, vaulting gates, whistling with the bird chorus. One part of him made him want to stay, but the other part wanted to see Three Gables, in spite of the unhappy times it sometimes conjured up.

Queenie's cottage came into view and he saw her milking a cow. He paused to watch her and there was

50

a warmth inside him for this gaunt-faced woman, with her tousled head pressed against the animal's flank as she tugged rhythmically at the cow's teats. He walked on and could hear her talking as the milk spurted into the pail.

'There, girl, there, you've done well. 'Twas no good getting into a paddy. The little lad only wanted to pat you.' She drew the bucket away, made the sign of the cross on the cow's hindquarter and said softly, 'God bless you, girl.'

When she turned and saw him approaching she called, 'Mr Ferris, sir. Is something wrong?'

He came up. 'I know it's early, Mrs McKnott, but I'm leaving before nine o'clock and wanted to let you know and to find out if you've heard anything from Rosin.'

'Not yet, it could be this very day. I never really know. And you're leaving. I'm sorry, sir. I've enjoyed talking to you.'

'And I very much enjoyed talking to you, Mrs McKnott.'

Queenie said, 'I could ask Rosin to write to you, or if she didn't have time I could pen a few lines to you, if it's not a liberty I'm taking. I could drop it in at your aunt's house and she could perhaps send it on to you.'

'That would be splendid, Mrs McKnott. It's most kind of you.' Ross stood hesitant a moment then said, 'Rosin is rather a strange person. I don't really understand her.'

'I sometimes think that the good Lord himself must be a bit bewildered at his handiwork after he made her,' Queenie replied. 'I wouldn't worry about her if I were you, sir. She likes you, I know that. She ran away from you because she liked you too much. That's a good sign.'

He took both her hands in his. 'Thanks, Mrs McKnott.

51

That gives me hope. When I'm back in Ireland, I'll come and see you.'

'Take care of yourself. May the Good Lord hold out a hand to you if you need help.'

'And to you, Mrs McKnott. Goodbye for now.'

Queenie shaded her eyes again from the sun as he went striding away. A lovely man. He belonged to the gentry but he treated her as if she were his equal.

The journey to Dublin took Ross over seven hours. He had done it too many times in the past to want to take an interest in the scenery. He had hoped to enjoy an empty carriage where he could do some thinking, but at various stations there were changes of passengers who all seemed to be talkative.

Eventually, however, he had the carriage to himself and he went over his meetings with Rosin, starting with the Puck Fair to the last time he saw her when she had told him about seeing the birthmark under his father's chin. Not that she had known it was his father. At that moment Ross felt the same uneasiness as he had when he received the telegram from John Davies. He shook himself free from his depressing thoughts as he realized they were approaching Dublin.

When he arrived at Kingsbridge Station, he travelled by cab, which took him along the quays into the centre of Dublin and on to Westland Row Station to catch the Bray train to Killiney. On the platform he met a friend with whom he had shared childhood summers. Recognition was instantaneous. 'Ross Ferris!' . . . 'Liam McLane!' Hands gripped and smiles were wide.

As they talked they realized the coincidence of their meeting, with Liam coming a week later than he had intended.

'It was fate and nothing else,' declared Liam, a tall, slenderly built young man, with thick jet-black hair and vivid blue eyes, who lived about a mile away from Three Gables. His mother had come to call on Ross's mother in the early days and the friendship had grown. Liam had shared the cousins' adventurous spirits. No, he said, he was not married either. He had not met anyone he wanted to marry and, added laughing, perhaps he had been waiting to meet the girls, who were now young ladies.

Ross chuckled and told him he would get a surprise.

The small-engined train came puffing in, clouds of steam enveloping it, which had them full of nostalgia, and they spent the journey talking of the good times they had had. The railway ran around the coastline and Killiney station was at the foot of the steep rise where a road on the left led to the house and curved to the right to Killeney village and on to Dalkey.

Liam had said that Ross could share his carriage, but as it had not yet arrived they stood talking about the short cut to the sea that they had taken as boys, a mixture of grass, bracken, heather and rocks and boulders galore.

Liam laughed. 'I'd like a pound for every time we fell and grazed our knees. Ah, here's the carriage.'

In Killiney village were a couple of shops and two pubs, but on the road to Dalkey a large park had been built. As the horse plodded up the steep incline Ross concentrated on the left of the road where more houses had been built since he was a child and when they came to the part where they turned left in the direction of Three Gables, Ross felt ashamed that he had neglected it.

As the house came into view Liam said, 'It never fails to fill me with nostalgia when I see it. An imposing place even now. You'll soon get it put right.'

When they drew up at the gate and Ross asked Liam if he was coming in, he said, 'No, my aunt will be expecting me, but I'll see you tomorrow.' He grinned. 'I'll be with you for breakfast.'

'That's a promise,' Ross said.

From the gate Ross could not see the true condition of the house. It was a many-windowed Georgian building, the wide elegant front door with a beautiful fanlight, and with the three gables at the right. The gardens were wild, some flowers showing through the undergrowth. How could he have allowed it to get into this state?

There was no movement anywhere and he felt reluctant to go into the house. He opened the gate, put his bags inside, then, crossing the road, he walked to the edge of the rise that overlooked the enchanting bay. To the right he could see Bray Head; to the immediate left was Dalkey Island and further beyond was the jutting islet of Howth. In the curves of the bay the purple and pinks of heather mingled with the gold of bracken and the greens of ferns and grass. It was wild and beautiful.

The weather had been stormy the first time he had seen it and he remembered how awe-inspiring it had been and how, as a small boy, he had tightly clutched his mother's hand. Huge waves had come rolling in and had spread all over the strand, as though seeking escape.

His mother had said, 'Don't be afraid, Ross. Tomorrow the sea will be in a different mood. Your father says so.'

It had been. Then, as was now, waves rolled in slowly, receding with a gentle swish. Ross, feeling soothed, turned to go back to the house and saw Mr Colhoun, his steward, come from the side of the house. Ross gave him a wave and the old man raised his stick in greeting.

Mr Colhoun, a small tubby man, had been steward as far back as Ross could remember. He had been vigorous once but now walked slowly with the aid of his stick.

He waited at the front of the house and when Ross

came up he said, 'Well, there you are, sir. I didn't hear you arrive but I'm getting a bit deaf. My wife and daughters have seen to the beds and the cleaning. My wife's mother is ill and she's gone to attend to her. But there's a cold meal ready for you and she'll be back in the morning to see to your breakfast.'

Ross said, 'That won't be necessary, Mr Colhoun. I can manage to cook myself some bacon and eggs. Now I mean that; your wife has enough to do.'

The old man said, well, if he was sure he could manage, and went on to talk about the repairs, which had been discussed on his previous short visit. He pointed out once more cracks in the walls, paint peeling, window frames that needed replacing, and shook his head.

'It's sad to see it in this state but there was nothing I could do. Can't even see to the garden with my rheumatics, but my nephew will do a good job at a reasonable price. I'm glad you've come back, sir, before another winter. Don't you worry, we'll get it shipshape again. Shall I take your bags in?'

'No, no, I'll see to them, Mr Colhoun. You go home and have a rest.'

'I do get a bit weary at this time of day, but I'll bring my nephew Niall round in the morning to see about the repairs. So I'll bid you good night, sir.'

Ross watched the old man hobbling away to the cottage that was on the land at the back of the house. Then he put the key in the lock feeling a reluctance to go in.

The oak floor of the hall was gleaming and there was the lovely fresh smell of lavender. He was about to take his case upstairs when he heard the sound of a carriage approaching. There were only two other houses along this road: Liam's, and the residence of Colonel Bradshaw.

Ross looked out and saw an open carriage with two

ladies inside. As it drew nearer he tensed. It couldn't be . . . No, of course not. Sitting beside a middle-aged straight-backed lady was a girl in a cream dress and cream straw hat who was so like Rosin he could hardly believe it. He hurried down to the gate. The carriage passed and his heart began to pound.

It *was* Rosin!

He ran after it calling, 'Wait. Stop, please!'

The horse was brought to a halt, and as Ross reached the carriage the girl's companion eyed him through a lorgnette.

'And who might you be, sir, to claim our attention?'

He bowed and gave his name. 'Forgive me, madam, but the young lady is so like a friend of mine I felt I could not let the carriage go by without making myself known.'

The eyes of Rosin met his. She was her double in looks, but this girl was elegant. She smiled. 'I hope, sir, that the lady I resemble is attractive.' Her voice was cultured and had a musical resonance.

'Oh, yes, very attractive indeed.'

The older woman's lips tightened. 'I am Lady Kereslake and this is my niece, Miss Alicia Sylvain. May I ask, sir, now that you realize she is not the person you expected, that we be allowed to continue our journey?'

Ross stepped back. 'Of course, Lady Kereslake. I offer my most humble apologies for having delayed you.'

Her niece said to him in a low voice, 'I regret I am not the young lady you expected,' and was scolded by her aunt for being so forward.

As the driver was ordered to continue the journey the girl smiled at Ross and it was with Rosin's delightful impish grin. Then she looked straight ahead but surreptitiously raised a hand, wiggling her fingers in farewell.

Ross's heart leapt. He had no idea how this transformation had taken place, but he was determined to find out.

5

Ross went to bed early and woke at six o'clock the next morning. He decided to walk down to the bay, guessing that Liam would not arrive for breakfast until eight o'clock at the earliest.

There was a light sea mist, but by the time he had come down the steep slope, taking the short cut of youth, the mist had cleared. He went down to the strand and stood taking deep breaths. It was good to be back.

He decided to have a paddle. Taking off his shoes and socks, he pushed the socks inside the shoes, tied the laces and slung them over his shoulder. He felt young again and full of vigour. He shouted at the coldness of the water, then laughed, reliving past days.

He walked back and forth, stopping now and again to dig his toes into the fine shingle or pick up a few pebbles and skim them over the surface of the water. There was hardly a ripple on the sea.

His mind switched from one thing to another, but he carefully avoided thinking of Rosin and Alicia Sylvain, knowing he would gain nothing until he had spoken to Liam. He thought of Three Gables and how he had neglected it.

The house had belonged to his maternal grandparents and willed to him on their death. Although they had left money for its upkeep for a number of years, this was finished and his father refused to pay anything towards it. Ross would have sold it had his mother not begged him to try to keep it for when he married and had children of his own.

He had been too wrapped up in his work and leading

a busy social life to worry about a house he never visited. Now, however, feeling that his life was assuming a different pattern, he felt a deep regret for his neglect, especially after he had seen the loving care Mrs Colhoun and her daughters had taken of the inside of the house.

His mind switched to John Davies and he wondered once more why he had a feeling that something was wrong.

Ross was suddenly aware of someone shouting. He turned swiftly and saw Liam coming towards him, his left arm held up. His wrist was bandaged.

Ross called, 'What have you been up to?'

Liam grinned. 'Fell over the front doorstep, would you believe it, and ricked it badly.'

'Lucky it isn't your right wrist. I need some weeding done. If I pull them out you can gather them in.'

'It's a good job I know you,' Liam replied laughing as he came up. 'I am going to laze for a few days.'

They walked to the low wall where Ross sat to put on his shoes and socks, saying, 'We had better go up by the road. If we took the short cut and you tripped and ricked your other wrist your aunt would have something to say.'

'I've already been lectured.'

Liam's mother had died when he was twelve and his aunt, who had never married, moved in to take over the care of the house, Liam, his brother Dermot and their father. She was a much-loved woman who had refused to marry Mr McLane because he had been married to her sister. Useless to tell her that her sister would have been delighted had she married her husband.

As they walked slowly up the road, Ross chose his moment to tell Liam about meeting Alicia Sylvain and her aunt and asked if he knew them.

'I know of them. They're staying with Colonel

59

Bradshaw and his wife. I've heard a lot of talk about the attractive Miss Sylvain, but I haven't yet had the pleasure of meeting her. I am, however, hoping to rectify this next Monday evening, having been invited, with Dermot, to a ball at the Gresham Hotel in Dublin. Liam looked at Ross, then added with a grin, 'It's a fool I am to have competition from you, but I think I could get you an invitation.

'You could?' A slow smile spread over Ross's face. 'Well, there's a friend for you. I'll do the same for you someday.'

'I'll hold you to it. By the way, you say Miss Sylvain is very like another young lady you know.'

Ross, not willing yet to discuss Rosin, shrugged his shoulders. 'She does have a resemblance. It was a good way of meeting the lovely Miss Sylvain, wouldn't you say?'

'You schemer! I'll tell her.'

'You dare!'

At the house, Ross cooked the breakfast and they ate it leisurely, chatting over various aspects of their lives. Later Liam sent a message home to say he would not be back until this evening. He was going to stay and meet Ross's aunt and cousins, arriving that day from Killorglin.

The two men reminisced during the morning, Ross lazily dealing with weeds and Liam, equally lazy, drawing them together with a rake. In the afternoon Ross talked to Mr Colhoun and Niall about the repairs, and felt satisfied with the dedication of the nephew who would be in his forties.

The family were due to arrive at the same time as Ross had done, and both men were changed and ready when a carriage drew up.

Tara shrieked with delight on seeing Liam and he swung her around as he had done when she was a child. Fiona, although less boisterous than her sister, was obviously pleased at seeing him again, while Ashling greeted him with her shy smile. Then Liam was greeting Eileen and Brendan and for a while the evening was alive with talk and laughter.

Mr Colhoun, his wife and a daughter were waiting at the door, the two women curtsying, their faces shining with pleasure.

'Oh, ma'am,' Mrs Colhoun said, 'How good it is to see you all again. We often talk of you.'

A savoury smell drifted out and when Eileen sniffed the air the housekeeper said, 'Rabbit pie, ma'am, your favourite.'

Ross chuckled. 'The favourite of all of us. I can't wait.'

Eileen pulled a pin from her hat. 'As the luggage won't be here until later and we can't change, I suggest we go in, wash our hands and then we shall be ready to eat.'

The dark oak floor and well-polished furniture in the dining room gave a mellow look to the room. The long table, covered with a snowy white linen cloth, was set with silverware and handcut crystal. Ross, remembering earlier days, felt suddenly emotional and noticed that his aunt gave a little sniff and flicked a finger across each eye. Everyone started talking at once, each one recalling a different occasion: 'Do you remember when . . .?'

The rabbit pie was followed by bilberry pudding, another favourite, and they were all saying they couldn't move an inch.

What bothered Ross was Tara looking at Liam as though hanging on to his every word, which had gone on all through the meal. She had always liked boys and they liked her, but there had never been this utter absorption with any of them.

The evening had turned cool and a fire had been lit in the drawing room. Liam had gone in for

61

accountancy and while Brendan was asking how the business was going Tara got out of her chair, gave a shiver, and sat at Liam's feet where she was closer to the fire. Eileen looked disapproving but refrained from saying anything.

Liam talked of how his work took him around the country and Tara kept glancing up at him. Still her mother made no comment, but when Tara gave a sigh and laid her head against Liam's knee she told Tara to go back to her chair, she was being a nuisance to Liam.

He laughed and said that it was the first time he had had a slave to which Fiona replied wryly, 'My sister will be any man's slave if he smiles at her.'

Eileen said sharply that there would be no more of that kind of talk and asked both girls to come outside with her. Fiona shrugged and got up and Tara, pouting, followed.

Then Liam was full of apologies, he was to blame, it was a stupid jest to make.

Ashling said quietly that he must excuse her mother, she had had a very busy time trying to get ready to come away, and the girls had been over-excited at coming back to Three Gables.

When Eileen and the girls came back into the room both girls apologized for having caused an upset, Tara looking contrite, Fiona with a tongue-in-cheek air, which had Ross thinking how much Fiona had changed over the past few years. She had always been a rather difficult child to control but now she had become confident in a not-too-pleasing way, always slipping in snide little remarks, more like an adolescent girl who is a little unsure of herself and wants to impress how clever she is.

The next day Liam told them that not only Ross had been invited to the ball, but the family too. When the first excitement had died down, the girls began wailing that they did not have suitable dresses with them.

Eileen told them calmly that they would have to improvise with summer dresses, and that she would go into consultation with one of Mrs Colhoun's daughters, who was a dressmaker.

When Tara announced she would not go to the ball unless suitably clad her mother turned to Liam and said cheerfully, 'Would you kindly inform the Colonel that there will one less in our party?'

Fiona protested that her mother was not taking into account their feelings. They did not want to go to the ball looking like paupers.

'Paupers?' Eileen exclaimed. 'Have I ever allowed you to look like paupers? Mrs Colhoun's daughter is a very accomplished young lady. I know her work, know what she's capable of, but if you want to withdraw from the evening, say so now.'

Tara gave in, as Ross had expected, and Fiona changed her mind. If her mother had faith that all would be well for the evening, she would like to go too. This was given grudgingly.

The girls worked hard at tidying up the garden, but, of course, so far as Tara was concerned, Liam was a big incentive. That is, until he began to show more interest in Fiona. Then she began to make excuses – she was hot, she was tired, had a headache.

Fortunately for the benefit of the garden, Liam's brother, Dermot, arrived to lend a hand, and as he was as good-looking as his brother and showed a great interest in Tara, it was a happy and satisfying afternoon.

But the early evening brought more conflict. The young people decided to go down to the strand.

Tara immediately slipped her arm through Ross's and smiling up at him, said, 'I could always trust you to get me down safely. You're so strong.'

Fiona remarked that if she looked carefully where she was going, she wouldn't need support.

Dermot said to Fiona, 'We're just going down to the strand, for heaven's sake, why the ill feeling?' To Tara he added, 'If you wish you can follow me, then if you do happen to stumble I shall cushion your fall.'

Tara's face flushed and, no doubt realizing how childishly she had behaved, she managed to answer lightly, 'Thank you, kind sir, that will be a great help.'

It brought smiles to everyone, apart from Dermot, who would not suffer fools gladly. Ross remembered how Dermot had been a steadying influence on Tara and Fiona when younger and hoped he might have some effect on both of them now.

All was well for a time. They strolled by the water's edge but when they decided to go for a walk over the strand Tara made sure she was next to Ross and when they stopped to skim pebbles across the water she was there again, pushing in next to him. He became irritated and moved away to Ashling.

'You always were the expert skimmer and still fill the role.'

She gave him her shy smile. 'Not really, I'm out of practice, but I always enjoyed our games.'

'Then let us have a competition.'

They all joined in but Tara soon quit, saying she was not in the mood and when Ashling was pronounced the winner and they all walked on, Tara dropped behind. Dermot, who was about to go to her, was told by Brendan to leave her alone, she would get out of her stupid babyish mood.

Tara heard and called out that she was not being babyish, her toe hurt, she had bruised it on a stone that morning, to which Fiona said, 'Ahhh, poor, poor little girl.'

'Stop it!' Ashling exclaimed. 'You're both behaving like children. If your toe hurts, Tara, you'd better stay in tomorrow.

'It's not as bad as that,' Tara mumbled. 'I can manage.'

They had almost reached the top of the short cut home when somone shouted from above. It was Eileen.

'Maeve is here,' she called. 'Such a surprise! Don't linger, she won't be staying long.'

Ross was astonished at the change this news made. Tara and Fiona were immediately the best of friends and, once they reached the top, went hurrying ahead, arm in arm, with Tara saying, 'I do hope she's brought the runes with her.'

Brendan spread his hands. 'No wonder men don't rush to get married.'

Liam grinned. 'Marriage tames women.'

'I'll tame the woman I choose for wedlock before we marry,' said Dermot.

Ashling said quietly, 'Don't underestimate women, they're cleverer than men.'

'Did you hear her?' scoffed Dermot. 'Clever than us? Never!'

'Well, let me ask you something,' said Ashling. 'Who would make the best wife, a woman who was coaxed with love to submit to her husband's demands, or one who was bullied and made ill by him?'

'Ho, ho, ho!' exclaimed Dermot with a grin. 'Isn't she the pert one now. I take your point, Miss Ashling McCoy, and I might just put you on my list of possibles.' His eyes were twinkling.

'Don't bother. I refuse to be on any man's "possible" list.'

Brendan said. 'I've always known that Ashling was the most sensible of the bunch, but most men go for the empty-headed, good-looking ones.'

Liam teased him. 'You surely are not referring to your two other sisters?'

'Well . . . they're both very good-looking, but both mislay their brains every now and then.'

Ashling looked at him aghast. 'That's a treacherous remark to make. They're your sisters.'

Brendan warned, 'Don't tell them I said it, or I shall be found lying dead in a ditch and yelling for help!'

Liam and Dermot roared with laughter. Brendan grinned. Ross was silent.

Ashling said, 'Really, the three of you are more childish than Tara and Fiona,' and walked on.

When they reached Three Gables, Liam and Dermot said they would go on home but Brendan insisted they came in. They could have their fortunes told. It would be fun. Ashling pointed out they must take it seriously and they agreed.

Nine of them were congregated in the drawing room and the one who dominated the scene was Eileen's friend Maeve, not because she was a tall, big-boned woman but because of her serenity of expression. Ross thought he had never seen anyone who embodied saintliness more. Her voice was soft, her smile gentle. All Ross's ill temper vanished. He felt completely relaxed.

Eileen explained that her friend was visiting relatives in Dublin and had made time to be with them. She encouraged Maeve to talk about her travels, the people she had met and what she had learnt about runes.

Maeve said that runes were clouded in mystery and secrecy, and right from the start she had a captive audience. There were many different alphabets, she said, each with its own signs. There were some folk who insisted they were the letter symbols of an ancient alphabet that originated among the Nordic peoples of Europe, centuries before the Christian era, and that the Vikings and Germanic peoples divined the future by the symbols.

Ashling spoke up. 'Mother said that her signs were made by the person who gave them to her.'

'Yes, one can do this. There are many, many different

kinds. Some people accept that they began as pictures in ancient tombs, others that they had been created by secret codes from sophisticated arts among the Arabs, who were renowned in the early Middle Ages as magicians. I prefer to use the regular ancient alphabet. The runes I use are made of oak, one of the sacred woods.' She opened a black linen bag with a drawstring and cast the runes on to the white cloth. 'The symbols on the black stones are usually painted in white. My symbols are in red, green and blue. No one can claim that a certain method is the correct one. Runes have been found in places as widely separated as Ireland, Northern Sweden, Iceland and the Ukraine.'

Eileen said, 'I understood that you found stones in Mexico.'

'Ah, yes, the black stones. These are found in the river beds of many countries. You can have circular runes and divide them into four quarters – air, water, fire, earth – but I think it would be wise to keep things as simple as possible at the moment.'

She picked up a rune. 'Every symbol has a different meaning. Take for instance this X sign. Basically, it means harmony, all things to do with life in general, partnerships, in marriage, in business . . . This has taken only seconds to tell you, but one must allow for the variations of meanings, which depend on the way the other runes have fallen.' She picked up another rune. 'This one is blank and is the hub in this set around which everything is built. To read the message could take some time. I have been studying for a very long time and I must admit that I am still learning.'

Her gaze went slowly over the runes where they lay. She appeared to be absorbed in her task and while this took place there was complete silence.

When she at last looked up she spoke softly, 'We-ll . . . ! What have we here?'

'What is it?' Eileen asked.

Maeve shook her head. 'A very strange thing. With so many of you here I had no intention of doing a reading, but there is such conflict here.'

'Conflict?' This from Brendan. 'I think I can safely speak for all of us when I say this can't concern any of *us*. We are all in a happy mood, we're on holiday.'

'Oh, but it does concern all of you. Indeed, it does. The mood is heavy with stress, animosity, worry. It's so strong, it's almost overpowering.' She closed her eyes momentarily. 'I've never experienced this before.'

The tension in the room was almost tangible.

Maeve began studying the runes again. She picked up three. 'Money, the loss of it, is causing a problem. Fraud is involved.'

Dermot said, 'Who is concerned?'

His brother motioned to him to be quiet.

Maeve, who was studying the runes once more, was silent for a long time. Then she said softly, 'Hate and jealousy are two very strong forces and must be controlled or unhappiness will prevail.'

Ross noticed that the cheeks of both Tara and Fiona were flushed.

Then Maeve continued, 'There's a celebration, where everything seems to be quite wonderful on the surface, but sadly, there is friction here too, uncertainty, jealousy.' She paused. 'How strange . . . A young lady . . . Are these one or two?' She shook her head. 'No, no, I . . . don't think so . . . It could be . . . No, oh dear, this is all so strange.'

Ross's heart was pounding. Although he had no wish to draw attention to himself he very much wanted to know the answer.

Maeve drew her fingers across her eyes. 'There's a mystery here that I have never encountered before.'

Liam asked in a quiet, respectful way, 'Is the lady wealthy?'

'There is money, yes, and position.'

'Is she a married lady?' This from Dermot, who also spoke quietly.

'No, she is unattached.'

Fiona changed the question by asking, 'Can you see any marriages for my sisters or myself, Mrs Warwick?'

'Y-yes.' Maeve rubbed her eyes again. 'I'm so sorry, but I shall have to stop. Everything has become blurred. I just can't understand it.' She began to gather up the runes. 'I shall be staying in Dublin for a week at least. We shall have another study of the runes. There's a strange influence on them this evening which I simply cannot explain. I've never experienced anything quite like this before. Perhaps I am tired. I haven't seen my relatives for some time and we have talked and talked.'

Ross only hoped she would come again before the ball so he might find an answer to the mystery of Rosin and Alicia.

6

Maeve did not manage to get back for another session with the runes before the ball, and at first Ross was not sure whether he was pleased or sorry. Later he realized how foolish he would have been to depend on fortune-telling, spiritual though it might have been, to make a decision for him. In spite of this he could not get caught up in the excitement of the coming ball until the girls had their dresses to try on.

'No one would ever guess the dresses were not new,' Eileen told him. 'Mrs Colhoun's daughter is really gifted. She's transformed simple summer dresses into creations. The girls agreed to leaving the choice to her. I feel sure that Ashling will accept hers, but supposing Tara and Fiona don't like theirs?'

'There's a simple answer. If they don't want to wear them then they stay at home.'

'I know I threatened to do that when Tara was being awkward about wanting a new dress but −'

Ross, realizing that it must be a worry trying to please three daughters, said gently, 'Tell me about the dresses. Then I shall know what to reply if there's any grumbling about style.'

'Tara's, of pale pink silk, has short sleeves. Bridie put in new sleeves of pale pink chiffon, which are full at the top and have frills at the elbows. The skirt has an addition of floating panels of the chiffon and on the panels are a scattering of tiny sequins in pale green and deep rose. The neck is high and Tara shall wear a diamond brooch. I thought it very attractive.'

Ross said smiling, 'I would say it was perfect for her.'
Eileen looked relieved. She then described Fiona's

dress, which was apple-green taffeta. Bridie had opened up the front of the skirt and inserted a panel of a darker green velvet and stitched narrow velvet ribbon down the fronts of the skirt and around the hem in a most intricate pattern. At the back, a velvet bow rested on a small bustle. The sleeves were plain and tight fitting at the wrist. Eileen said she felt it was right for Fiona, who did not like fussy clothes.

'Then I'm sure that Fiona will like it too,' Ross said.

Eileen then spoke of Ashling's gown and there was a dreaminess in her eyes. 'It's white, a virginal dress. Bridie, using chiffon again, made an overskirt with the hem ruched up at intervals, with tiny white satin rosebuds nestling in each loop. Chiffon is looped at the top of the sleeves, draped across the neck and caught at the shoulders, where long ends will float behind her when she dances.' Eileen sat up. 'Ah, here they are now.'

Tara came in first and, after twirling around, curtsied in front of Ross, her expression demure. 'And do I meet with your approval, cousin, dear?'

'You do, cousin Tara, you look beautiful.' Ross meant it. He had never seen her looking more lovely.

Tara floated away and Fiona came forward. She paraded like a mannequin, then stopped in front of him, her head held high, her right hand on her hip. She was unsmiling but there was no mistaking her excitement.

'You make a perfect mannequin, Fiona,' Ross spoke quietly and he knew she was pleased with his reply.

Ashling made no effort to come forward until Eileen said, 'Come along, let us see your gown. You are in the shadows at the moment.'

She came forward slowly, saying, 'I feel strange, more like a bride than being dressed to go to a ball.'

'It's a Cinderalla dress,' declared Eileen.

'And don't forget,' Ross said smiling, 'she went to the ball and met the Prince.'

Fiona, head inclined said, 'I think it might have been better if there had been some colour on the dress.'

'No,' Ross spoke sharply, not wanting Ashling to lose the look of wonder that was in her eyes. 'The dress is so right, I feel it could not have been bettered.'

'Thank you,' Ashling whispered, colour touching her cheeks.

'It's a good job Bridie has handy sisters who helped her,' said Eileen. 'I understand they worked through the night last night.'

'I can't believe it,' Tara declared. 'How could they possibly stay awake all night?'

Fiona replied wryly, 'You would have had to keep awake if you had been born into a poor family and had to work for a living.'

Tara's head went up. 'But we're not poor, are we?'

Eileen suggested that the girls go upstairs and get changed. Liam and Dermot would be here soon to have a game of cards with them.

'Sometimes I feel it's a shame they have to grow up,' Eileen said, when they had gone. 'When they were small they were a happy threesome. Oh, Tara and Fiona would throw tantrums, and Ashling too on occasions, but at bedtime, after their bath, all sweet and clean and loving, there was an angel-shine about them. One of them had only to put her arms around my neck and say, "I love you, Mama", to bring tears to my eyes.' She sighed. 'Now little jealousies seem to be creeping in. Tara can be petty and Fiona make nasty remarks at times.'

Ross told her how, on the strand, they were the best of friends the minute they knew that Mrs Warwick had arrived, adding gently, 'You worry too much, Aunt Eileen.'

She gave a faint smile. 'It's becoming a habit.'

The grandparents of Liam and Dermot had agreed to put the whole party up on the evening of the ball and this was regarded as an extra exciting bonus, seeing that they lived in a Georgian house near the centre of Dublin. Patrick had joined them by this time.

The girls wanted to go to Dublin early in the day and look at the shops, but Eileen said no, the ball was the reason they were going and it would be foolish to arrive worn out. As they were staying overnight they would be able look around the next morning.

Their evening clothes went in a trunk by road to Dublin and the party went by train late afternoon and were welcomed by Liam and Dermot's grandparents, who were a rather gentle couple, also caught up in the excitement of the occasion of the ball. In fact there was so much talk that there was a little rush at the end to get ready in time.

When the girls came downstairs their hostess clasped her hands together and exclaimed, 'Now did you ever see three more beautiful young ladies?'

They certainly were eye-catching. Tara, with her willowy figure, had golden curls caught at one side of her face. Fiona's curly brown hair, had been lifted to the back and was fastened with a beautiful jewelled hair slide, while Ashling's fair curls had been lifted to the top of her head and circled with forget-me-not-blue ribbon. They were all slightly flushed with excitement.

Surprisingly, when the carriages came to take them to the Gresham Hotel, the girls had calmed down to such an extent that they all had a subdued air and it was not until they arrived and were just one of the parties stepping out of a line of carriages that they blossomed again, with Tara, shiny-eyed, murmuring, 'Oh, Mama, isn't it all wonderful, the beautiful women, the exquisite gowns?'

Fiona said, 'Aren't you forgetting the well-groomed, handsome young men?'

To which Ashling replied quietly, 'I think other women will be envying us *our* attractive escorts.'

Brendan laughed. 'Isn't my sister splendid? She always comes up with the right words to say.'

Ross nodded, but his attention was focused on the people stepping out of carriages as he looked for Alicia Sylvain and her aunt.

In the large reception area groups of people greeted others. Patrick and Eileen were being hailed by a couple and the young ones were greeting a small party of young men and women when Ross caught a glimpse of Alicia and her aunt, and was taken aback when he saw they were escorted by a tall, attractive young man and a silver-haired man with a soldierly bearing. A moment later he wondered how he could have been so foolish as to expect Alicia and her aunt to be unaccompanied.

Her party were moving into the ballroom. He might have followed had not the family come up at that moment with Eileen saying to her husband, 'I know you don't like these affairs, Patrick, dear, but try to make an effort and appear as if you do, for all our sakes.' She looked over her shoulder. 'Are we all here? Good, then shall we go in?'

The orchestra was playing softly. Eileen and Patrick stopped to speak to friends. Ross and the rest of the party were introduced but, anxious to find Alicia, he made an excuse that he had seen an old friend and left them.

The dancing was not due to start for another half-hour and although people were already seated around the ballroom, quite a number were on the floor talking.

He paused and let his gaze wander round the room, but with the constant movement of people it was difficult to pinpoint anyone. After a while he stopped and quite suddenly he was reminded of a painting he had seen once in an exhibition, a similar ballroom, the oak panelling, the glow from the candles in the beautiful crystal chandeliers reflecting on the dark oak polished floor. There was so much colour in the dresses of the ladies, a feeling of gaiety and yet now, as there had been then, he was aware of the more sombre tones of the men in evening dress, as though one must be aware that even on such an occasion all was not beauty and joy.

Ross gave a little shiver. Heavens, what was the matter with him, thinking such morbid thoughts? He made to move away and it was then he saw Alicia. She was with one of the groups of people on the floor. She was wearing pale blue satin. Her creamy shoulders were bare. She fluttered a lace fan but although she was looking up at her tall, good-looking escort there was little interest in her eyes.

Some people moved and Alicia was lost to Ross again. Then he looked around, startled as his arm was gripped. It was Brendan.

'What are you doing standing here looking like a lost soul? The family are getting worried, especially Mama, wondering if we've offended you in any way.'

'No, of course not.'

'Well, the wanderer returns,' Eileen greeted him, smiling.

Tara jumped up. 'You must sign our dance cards, cousin Ross. Already we've been asked for dances.'

Her mother said, 'Tara, will you please sit down and stop behaving like an excited child.'

'I *am* excited.' She sat down but handed Ross her card saying with a teasing smile, 'You had better sign before my card is full.'

He signed the cards of all three girls, then turned to his aunt. She was wearing a black silk gown with silver stitching, a lovely diamond and ruby brooch in the shape of a heart at the high neck. With her fair colouring she wore black successfully and looked ten years younger than her forty-four years.

Ross said, 'And how many dances may I have with my beautiful aunt?'

She looked at him over her silver fan. 'I should like to dance every one, sir, but I am a matron and my

75

husband is such a jealous man.' She glanced towards Patrick, who was in earnest conversation about politics with an elderly man, and added with a mischievous smile, 'A *very* jealous man.'

Ross gave her a bow. 'You will never be a matron, ma'am, and I demand three dances at least, though it end in a duel.'

She laughed delightedly. 'Oh, I am going to enjoy this evening.'

A family came up then and greeted Eileen. There were sons and daughters, and while card signing was going on between the young people Ross suddenly caught sight of Alicia again. He excused himself hastily and wove his way among the groups of people, then came to a stop. She was no longer there. He moved on slowly and suddenly came face to face with her.

Alicia looked startled for a moment, then she smiled. 'I'm so glad I found you, Mr Ferris.'

'Are you?' He was as delighted as a schoolboy who has won a most prestigious honour.

'I saw you and slipped away. I left hurriedly before my aunt could say she would accompany me. Could we please stand behind these tall people and be prepared to leave should they move away?'

She looked up at him with Rosin's lovely amber eyes and she had Rosin's delightful impish smile. 'When I saw you I just had to satisfy myself about the girl you said strongly resembled me. Who is she?'

Ross gave a very brief account of Rosin and Alicia said, 'Everyone is supposed to have a double. Are you in love with this young lady?'

'I'm interested in her,' he said noncommittally.

'Would you want to marry her?'

Ross parried her question with another. 'The young man who was with you, is he your fiancé?'

'He wants to be and my aunt approves, but I have no wish to get married, not yet.'

Just like Rosin.

Alicia said, 'I'm afraid I must go. My aunt will be restless. She would have me on a chain if she had her way. But first, may I ask something? I know I am being most unorthodox, but if I gave you my dance card would you sign it?'

'For every dance?' he teased.

'That would be very pleasant, but I'm afraid it must only be one for the moment. I shall see what can be arranged later.'

He signed the card, she took it and, after giving him a quick smile, was gone.

Ross made his way back to his aunt in a bemused state. So Alicia was attracted to him.

He had just reached his aunt when a man came up, bowed to her and said, 'Mrs McCoy?'

Eileen's expression changed, first to astonishment, then to dismay. She whispered, 'Preston,' then looked frantically around her as though seeking escape.

Ross, realizing who the man was, said, 'My name is Ross Ferris, Mrs McCoy's nephew. I think you've startled my aunt.'

The man introduced himself then, turning to Eileen, apologized, adding softly, 'I just couldn't believe it when I saw you, Eileen. It must be about eighteen years since I was at Killorglin.'

'Is it that long? Good gracious, how time flies.'

Ross was glad to see that his aunt had recovered her equilibrium, outwardly, at least. She asked Preston Rafferty if he was living in Dublin and he told her no, just visiting. No one would have guessed he was the man who had left her pregnant, taking all her jewels.

Then Eileen said suddenly, 'Oh, a friend is beckoning to me. Will you excuse me, please, Mr Rafferty?'

He bowed. 'Of course. I hope we shall meet later. Please save me a dance.'

He withdrew and Eileen appealed to Ross, 'What am

77

I going to do? My heart is threatening to jump out of my body.'

'Forget him,' he said grimly.

'I can't. And don't tell me I must. You refuse to forget Rosin.'

'That is a different situation. I have not made love to her.'

'Be thankful for that,' she said fervently. 'What you've never had you never miss. I still suffer torment.'

'I also suffer torment. The saying is wrong. What I've never had I *do* miss.'

There was a roll of drums and the Master of Ceremonies came forward to ask the assembly to take their partners for the Grand March. Families usually kept together for the opening so there was a great deal of movement and chatter before all were ready.

As Patrick disliked dancing, and was certainly not good at it, Ross accompanied Eileen. Brendan took Tara, Liam held out an arm to Fiona and Dermot offered his to Ashling.

The orchestra struck up with the Grand March. The Honourable Henry Faycourt, brother-in-law of Colonel Bradshaw, and his wife led the march. Several couples behind came Alicia and her handsome escort.

They were a well-matched pair and Ross experienced a stab of jealousy. A number of other couples followed so that when Ross and Eileen moved into place he was able to study Alicia as she and her partner were just round the first corner in the room. It was only then that he saw the full beauty of her gown. The skirt was full and swung as she walked. At the hem were insets of lace and tiny flowers, looking as if they had been set in little grottoes. Eileen brought his attention to it, not aware it was Alicia. She whispered, 'Exquisite.'

Ross nodded, but refrained from saying who it was, wanting to keep Alicia's identity to himself for a while.

The march began and Ross gave his full attention to

Eileen. She was an excellent dancer and when she missed a step Ross realized it was because she had seen Preston Rafferty. He escorted an attractive young woman in an emerald-green dress that Ross thought very much overtrimmed. Eileen was now staring straight ahead, a forced smile touching her lips. He guessed what she must be suffering.

When the march ended, as Ross was guiding his aunt to her seat, she said, 'Thanks, Ross, I enjoyed that. I only wish that —'

She stopped and he finished for her: 'That Preston Rafferty had not come back into your life.'

'Yes. Now the old restlessness is back. How do I overcome it? I want to, I must.'

Patrick got up as they approached and was beaming at them. Ross said to Eileen, 'We'll talk about it later.'

The rest of the family, with Liam and Dermot, came up, full of chatter, but Ross longed to get away on his own where he could think things over. Alicia was Rosin's double, same eyes, smile, dark hair, same dainty figure . . . yet she had said that her aunt would keep her on a chain if she could, so it would seem she would have no chance of travelling.

Then Colonel Bradshaw came to ask Eileen to save him a dance. He mentioned Alicia, saying with an indulgent smile that he wished he could see her more often, but she was here, there and everywhere. One time she would be in France, another in Italy, or even India.

Ross would have questioned him, but Eileen had another man approach her for a dance and the Colonel, chuckling, said he was glad he had been in time to claim at least one, and left.

They had a number of visits from matrons with eligible daughters, some attractive, some not so attractive. Ross, doing his duty, signed some dance cards, then said to Eileen, 'That is all. I have dances with the girls, starting with Tara now. May I be excused?'

'You may, sir,' she answered lightly, then added softly, 'Thank you for asking the plain ones as well as the more lovely ones, Ross. I was a wallflower once when I was younger and I wanted to crawl into a corner and die.'

'I couldn't imagine you ever being a wallflower, Aunt Eileen.'

Ross hoped to catch a glimpse of Alicia, but Tara had already grabbed his hand. While they waltzed, Tara prattled about all the attractive young men who had claimed dances. He made up a group of eight with Fiona for the lancers, with her grumbling about Tara nearly knocking her out of the way to catch men. And then came Ashling's turn when he hoped to have some peace.

Ashling said when he led her on to the floor, 'I feel that Papa should have paid you a fee to dance with us when you have so many attractive ladies wishing to claim your attention.'

'Oh, he did,' Ross said.

'Might I enquire how much?' Her expression was serious, her eyes twinkling.

'The amount cannot be revealed, but I'm delighted to say I won the prize.'

'Sorry it was such an ordinary one,' she replied lightly.

'Do not belittle yourself, Miss McCoy. Sometimes the most beautiful woman can be a bore. Heaven endowed you with a lovely nature.'

Ashling pulled a face. 'Oh, please, sire, stop, or I shall swoon.'

'If you do I shall leave you to your fate.'

She laughed. It was full-throated, infectious. 'Ah, an honest man, a rarity nowadays. I salute you.'

'Your tongue delights me, Miss McCoy. How rewarding to have the truth from a woman. 'Tis the first time I have experienced such a thing.'

'There are plenty of honest woman, sire, but they are mostly those who end up being left on the shelf.'

'Not on *my* shelf.'

'That is nice to know. I shall spread the good word abroad.'

Ross chuckled and gave her a quick hug. 'Never change, dear Ashling.'

As he was walking her back to her seat he felt someone touch his hand. It was Alicia, who gave him a quick smiling glance that set his heart pounding. Her partner led her in a different direction.

Ashling looked up at him. 'Do you know the lady?'

He nodded, but put his fingers to his lips.

'Oh, I see,' she whispered, a mischievous look in her eyes. 'Is she married?'

'No. I'll tell you about her sometime.'

'That is a promise. Assignations are exciting. Anything I can do to help?'

'You are wicked,' he teased her.

'I would like to be.' There was a delightful smile on her lips. 'Even if it's just for once.'

He looked down at her and said in a conspiratorial way, 'I'll see if it can be arranged.'

When they returned to the family, Ashling assumed the expression she usually wore when she returned home from church. Ross reflected there were depths in this young cousin that had not been plumbed.

It was not until the break came for the buffet supper that Ross and Alicia managed to get together again. Her aunt was talking to some people a short distance away while the young man and the Colonel were at the long table filling plates with titbits for the ladies. Ross was seated behind a potted palm and Alicia had moved her chair closer.

Ross said, in a low voice, 'Why all this secrecy? The Colonel was speaking to my aunt some time ago. They're acquainted.'

'I know, but my aunt took umbrage that you stopped her carriage that evening and was upset that you should remark on my likeness to this other girl you mentioned. She thinks you very forward.'

'If this is so, how am I going to claim a dance with you?'

She sighed. 'I was hoping she would retire early, leaving me with the Colonel and his nephew, but she seems in good state. Oh, my aunt is on her feet. She will be here any moment. You must go. I shall try and arrange a dance. Go quickly, please.'

Ross was able to escape unnoticed with the aid of the potted palm.

He had been back with the family about five minutes when Eileen said in an undertone, 'Look.'

Following her gaze he saw, to his surprise, Colonel Bradshaw, his nephew, Lady Kereslake and Alicia coming in their direction. And moments later, he felt utter astonishment when, after introductions had been made, Lady Kereslake acknowledged him with a gracious smile and said, 'I must apologize, Mr Ferris, for being so abrupt when you stopped my carriage the other evening. I had had a most trying day.'

He assured her in soothing tones that he was entirely at fault and apologized for causing her distress. He requested a dance, which she waved aside and added that he had her permission, if he wished, to claim one with her niece.

It had all happened so easily, so quickly, he felt overjoyed. He turned to Alicia, who was sitting looking so circumspect. Then he became aware of a smile touching her lips and a look in her eyes that he could not quite fathom . . . just as it had been with Rosin.

There was gaiety around him, soft music, laughter. He found himself thinking of how earlier he had stopped to take in the scene, the beautiful colours, the lovely crystal chandeliers, and of how seconds later he had become aware of more sombre tones.

He gave a little shiver. Was it possible that two women, looking identical, could pull the wool over his eyes about their lives? If only he could see them together.

7

The dance with Alicia was a polka. Ross would have preferred it to be something more romantic, like a waltz, but she declared it to be vigorous, exciting, releasing all tensions. He would have liked to have known what tensions she suffered from but at her request there would be no talking; their full attention must be given to the dance.

Ross had danced many polkas but had to admit that with Alicia it was an experience. There was a sensuality in every movement that had his blood pounding. As they danced he had crazy thoughts, like picking her up and carrying her away to somewhere they could be quite alone.

He told himself he was mad, but the heat in him persisted. When the dance ended she looked up at him, her eyes a dark liquid amber that he felt he could drown in.

Before they reached her party he said, 'I must see you again.'

'We can't dance together again this evening.'

'We must, you can't deny me that.'

'I'm sorry, but it's impossible. We can meet soon. That is a promise.'

'Where?'

'I shall let you know . . . somehow.'

Ross delivered Alicia back to the care of her aunt, talked for a few moments, then returned to his own party, feeling that the evening had finished for him.

It was the fact of his aunt making an effort to put on a bright face when she must be in torment at having her former lover turn up unexpectedly that gave Ross the impetus to try to behave normally.

Tara was sailing on clouds because she had had so many claimants for dances. Fiona seemed content with the fact that Dermot was happy to share her company, while Brendan was full of talk of a young lady who, although seemingly quite shy and a little on the plain side, had a lovely sense of humour.

Ashling, always discerning, seemed to be the only one aware that all was not well with Ross.

When she asked him if he had fallen out with his lady friend he said, 'No, we are on amicable terms.' Then, suddenly finding a need to talk about Alicia, he went on, 'She will arrange for me to see her again, but I can't quite weigh her up. She led me to believe that her aunt was a dragon who restricted her movements, yet Lady Kereslake was most gracious towards me and suggested I ask Alicia for a dance. Who is wearing the mask?'

Ashling sat studying him for a moment, then she said, 'I've always thought of you as a strong man, cousin Ross, not only in body, but in mind. I simply cannot imagine you letting a woman dominate you.'

'But I don't. I would never let any woman dominate me.'

'Alicia does. You jump to her bidding and are demeaning yourself. I don't like you in that role.'

Ross felt shocked. Was that how he appeared to Alicia? Humble? What a fool he had been, mooning over her like a lovesick youth. Well, from now on all that would change. There would be no fitting in with her arrangements, her clandestine meetings.

Ashling said suddenly, 'Oh, you'll have to excuse me. A young man is coming to claim the next dance with me.' She was blushing and he thought how sweet and lovely she looked.

He squeezed her hand. 'Enjoy your dance and

thanks, Ashling.' He stood up to be introduced to her partner.

Before they left she gave him a worried look and whispered, 'Don't be upset. You are still my favourite cousin.'

'And you mine,' he replied with a warm smile.

Fiona replaced Ashling, saying, 'I need a rest.'

'I was glad to know that you have so many admirers and are getting on well with Liam.'

The word *demeaning* kept going over and over in Ross's mind. He suddenly became aware of Fiona saying in a peeved voice, 'If I'm not welcome, please say so.'

'I'm sorry, it was just that something came into mind I have to remember. You were saying that you were getting on well with Liam.'

'Correction. *You* said it. He's all right. A little too demanding, perhaps.' She glanced at him. 'Why are you sitting out. I thought you were cavorting with Miss Sylvain. She certainly knows how to polka.'

'I believe it is her favourite dance,' he replied stiffly.

'By what I hear about her it might be wise to avoid her.'

Ross tensed. 'And why might that be?'

'I overheard two men talking. One man said, "I believe our dear Miss Sylvain is hot stuff if she fancies a man." The other man laughed and replied, "I'd be delighted if she took a fancy to me." Then after a pause he went on, "She has something that I've never found in any other woman." '

Ross's heart beat a little faster. It was what he had thought about Rosin. 'Oh, and what was that?' He tried to speak casually.

'He didn't know. He said it was something more than sensuality.' She spoke as though she used the word every day. Showing off, Ross suspected. 'The other man suggested it could be a sort of mesmerism and his companion agreed. They then walked away.'

Ross could not resist saying wryly, 'And what does your clever mind suggest?'

'I'm afraid I am not experienced enough to answer that,' she replied in a mock demure way.

To which Ross replied, 'I'm glad to hear it, as your use of a certain word suggested you might have had a great deal of experience on the subject.'

'Chance would be a fine thing,' she retorted.

'Chance would *not* be a fine thing, Fiona. And I suggest you disregard the comments made by the two men you overheard maligning Miss Sylvain's character. Men who have not been successful in capturing a certain lady's attention will call her names to get revenge. They are to be despised.'

As Ross spoke he realized that he had jumped very readily to Alicia's defence. He had hardly met the girl. Ashling's words to him needed a great deal more thought.

He longed for the evening to be over. Despite himself he looked round for Alicia, but neither she nor the Colonel's party were there. Had they gone home?

The girls begged to be allowed to stay until the ball ended but both parents insisted they leave then, with Eileen pointing out that they wanted to explore Dublin the next morning and they would be in no state to do so if they were droopy-eyed. The young men decided to leave too, Liam saying that his grandmother was a worrier and might be waiting up until they were all back and safely in their beds.

The old lady was up and eager to know all about the ball. It was three o'clock when they got to bed, and as the men were sharing a room there was much talk from Liam and Dermot about all the girls they had met so that when they did drop off to sleep, Ross was wide awake.

His mind jumped from one thing to another without coherent thought. At four o'clock, feeling that nerve ends were shooting out of his fingertips, he got up, put on a dressing gown and crept downstairs.

It was light enough to see his way to the sitting room. He opened the door and stood, startled, as he saw a white clad figure.

'Ross! Oh, what a fright you gave me. I couldn't sleep.'

It was Eileen. 'Nor I,' he said. 'I thought for a moment I was seeing a ghost.'

She drew her large shawl closer to her. 'I found this on the sofa. It's not the warmest time of day. I feel like running away. I curse Preston Rafferty for coming back into my life. When I danced with him – although I had made up my mind I would say that my card was full – I was in a seventh heaven.'

'And you want to see him again?' Ross asked gently.

'Yes, I do, may the Good Lord forgive me.' Her head had been bowed, now she looked up at him and her eyes were full of torment. 'What am I to do, Ross? Help me, please. I feel I'm being unfaithful to Patrick just lying beside him in bed.'

Ross hesitated a moment then said, 'I've been going through a much lesser torment but I would like to tell you something that Ashling said to me. It has made me think.'

He told her about Ashling saying he was demeaning himself allowing Alicia Sylvain to dominate him, concluding, 'My problem is less difficult to solve, but I'm still asking myself is Ashling right? And now I ask are you demeaning yourself by craving to be with Preston Rafferty?'

'How strange,' Eileen mused, 'that Preston's own child should come up with such a criticism. Demeaning.' She nodded slowly. 'Yes, that is how I am behaving. I'm as weak as a piece of rotting rope. I did half promise that I would try and meet him again, but I won't and from now on I shall try and put him out of

88

my life. It's what I should have done years ago.' She
threw a corner of the shawl over her shoulder in an
abandoned way and smiled. 'I'm a free woman at last.
It feels wonderful. Every now and then that wretched
man used to come into my mind and I would feel all
silly and sentimental, as though he were the most
loving, the most romantic man in the world.' She fell
silent for a few moments, then she looked at Ross in
a sombre way. 'I'm fooling myself a little. It won't be
easy to forget him.'

She sighed and got up. 'I must go back to bed. If
Patrick misses me he'll be down.' She laid a hand on
Ross's shoulder. 'Thanks for listening to my tale of woe.
I don't know what I would do without you. There's no
one else who would have understood. What have you
decided to do about Alicia?'

'Nothing yet. I hope you manage to sleep.'

'I think I will. My mind is more settled. I'll see you
in the morning, Ross. Thanks again.'

It was first light, the heavy oak furniture in shadow.
Then the sky lightened a little and each piece materialized. Ross got up from the sofa. There was no sleep
in him, but he felt calmer and decided to go back to
bed.

His three companions were all snoring and he smiled,
envying them. He nipped the nose of Brendan, who
was sharing his bed. He spluttered, shuffled around and
settled on his side. Ross repeated his tactics on the
other two but only Liam quietened. Soon he became
aware of the traffic, the clatter of hooves, iron wheels
on the cobbled street and the raucous shouting of
drivers, which became a chorus to Dermot's rendering
of grunts and snorts.

When a maid, stooped and toothless brought early
morning tea, Ross was astonished to find he had slept.

Liam called, 'The top of the morning to you, Bridget,
me darling.'

'And to you, sir, and your friends, and a fine morning it's going to be, to be sure.'

The sun had just broken through the clouds. Bridget urged them all to drink the tea before it got cold, then told them the mistress had said they were to get up when they pleased, but to let her know when they would be down for breakfast.

Dermot, who was still humped under the bedclothes, told her to say they would let her know when they were down and Brendan, laughing, threw a pillow at him and said, 'You speak for yourself, I am ravenous. I could eat a horse.'

Bridget, in a droll way, replied, 'Ah now, we can't supply a bit of horse, sir, but I'm sure Cook can cut you a bit of an ould sow that might be to your liking.'

The other three men roared with laughter and complimented Bridget. Dermot groaned and pulled the bedcover over his head.

Everyone was downstairs at nine o'clock and they all breakfasted together, the girls impatient to get to the shops.

Eileen said with a sigh, 'I shall have to go with them but I would rather just laze.'

Liam and Dermot wanted to visit friends and when Ross told them he had planned to go to the library at Trinity College to look at the Book of Kells, Brendan said eagerly, 'I should like to come with you, if you don't mind.'

Ross said he would welcome his company, but deep down he had hoped to spend the time alone, to browse and think.

When they were all ready to leave Liam and Dermot's grandmother made them promise to be back for lunch.

'I am very, very selfish,' said the old lady, beaming at them. 'I love seeing you all and I want to know about all your experiences.'

As Liam said despairingly when they left, 'What could one reply to that? Dear Grandmama, we all love her, but it seems impossible to get away from the dominance of women. My mother used to be just the same. Now it's my aunt who gives the orders at home. One of these days I'm going to rebel.'

'And break poor old Aunt Edith's heart?' replied Dermot. 'Keeping the house going is her life.'

They discussed this until they reached, Sackville Place, where Liam and Dermot left them.

As they neared Nelson's Column, Ross said to Brendan, 'How about climbing the column and viewing the city?'

Brendan hesitated. 'Well, I, er, did want to talk to you about a young lady I met last night. She really is a very nice person, Ross. Not a beauty by any means, but so sensible and she does have a lovely sense of humour.'

'So you said,' Ross replied drily. 'I have my own problems and am not in the mood to discuss your affairs.' In the next breath he apologized. 'I'm sorry, Brendan. I'm behaving like a bear with a sore head.'

'That's all right,' Brendan said happily. 'I offered to come with you. To be honest I did want to call on Celina. I invited myself. I don't think her parents were very pleased, but if I don't see her I won't get to know her, will I? You go off on your own and I shall go visiting.'

'No hard feelings?'

'With you?'

Ross gripped his cousin's shoulder. He had been a good friend.

Brendan left him and Ross paused, wondering if he should go back and climb to the top of the column. Viewing the wide horizon of the city might help to clear his head of the petty things that had started to surface again, such as Alicia wanting to arrange time and place when he could see her again. No. He walked on. He would decide what to do without needing the sop of a greater horizon to help him.

For a time his thoughts centred on the events of the evening before, but when he reached the junction of College Green and Westmoreland Street he became aware of the extra noise of traffic and hustle and bustle. He turned through the entrance gates of Trinity College, passing the tall statues of Burke and Goldsmith and continuing under the archway leading to the beautiful stretch of emerald-green lawns. Suddenly he felt a great peace as though a heavenly hand had touched him, shutting out all sounds. At the Porter's lodge he chatted with the Porter, whom he had known for years. Ross then crossed another quadrangle to a door leading to the library. He climbed the wooden stairs that led into the middle of the Long Room and as he stood looking around he experienced the familiar feeling of awe, of being involved in the lives of people of past generations.

On both sides of the room were alcoves with shelves holding leather-bound history books, some quite ancient. Outside each alcove were marble busts of people dating from the eighteenth and nineteenth centuries, some past members of the College, including Jonathan Swift, Burke, Wolfe Tone; others also men of fame and learning, from Homer and Socrates to Newton and the Duke of Wellington.

Ross moved to the glass-covered case that held the Book of Kells, one of the most beautiful illuminated manuscripts in the world. A page would be turned every day to allow visitors the opportunity of seeing all of it in time. As Ross studied the present pages displayed, he marvelled as always how the brilliant colours of the manuscipt had kept so perfect over a thousand years. In a space about a quarter of an inch square could be counted, with the aid of a magnifying glass, no fewer than a hundred and fifty interplacements of a slender ribbon pattern, formed of white lines edged with black ones on a dark ground. It was said that these unerring lines were traced by angels.

The sudden clatter of footsteps on the stairs had him look up. A burst of laughter became suppressed as someone said, 'Shush.'

A group of young people came into the room, accompanied by an elderly woman. They stopped on seeing Ross, then at a whispered remark from the woman the gaze of all went to the high ceiling. Ross moved away from the display case, then they came to the case one by one, some on tiptoe, with the woman apologizing to Ross for disturbing him.

'Not at all,' he said politely, but left. The atmosphere of the room was still with him, however, when he was outside and as he walked along the path he found himself saying softly, 'Traced by angels.' Then: 'A tracing of angels.'

It was like life, in a way. The colour, the beauty, the intricacies, the white lines edged with black on a dark ground.

He found himself recalling his mother's words, when she had scolded him gently as a boy for complaining that the library was boring. 'The books record centuries of living, Ross. There was love, hate, envy, greed. Wars were fought for power. At times, brother fought brother. Some people lived in poverty, some in luxury, yet in the end rich and poor alike ended under the soil.'

In this relaxed state, Ross allowed Alicia to drift back into his mind. He found himself thinking that quite soon he would be returning to London and Alicia, she had told him, would return to Bath, and it somehow seemed unimportant whether he met her again or not. He had tormented himself wondering whether she and Rosin were one and the same person or two different people, but why should he care? It was unlikely he would ever meet either again. And heaven knew there were plenty of women to choose from in the circles in which he moved.

He squared his shoulders. He would have a walk to the docks, another place he enjoyed visiting, and was about to step out when he heard someone call his name.

To his surprise it was his Uncle Patrick, who had said he wanted to rest after the activities of the previous evening. He came up a little breathless and Ross was about to ask him if he had changed his mind and was coming for a walk with him when he noticed his worried look.

'I'm glad I've found you, Ross. I remembered you saying you were going to the college.' His uncle paused for breath. 'A telegram came for you. It must have gone home and Cook sent one here with the message repeated. I opened it. John Davies is ill.'

Patrick brought it from his pocket and held it out. Ross read it aloud. *Mr Davies in hospital. Worried. Bertha Fox.*

He looked up, his heart pounding. 'It must be serious. Mrs Fox is the housekeeper and one of those stolid people who never gets upset. I must get back to London.' He pushed the telegram into his pocket. 'I'll go to the station and find out the times of the trains.'

'Look, Ross, you go back to the house and pack a bag. All your other luggage at Killorglin can be sent on. I'll go to the station for train times, then I'll find Eileen and the girls. They were going shopping.'

'No, don't tell them, it would spoil their day. I'll go to Killorglin and pack. I have some business papers and money to pick up there, but I've left nothing important at Three Gables. I'll come back to the house here.'

John had seemed to enjoy good health. During the train journey to Killorglin Ross worried about what could have happened. He got talking to a fellow traveller who had a timetable and learned that it would best to start off in the late afternoon for London.

When he arrived at the house he was met by Cook who held out another telegram saying, 'This came about five minutes ago, sir. I'm glad you're here.'

Ross had a sinking feeling in his stomach as he opened the telegram. Was John worse?

It was from John himself, and said, *Greatly improved. I am home. Don't rush back. John.*

Ross heaved a sigh of relief and said to Cook, 'It's good news this time, thank goodness. I can relax, for a while at least. I'll send a telegram to my uncle. I shall be going back to London, but not in a mad rush, as I might have been doing.'

Once Ross had sent word to John Davies, informing of his time of arrival, and also to his uncle, a plan began to form in his mind. He had wanted to see Queenie McKnott again to find out if Rosin had been back to the cottage and decided that after he had packed he would go and have a talk with her.

On the way to Queenie's cottage he called himself all kinds of fool for bothering to pay a visit. If Queenie had seen Rosin what would he gain? Well, he would at least know for certain that she and Alicia were two different people. But what then? He would be back in London. There was a possibility that Alicia might come to London but certainly not Rosin.

When he drew near to the cottage he stopped. Queenie was handing a package to an elderly man, saying, 'It's not much, Mr McCloud, but it'll perhaps tidy you over.'

The man touched his shabby hat. 'It will that, all right, ma'am, and me good wishes to you. May you be in heaven an hour before the Divil finds out you're there.'

'And the same to you, sir.'

The man touched his hat and shuffled away. Although he was shabbily dressed and obviously an itinerant, he was reasonably clean.

Queenie picked up a bowl at her feet and started to spread some washing over the bushes. She had her back to him and when Ross came forward and called, 'Good morning, Mrs McKnott,' she jumped then swung round.

'Why, Mr Ferris, sir.' A smile spread over the rough-skinned face. 'Now isn't this a grand surprise. I thought you had gone to Three Gables.' She began to pin up strands of hair. 'Come away in. I brewed some tea not long ago. Mr McCloud wouldn't come in to have any. Said he didn't want to ruin my reputation.' She chuckled at this. 'Reputation? Him about seventy and me like Todd's rock.'

Todd's rock was a big piece of stone that from a distance looked like a giant figure of a woman.

'Love sees only beauty,' Ross teased.

She roared with laughter.

As they went inside Ross said, 'I have to return to London. There's some business I must attend to.'

Queenie pulled out a chair for him. 'I'll miss you, Mr Ferris, sir. So will Rosin.'

His heart skipped a beat. 'You've seen her recently?'

'Not since the day after you were here. She had nothing to say, which was unusual. When I asked her if she thought she was sickening for something she said she could be, it was called uncertainty.'

'Did she say what she was uncertain about?'

'She did not, she was as closed up as a clam. Said she was going for a walk, she needed to think. That's when I lost me temper and I asked her what she thought she'd been doing for the past few hours, making me feel like an eejit, like me husband used to do, and then I told her if that was how she thought of me she could take her stuff and find someone else to treat in this way.'

'And what did she say to that?'

'Oh, she got herself into a terrible state, to be sure. Flung her arms around me and begged that I would let her stay, said that she had never for one moment thought I was an eejit. There was nowhere else where she felt so at home. Then she talked about the people she had met, but I never got into what she was thinking inside, if you know what I mean, and I began to realize that I never had. Strange how I'd never been aware of it until then,' she mused.

'When she left you did she give you any indication that she might be away for some time?'

'She did not, but then she never does. She would just turn up any old time and I accepted it. She knew I would always be here.'

'Was she any happier when she left than when she arrived?'

Queenie pondered this then shook her head. 'Not really. She was like a girl in love who didn't have her parents' blessing to get married.'

'And the man?'

'Why you, Mr Ferris, to be sure. There's no doubt about that.' A clock struck the hour somewhere in the distance and Ross got up saying he must go.

When Queenie wailed that she had forgotten to pour out the tea she had made he laid a hand on her arm. 'I'll be back one day and we'll share a brew together.'

'That's a promise now.' She gave a little sniff and walked with him to the door.

'And when I do come back you'll have a lot to tell me about the visit of your family.'

'So I will.' She paused. 'I could let you know about Rosin, Mr Ferris. She's bound to be back sometime. I can drop the letter in at your aunt's house, like I said.'

'I would be very grateful if you would, Mrs McKnott. Thank you very much.' He paused then said quietly, 'You've been a good friend.'

She gave him a little wavering smile. 'That's the nicest thing anyone's ever said to me, sir. Look after yourself now.'

'And you.' They shook hands and he left. When he turned before taking the bend in the road she gave him a wave. He waved back, thinking of her during the winter living alone, perhaps not even having Rosin to call.

Then he squared his shoulders, chiding himself for getting emotional. There were many people who were much more isolated than Queenie. People in remote farmhouses who seldom saw a soul.

He started to go over all that Queenie had told him about Rosin then dismissed it. It could be months before he saw Rosin again, if ever . . . or Alicia. The most important thing to think about at the moment was John Davies. Was he perhaps making light of a heart attack?

8

Ross arrived in London at eleven o'clock in the evening. He was in a bad mood. His travelling companions had been missionaries who, having been out in Africa saving the souls of natives, were determined he should be acquainted with every detail of their good work. He gave them a brief farewell before he hailed a porter. His luggage had just been put on a barrow when he saw John Davies's nephew hurrying up to him.

He said, a little breathless, 'Oh, Mr Ferris, I'm so glad I found you. Uncle John asked me to meet you. It was short notice.'

'How is he, Richard? What happened? I've been so worried.'

'He had a fall, but look, I have a cab waiting, I can tell you all about it on the way.'

Richard told the story as they set off for Kensington.

'Four days ago, Uncle John was coming down the stairs at home when he tripped and fell, hitting his head on the tiled floor of the hall, and was made unconscious. As it happened, his own doctor was visiting at the house next door so he came at once and, after examining Uncle, had him transferred to a nursing home close by.'

'Was he unconscious for long?'

'Several hours, and when he did come round he had no idea where he was or who he was, which was most worrying. Unfortunately, he did not recover his memory until yesterday and then it was sudden and, as the doctor said, no one would ever have guessed he had been ill. He was full of vigour, demanded to go home and the doctor agreed but on one condition – that he stayed in bed for a few days. Uncle accepted the terms but once home refused to go to bed. He felt normal, felt fine, and when he found out that Mrs Fox had sent you a telegram saying she was worried about you, he insisted that another telegram be sent to let you know he was home and to tell you that you were not to rush back to London.'

'Well, I think that John is very lucky to have recovered so well after such a fall.'

'That is what the doctor said. Uncle did go to bed this afternoon for a rest, but with the sole purpose of being determined to be up when you arrived. Although he told you not to hurry back I know he'll be pleased to see you.' Richard paused, then went on, 'I hope you will excuse me for saying this, Mr Ferris, sir, but try not to let him get excited. The doctor thought he should take it easy for a while.'

Ross, knowing that John was one of the calmest people he had ever known, gave his word without hesitation.

He had rooms in John's house, but although they spent quite a time together in business, it was only occasionally that they mixed socially.

Mrs Fox, who acted as housekeeper to both men, opened the door and bemoaned the fact that she could not persuade Mr Davies to go to bed. She appealed to Ross. 'You must insist on it sir. He'll kill himself sitting up this late.'

Ross promised to try then said goodnight to Richard.

John came into the hall and was shooed back into the drawing room by Mrs Fox, who complained that men took more looking after than children.

'Ross, how are you?' John's smile was wide and welcoming, his handshake firm. 'All this fuss that is being made because I had a fall down a few stairs.'

'I must say you look well,' Ross said, which was true.

'I feel fine, I'm ready to get back to the office. Come

on, let me pour you a drink, then you can tell me news of your family.'

Mrs Fox looked in to say she was going to bed and that a cold meal was in the dining room if they wanted it, then begged them not to sit up to late.

They ensconsed themselves deeply in dark green velvet armchairs and, their hands cupped round brandy glasses, Ross gave John a brief account of his visit to Ireland. He made no mention of Rosin of Alicia.

They started to talk about business and John said, 'You'll remember when I told you not to touch Fray and Hulton shares. I regretted it when they shot up. Well, today they plummetted.'

For a moment Ross felt he was encased in ice. He said in a low voice, 'I did buy. You were away at the time. They were strongly tipped to be on the acquisition trail and the shares jumped. What happened?'

'I don't know, Ross. There could be many reasons. One of them could be that the takeover was rejected. I would say sell, cut your losses.'

'I invested heavily. This will affect my future.'

'I've never known anyone who hasn't made a loss at some time. You have other investments.'

Ross sighed. 'Very few and very small. I drew on them to buy the Fray and Hultons.'

'I see.'

His voice sounded tired and Ross noticed that John had dark lines under his eyes. He said, 'It's bed for you, John. We'll see what happens in the morning.'

'I'm all right.'

'No, you're not. Come along, on your feet.'

When John got up he gripped Ross's shoulder. 'Remember this. You are not the first to make a big loss and you won't be the last. I made a big mistake years ago but I came bouncing back. You'll pick up the pieces as we all do.'

It was an almost sleepless night for Ross. He tormented

himself for ignoring John's advice about the firm. He had been good to him right from the start, talking endlessly about the market. He had spoken of his own mistakes, introduced him to people he knew. Why had he ignored him? He had wanted to be clever, to show that he could manage without John's advice. Fool.

And yet, he didn't want to sell. But then the shares could drop still further. What the devil should he do? He only hoped his father wouldn't get to know what had happened to him or he would have cause to sneer.

At six o'clock, unable to lie any longer, he got up and went downstairs. John was already up.

'Hello, Ross. I had to get up early. I wanted to telephone Clive Evans, who has been steeped in the stock and share market all his life. He gets up at five every morning. I've learned a few things.'

'Such as?'

'Apparently whispers were going around yesterday about your father who, having bought shares on behalf of a nominee some time ago, sold them at their peak and made a handsome profit.'

'There's nothing wrong with that.'

'No, but later the shares began to drop and fraud is suspected. It's rumoured that false accountancy showed increased profits which had boosted the value of the shares.'

'But my father can't have anything to do with this.'

'Not obviously, but the rumours are apparently gaining momentum because your father was once a directer in Fray and Hulton and is a crony of the man in charge of accountancy. I myself can't believe your father capable of such behaviour. He's not a likeable man but he is a man of integrity.'

'He's ambitious. Greed could have driven him.'

John shook his head. 'No, I can't accept that. Evans said he would let me know later how things were going.'

'What did he say about the Hulton shares?'

'Oh, sell.'

Ross did sell and was glad he had when he learned the the shares had tumbled still further.

He sat slumped in a chair and John said, 'Look, Ross, I went through the mill when I was your age. I think I enjoyed those years the best. There was always a challenge. Now I have no goal. I just amble on.'

'No, never, John, not you. You have a calm way of handling things but your interest in your work rubbed off on to me. I became fascinated in the way you handled shares, your very shrewdness inspired me. If I had taken your advice about the Fray and Hulton shares I wouldn't be in the state I'm in now, would I?'

'We're two of kind, both gambling men.'

'The difference being that you have more common sense,' Ross replied wryly.

'Stop belittling yourself. I'm going to the office later. I feel quite fit. Do you want to come with me? I can always find you a job to do.'

Ross not quite knowing what he wanted to do said he might look in at the office later.

It was not long, however, before he had an awful feeling of aloneness. It was natural, of course. He had lived with a lively family for some time, been to different places, met Rosin and Mrs McKnott. He had met Alicia . . .

No, he was not going to go over all that business again. He would call in at the office.

John's offices were at St Katharine's Dock in the East End. There were three great basins with ships lying close to the wharves. Gigantic warehouses, grimed with soot, towered above, and below was a maze of deep cellars.

Ross stopped to take in the scene. When he was a boy, Uncle Edward had brought him here as a treat and he remembered how awed he had been at seeing so many ships. Sailing ships had predominated then, but there were also steamships, cargo boats, little tugs going busily up and down the river and barges with reddish brown sails, the canvas having been dyed with the bark of a tree, which, according to his uncle, made the canvas stronger. As Ross walked on he was aware of the rather mournful hooting of tugboats, the deep throated 'oooo' of a steamship about to leave, black smoke billowing from the funnel and the shouting and curses of men giving orders.

Another memory came to Ross then. His uncle had promised that he would take him on a trip abroad but the trip had never materialized because his father had refused to let him go. Bitterness rose in Ross as he remembered his disappointment. His uncle had consoled him with the thought that when he came of age he could go where he liked. He had been to several countries, but he had never experienced the pleasure he had known when his uncle had made his promise. He moved on and after a few moments he turned right and cut through narrow cobbled streets to where John had his office. Outside was a notice which said, *John Davies & Company, Shipping Agents.*

Ross made for John's office. It was empty and he crossed to the main office opposite. Here five staff were employed; the rest worked upstairs.

When he went in two young men who were dealing with customers glanced up, but concentrated immediately on the business in hand. The other three, however, greeted him with smiles.

Mr Cole, an elderly man with a brilliant mind for figures and a knowledge of shipping that had been passed down from grandfather to grandson, raised his hand and gave a nod. 'Good to see you back and looking so well, Mr Ferris.'

Miss Simpson, the shorthand typist, a spinster of thirty-five who still held out hopes of finding a husband, beamed at him and said, 'You've been greatly missed, sir.'

Herbie, the skinny little office boy, whom Miss Simpson said had an ambition to become a shipping magnate but who couldn't multiply three hundred and seventy-seven by nine without using pen and paper, gave a cheeky grin and asked Ross if he had found any four-leaved shamrocks.

To which Ross replied solemnly, 'No, only four-legged hens.'

Herbie looked bewildered 'Never 'eard of them, sir.'

'Haven't you?' Ross remained solemn. 'They wear goloshes over their boots and sou'westers when it rains.'

The boy suddenly dissolved into laughter. 'You're funning, sir.' Then he clapped his hand over his mouth. 'Oh, I'm sorry, sir, I forgot me manners.'

The door opened and John looked in. He smiled. 'I thought it must be you, Ross. I haven't heard such mirth since you went to Ireland. Come into the office.' To Herbert he said, 'A pot of tea, Herbie, with sugar lumps *in a bowl*, please, not on the saucers. Jump to it, boy.'

'Yes, sir, yes, right away, sir.'

Ross said 'Your office boy is quite a character.'

'He is. Our *dear* Miss Simpson complains that he's disrespectful to his elders and, I suspect, wonders why I employed him.' In the office John pulled out a chair for Ross. 'I like the boy because although being one of a family of seventeen who live in poor circumstances, he is scrupulously clean, his clothes neatly darned. He's keen to learn the trade and Mr Cole told me yesterday that the boy is extremely bright. And now, Ross, after all that, how are you feeling?'

'Not so good. I can't get used to the idea that I made such a bad investment.'

'You're luckier than some, you still have capital. It isn't as if you are on the breadline. You'll soon recover.'

'It's waiting to recover that's the problem.'

'I can find you plenty of jobs here, if you feel like it.'

'I'd be grateful.'

'Well now, I have something here that might interest you.' John took a roll of paper from a drawer. 'I want you to convert some of the Dell Line cargo ships to take a few passengers, say six to eight. The ships I had converted to cargo and passenger in the other lines are showing a handsome profit.' He cleared the desk and spread out the paper. 'I drew up a rough draft. I thought you might give your opinion.'

Ross studied the plan for a moment, then asked, 'But why me? You need the opinion of someone more experienced. I can only speak as a traveller.'

'And that is exactly what I need. Last year, after your trips abroad on the *Eagle* and the *Dolphin*, you made some valid comments about improving not only the comfort of the cabins, but the position of them on the ship and your comments slipped my mind. This morning I recalled what a help you had been. But there is more competition now.' He pointed to the plans. 'I have done some of the changes you suggested. You might get further ideas if you study them. Would you do that for me?'

'Of course, I shall be glad to.' Ross rolled up the plans. 'I'll take them upstairs and get out of your way.'

By the time the two men left at six o'clock, Ross was so full of enthusiasm for the work he had done that John laughed and told him he had better move into the office permanently.

Ross shook his head. 'No, but I would like to spend a few days on the plans. Then I shall probably go back to investments.'

The following morning he was up early. He looked at the paper first and found that Fray and Hulton had been suspended. He put the paper aside to read over breakfast because he had noticed a letter from his Aunt Eileen on the top of his mail.

The letter, in spite of all his troubles, sent his heart racing. Alicia Sylvain had called and asked Eileen if she would tender her apologies to him for having left the ball so suddenly without explanation.

'It was apparently the fault of her aunt,' Eileen wrote. *'She had developed a migraine and wanted to be away from the noise of the ballroom. I quite like Alicia. I asked her in and we had a long talk. Although she seems to know many people I have a feeling she's a rather lonely person. She and her aunt are spending some time in London before returning to Bath.*

They are staying at the Savoy Hotel. She mentioned this twice and she also mentioned that her aunt has had tea in her room but that Alicia had hers in the lounge at four o'clock. I presume she would like the opportunity of apologizing to you personally. I gave her your address, but perhaps you could write her a short note. I guessed you were taken with her when I saw you dancing together and Alicia Sylvain is certainly a lady in love. I wish you well!'

Ross sat back. Well! How very interesting. In love with him? Mmm, he would have to make a point of going to have tea in the Savoy lounge one afternoon. Perhaps tomorrow? Having decided on this he read the rest of the letter.

'Fiona and Ashling have asked to be allowed to leave school. Tara left this summer anyway. We had a family discussion and it ended up with Patrick giving his consent. I am not happy about this. I've told the girls if they stay at home they will have to help me care for the tenants. Ashling is willing and, to my surprise, so is Fiona, although she insists that eventually she wants to follow a career.

Tara was furious when she knew that Miss Sylvain had

called, saying that the apology was just a ruse to get in touch with you. Tara still feels you belong to her but trying to convince her that you are your own man is like trying to blow down an apple tree. Oh, Ross, what am I to do with my temperamental daughter? I can only pray that she will fall in love with a man who wants to marry her.

Incidentally, Brendan is also in love. He met the young lady at the ball. She's a gentle girl, painfully shy and with no looks to speak of, but Brendan can praise her qualities for ten minutes without repeating himself. He's talking about marriage. I do hope that he's made the right choice, bless him.

And how are you settling down? It is not easy to settle down after a holiday. We all miss you terribly. Write when you can.

Love from all of us, Aunt Eileen.'

Ross put the letter aside and was getting ready to go to the office when he suddenly made up his mind to call and see his father.

Addison Ferris was not an affable man. He had plenty of business acquaintances, many enemies, but according to what Ross had been told, his father did not know one man he could call a friend.

When Ross was shown into his office Addison did not even look up to acknowledge his son, but went on putting his signature to several letters. Ross, steeling himself not to walk out, picked up a morning paper, sat down in a chair by the window and opened the paper. The next moment his father said in a sarcastic tone, 'Do make yourself at home.'

Ross forced himself to reply in a vague way, 'Pardon?' then went on, 'Oh, yes, yes,' and giving the paper a shake made a pretence of reading. He longed to say something about Fray and Hulton, but refrained.

His father laid down his pen carefully. 'May I enquire the reason for this sudden visit?'

'Before my mother died she begged me to look in on you from time to time, which I have done. I must point out, however, that my visit is no more than a duty call.'

'Your mother was a stupid woman.'

'My mother was endowed with a great deal of common sense if you had taken the trouble to find out. Her fear of you was because of your brutality.'

Addison dismissed this with a snort and a wave of the hand. 'I never laid a hand on her. It was all in her imagination.'

'Imagination, however vivid, does not bruise the flesh!'

Addison turned to his desk. 'You are stupid, like your *dear* mother. Every bruise on her was self-inflicted.'

It took all of Ross's control not to jump up and punch his father in the face. 'You are the stupid one for expecting me to believe that my mother, or any other woman, could inflict bruises between her shoulder blades.'

'It's obvious that you've never dealt with an hysterical woman,' his father sneered. 'A wooden back brush can wreak havoc on the flesh. You should try it sometime.' He picked up his pen. 'And now, if you will *kindly* excuse me, I have work to do, even if you haven't.'

Without haste Ross got up. 'Oh, I have plenty to do, more than I can cope with at the moment. But then, money seems to cling to me as it does to you. Thanks to the advice of John Davies, I've made some excellent investments. I have nothing to grumble about.'

His father, who was normally so poker-faced when discussing business affairs, showed surprise.

Ross walked to the door. 'I'll bid you good day, sir.' He glanced back at the statue-like figure and felt no regret at having told a lie. It would give his bombastic father something to think about.

Unfortunately, the meeting had dredged up other

thoughts. Had his father been right when he claimed that his mother's bruises had been self-inflicted? He recalled Aunt Eileen saying once, 'I loved your mother very much, Ross, but she must have been very trying to live with at times. She became neurotic and would complain of feeling unwell simply to get your father's sympathy. She was a very loving person and desperately needed to be loved in return, and your father had other women. It must have hurt her terribly.'

After weighing up the conversation with his father and recalling his aunt's comments about his mother's poor health, Ross began to understand the needs of both parents. His mother's desperation for her husband's love and her constant demand for attention must have sent his father seeking other women who were willing to accept what he wanted to give.

Thoughts of the complexity of women naturally led to Alicia. He just had to know more about her. Well, he had been given the opportunity. He would go to the Savoy that afternoon.

The scene in the lounge of the hotel was one of decorum. At some tables were young ladies chaperoned by a mother or aunt, all nibbling at delectable confections and drinking tea, with many of the young ladies casting surreptitious glances towards well-groomed, eligible-looking young men, or gazing with envious looks from lowered lids to where the parties were mixed. Violinists in the background gave a rendering of sentimental ballads.

All very romantic, Ross thought, as he looked around the room for Alicia. With people barring his view he began to weave his way among the tables and was conscious of claiming attention, not only from young ladies but also their chaperones. He was praying he would not be recognized by anyone when he saw Alicia and made a beeline to where she was seated alone at a table in a corner. When he approached her she said,

'Why, Mr Ferris, how nice to see you. Are you meeting someone?'

'I came especially to see you,' he replied softly. 'My aunt told me in her letter that you took afternoon tea alone at four o'clock.'

Another woman might have made a pretence of being flustered and say coyly, 'Oh, dear, I wasn't aware of having it mentioned it.' But not Alicia. The smile she gave him held mischief.

'I'm so glad you found me. Do please sit down.' A waiter came up to take his order and when he had gone, Alicia continued, 'I wanted to apologize to you personally for having to leave so suddenly on the night of the ball. It seemed so rude.'

'My aunt explained the reason. I understand. May I say you are looking extremely well.'

She was wearing a cream linen dress, the only embellishment a small diamond-shaped brooch in turquoise and although the dress was simply styled she looked elegant. She inclined her head, acknowledging the compliment.

Tea and cakes were brought and after the tea was poured, Alicia was indecisive about which cake to have. Ross suggested a heart-shaped one, with a cherry set into the cream. Alicia accepted his choice and said with a singularly sweet smile, that reminded him of Rosin, 'I think you are a romantic, sir.'

'A man without romance in his soul would make a poor lover indeed.'

'I like you, Mr Ross Ferris,' she said lightly.

'I'm glad.' He touched her hand and she withdrew it quickly, her expression changing, bringing Rosin immediately to his mind. He would be aware that she was enjoying his company, but touch her and she would withdraw into herself.

He said, 'I understand that you and your aunt are staying in London for a while, Miss Sylvain.' He spoke briskly so she would not get the impression that he wanted any closer association and was pleased that she seemed taken aback by his manner.

'Y-yes. My aunt has several business appointments. It's all very dull to me. I always try to get out of going with her.'

Ross wiped his mouth with his napkin. 'I'm sure you must have many friends who will be pleased to have a visit from you.'

'Not really. The people I know are mostly my aunt's friends. They are all older.' He was aware that she was trying to weigh him up. She asked him if he wished for more tea and he declined. They talked about various places in Ireland, then Ross, not wanting to outstay his welcome said he really must be going. He made to rise and she asked him if he could stay for a little while longer, explaining that even ten minutes would help to get her over a very boring day. There was nothing forlorn about her manner. It was a simple statement of fact.

He sat back. 'Do you have to live with your aunt, Miss Sylvain? Surely you would be better living with a relative who has a family.'

'My aunt is my only relative, my parents are dead, I never knew my grandparents. My aunt is trying to marry me off, but I refuse to marry any man whose sole interest is getting his hands on my dowry, which is quite substantial. I'm not expecting a man to fall madly in love with me, nor I with him, but I must have some respect for the person I am going to marry. Love can grow with time.'

Ross leaned forward, 'May I put a mythical case, Miss Sylvain? You and a young man are deeply in love, you want to get married but your aunt refuses her permission because the man is not able to keep you in the style to which you've been accustomed. Supposing the young man begged you to run away with him and get married, would you do so, knowing you would forfeit your money?'

'No, because I've had it drummed into me that where there's a lack of money love flies out of the window.'

'And you believe it?'

'Yes, I do.'

'So you have never really been truly in love?'

'And you have?'

'Yes, many, many times,' he replied airily.

She inclined her head. 'Have you ever lived in poverty?'

'No, I can't say that I have.'

'Then how can you possibly judge the real meaning of love?' She spoke sharply. 'Men enjoy boasting about the affairs they've had, which are really no more than passing flirtations to boost their egos.'

'You seem to know a great deal about it,' he said, making an effort not to get rattled, yet knowing there was truth in her statement.

'I've mixed with many men, Mr Ferris, more often than not against my will. They talk a lot about their conquests, no doubt hoping to impress me with their prowess as a suitable lover or husband. They sicken me.'

'How fortunate that I made no attempt to speak of my peccadilloes, Miss Sylvain, otherwise I might have been banished from your little domain.' She flushed and, realizing how petty he must have sounded, he said, 'Forgive me, I'm afraid I phrased my words rather badly. What I meant was –'

'It's all right, there's no need to apologize.' She interrupted. 'At times I let myself get carried away on certain subjects, men being one of them. Or should I say, certain men.' She flashed a quick smile and then her expression became earnest. 'I must say that I've been grateful for your company, Mr Ferris, and now I'm afraid that I must go. I've just caught sight of my aunt. It's unusual for her to seek me out at this time of day.' Alicia got up and held out her hand.

They shook hands and she was about to move away when Ross said, 'I'll be here the same time tomorrow, Miss Sylvain.'

Her look of pleasure was all he needed. It would be something to look forward to.

Unfortunately, they were to meet sooner than expected.

9

It was not until Ross had left Alicia that his present position hit him hard. Until then he had made an effort to accept his loss on the stock market. It was something that John had always drummed into him. 'Always be a forerunner, Ross, and if you do fall, get up at once and tackle the road ahead, never look at the ground.'

Ross had met men who, having lost heavily, would treat it as knowledge gained. He even heard one man say cheerfully that the bankruptcy court was the ante-room to the boardroom. Unfortunately the outlook of others at that moment did nothing to help him start building his life again.

At the office Ross and John talked about the stocks and shares market for a while, John saying there were no further whispers about Fray and Hulton, so they would just have to wait and see what developed.

Ross then produced the cargo ship plans he had been working on. John declared he was delighted at the changes, but Ross said he could see a possibility for making further improvements and would work on them for a couple of hours.

They had arranged to meet colleagues at their club that evening for dinner. It was a lively and satisfying evening and when they arrived home John asked Ross into his study for a final drink. Before the drinks could be poured, however, there was a wild clanging of the front door bell.

The two men exchanged glances. John said, 'Who the devil –?' The bell was pulled for a second time and he put down the decanter and went into the hall. Ross followed.

When John opened the door a woman all but fell in. He caught hold of her. Ross gave a gasp and hurried forward. 'Miss Sylvain?'

She looked as if she had dressed hurriedly and she gazed at him in a tormented way. 'Help me, Mr Ferris, please.'

He put his arm around her and John said briskly, 'Bring her into the study and I'll pour some brandy.'

By the time Ross had managed to get her into a chair Alicia's face was paper white and she seemed to be on the verge of fainting. He chafed her hands.

John brought the brandy saying gently, 'Try and take a sip of this.'

She managed to take some, then leaned back and whispered, 'I'm sorry, Mr Ferris. I didn't know who else to go to.'

'It's all right, Miss Sylvain. Don't worry about that. When you feel a little better you can tell me what happened.' Then as an afterthought he asked, 'Is your aunt all right?'

She nodded. 'She knows nothing about it.'

Alicia gave a shudder and to John's querying glance Ross said to him, 'This is Miss Sylvain. We had tea together this afternoon. She and her aunt are staying at the Savoy Hotel. We met in Ireland.'

Alicia began to shake uncontrollably and John hurried out and returned with a fur-lined travelling rug, which he tucked around her. He then told her if she would like to lie down he could call his housekeeper. Alicia shook her head and said she would be all right in a moment, she had had a shock. John said he would make some tea and left once more.

It was then that Alicia looked up at Ross, her eyes brimming with tears, her expression one of despair.

'It was terrible. Two men broke into my room. I was in bed. One man came over –' She began to sob and Ross thought: Oh God, has she been raped? He drew

116

her to him and tried to soothe her. By the time John came in with a tray the sobbing had stopped but Alicia looked utterly drained. She sat with her eyes closed and when Ross suggested that she lie down on the sofa for a while she gave in without protest. He put the rug over her and within seconds she was asleep. John picked up the tray and motioned to Ross to leave.

In the drawing room with a cup of tea each, they talked over the problem, with John thinking of possible explanations. 'Has she suffered a nightmare? They can be quite terrifying. I had a dreadful one once, which remained so vivid that I couldn't accept until hours later that it had been a-dream. I was fifteen at the time.'

It was over half an hour before Alicia roused and in that time Ross had told John the story of Alicia and Rosin. 'You've certainly met some interesting people, Ross,' said John. But then you've always been caught up in adventures, haven't you? It will be interesting to hear what exactly happened to Miss Sylvain – or is it Miss Dannet?'

The men had taken turns to look in on Alicia and it was Ross who found her awake and sitting up. Although still pale she had lost the desperate expression. She swung her feet to the floor.

'I owe you and your friend an explanation, Mr Ferris. You must have thought a madwoman had escaped from an asylum.' Although she had made an attempt to speak rationally there was a quiver in her voice. 'It was the most frightening experience I've ever known.'

John looked in then and, seeing that Alicia was awake, was about to withdraw when she said, 'Please come in, sir. I think you deserve an explanation for my irrational behaviour. I can't believe that it actually happened, but believe me it did. Between you, you might be able to offer an answer.'

Ross introduced John, who asked her if she would like some tea before she started and she said she would prefer some brandy if he didn't mind. It was easy to see why. In spite of attempting a show of calmness her hand shook and the glass tinkled against her teeth. She sipped at the brandy then, putting down the glass, she squared her shoulders.

'I think I did tell you that two men came into my bedroom. I must point out that my aunt introduced me to two friends at dinner. Both men were middle-aged, both charming and good company. My aunt drank three or four glasses of wine, which was not unusual. I had only one glass but even then did not drink it all.

'The men left before ten and my aunt and I went up to our rooms. I had a slightly hazy feeling and put it down to the wine. Later, when I went to my aunt's bedroom to say goodnight, she was asleep and gently snoring. As my aunt suffers from insomnia I thought it strange because although she takes sleeping tablets they usually take a while to work. She likes to have an oil lamp left on low so I turned the lamp down and left. By this time I began to feel strange, light-headed, and decided I would forfeit my bedtime reading and settle for sleep.'

Alicia paused then went on: 'I have no recollection of removing my negligée or getting into bed, but when a sound woke me suddenly, I was in bed, the lights were on and I was not ... wearing my nightdress.' Alicia took a deep breath. 'It was then I became aware of two men in the room. Everything was still a little hazy but to my utter astonishment I saw they were setting up a camera.'

'A camera?' Ross and John said in unison.

Alicia nodded. 'I thought I must be dreaming. But then I heard one of the men say, "I'm ready. Get her ready." The other man came over to the bed and I shut my eyes and pretended to be asleep, praying they would go away. He shook me. Then, sitting on my bed, he put his arms around me.' Alicia swallowed hard. 'I

118

tried to scream but no sound came. Then he pulled me up, dragged down the bedclothes and putting his hand under my . . . my . . . he kissed me. At that moment there was a flash, I screamed and the man holding me struck me. Then anger surged. I clawed at his face and tried to scream again but the man hit me another blow. Then the man at the camera shouted, "Come on, you fool, we'll have to get out of here, quick."

'I saw them leave and then the maid was knocking on the door and asking if I was all right. I put on my negligée and, opening the door slightly, I told her yes, I had been dreaming, and she left. I was shaking so much I could hardly stand, but even then the implication of the incident struck me and I knew I had to get away and tell someone what had happened.'

'Why didn't you ring reception and report it?' John asked.

Ross was wondering the same thing when she said quietly, 'Are you aware of all the implications? That man took a photograph of me naked in bed. He was kissing me. And why?'

'Blackmail?' Ross queried, sounding as though he were not ready to believe it.

'I can't think of any other reason, can you?' She turned to John. 'What do you think, Mr Davies?'

He nodded slowly. 'It seems to be the only explanation. No doubt in a day or two you will get a demand for money or the pictures will be shown to someone. Are you engaged, Miss Sylvain?'

'A gentleman has asked my aunt's permission to marry me. She wants me to accept, but I have no intention of getting married at the moment.'

'So if the picture was sent to your aunt it would force you to accept the gentleman's proposal?' Ross said.

'Why should it? My aunt would know I wouldn't allow a man into my bedroom, much less into my bed.

119

If I wanted a secret assignation it would not be in the bedroom next to hers.'

'But you say you thought she was drugged.' This from John. 'She might think that you were responsible.'

'It would never occur to my aunt to think such a thing. She knows me through and through.'

Ross raised his eyebrows. 'Do we ever know each other?'

Alicia tensed and she held up clenched hands. 'Are you suggesting that I –?'

'I'm not suggesting anything, Miss Sylvain. I'm looking at the situation from your aunt's point of view. If the picture is submitted to her by these rogues she will naturally wonder why you didn't complain to the management. My friend and I know the reason. We saw the state you were in and understand why you came here.'

The tension went from Alicia. 'Yes, I see your reasoning. I've behaved foolishly.' There was a wry note in her voice. 'If the men were found and I had to go to court I could see the headlines in the newspapers: *Blackmailed Heiress Seeks Help of Men Friends in the Early Hours*. Oh dear, I have made a mess of everything.'

'Miss Sylvain,' John said, 'can you describe the men who came into your bedroom? You said your vision at first was hazy.'

'Yes, but later –' She sat, her fingertips to her lips. 'The man taking the photograph was older than his companion. He was big, stout. He had dark hair and a moustache and beard. Yes, and his hair and beard were thick. His coat was –' She frowned as she tried to recall it. 'It was black but I'm not sure whether it was a tailcoat or not. I didn't note any particular distinguishing marks, in fact, I'm surprised I noticed that much considering the state I was in.'

Ross told her she was doing excellently and asked if she could describe the other man. Alicia shuddered. 'I doubt whether I'll remember anything at all about him. He was so awful, fondling my – body.' She shuddered again. 'I know his breath stank of drink and garlic, but that's all.'

'Was he dark, medium, fair? How old would he be?'

Alicia shook her head. 'I have no idea of his colouring, but I would say he was younger than the other man.'

John urged her to go on. 'One observes details without realizing it. He kissed you – was his skin rough? Would you say he was unshaven?'

She touched her chin. 'Yes, yes, it was and I think I can remember him now.' She closed her eyes moment-arily and when she opened them she was excited. 'I can see him clearly. He had a thin face and a long nose, pinched at the end. He was swarthy-looking. Oh, yes, something else. The older man spoke in English but the other spoke in a foreign tongue. It wasn't French or Italian. I didn't understand what he said.'

'He could have been a seaman,' John mused. 'Did you notice anything else strange about him?'

'I'm afraid not.'

She sounded suddenly weary and John said quickly, 'We've been very probing with our questions, Miss Sylvain. You've done very well indeed.'

Alicia put her hand to her head, then got up. 'I must go. My aunt could wake and might need something.' Both men offered to go with her and when she begged them to let her go alone so as not to draw attention to herself, Ross pointed out gently that she would feel safer if she was accompanied to her room and the door locked. She gave in.

There was even a little light relief when John sug-gested a camouflage for Alicia and brought a white silk cape with a hood. Ross asked how many camouflages for young ladies he could produce, and John laughed and said he was an expert. It made Alicia smile.

She had brought the key to her room with her, and

121

as the staff were busy at reception with late arrivals they reached her room without being noticed. Ross and John went in with her, looked around for clues, opened the wardrobe door and, finding nothing untoward, prepared to leave. Ross promised to call the following afternoon to take tea with her.

She thanked them for their kindness and seemed on the verge of tears. Ross longed to take her in his arms and comfort her but had to be content with saying softly, 'We'll do all we can to find these villains, Miss Sylvain,' and was rewarded with a fleeting smile.

John said as they went downstairs, 'Was it only this afternoon that I said you led an adventurous life, my friend?'

Ross replied, 'I would say, without doubt, that these are the most adventurous times of all.'

10

It was not until Ross and John were back home and went over Alicia's story in detail that they came to the conclusion there was something wrong in the telling.

'But what?' Ross flung out his hands. 'I believed it when she described all the incidents. I felt terribly sorry for her when we had to leave. She did look genuinely drained.'

With both hands cupped round the brandy glass, John swirled the liquid gently for a moment, then looked up and said, 'My sympathies were with her at the time. Is it because the story seems too glib in retrospect? With prompting she gave good descriptions of the men. She was distressed but was she distressed because she was not telling the truth?'

Ross sat up. 'But why lie? Yet I think I felt deep down that she was withholding something.'

They went over the whole story once more without discovering any real reason why Alicia should lie about the incident.

Then John said, 'Could she have manufactured the whole thing because she wanted an excuse to visit you?'

Ross said, 'No, never,' but John persisted.

'Her behaviour towards you at the ball suggested she's a tease. There are many such young ladies. Alicia promised to arrange to meet you but left without saying goodbye. She writes to your aunt, explaining she felt awful for not making her apologies to you, but makes it clear she wants your aunt to tell you exactly where she will be at a given time. At the Savoy she again leaves you, explaining she sees her aunt and must go. Did you see her aunt?' When Ross told him no, John continued, 'So she has you interested in seeing her again. But, she wants to see you alone at home. She concocts the story, not knowing at the time that anyone else lives here.'

Ross nodded. 'Could be. I shall know more tomorrow.'

'*If* you see her,' John said wryly. 'Her plan went wrong and no doubt she will avoid you until the incident has died down.' He stifled a yawn. 'I suggest we go to our beds. It's been a busy day.'

Ross, unwilling to think further on the subject went to bed and gave himself up to sleep.

He was up early and was surprised to find a letter from Alicia, which had been delivered by hand. She wrote that knowing she would not be able to sleep in the bed with its awful memories she had pulled the counterpane off to sleep on the sofa and had found a man's handkerchief. She had kept it up for him to see. She added that she had remembered that the younger man had had an anchor tattooed on the back of each hand. Might this be of help? She thanked them both for their extreme kindness, and hoped to see Ross that afternoon.

Ross showed the letter to John. 'A sensible young lady, offering evidence.'

'Oh, so now you approve of her? Last night you were unable to say one good thing about her.'

'Ross, don't get on your high horse.' John spoke quietly. 'This letter has not solved anything. Maybe you will get to know more this afternoon. In the meantime, I know just where to pursue the man with the tattoos. There's a pub near the office, the Dog and Gun. They always know what's going on there.

At lunchtime, Ross gave John a head start, aware that he was well known and trusted among the dockside community. Then he went into the Dog and Gun and saw John at a corner table, talking earnestly to an elderly man. The pub was fairly full. Some of the men were fishermen, some sailors, the rest a mixture of dock workers and others. They were a rough-looking bunch. A few gave Ross a passing glance, but that was all.

When Ross went up to the table John introduced him, and then the old man to Ross in turn – Nat Richards, who used to work for his father.

Tankards were on the table and John said, 'I was asking Nat if he had happened to notice a foreign sailor-type of chap who had an anchor tattooed on the back of each hand and he said no seaman would have such a thing because it would be tempting providence. It could mean he would lose an arm.'

The old man man shrugged. 'Just one of those superstitions. My uncle used to tell us hundreds of them when I was a lad. Mind you, if every sailor believed them all they'd never have gone to sea.'

'So you weren't a sailor?' Ross queried.

'Not me, I would be sick in a rowing boat. And yet I like living by water. I like the activity, ships leaving, returning. There's never a dull moment beside the docks.'

They finished their drinks, chatting about the old days. Then John said they had better be going, adding that they would give up looking for a thug with anchors tatooed on the back of his hands.

When they were outside, John said, 'I'm wondering if you are thinking what I am thinking, about Miss Sylvain, I mean, and the two anchors?'

Ross squared his shoulders. 'I would say she has a vivid imagination.'

'Exactly.'

'But why, John, why? Is it boredom? My cousin Tara does foolish things to be noticed, yet she has no need to, she's attractive and draws young men to her without even a coy glance. But Alicia Sylvain knows I'm attracted to her, so why all the subterfuge? I know this, I shall certainly not mince my words when I see her this afternoon.'

'If she is there,' John replied quietly.

Alicia *was* there, sitting at the same table in the Savoy where she had sat the day before but she looked so pale, so desolate, that Ross's intended angry speech was never made.

As soon as she had invited him to sit down she said, 'Mr Ferris, I have a confession to make. I gave a false description to you last night of the men who invaded my bedroom. It was wrong of me, but at the time I felt I was doing the right thing.'

'You caused Mr Davies and myself a great deal of inconvenience,' he said, but the rebuke was mildly given.

'I know, but if I can explain. It's difficult because it involves my aunt. Or rather I feel sure it does. You see, Mr Ferris, the men my aunt and I had dined with earlier last evening were the ones who came to my room.'

'It had occurred to me, but I could see no reason for withholding this information.'

She gave a deep sigh. 'I know how bizzare it must all sound, but I shall try and explain it as it came to me. Naturally, when I saw these two men in my room I was shocked. Then when they began setting up the camera and I realized why, I felt horrified, especially as I had begun to feel that my aunt must be involved in some way.'

'Why should you think that?'

'She was on good terms with them and I had the impression during the meal that she knew them extremely well, even though she told me they had met at a friend's house for the first time a few months previously.'

The waiter came for the order and when it was given Alicia continued, 'I have no love for my aunt, Mr Ferris. She's a devious woman and I am only sorry that she has been made my guardian. She not only controls me, but my money too. Now then, I'll come to the crux of the story. When I came to your house after my awful experience I was in a state of shock and it was not until you asked me to describe the men that I knew I had to be careful. How would this affair affect me?'

'You have a very quick thinking mind, Miss Sylvain, considering you were in shock.'

'So I've been told a number of times. A friend of the family once said if I had been a son instead of a daughter I would have made my way in the world.'

Alicia never failed to surprise Ross. He had made no effort to disguise his sarcasm, but she had replied in the most matter-of-fact way. He could not resist saying, 'You would also have made a very good actress, Miss Sylvain. You fooled Mr Davies and myself. We've been making enquiries about the man with the anchors on the backs of his hands.'

'I'm sorry about that. I had not expected such quick action. It was my intention to confess what I had done this afternoon.' She nibbled at a piece of cake in an abstract way, then put the cake down. 'After a great deal of thought since last night I feel that this whole incident was planned by my aunt and Mr Bradshaw, the man she wants me to marry.'

'What would your aunt gain? If you were to marry, your husband takes over your affairs.'

'I was led to believe by my aunt that Mr Bradshaw is a wealthy man. I don't think he is. I overhead a young husband and wife talking about him at the ball. The man called him a ne'er-do-well and the wife accused her husband of being jealous.'

Ross shook his head. 'I still can't see how your aunt would benefit by arranging for you to be blackmailed.'

'It's simple. She arranges for Mr Bradshaw to engage the men to take the photograph. They get their fee, my aunt uses my money to supposedly pay the black-mailers, then she and Mr Bradshaw share it.'

'I'm not really believing all this, Miss Sylvain, but might I point out that if this were so, it would not let Mr Bradshaw win you as his bride.'

'Not at the moment, but that would follow in time. The blackmailers would produce the plates of the photographs, which they had not destroyed. Mr Bradshaw would supposedly pay the money to have them destroyed and my aunt would insist I marry him in gratitude.'

'There are still some unanswered questions. In view of all this, why did you think it necessary to give false descriptions of the two blackmailers?'

'I was so confused. The men had dined with us – my aunt knows them. They should have been friends. Now I'm convinced that my aunt and Mr Bradshaw are involved I shall simply face them with the facts.'

'And risk being certified insane?'

'Insane?' She looked at him puzzled.

'What proof have you that men were in your room? A man's handkerchief could have been placed there by you?'

'It was there,' she protested. 'I have it.'

'If, as you say, your aunt is a conniving woman and you accused her and Mr Bradshaw of being involved in blackening your name and of rogues being engaged to set it up, what do you think the result would be? Lady Kereslake is a very imposing figure and I feel she would have no trouble in convincing a court that you had been acting very strangely of late and had concocted this tale against her.'

'But it actually happened!'

'Think it over carefully. Think how it would sound to the average person, much less to legal men. You were in bed and asleep and you awoke to find two men in your room. One was setting up a camera. The other man came over and pulled down the bedclothes and you discovered that you were naked. No, you say to counsel, you had no idea how that happened. Someone must have drugged you. You felt hazy when you woke. The man put his arm around you and kissed you. You tried to push him away and scream but no sound came. Your aunt then says she was in an adjoining room and was wide awake and heard no sound. Need I go further?'

'And that is how it sounded to you and Mr Davies?' Alicia asked in despair.

'We both agreed there was a flaw in your story but had no idea what it could be because we had seen you distressed. But now you say you lied about the description of the two men, and you know, Miss Sylvain, if we were in court as witnesses, and on oath, we would have to tell the truth, wouldn't we?'

Her shoulders suddenly sagged and she looked at him like a child who had been caught pilfering. 'And I thought I was so clever.'

'You may be right about your aunt planning the whole thing but you would have to have more proof than a man's handkerchief that you insist had been left behind.'

'It was, I say that in all honesty, and the only part of the story I changed were the descriptions of the men.'

'Right, then shall we start there? Describe them.'

A look of hope came into her eyes. 'You are willing to help me after the foolish way I behaved? Thank you, Mr Ferris. I can't tell you how much I appreciate it.'

If she had been maudlin in any way Ross knew he would have regretted the offer, but she immediately became businesslike.

'Their behaviour during dinner could only be described as impeccable. They spoke in an educated way and were well groomed. I think I told you that they were both charming and good company. They talked about travel quite a lot and gave some amusing incidents that had occurred in different countries. They were middle-aged, but I would say that Mr Storton was the elder by a few years. He was of medium build, had brown hair streaked with grey, which was thin on top. He was an aristocratic-looking man.

'Mr Gault was tall and fair. His eyes would look blue sometimes and grey at other times. There was a twinkly look about them when relating a story and he had a quite infectious laugh. Although he did not have Mr Storton's aristocratic air there was nothing to hint whatsoever that they were not what they seemed.'

'Most rogues in higher circles have a charming manner. It's their stock in trade. Why not mention them casually to your aunt? If she is involved then she must be very surprised that you did not wake her after your terrifying experience.'

Alicia inclined her head. 'I don't know that I will mention the men. She would know that I went out, and when I came back, but I think I shall keep her in suspense. She must be wondering what plan I have in mind.'

'I think you must be prepared to get a letter demanding money for the return of the photograph. Your aunt will also get a photograph showing you in bed, so what do you do then?'

'Their plans have gone wrong. They might step down. I shall wait and see.'

Ross had a feeling that Alicia was beginning to treat the incident as an adventure and warned her against being too complacent.

Her expression changed, a haunted look came into her eyes. 'Please don't misjudge me, Mr Ferris. I don't think I shall ever forget my experience last night. I'm trying desperately not to think about it. When I do, I feel sick, soiled. An anger is there deep inside me. I would like to know if my aunt is involved and if it could be proved, I would be free of her dominance for

130

ever more. She's like a thorn in my flesh. I shall try and find out who these two men are.'

Ross had little faith in her finding them. That type of blackmailer would most likely be miles away by then, seeking further victims. Before he left Alicia he told her he would call again the next day and when her eyes suddenly filled with tears he found himself relenting towards her and promised to help if he possibly could.

After relating all the details to John, he said, 'I felt like washing my hands of the whole affair, but then she looked so lost, so forlorn, I felt I must try and help.'

John replied quietly, 'There are rogues who are blackmailers, but there are also well-bred women who are blackmailers, who trade on the feelings of vulnerable men.'

Ross looked up. 'And you think that I am one of the vulnerable male victims?'

'I don't know, Ross, I just don't know. In the past I've usually managed to weigh women up, but Alicia Sylvain is an enigma to me and I would like to know why. She's such a dainty person yet I feel there's an iron will hidden in her. I was willing to help when she first talked about the men who invaded her privacy, but now with all you've told me I'm not so sure that she needs help.'

Ross explained there was a gentle side to her, but when John reminded him of his remark that she would make a good actress, Ross was forced to do some further thinking. He was no nearer knowing what was truth and what was fiction. John was right, she was an enigma . . . like Rosin. Well, he would see her once more and try to pin her down to something more positive, and if he was still not satisfied he would forget about her.

When he went to the Savoy the following afternoon, however, she was not there and after waiting nearly half an hour he enquired about her at the reception desk.

The receptionist said, 'I'm sorry, sir. Lady Kereslake left with Miss Sylvain at seven o'clock this morning.'

'Left? Are you sure?'

'I'm positive, sir. I had just come on duty. They might have been unexpectedly called away. Lady Kereslake seemed to be in a hurry and Miss Sylvain looked a little – well, dazed, as though she had been roused from sleep.'

Ross's heartbeat quickened. Sleepy? Lightly drugged perhaps? He asked if there was anyone else with them and the woman, after hesitating a moment said, 'There were two men, who, although not appearing to be with them, knew the ladies, because they had all dined together two evenings before.'

At this his spirits sank to zero. Had Alicia been kidnapped and would she be forced to submit to marry a man she didn't like, or . . .

Ross's mind would not go further than that.

11

Ross had been reluctant to tell John Davies of his worry about Alicia and her aunt leaving the hotel so suddenly, feeling he might think he was making too much of the incident. John, however, showed an immediate interest.

'So now there are three possibilities in connection with the blackmailers: One, Lady Kereslake could be very friendly indeed with the rogues and they were abducting her niece. Two, Miss Sylvain might have made the whole story up and it was just coincidence that the men left right after them, and three . . . Lady Kereslake might not be friendly at all with them and both she and her niece were being abducted.'

'*Both* abducted?' Ross looked up startled. Such a thing had not occurred to him.

'Why not? I don't think we should ignore the fact that Alicia has nothing good to say of her aunt, yet you found Lady Kereslake quite pleasant to you.' John was silent for a moment, then he said, 'There is also a fourth possibility to consider. Our lady could have had an urgent message from home and this was the reason for their hasty departure.'

'No.' Ross shook his head slowly. 'I can't accept this. It's too simple an explanation. You are forgetting the blackmailers. They followed the women out.'

'The question remains, Ross, were there ever any blackmailers? When I weigh up this situation there seems to be a number of discrepancies in the story. Why don't you question the cabbies who picked up early passengers from the hotel this morning and find out where they were bound for?'

Ross seized on this suggestion and went back to the

Savoy, where regulars drove the route to and from the hotel. Although he was lucky enough to find the cabbie he wanted at the third try he was disappointed at the results. The man had taken the women to a house in Kensington Gardens Square where, apparently, the old lady's sister-in-law had died. All the blinds were down, he said, and the curtains drawn. No, there were no men with them. The women travelled alone.

When this was related to John Davies and he asked if this was now the end of the story, Ross said, 'No, I have to find Alicia. I won't be satisfied until I've talked to her. I shall go to the house tomorrow. I may not be allowed to see her, but I shall try and find out something about her. I won't rest until I know the truth. If I find out that she's been lying to me in any way then that will be the end.'

'So be it,' his friend replied with a helpless shrug.

Ross arrived the next morning in Kensington Gardens Square at ten o'clock and stood staring at the house. The blinds were up and all the curtains drawn back. The only person in sight was a little maid next door, who was polishing a brass plate at the side of the door.

When Ross asked her if she knew if a funeral had taken place next door, she said, worriedly, 'I know nutthin', mister, an' I'm not supposed to talk to anyone.'

She gave a quick rub to the plate then scuttled inside and closed the door. This was to be expected. Skivvies were underdogs who kept their places, mostly in the kitchen. He went up the steps to the house he had come to see and raised the knocker.

The ratatat had a hollow sound and no one came in answer to its summons. Nor was a second knock answered. Then Ross, seeing a young man come out of a house two doors away and walk in his direction, went down the steps and hailed him.

After Ross had explained his errand, the young man said, 'I'm afraid I don't know much about the lady who lived here but I did overhear two of the servants talking last night about the undertakers having been and, apparently, after a van had taken some goods away the staff left. I don't think anyone's here now. I'm sorry I can't tell you any more than that.'

Ross thanked him but made no move, realizing he might get more information if he spoke to the servants in the young man's house. There might be other members of the family there. He could at least try.

A young maid opened the door and when Ross told her he needed some information about the people next door she said she would get the housekeeper to talk to him.

Although the middle-aged woman in black looked severe, she seemed very willing to talk about the neighbours when Ross said he was a reporter and he understood that the lady who had died the day before was the sister-in-law of Lady Kereslake.

'That's right and never been near the poor woman until she was dead. Mrs Travers was a bit of a recluse, never went out, but she could have called on her. I don't know what she hoped to get. The money and house go to a nephew. Perhaps she thought she might have got some jewellery. Greed, that's what it is. No relatives turn up when a pauper in a family dies, do they?'

Ross tried to find out if the two men he called the blackmailers had been, but the woman said she hadn't seen anyone else apart from the undertakers and Lady Kereslake and the young lady with her, and added that she wouldn't have known who they were had it not been for Mrs Travers's nurse telling her. He thanked her for the information, but left feeling none too pleased with his efforts.

He knew that Alicia and her aunt had been there, but he had not solved anything of the mystery, nor did he know where they were now. Possibly they had gone to Bath.

Feeling thoroughly frustrated and not being in the mood to be questioned by John about Alicia and her aunt, Ross decided to go to his club, where at least the conversation would be centred on business.

On the way, he felt suddenly angry that he had become involved. He must forget the whole thing. He and John had discussed the market the night before and he had decided to go and see his broker this morning and what had he been doing? Chasing around after Alicia Sylvain and her aunt when nothing about Alicia's story held any feeling of reality. The trouble was he had been so flattened by his heavy loss in his investment that he had purposely avoided taking up the cudgels again. He could delay no longer. He must go to his broker.

After he had discussed the firms he had decided to invest in, he felt as though he were re-entering the world. The sale of a couple of paintings he owned would provide the money. All his old confidence was returning.

John was quietly pleased when Ross told him he was back in the swim again and after he had related the events regarding Alicia and her aunt, John said, 'Well, Ross, I'm glad you came to the decision to put Miss Sylvain out of your mind because I saw her this evening on my way home, coming out of a small private hotel on the arm of a gentleman, her aunt with her. Our dear Alicia was smiling happily up into his face and I can only conclude this must be the man her aunt wants her to marry.'

Athough Ross had been determined to forget the Alicia affair he felt shaken by John's news. 'I knew there was something underhand going on in some way, but I find it difficult to believe that they were a blackmailing gang.'

136

'They were obviously after money. They would know your father is wealthy, but would not know of your losses with the Fray and Hulton affair. You should be thankful that you were not more fully drawn into their scheme.'

Ross was silent for a moment, then he looked up. 'Supposing I come across Alicia. What excuse is she going to make?'

'I doubt whether you will have that problem. They would have gone to Kensington Gardens Square yesterday hoping for money. They might even have found some valuables to make their journey worth while – paintings, ornaments, some special pieces of furniture, perhaps.'

'The van,' Ross said. 'The housekeeper next door said that a van had taken items away. Oh God, I can't believe Alicia could behave like this.'

John sighed. 'I've met many such gangs during my travels, Ross. They are all over the world, although I must admit I was a little taken in by Miss Sylvain. Of course, the discrepancies in her story were suspect from the start. You yourself were aware of it too.'

'But what was the point of it all? What could she hope to gain?'

'She knew you were attracted to her. In time I suspect she would have asked you to lend her the money to pay the blackmailers and would have promised to pay you back somehow. The sudden death of the relative changed all that.'

'You may be right but I still feel there is a piece of the jigsaw missing. I am not, however, planning to look for it. I've wasted enough time already.'

For the next months everything seemed to go well for Ross. Although Alicia came into his thoughts from time to time it was only briefly, then was gone as he became

137

involved in the market again. There were no swift share rises, some were static but others had risen and he was content with that.

Letters had come from Aunt Eileen with notes from each of the girls who, it seemed, were enjoying being at home. Then in his aunt's last letter, a note from Queenie McKnott was enclosed, saying that although she had not seen Rosin since Ross had left Ireland, a man passing by had left a message from her to say she would be seeing Queenie in a week or ten days time. *So that is good*, Queenie added. *I was getting worried about her. I thought that you, too, Mr Ferris, would be pleased to know that she's all right.*

This did set Ross thinking once more about the possibility of Alicia and Rosin being one and the same person, but the question was soon at the back of his mind when he read the papers announcing that the receiver had been brought in to Fray and Hulton, Property and Land Developers.

Then, more startling yet, came a short piece in the next column, stating that Addison Ferris, a merchant banker, had been missing from his home for two days, and added that the last time he had been seen was two days before on a Channel ferry bound for Calais.

Ross, who had just started his breakfast, put down his knife and fork and sat staring at the folded newspaper, which was propped up against the coffeepot, feeling as though he were suffering from paralysis. There was a tap on the dining room door, then John came in, a newspaper in his hand.

'You've seen the news, I take it?'

'Yes, I've seen it. It seems hard to believe. I just can't imagine my father running away. I've always felt that he was the sort of person who would face up to a dozen barristers and manage to prove he was innocent, even if he had been guilty of any wrong doing.'

'I should imagine that everyone who knew him would

feel the same way. He was that kind of man. What I can't understand is not hearing any whispers that he had gone missing.'

Ross moved the newspaper and poured John a cup of coffee. 'The trouble is, I feel I should be doing something, but what can I do?'

'I think it might be wise to stay out of the limelight for a few days. The journalists will be on your trail, trying to find out how much you know about your father.'

Ross could not help thinking how feeble his own investigative efforts had been when trying to get news of Alicia and her aunt. He said, 'I'll stay here for today at least and work upstairs. Mrs Fox will keep them at bay. I'll tell her to say I've gone to France to look for my father.'

'France?' John repeated, looking thoughtful. 'Do you think he would find a hiding place with your Uncle Edward where he stays in Paris? I know there's no love lost between them, but Edward has always been willing to help anyone in trouble.'

There was a loud ratatat at the front door and John said quickly, 'I'll hurry and tell Mrs Fox what to say.'

By mid-morning Ross came to the conclusion that Mrs Fox too would have made an excellent actress. From behind the lounge door he heard her telling a very believable story to the journalists that Mr Ross had gone rushing off during the early hours of the morning after a man had delivered an urgent message. She added that she was sure that Calais had been mentioned, but why he should go there she had no idea.

It did the trick. The knocks at the door ceased just before eleven o'clock. Ross had had several telephone calls from John, wanting to know what was happening. His office too had been besieged but after he said he had not seen Mr Ross Ferris for the past three days the press tailed off.

It was late afternoon and Ross was downstairs looking for some papers when he heard a knock on the front door. He heard Mrs Fox go to the door but was unable to hear what she said.

The next moment she was with him, saying, 'It's your aunt from Ireland,' in as matter-of-fact a voice as if his aunt were in the habit of dropping in every day.

Then Eileen burst in wailing, 'Oh, Ross, I just had to come.'

Ross, bewildered, took her in his arms. 'What is it, Aunt Eileen. What's wrong? What's happened?'

She looked up, tears rolling down her cheeks. 'It's your father, Ross. He came to us wanting somewhere to hide.'

'My father?' He stared at her. 'Came to you? I can't believe it. It's the last thing I would have expected him to do.'

Eileen made an effort to pull herself together. 'I'm sorry to have behaved in this way but you know how much I dislike him and he's no different in his ways seeking sanctuary. Such arrogance. You should hear him giving his orders. He wants a certain room, certain meals, he doesn't want to be disturbed . . .'

Ross was about to say he would order some tea when Mrs Fox looked in to say she had taken tea and cakes into the lounge. Ross helped Eileen off with her hat and coat.

'I don't know how you've managed to cope with all this trouble. Come along, we'll go and sit down and see if we can sort something out.'

When they were sitting down and the tea was poured Ross asked how the family had taken all this upset. Eileen sighed.

'You know Patrick's maxim: one must help the sinner on the way.'

'So my father has confessed that he's guilty of –'

'He hasn't admitted anything. According to Addison,

someone has betrayed him, but he has no chance of proving it.'

'It all seems so crazy. It simply doesn't make sense. How have the girls and Brendan taken it?'

'The girls, as it happens, are staying with friends for a few days, and thank heavens for that. Brendan seems to think it's a big adventure having a criminal in the house.' Eileen looked up and added quietly, 'Because he *is* a criminal, Ross. He hasn't told us exactly what has happened, but his very manner tells me he is. I want him out of the house before Patrick insists that he becomes a permanent guest. Addison takes it for granted that because he was married to your mother I should give him sanctuary by rights. Why should I, after the brutal way he treated her? Your father is a schemer, Ross, always has been and always will be. I should imagine he had his route all planned out before the trouble broke. He's extremely pleased that he hood-winked the police. He told me, enjoying it, that he led them to believe he was bound for France, but before the ferry sailed he managed to slip away and hide. Then, disguised, he arranged to travel to Ireland.' Eileen paused then looked at him appealingly. 'I want rid of him, Ross. How do I do it? He just ignores me and Patrick just says that the poor man needs help.'

'I'll come back with you, I'll get him out of the house.'

'Oh, Ross, would you? I would be so grateful. It's not only the fact of losing our good name should we be accused of harbouring a wanted man, but I worry about Tara. Like Brendan she will see it all as a big adventure. And she'll love Addison, because if he puts his mind to it he can be a real charmer, especially where attractive young ladies are concerned. What's more, Tara simply cannot keep a secret.'

Ross looked thoughtful. 'I could take him to Three Gables. Mr and Mrs Colhoun are the souls of discretion.

141

Father must have some eventual plan. He's not the kind of person to lead the life of a recluse. I imagine he'll assume a new identity and go and live abroad somewhere. His work is his life. What's more, he'll have the money to do it. I should imagine he will have a small fortune hidden in some bank abroad somewhere.'

John was out late that evening so that Ross and his aunt had covered a lot of ground by the time he arrived home. Eileen had gone to bed, as she and Ross had arranged to travel back to Ireland the following morning. Ross told John the whole story, knowing he could trust him to keep it to himself.

'What on earth is your father doing running away?' John exclaimed. 'According to the present rumours, someone else is involved in the fraud. But then, of course, it *is* all just rumour. Heaven knows what the truth is. How do you plan to get him away from your uncle and aunt's house?'

'I shall deal with that when the time comes, but I will suggest his going to Three Gables. If he refuses then I shall threaten to tell the authorities where he is.'

'And would you have the courage to force him to leave?'

'Oh, yes, without a doubt. He's walked over many people in his time, including me. It's move, or else.'

Although Ross usually enjoyed the sea crossing to Ireland, this time it was simply something to be got over. He was certainly not looking forward to doing battle with his father, knowing that he too would have to take as ruthless an approach as his parent.

He was on deck, leaning on the rails, when Eileen, who had been in the saloon, came lurching towards him.

'Thought I would have some air. It's certainly fresh.'

'And rough.'

There were white horses on the water and Ross suddenly began to enjoy the pitch and toss of the ship. His aunt was a good sailor too, and after a while when she asked him if he could bear to hear her other two tales of woe, he smiled and said, 'What better opportunity than now?'

'I'm going to be honest, Ross, and say that when I first thought of coming to see you and enlist your help it was in my mind to see Preston, who is in London at the moment. But no sooner was I there than I realized how feeble-minded I was behaving. I would not only be chasing a man who was no good, but even if we never even touched, I was being disloyal in thought to my husband.' She paused. 'So having confessed that sin, I shall confess that I do not want Brendan to get married in July, which he has announced as his intention, for the simple reason that I am not ready to lose my son.'

Ross turned to her. She had tied a fine silk shawl over her head and the ends were flapping this way and that. One end flopped across her face and stayed there. Ross pulled it away and said gently, 'This is not you at all, Aunt Eileen. You've always done your very best for your children. Brendan was going to be married years ago, remember. Why should you now deny him the right to marry the girl he loves and leave home? It can't be because you're jealous of her.'

'No, I'm not jealous. It's because I feel that Celina isn't right for Brendan. She has no mind of her own and has always done what her mother told her. Her mother will run their lives.'

'No, she won't. Brendan won't allow her. I know you are always saying that he's easily led, but you were not at college with him. Your son, my lovely aunt, has a mind of his own and will wear the trousers in the house.

He has given in to you many times to please you, because what you've asked has not been important, but when he digs his heels in over something important, there's no moving him.'

Eileen, who had been staring out to sea, nodded slowly. 'I'm probably like other women who have only sons and find excuses to keep them at home. I shall have to rethink my motives.'

With the sea journey, then the train journey behind them, Ross was getting himself keyed up to meet his father and, instead, was faced with a joyous greeting by Brendan and, unexpectedly, his three sisters.

Brendan just about pumped his hand off. 'Well now, and what a pleasant surprise this is! How long are you going to stay?'

The girls interrupted by greeting Ross, Tara exuberantly flinging her arms around him, and although Fiona and Ashling's greetings were less lavish, they left no doubt about their pleasure at seeing him.

When Eileen asked the girls what had brought them home sooner than expected, Tara announced, 'Because Cook sent a message that Mama had been to England, that she was coming home and that cousin Ross was with her.'

Eileen gave a forced laugh. 'Anyway, here you all are. We'll have something to eat, then you must tell us all your news.' To Ross she added, 'I'm sure you must want to freshen up. Brendan will go up with you. I know you'll both have plenty to talk about.'

The cousins made small talk until they reached the first landing, then Brendan stopped and raised his eyebrows. 'They would come home now, wouldn't they, complicating things. His lordship is in the end room. Although Mother insists he stay in his room, and the girls sleep on the next floor, they couldn't avoid knowing he's in the house. When he gives his orders you can hear him at the other side of the lake.'

'Well, as soon as they do know I'll talk to him. I'm expecting plenty of opposition.'

They walked to the other end of the corridor where Ross usually slept when he visited. While he was emptying his bag, he asked where his Uncle Patrick was.

Brendan said, 'He stays out as long as possible. It makes Mother annoyed, but you know what a peaceable man he is. He hates trouble.' Brendan gave a wry grin. 'He does come in for meals.'

Before the two cousins went downstairs Ross had offered to explain the situation to the girls, adding, 'I think your mother has had more than enough to cope with. I'll try and have a quiet word with her.'

'They have to be told, but the staff are loyal. I'm sure they won't talk.'

When they went downstairs Patrick was there and seemed greatly relieved that Ross was planning to stay a few days, and he was actually quite lively over supper. The girls, of course, were full of chatter and it was Tara who brought up the news of Brendan's coming wedding with the added information that she, Fiona and Ashley were going to be bridesmaids.

Brendan teased them saying that he and his bride-to-be were going to elope, which brought an outcry from Tara, but both Fiona and Ashling said they thought it an excellent idea that would save a lot of fuss and expense.

Ross had spoken to Eileen about letting the girls know about his father, and although outwardly calm during the meal he was conscious of giveaway signs that his aunt was under stress by the way she kept moving the cutlery in between courses, pulling at the edge of her table napkin and toying with her food.

After the meal Ross broke the news to the girls about his father. The first reaction was complete silence, the gaze of his three cousins directed at him.

Then Tara said, 'Well, I'm glad we came home. How

terrible it would have been had we missed all this lovely drama.' Excitement oozed from her.

'It's not exactly a lovely drama,' Ashling protested.

'No, it's certainly not,' snapped Eileen, 'and what is being told now must go no further than these four walls. Is that understood?'

All the girls, with Tara now sober-faced, agreed. Tara, however, having an avid curiosity, said she felt it only fair to know exactly what crime their uncle had committed.

After Ross had explained the situation as fairly as he could, Tara had reached the fact that her uncle was being victimized.

'He is not being victimized!' her mother exclaimed angrily. 'And he will be removed from this house as soon as possible. What is more, there will be no more discussion on the subject.'

Tara, however, would not accept the verdict and appealed to her sisters and Brendan to back her up. It was unfair that the poor man was being proved guilty without a trial.

Ashling declared that she must agree with Tara.

Then Ross explained to the girls that his father had no right to seek sanctuary with their parents as he could be involving them in his activites and, if they were criminal, their parents could be taken to court too.

Ashling apologised, said she had not really fully understood the position. Tara, however, began mumbling that her sympathies were still with her uncle.

'That will do, Tara,' said Ross. 'You've had your say. Apparently you are not really conversant with the law. My father will be out of this house tomorrow and I hope there will be no more mumbling about him.'

Tara's face flushed a deep red, but Ross was not repentant. It was bad enough having to confront his father without Tara's sympathies being with him. He would have liked to have spoken to his father that evening, but Eileen – having taken his meal up and been first of all ignored, then told she need not show her face again that evening as he was going to have an early night – knew he would have to wait until the morning. Ross wished for the whole thing to be over.

12

Ross spent a restless night going over and over what he would say to his father and how he would act should he refuse to leave the house. Threaten to report him to the authorities? But was he guilty of a crime? His mind jumped from one thing to another: Tara's stubborness, Ashling's quiet manner, but her willingness to support Tara against any victimization. Fiona had had little to say but she had a shrewd mind and would be weighing everything up. He turned over in the bed and plumped up his pillow. Why did this all have to happen just when he felt that his life was beginning to run smoothly again?

He semi-dozed until six o'clock, then got up feeling jaded. He was standing at the window stretching his muscles when he tensed as he saw a figure making in the direction of the house. It looked like Queenie McKnott. But why should she be coming here at this time in the morning? As she drew near he made out that it *was* Queenie, an odd figure taking long strides.

Ross hurried downstairs and went outside. Had Rosin perhaps arrived and Queenie was leaving a note for Eileen so she could tell him? He was surprised at the feeling of anticipation this thought aroused. When Queenie caught sight of him she looked as though she were seeing a ghost, but then a delighted smile spread over her gaunt face.

'Why, Mr Ferris, sir,' she said as she came up to him, 'I could hadly believe it was you. When did you arrive?'

'Yesterday. I came because of family business.'

'I called to leave a note for your aunt to let you know

148

that Rosin has arrived at last. Thought you would want to know.'

'Yes, I did. Thanks, Mrs McKnott. How is she?'

'Nicely, nicely, looks well and is more talkative this time than when she was here last. She'll be pleased I've seen you. She did mention you last night. Cautiously, if you know what I mean. Didn't want me to know she was interested, but there was no mistaking the look in her eyes. Would you be thinking of coming over?'

'I would like to very much, but I shall have to see how the business goes this morning. But, depend on it, Mrs McKnott, I shall call as soon as I can.'

She said she knew he would, and made tracks to leave. Ross offered to walk so far with her, but did not learn any more. Rosin, like Alicia, told only what she wanted people to know, which made Ross all the keener to talk to Rosin, find out how far she had travelled. He realized she would never admit to being at a ball in Dublin.

He came back deep in thought and was met by Eileen, who asked if he too had had little sleep. He told her about Queenie's visit and the reason for it. His aunt searched his face, then asked him if he still wanted to be involved with Rosin.

He nodded. 'Yes, I do, in fact I want to more than ever.'

She made no comment, but when they decided to walk round the garden he told her the story of Alicia and she exclaimed, 'Holy Mother of God, as Cook would say. What a tale! Whoever concocted it must certainly live in a fantasy world.'

'Apparently not. According to John, these con tricks are going on all over the world. In different forms, I should imagine.'

'So the lovely Miss Sylvain and her aunt, Lady Kereslake, are cheats?'

Ross hesitated. 'I'm not quite sure about that. There's a lot that doesn't ring true, but on the other hand there are certain things that I do believe happened. Alicia's distress was so real. Even the most consummate actress would be hard-pressed to simulate her terrible fear. Yes, I know that John said he saw her smiling up at a man who is probably the one her aunt wants her to marry, but maybe we guessed wrongly about him.' Ross shook his head. 'I decided to forget the whole thing, but now it's all back to torment me. First, however, I shall have to deal with my father and I'm certainly not looking forward to that.'

'You can take him his early morning of cup of tea. I usually take it but he just ignores me at this time of day. He gets up early. He doesn't even say come in when I knock, so if you get no response just go in. There's no key.'

Ross found himself suddenly calm when he did go up with the tea. There was no response to his knock so he went in and put the tray on a side table. His father was standing at the window, his back to him, dressed in a well-tailored suit as if he were ready to go to the office. Ross said, 'Good morning,' and his father turned slowly and glared at him.

'What the devil are you doing here?'

'I've come to take you to Three Gables.'

'Oh, have you? Then you've made a wasted journey. I am staying here.' He spoke with his usual arrogance.

'I think not. You had no right to come here in the first place.'

'I have as much right as you. *Dear* Eileen is your aunt but she is my sister-in-law. Will you please leave and let me enjoy my cup of tea in peace. There's little else to enjoy.'

'I see we need to have a talk.'

'Then you shall be talking to yourself. I have nothing to say to you.' His father poured himself a cup of tea.

Ross pulled up a cane bedroom chair. 'Then I had better sit down because I have a lot to say to you.' He straddled the chair. 'I understand you say you are not guilty of anything, so why come here seeking sanctuary? Your expression, apparently.' When his father made no reply, Ross went on, 'You may as well reply because I shall stay here until you do.'

'You are a fool, always have been and always will be.'

'And you aren't,' Ross said quietly.

His father was silent and Ross had to admit he was an imposing figure, with his strong, handsome face and his upright bearing.

'All right, don't reply,' he said, 'but I shall keep on talking. You say you have every right to come here. I wonder what gives you that idea. When we stayed at Three Gables in the summers, Uncle Patrick and Aunt Eileen were father and mother to me. You seldom even spoke to me. More often than not you were away cavorting with your lady friends.'

'That's a lie! I left to get some peace. When I was there your mother was always on to me, accusing me that I had other women. She never gave me a moment's peace. She would accuse me of not loving her, of never having loved her. She drove me away. All I wanted was some peace and I found it walking among the mountains here. I don't suppose it would occur to you that I would ever want to do such a thing?'

'No, it didn't.'

His voice had trailed off and he looked suddenly drained. 'There was all the talk of fraud in London and I was condemned by some people and yet I was not involved in any way.'

Ross sat looking at him, trying to weigh him up. Was he telling the truth? He had never ever seen his father in such a mood.

'I went to Connemara for three weeks once. It was

151

the most peaceful time I knew in my whole life. I could walk for days and hardly meet a soul.' He looked up. 'I don't expect you to believe me, you've never seen that side of me. I sat some nights with shepherds and began to learn about living, about the earth and the skies.' He sighed. 'But then I came back to your mother and she accused me of fawning over her to make up for my sins. Sins,' he repeated, a sadness in his voice. 'Once I admired a farmer's daughter who was truly beautiful, but I never even spoke to her.'

Ross wished he could believe his father, but he felt it was like talking to Alicia – impossible to tell what was fact and what was fiction.

His father got up, took a piece of paper from a jacket pocket and handed it to him. 'This is a map I made of the route I took in Connemara. During my wanderings I came across a shepherd called Conal. I talked to him for two nights. He had lived in a monastery for ten years and left because he said he had a sudden yearning to see the world.'

'And he ended up looking after sheep?'

Addison Ferris nodded. 'Yes, and he told me more about life in two nights than I had known in all my years of so-called high living. He said to me the day I was leaving to return home, "May you have warm words on a cold evening, a full moon on a dark night and the road downhill all the way to your door." '

Although Ross was touched by the words, he could not help but remind his father that he had never been the kind of man to encourage good wishes.

His father gave him a sharp look. 'You don't believe it happened, do you?'

'I don't know what to think.'

His father showed him a point on the map which was marked with a small red cross. 'If you happen to go to Connemara, seek this spot. There you will find the shepherd. Ask him about the man who showed him a silver watch that chimed the hours, which has an inscription inside that says, *To my son Addison on the day he became a man.*'

'Your father gave it to you on your eighteenth birthday,' Ross said. 'You gave me a good hiding one day when you found me listening to the chimes. I hated you.'

'I hated you, too.' The arrogant manner was back. 'You were a defiant wretch and the image of your mother's lover.'

Ross jumped up and pushed the chair aside. 'I won't have you sullying my mother's name.'

'It's true whether you believe it or not. She admitted it once, then as quickly denied it when I flew into a temper. And I don't think anyone can blame me for that.'

'I never knew you in anything but a temper,' Ross snapped. 'I can't remember one time in my life that you picked me up or spoke a kind word to me.'

'Because I knew you were not my child.' His eyes blazed. 'The deceit of your mother . . . I was delighted when I knew she was pregnant but the birth was earlier than expected. I was away at the time. I had a telegram to say I had a son. Overjoyed, I rode the forty-mile journey. It was a wild night when I arrived and I was soaked. I rushed upstairs and found your mother in another man's arms. No, I don't suppose you were told this. Everyone was anxious to pass him off as a distant cousin and because your mother had worked herself into such a state I accepted it as truth. I cossetted her because of the baby. Then one day I overheard your Aunt Eileen assuring your mother that I would never know the baby was not mine.' Addison nodded slowly. 'This was when your mother admitted it, then as quickly denied it. I stayed with her because, God help me, I loved her in spite of it. I tried to make the marriage work, even though I could never take to you. So now you know why I have no affection for you.'

Ross stood stiffly, looking away. 'I don't believe it. I don't think you are the type of person who would go on living with my mother, not when you could have a choice of women.'

'I loved your mother until the day she died and hated myself for being so weak.'

Ross, turned to the window, not wanting to believe a word of what he had heard yet, at the same time, feeling there must be some truth in it.

His father was silent for a long time. Then he said in a low voice, 'It may seem nothing to you but bringing up another man's son was like doing a daily penance.'

Ross turned slowly and on impulse said, 'Why don't you come to Three Gables with me?'

'Give me today to think about it and please just leave me alone until I decide.'

When Ross went downstairs Eileen was waiting in the hall.

'Well?'

He cupped a hand under her elbow and led her outside. They walked in silence for a while and when he told her the story, Eileen vehemently denied it. 'It's just not true! There's not a word of truth in it. Why does he bother to lie?'

Tara came running out to them. 'Breakfast's ready. We are all down, Papa too.' She linked her arm through Ross's as they walked in the direction of the house. 'And what have you planned today for us, cousin Ross? We're invited to a party this afternoon and you can come with us, but where shall we go this morning?'

'Ross has business to attend to,' her mother said quickly, 'You run on ahead, Tara, and let Cook know we're on our way. Go on, go, I have something I want to say to Ross.'

Tara left reluctantly, calling over her shoulder, 'Don't dare plan anything in which we aren't involved.'

Eileen then asked Ross what plans he had made with

his father and tutted impatiently when told that he had asked for the day to work things out.

'He's prevaricating, Ross. Can't you see it? Give him one day and he'll want another and another. I'll never be rid of him.'

'I told you I would move him, Aunt Eileen, but just allow me this one day, will you?'

Ross knew he had been short with her and Eileen snapped back, 'Why? So you can go and see the gypsy girl? I'm sorry, Ross, but this situation will make us enemies if we're not careful.'

Ross, knowing deep down that she had spoken the truth, said, 'And I'm sorry too. Yes, I do want to see Rosin. Foolish perhaps, but I'm left with so many untied ends and I wanted to take the opportunity to try and tie up one at least.'

Eileen said she agreed and they went into the house where Tara was having a heated argument with her father that Uncle Addison should be allowed to have his meals with them.

'It's barbarous,' she declared, 'to keep him locked in his room.'

Patrick, ever patient, was trying to explain that Addison was not a prisoner when Eileen interrupted.

'Whoever wishes to make complaints about our unwanted guest will kindly leave this table and continue their discussion out of doors.'

Tara stood up and looked defiantly around the table. 'Any offers?'

There was silence and Brendan asked Ross in a bright voice if he would like to have a walk around the estate after breakfast.

Ross took the cup of coffee his aunt had poured and smiled. 'Perhaps later. I have some business to attend to.'

'Such as getting your father out of this house?' Tara demanded.

Patrick thundered, to everyone's astonishment, 'Sit

155

down, Tara, or leave this table!' She sat down and stared at her father in an astounded way. 'And get on with your breakfast.' To Ross, he added, in his normal quiet voice, 'If you have time I should like to show you a new seed drill I've bought. It has some interesting innovations.'

Within minutes a stranger coming in would have found them all chatting away in a pleasant family atmosphere, which included Tara, who described some puppies they had been to see at a friend's house.

She said, addressing Ross, 'They're so delightful to watch. Their parents are pedigree animals. Our friend's father sells them.' She turned to her father. 'Could we buy one, Papa?'

'We really have enough animals to contend with, but I shall think about it.'

Fiona spoke up. 'I don't think you should buy her another pet because it will end up like all the other ones she's had – the rabbits, the canary, the hedgehogs – Ashling and I will end up feeding and caring for them.'

When Tara began to protest Patrick said amicably, 'We shall discuss it later. Now if I may be excused I have work to do. Brendan, are you ready?'

After they had gone Tara threw down her table napkin. 'If ever I want anything I'm always thwarted.'

Fiona said, 'I don't wonder cousin Ross wanted to stay clear of you. Such behaviour. Standing up and shouting at the table.'

'I wasn't meaning Ross, I was talking about the puppy. If you must know, I need something to love.' Tara's voice broke and she rushed out.

Eileen sighed. 'Oh, dear, off we go again and I thought that everything was beginning to run more smoothly. Why do you torment her, Fiona?'

'She only has herself to blame. She drools over Ross, wants always to be next to him, then starts shouting at him about his father. She's the eldest of the three of us but the most childish.'

Ashling said quietly, 'It's awful for someone like Tara to be in love. She feels so deeply. She lets her feelings run away with her and gets hurt because of it. She's hurt for Ross's father being cut off from the family. She suffers for people.'

Tara, was at that moment wandering about the garden, tears running down her cheeks, railing inwardly about her lot. Why did everyone treat her as though she were a child? Especially Ross. She had tried to fall in love with other young men, but although she could like them a lot she could never feel the same about any of them as she did about her cousin Ross. He was so very special. It was not only because he was so forceful and handsome, but it was something else. Ashling had once used the word charisma, which could not be cultivated like acquiring a charm. Tara wished that she had been born with this charisma and then Ross might have fallen in love with her.

Not that she was going to give up. Oh, no, she would go on trying, but she must behave differently. Perhaps if she could be a little more aloof with him, behave as if he were not important to her? Yes, that might work. Her tears stemmed.

She had walked round to the back of the house, and with a new determination decided to see if she could worm her way into her mother's good books by offering to do something useful, when she caught sight of the figure of a man at a first-floor window.

Of course. It was Uncle Addison in hiding. He was staring at her. Poor man, he looked sad. On an impulse she waved, then made signs indicating that she would come up. He simply shrugged, which was not very encouraging. She gave another wave and decided to go in the back way.

To her knock a weary voice called, 'It's open.'

She peeped in and, getting an unexpected smile, entered, closing the door behind her. She said, 'I am Tara, Uncle Addison. I don't suppose you remember me.'

'Certainly I do. You've grown into a very lovely young lady. Do please sit down.'

Well, Tara thought, criminal or not, he certainly had an abundance of charm. She had not seen a great deal of him at Three Gables when she was young, but she did remember him as a handsome man.

He asked if she would like a drink of wine and in a fit of recklessness she accepted. Then he asked her about her life, how she filled her days.

She was telling him about the friends she had and the parties she went to when her mother burst in and, grabbing her by the arm, yanked her to her feet, exclaiming, 'How dare you come in here when I forbade it?' To Addison she added scathingly, 'Trust you to take advantage of a young girl.'

She pulled Tara out of the room and pushed her in front of her along the corridor. 'Go to your room and stay there until I give you permission to come out. If you attempt to leave you shall be out of this house and will be sent to live with your Great-Aunt Henrietta.'

The threat was enough to keep Tara in her room, but the injustice of the whole thing made her blood boil. How could her mother behave in such a way? She had always been fairly strict, but Tara had never seen her in such a temper. What on earth had her Uncle Addison done to make her behave so badly? They were not doing any harm talking and, heaven only knew, the man would be lonely stuck there in one room.

Fiona and Ashling, who were waiting for Tara to go with them sick visiting, hardly recognized their mother when she came into the sitting room and began throwing cushions around and ranting on about Addison Ferris not only being a criminal, but he had got Tara into his bedroom and heaven only knew what would have happened if she had not found her.

When Eileen started picking up ornaments and banging them down, Ashling jumped up and smacked her across the face, at the same time apologizing. Eileen stared at her in a dazed way, then burst into tears. Ashling put an arm around her and sat her on the settee. She then told Fiona to get some tea with brandy in and sat down beside her mother, talking soothingly.

'It's all right, Mama, you were overwrought. Now just try and calm down. After you've had a drink of tea and brandy I shall take you upstairs and you shall lie down.'

Eileen turned her head. 'I was so unkind to Tara.' Tears welled up and slid down her cheeks.

'Tara behaved stupidly. She had been warned not to go into the room. It's time she had some sense. I shall have a talk to her later. You've had far too much to carry on your shoulders.' She put her arm around her mother and began rocking her gently. 'There, there, you'll be all right.'

Fiona, who had gone to the kitchen for the tea, thought that everyone in the house must be going mad. First their uncle planting himself in their house, her mother rushing to London and coming back with cousin Ross, and now he was off to see some woman called Rosin. She had overheard Ross and her mother talking about her while she was getting ready earlier on. Who was she?

Cook made the tea, and Fiona carried the tray to the sitting room and found her mother calmer. She poured the tea, Ashling put some brandy into it and held out the cup. 'Drink this, Mama, then you are going to lie down.'

Eileen, suddenly tearful again, apologized for all the fuss she had made, then added that she could never remember having got into such a state before.

'Nor can we,' declared Ashling, 'and that is why you must take things easy. Fiona and I can see to whatever has to be done.'

Eileen, realizing then how utterly drained she felt, allowed the girls to take her upstairs and, after partially undressing her, made her lie down and drew up the cover. Ashling had pulled the brocade curtains across and they left.

The girls discussed their mother's hysterical condition without actually coming to any firm conclusion. After all, she had had to cope with many problems over the years, which to them seemed much more important.

Eileen McCoy, however, knew exactly the reason for her hysterical outburst. She was carrying too many secrets and they were beginning to become too big a burden. The trouble was, of course, she had sworn on the Bible not to tell. She would have to take care to control her emotions. Swearing an oath on the Bible was a very sacred thing.

13

Ross knew of the upset with his aunt but had no idea what had brought it about. He was anxious to go to see Rosin in case she suddenly decided to leave, but felt he must wait to see if everything was all right here. He was in the garden when Ashling came out. She looked worried at first but when she saw him her frown vanished. An unexpected wave of affection for her swept over him.

'Ross, I thought you had some business to attend to.'

'I have, but I felt I must wait and see if your mother is all right. What happened?'

'Oh, Tara decided to go and see your father, which she had been forbidden to do and Mama went and dragged her out and ordered her to her room. Then Mama . . . well, was slightly hysterical. She's all right now. She's lying down.'

'Your mother has had a lot of worry recently. My father should never have come here. Tomorrow, however, I shall take him somewhere else. Walk with me as far as the river and we can talk.'

They walked away, Ross's arm around Ashling's waist.

Fiona, who had been watching them from the window, felt an unexpected stab of jealousy. She had always been drawn to Ross, had even thought she might marry him one day if he would agree to her having a career. He was always praising her for her sensibility, her efficiency. Ross did not suffer fools gladly. Although she knew that Tara was determined to have him she had never thought of her as opposition. Tara behaved stupidly, always hanging on to him, drooling over him and no man would accept that kind of behaviour. But then neither had she ever thought of Ashling competing for his favours. She had no looks to speak of, was quiet and self-effacing at times. Now, however, after seeing the affectionate way Ross had been looking at her younger sister, and remembering the other woman he was planning to see, Fiona decided she might have to fight for what she wanted.

Ross, thinking there was more to his aunt's sudden hysterical outburst than having his father seeking sanctuary with them, tried to draw Ashling out, but had little success.

She did say that her father could be trying in certain circumstances but added that this was not often, her father hating confrontation.

Then, after a pause, she glanced at him. 'Will you satisfy my curiosity? What kind of business can you be conducting going in this direction?'

'If I say I have to meet a young lady, will that satisfy you?' He said it in a teasing way and Ashling replied in an equally light vein.

'And I shall make a guess and say it's the one who stays with Mrs McKnott.'

This really took him aback. 'Who told you this?'

'I knew you had met her at the Puck Fair and later heard you had been to the cottage.'

'I thought Brendan would have been more discreet.' He had difficulty in controlling his anger. 'I don't go telling everyone about his affairs.'

'It wasn't Brendan. A friend of mine saw you coming out of the cottage, saw the girl who was at the fair. I don't think that Tara or Fiona know. I haven't told them.'

'Well, thank you for that!'

Ashling stopped. 'I'll leave you here, Ross. Sorry I've upset you. I would be very pleased if you had fallen in love. It's time you settled down.'

Ross suddenly found himself laughing. 'Yes, Grandmama. I shall do my best to find a bride.'

Ashling, who had looked so solemn, dissolved into laughter too. 'How prim and proper I must have sounded.'

He spoke softly. 'Forgive my boorish manner. Like your mother, I have had my worries too. You go on home. I won't be long. When I return I shall tell you if I've proposed to the young lady or not.'

'And if not, I shall want to know the reason why.'

She was so light-hearted now that Ross felt like asking her to walk a little further with him, but she was away, pausing once to give him a wave.

There had been heavy rain for several days before he had arrived in Ireland and the river was in full spate, rushing over rocks as though impatient to reach wherever it was bound for. Just like himself, he thought, as he jumped across stepping stones, where some of the stones rocked when he trod on them.

The grass, in spite of the rain, had lost that lovely emerald green and the hills were grey.

As he neared Queenie's cottage Ross noticed that Rosin's little pony trap was there and the pony grazing nearby. In spite of his trying to keep calm, his heartbeat quickened.

Queenie, who came to the door, gave him a wave and a moment later she had Rosin by the hand. Rosin, he noticed, was trying to draw back but was tightly held by Queenie. It was she who greeted him.

'Good morning to you, Mr Ferris, sir.'

Ross swept them a bow. 'And a very good morning to you both.' To Rosin he added, 'It's good to see you again.'

Until that moment Rosin had worn her closed in look but at the bow she smiled her lovely smile, which had Ross bowing again and addressing himself to her. 'Miss Dannet, may I have the pleasure of your company to stroll along the lanes?'

Rosin had started to say she was sorry, but Queenie

gave her a push. 'Indeed she will. It will give her some exercise after sitting in that pony trap for days on end.' When Rosin seemed about to protest Queenie said, 'It'll do Mr Ferris good, too. He's had a lot of worry on his mind.'

When Ross looked swiftly at her she gave him a wink and a saucy grin.

Rosin said with a sigh, 'It seems we are both being bossed around, Mr Ferris, but Mrs McKnott is right, I do need some exercise. Thank you for asking me to accompany you.'

At that moment it was as if Ross were hearing Alicia speaking, the words slightly stilted. He held out a curved arm to Rosin and she played up to him, possibly for Queenie's benefit, and slipped her arm through his, smiling up at him in a provocative way.

'La, sir, I should be wearing a velvet coat, a wide-brimmed fur hat and be carrying a muff.'

To this he replied gallantly, 'You could not look more appealing, Miss Dannet, had you been wearing cloth of gold.'

In the voice she normally used she replied, 'Perhaps it would be better to keep to reality. I never did believe in fairy-tales.'

He eyed her seriously, 'I'm sorry about that. I think a child misses a great deal in life if he or she does not believe in fairy-tales or Father Christmas.'

'Children never miss what they've never had.' She drew her arm from his and waved a hand towards the snowdrops in the hedgerows. 'Aren't they lovely? I think they are better than ever this year.'

Ross, realizing she did not want to pursue the subject of her childhood said, 'I became so used to seeing the snowdrops in the hedges from being a child that I'm afraid I don't notice them. Tell me, have you done any dancing since we last met?'

He had hoped he might take her off her guard but

she eyed him with puzzlement. 'Dancing? No. Why do you ask?'

'Because I met a young lady in Dublin who is your double. It was difficult to accept that she was not you, she had the same coloured eyes, same dark hair, same build. You could have been identical twins.'

Rosin resumed her distant manner. 'It's said that everyone has a double. Who is this young lady you met?'

'Her name is Alicia Sylvain. Her aunt is Lady Kereslake.'

'It would be interesting to see this Miss Sylvain and see how I appear to other people, but, of course, she will be used to an extravagant life style.'

'Not really. Her aunt is her guardian and keeps her on a tight rein. You have much more freedom.'

'And you think that my life is preferable to hers?' There was a bitterness in her voice.

'If I had to choose between the two I would certainly prefer your kind of life. I know you are in danger of being molested, but I have a feeling if anyone attempted to do so he would get more than he bargained for.'

'I once broke a villain's nose, his arm and his other wrist and I have a feeling he would not be rushing to attack a woman for a long time. If ever.'

'Splendid. I shall have to take care how I treat you.' He spoke lightly.

'I had a great feeling of satisfaction at the time. Later I was angry that a woman should have to be put in such a degrading position.'

'I agree that it ought not to be this way, but it is and you tackled the problem. I applaud you.'

She glanced at him. 'So, you would approve of your wife fighting in this way to protect herself?'

'No. If I were married my wife would not work. I would keep her at home to run things, care for the children I hope to have.'

'So you disapprove that I earn my own living?'

'Miss Dannet, please stop putting words into my mouth. I admire your tenacity to be independent now, but one day you will fall in love and then you won't want to work either. I am quite sure you would want to stay at home and look after your husband and children, if you had them.'

'I have no plans for getting married,' she replied shortly and, leaving him, walked across the road and stood at a field gate staring across fields.

He followed her. 'What have you against marriage?'

'Nothing. I just happen to like my freedom.'

'Obviously you have never been in love.'

She turned to him, her deep amber eyes stormy. 'And it's obvious that you have never been in love or you wouldn't say such a thing! I've been in love, oh, yes, I know the joy of loving and I also know the terrible ache of waiting and the pain and the misery of rejection. Don't talk to me about not knowing the meaning of love.'

He was shocked by her hurt, her devastation, but when he reached out and touched her arm she drew back. 'Don't touch me. Don't add insult to injury by offering sympathy. You are the kind of man who picks women up on the way, has a good time, then discards them.' She put her hands to her face and whispered, 'Go, please, leave me.'

'No, I can't go. I want to help you. I did at one time take my pleasures where I wanted them, but that is behind me. I too need help. Can we talk? If you say no and mean it I'll leave.'

After a moment she lowered her hands. Her eyes were still brimming with tears. She brushed them away. 'Could we wait until tomorrow?'

'I'll be leaving tomorrow.'

'Tomorrow? Oh.'

He pointed to a huge tree stump a short distance

away. 'I think that a short talk might help us both.' She nodded.

They sat apart like strangers at first and were silent. Then Rosin said, 'I don't really feel I'm ready to talk about my life, but if it will help you to talk I'm willing to listen. Queenie said you had worries.'

'I can't talk about that particular worry because other people are involved, but I would like to talk about us. I was attracted to you the day we met. I tried to put you out of my mind when I left Ireland and I did manage because then I had personal business worries. They are more or less behind me now and I'm picking up the pieces.' He sat hesitant for a while, then went on: 'When I went to Killiney a while ago, where as children we spent every summer, I met Alicia Sylvain, who is your double. At a ball in Dublin, we danced together, but as with you, she put a barrier between us. And, in fact, a mystery developed, which I have not yet been able to fathom. This is something that I am unable to talk about, but I must say I have a strong feeling that you and Alicia are one and the same person.'

Rosin looked at him startled. 'Why on earth should you think such a thing? Your Miss Sylvain comes from the upper crust. I am nothing, a wanderer, a teller of fortunes. I sell knick-knacks, cheap jewellery.'

'And more expensive silver and gold items,' he prompted quietly.

She looked at him steadily, 'Which I steal from time to time?'

'I don't think so.'

Rosin moved closer. 'I simply cannot understand how you could come to such a foolish conclusion. Even if we happened to be identical twins, which is quite ridiculous, there would be differences, no matter how close we were. I knew identical twins who people said could not be told apart, but there was a difference. One girl had a mole on her right shoulder.'

'So I would have to see each of you naked,' Ross teased, then immediately apologized. 'Sorry for my remark.'

'It's valid and one no doubt you would find quite interesting to pursue.' Rosin, for once, spoke lightly.

'I would, but only to satisfy my curiosity, of course.'

There was an imp of mischief in her eyes and Ross had a sudden hope of delving further into the mystery when Rosin got up and said she had fortunes to tell to two wealthy ladies a few miles away who made it worth her while to go.

Ross took her hands in his and looked into her eyes. 'I think you are making an excuse to leave because I am getting a little too near the truth.'

'Mr Ferris, you have a long way to go to find the truth and I think when you get back to your aunt's house you will have a surprise that will set you on a different route to what you had planned.' She made to draw her hands away and he held them tight.

'You won't lose me. I shall come back to Ireland and learn the truth.'

'I might come and find you.'

'I'm not sure exactly where I shall be.'

'If I make up my mind that I want to see you I shall find you wherever you are.'

There was something about her eyes then that made him believe she would and when she made to draw her hands away he let her go.

'Goodbye,' she whispered and, turning, began to run. Strangely, it was not Rosin he was watching but the hedges that seemed to waver endlessly into the distance.

When they steadied, Rosin was out of sight. He walked back slowly, with a feeling that the mystery was deepening. Or was it that she had purposely created a deeper mystery, not wanting him to know any more about her life?

Before he arrived he saw Ashling hurrying towards him.

'Oh, Ross, I'm glad I found you. Your father has gone.'

'What do you mean?'

'He's left, taking his luggage. We have no idea where he's bound for.'

Ross felt a coldness stealing over him as he remembered Rosin's words that he would get a surprise when he returned to his aunt's house. Shock would have been a more appropriate word.

'How is your mother taking it?' he asked, as they hurried towards the house.

'She is surprisingly calm, saying it is the Lord's will.'

No, Ross thought wryly, it is my father's will.

His aunt was waiting at the door. She held out her hands. 'Ross, I'm sorry, it's all my fault. If I had not lost my temper —'

'I don't think it would have made any difference, Aunt Eileen. I would say that he already had plans laid where he would go. This was a resting space for him.'

'Where do you think he will make for? Three Gables?'

'I doubt it, although I will go there first.'

Eileen raised her eyebrows. 'You intend to follow him?'

'I must.'

'Why? He doesn't want you. He doesn't really want anyone.'

'That's the reason I have to find him. I think there's another man inside my father that we know nothing about.'

His aunt dismissed him with a wave of the hand. 'That is quite ridiculous. Your father is a man who loves only himself.'

'I thought so too until I spoke to him earlier.'

He described his father's wanderings in Connemara, his aunt and Ashling both listening intently, but at the end Eileen declared it was someone else's experience he had been relating. There was nothing in Addison Ferris that would merit such behaviour.

Ashling said she believed her Uncle Addison. Some people had many sides to their characters and it depended on circumstances which developed and which lay dormant. 'Circumstances make us react differently. We have always come first with you. As things stand, we've never really wanted for anything. But if you had been poor and you had no money to feed us you might have become a thief to get food for us.'

'Yes, but –'

'You told us once that when Uncle Addison and Aunt Maura were married they were very much in love.'

'That is true. Then your uncle changed.'

'I would say because he had a business to run and Aunt Maura wanted him with her all the time.'

'No, that's a lie.'

'It's true, Mama. Although Tara, Fiona and I were all young, we knew that Aunt Maura invented complaints to get his attention.'

'Who told you that?'

'We overheard servants talking.'

Eileen was silent for a while then she said, 'Ashling, Tara and Fiona have taken some food for old Mrs McMahon. They should be back soon. Go and meet them and keep them out for a while. I want to talk to Ross.'

Ashling got up at once and when she had gone Eileen said to Ross, 'Heaven knows how much they do know. Pray God they have no knowledge of Preston Rafferty.'

'I don't think you need worry. It happened years ago. Forget it.'

'Ross, even after all the points that Ashling made, I still don't believe your father's story. All he wants is a place to hide until he's ready to start a new life abroad.'

Ross straightened. 'But I have to go and find the truth. I won't be content until I do.'

170

Eileen said, 'Shall I tell you something, Ross, I don't think you believe your father's story either, otherwise you would not have planned to go to Three Gables first.'

Ross thought she could be right but at the same time he knew he would have to find this shepherd Conal. Then he would know the truth about his father at last.

It was decided that he would leave first thing in the morning to travel to Killiney and Three Gables.

He was in bed and on the verge of sleep when in his dreaminess he could feel Rosin's hands in his. They were smooth, the skin like satin . . .

Suddenly he was wide awake. Skin as smooth as satin, the hands of a gentlewoman . . . not a pedlar girl, who drove a pony and trap, who sold knicks-knacks at fairs, moved wooden boxes about . . .

14

When Ross arrived at Three Gables he learned, much
to his surprise, that his father had stayed there overnight and left early that morning.

'Told me that nostalgia had brought him,' said Mr
Colhoun. 'He seemed different somehow to how I
remember him, softer, if you'll forgive me for putting
it that way, sir. He wouldn't let me get the missus to
make up a bed. Said he would just lie on a sofa with
a cover over him. Didn't want no breakfast either. I
have no idea where he went.'

'That's all right, Mr Colhoun. I think I know where
he will be. I shall stay overnight and leave tomorrow
morning. And I don't want any fuss made either.'

The steward explained that his wife and daughters
were now away visiting a relative for two or three days
and offered Ross a bed at the cottage. 'There's a spare
bed made up and there's plenty of food.'

When Ross hesitated, Mr Colhoun said, a wistful note
in his voice, 'I'll be glad of a bit of company, sir, I'm
getting older and don't want to go wandering off as I
once did.'

Ross smiled. 'And I shall be glad of a bit of company
too.'

He talked of looking in on his friends the McLanes
but learned from Mr Colhoun that they were all away
and he felt a swift disappointment. He had been looking
forward to seeing Liam and Dermot and realized why
Mr Colhoun was lonely.

Over the meal Ross and Mr Colhoun reminisced
about the days when the families had come to Three
Gables for the summer and afterwards they sat quietly,

the old man puffing away on a meerschaum pipe, his eyes half closed. The evening was still and Ross was aware of the pungent smell of his steward's tobacco, mingling with the tangy smell of seaweed.

A neighbour came to see Mr Colhoun and while the two men were talking, Ross found himself thinking about his father. Where was he now? Was his story true about having met the shepherd in Connemara and coming back hoping to find peace again? He could be guilty of fraud and, feeling unable to cope with the indignity of the slur on his name, had run away. Then, suddenly needing an ally, needing sympathy, he had concocted the story.

It then occurred to Ross to question his own motives for following his father here. They had nothing but hatred for one another so why should he have gone to all this trouble to pursue him? A strong force had driven him. As a child Ross had had a great admiration for him and had thought him the most wonderful man in the world. His father had never been a demonstrative man but he had taken an interest in him when he was young, introducing him proudly, and encouraging him to ask questions. It was later he had changed, been cold and would not have him near.

When had the change come about? At eight years old? One morning he had been shocked to find his mother all bruised. She told him she had been dreaming and fallen out of bed and his Aunt Eileen had confirmed this. His aunt had eventually told him that his father was a brutal man and that was when Ross's hatred for him had begun.

More recently, however, his father had not only accused his mother of inflicting the injuries herself but had told him in no uncertain terms that he was not his son.

It occurred to Ross then that if he ever showed affection to his father then he would not only be disloyally to his mother's memory but he would be tainting the loving image he treasured of her.

When Mr Colhoun came back he said to Ross, 'My good friend Eamonn McGinn has a great respect for your father, who rescued his wee lad who fell over a cliff, and carried him two miles to a doctor knowing he needed urgent attention.'

'Mr Colhoun, you've had a lot of dealings with my father. Would you say he was the kind of man who would come to Ireland to find peace?'

'Oh, I would indeed, sir. A difficult man to deal with at times, a very impatient man, but at the same time a deep thinker. He had a kindness in him that some people would not suspect. My wife was very ill when she had our youngest girl and your father gave me extra money to get good food for her and medicines. When he came on visits during the summer months he would go off on his own from time to time and when he came back he would say to me, "I've been communing with nature, Colhoun," and somehow I would sense a sadness in him.'

And that was what Ross had seen in his father the day before when he had talked to him about Connemara and meeting the shepherd.

The two men stayed talking about politics until the fire embers glowed white. Then Ross walked to the top of the rise and stood looking down on to the bay. The only sound was the shushing of the water as it rolled leisurely over the pebbles and receded with a gentle sucking sound. He felt a reluctance to leave.

After the soundest sleep he had had for some time Ross wished more than ever that he could stay for a while at Killiney, but after breakfast he left with a promise to Mr Colhoun that he would try to pay another visit soon.

He went by train from Dublin to Galway and, at Mr Colhoun's advice, called at the home of his nephew

174

Boyd, who made journeys to Clifden delivering goods, and would often take a passenger. To Ross's pleasure and luck, the nephew was due to leave early the following morning and he and his wife offered to put Ross up for the night.

They left at six o'clock the next morning and for Ross the journey passed quickly because of his companion's lively chatter.

Unfortunately no one in Clifden knew the wherabouts of Conal the shepherd, in spite of the group of men and woman the question had drawn, all anxious to help.

'Now would that be the new man at McCasey's, only been there a few weeks though? . . . What about old McGuffy? He had a good line in talk. Grand to listen to . . . Or it could be Old Finnibar at Mick's Corner? No, now it couldn't be him, could it? Deaf as a post and never give you so much as a nod when you spoke to him.'

In the end Ross said he would do some walking and try to find this Conal, but he had begun to accept that his father could have concocted the story.

He and Boyd were about to leave when a toothless old woman suggested that Ross got himself to the mountains. It would be there he would find this Conal. She could see him in her mind's eye tending his flock, a man who had lived with saints but who had then left them because he was doubtful of their saintliness.

Ross was immediately interested but Boyd warned him in a kindly way not to take too much notice of old Meg whose mind got twisted into knots at times. But although the woman was physically quite bent, Ross saw eyes that looked clear and unwavering into his own. He touched her arm gently and thanked her. He would go to the mountains.

Boyd told him that if he was going walking in the

mountains he would need to carry bedding with him, plus a kettle, a tin mug and food, and suggested he could get these items for him if he would give him time to deliver some of his goods.

When Ross told him not to bother he would manage all right, Boyd said, 'There are no shops in the mountains and if you happen to find a place where people live those folks will be scratching a living from the soil. Oh, they'll share what food they have with you and probably starve the rest of the week.'

So Ross accepted Boyd's offer. Unfortunately, his companion's words had brought home to Ross what he could be tackling. Until then it had been just a big adventure to him.

Now he made for the sand dunes and sat down on the fine sand. He scooped up a handful and let it trickle through his fingers. The morning was perfect, sunny and the air so clear one could see miles away.

As he looked out to sea his mother became vivid to him, and he could hear her say in the gentle voice she used when he was small. 'Go and find me a pearl, my darling. I would love to have a pink one, but if you can't find a pink one a creamy one will do.' She had been happy then and in good health.

Ross walked slowly to the water's edge. When had the change in his mother taken place? He stooped and picked up some shells. Three had a creamy pearlized lining, the fourth was a delicate pink. How he had grieved that he had never been able to take her a pearl.

She would hug him and say, 'It's the gift that counts, my love, and these shells are just so beautiful. Isn't nature wonderful to fashion such delicate patterns?'

Soon it was time to go to meet Boyd. He had everything he felt Ross would need for his journey packed in a piece of oilskin, with straps attached to the pack to carry it on his back. Plus a map to go in his pocket.

While Ross secured his bundle, men who were standing around offered advice. He was to make sure he put one piece of oilskin under his blanket and another piece on top, against the damp. He was warned to keep his matches dry and always to carry a bundle of twigs with him or dried furze as kindling, and to be sure to keep them dry.

Ross smiled and told them he would probably only be away for a couple of days, but there was a shaking of heads and a reminder that if a man went into the mountains he could be away for weeks. The mountains cast a spell. Some men had never come back. He set off with their good wishes.

Houses and cottages became more sparse until he was beginning to find odd derelict cottages that made him realize how many people had had to give up their homes because of the poorness of the soil. By the time he reached a remote cottage where a man stood at the front door Ross felt subdued. The man offered hospitality, a rest inside and a drink of water and Ross accepted, not wanting to miss an opportunity to try to find out where the shepherd might be. The man, who lived alone, told him he had heard the name but had no idea where to find him and suggested he ask the Father at the chapel, which was further along the road. He knew everyone and would walk miles to be with a sick person.

'Don't you feel lonely here?' Ross asked the man.

'How can a person be lonely with the fairies around?'

Ross eyed him in surprise. There was a softening of his expression and he asked gently, 'Who are the fairies?'

'They are angels who were tricked by the Divil.' The man spoke as if he were surprised that Ross didn't know about them. 'God got up from His seat one day and cunning Lucifer slipped into it and within seconds had created hell. Although most of the Angels managed to stay in heaven, some were trapped on the edge of hell. God released them, but they were unable to get back into heaven, so He blessed them and they were committed to fly free and do good works. Unfortunately, some of them were tainted from their experience and now there are the goods ones and the bad. No, not bad, to be sure, but mischievous. They tease people, knock a piece of bread from their hand. Trip them up.'

'And you've seen them?' Ross asked.

'I have that. Mostly the good ones. The Scottish people, I'm told, have very bad ones in the Highlands and would willingly kill them, but in Ireland we treat them graciously. If you get lost they'll help you to find your way. Put your trust in them.'

'I certainly will,' Ross said.

By the time he reached the chapel he was beginning to feel he could do with the help of the fairies to ease his tiredness. And perhaps they did help, he thought, when he had a warm welcome from Father O'Toole, a gently spoken man who invited him into his small house and offered him a meal. Ross gratefully accepted and was delighted to learn that the Father knew Conal very well indeed. He did add, however, that he lived quite a distance into the mountains. He marked on Ross's map the paths he should follow.

'Conal is an academic and a rebel who does not see eye to eye with the ways of the Church, but he is an interesting man. It grieves me, of course, that he left the monastery. He did a lot of good work. Now he looks after sheep, which a youth could do.'

Ross was thoughtful for a moment, then he said, 'Surely he is more than that, Father? My own father was distressed when he met him. The shepherd gave him peace. Helping people to cope with life does more good than men in a monastery praying hour after hour hoping to save souls.'

'Ah, but you forget the power of prayer, my son. Think of the thousands of prayers that are being said all over the world. They reach the sick, give them comfort, reach the troubled and give them solace.'

When Ross was ready to leave, Father O'Toole thanked him for his company, adding that visitors were few. The holy man waved until Ross was out of sight, which had Ross wondering why a man would stay in such a barren place with so few parishoners. He also wondered why Conal the shepherd, a learned man, should choose to live with a herd of sheep in such forbidding-looking territory as this mountainous country.

As Ross began to climb, the ground became more stony, paths rough. Many of the stones were white, giving a lightness to the scene, and although the whole had a barren look there was colour in the golden-flowered furse. There were no trees around but he kept picking up twigs that birds must have dropped. Ross saved every tiny one.

There were plenty of flocks of sheep but most were tended by youths. Some of these young shepherds had heard of Conal but had never met him. The priest had told him he would not meet the former monk until the following day, but Ross had assured him he was a good walker. By late afternoon, however, he had to admit he was utterly weary. What was more, the sky was overcast and a dampness had come into the air. Even then, unwilling to give in, he plodded on for another half-hour. Then, coming unexpectedly across a suitable camping place, he stopped, undid the straps of his pack and, letting it drop to the ground, sat down beside it closing his eyes.

There was a natural incline in the rock here, and although it could not be called a cave, there was a deep overhang, which would give some protection should rain come. A traveller had built a fireplace under the overhang and a short distance away was a small spring.

There was some dried brush beside the fireplace and Ross laid out some of the twigs he had carried and put a match to them. The twigs flared, sparked, then suddenly died. Although feeling he could go to sleep standing up, he put on some more twigs and tried again. This time the twigs and the furse ignited. He put water in the kettle, set it to boil, then got out the food that Boyd had packed.

It looked like a feast, cooked chicken and pie, uncooked sausages and bacon, three different kinds of bread and some fruit cake. He laid some sausages and bacon on a tin plate and put them to cook at the other end of the fireplace. The smell as they sizzled made him feel ravenous. He was tempted to cook more but knew he would have to limit himself, not knowing how long he would be away from civilization.

The sky darkened early that evening and it brought light rain. Ross, sitting cross-legged beside the fire, found it quite cosy at first, but later thunder followed, bringing a deluge and he was glad to get under his blanket covered with the oilskin.

Rain gusted under the overhang, dousing the fire. Eventually he got up and, bringing in the largest stones he could find, built a wall around his bed. It gave some protection but before long he was chilled to the bone and his journey was no longer an adventure but an ordeal. Exhaustion finally brought sleep. When Ross woke he was stiff and cold. He got up to loosen his limbs and when he went outside he was awed by the beauty of the dawn, the skyline spreading from palest pink to deep rose tinged with orange, the whole edged with a delicate apple green. In places mist drifted and when it parted the wildness of crags were displayed. On the still air could be heard the bleating of sheep and the barking of dogs. They sounded quite close but Ross knew from experience that they could be quite a distance away.

Having used all the twigs he had collected, and knowing he would need exercise to loosen up his limbs, Ross packed his bed roll, drank two mugs of the clear cold spring water and set out on his journey again. Sometime this morning he should meet the shepherd.

The air was invigorating and he stepped out thinking he had never felt better in his life. Some of the paths that the priest had marked had been obliterated, possibly by a fall of stones and earth during storms, but he was able to pick up the paths ahead. A curlew, plummeting down from overhead, startled him with its mournful cry. Then he heard the sound of water and circling a bend he came across a small waterfall that leapt from edge to edge of rock until it splashed into a pool below. There were lakes in the valley, each one a misty blue, all so beautiful.

Ross began to pick up twigs again and, tying them up, slung them from his pack. Later the sun came out and the air was scented with golden furze. He came suddenly on a herd of goats that seemed to be unaccompanied and began to wonder when he would find the shepherd he was seeking.

It was late afternoon when he heard the bleating of a flock of sheep and, when he rounded a bend, saw a man in a linen smock talking to a small group of them, the animals gazing at him intently as though understanding what he was saying. He had pictured the shepherd who spoke to his father as being middle-aged and saintly looking, but although this shepherd would be about thirty, had long dark hair and in profile had a sharp nose and chin, he knew instinctively he was the man he was seeking.

The shephered turned suddenly and greeted Ross with a smile. 'Ah, you must surely be the son of Mr Ferris from London who spent most of yesterday with me.'

Ross eyed him in surprise. 'How did you know we were related?'

'Oh, I just know.' His piercing blue eyes held Ross's gaze and his voice was gentle. Ross was invited to sit down on a slab of rock and offered a drink of water.

'How unfortunate that you missed your father,' the shepherd said. 'He left yesterday morning. He had planned to go to India.'

'India?'

'It was apparently a dream of his.'

'I've wasted my time.' Ross could not keep the bitterness from his voice.

'No time is wasted, Mr Ferris. Your father felt sure you would follow him. He would have liked to have seen you, but he did not want you to persuade him to return to London.'

'If my father made up his mind not to do something, no one would ever have persuaded him to change it,' Ross retorted.

'I think your father is a sick man, Mr Ferris. He told me he was guilty of fraud but that no one could prove it.'

'My father has a devious mind.'

'To be successful in business a man has to be devious. He could have known of the fraud and although he was not involved nevertheless feels guilty.'

'You don't know him.'

'I would say that I know more about your father than *you* do, Mr Ferris.' The shepherd's voice was gently scolding. 'I think you have just touched the surface of his mind. He has great depths that no one has attempted to explore.'

'He's clever,' Ross persisted. 'He has a way about him of making people believe that what he is saying is the truth.'

The shepherd turned his head and studied Ross.

'Your father had little to say about himself. What I am telling you are things I deduced about him in the long silences we spent together. Silence is a great leveller.'

The group of sheep he had been talking to had wandered away but several others had come up and were standing motionless watching him. He shooed them away saying softly, 'Not now, I am busy. Off you go.' One gave a baa, then they all turned and trotted off to join others of the flock.

Ross, curious, asked him what had made him leave the monastery and take up shepherding.

'I had ceased to be an individual, which I felt was wrong. God fashioned us all to be different and here I was, year after year, doing the same things, singing the same hymns, saying the same prayers, going to bed at the same time and rising every morning at the same time.'

Ross could not help smiling. 'And you feel you are an individual looking after sheep?'

'Oh, definitely. I can do as I wish. I can swim in a lake, eat when I want to. I can plan to build a tower or a wooden hut where I can sleep, if I wish, or I can make my bed under the stars. I can compose poetry, write reams of words. Or I can just sit contemplating and there is no one to order me to prayer.'

'So you are contented?'

'There's not such a thing as a contented person, Mr Ferris.'

'Oh, come, what about spiritual men, those who have spent their lives in monasteries?'

'I shall tell you a story, Mr Ferris. A farmer put a big notice on a fence outside a field, saying, *This field will be given to a contented man.* The first man who applied, when asked by the farmer if he was contented said, "Oh, yes, indeed. I am financially sound, I have a loving wife and caring children." The farmer then said,

"If this is so, why do you want the field?" ' The shepherd smiled. 'And why did he? Because he was greedy. On the other hand, if there was no greed we would all be living in caves. Until two years ago I thought of myself as a contented man. Now I know I want more out of life. I want the love of a human being. I want marriage, children. God made us so that we could procreate children. There are those who want other things but that is inevitable. I don't think one can expect God's perfection in the world.'

'There are the saints.'

'I have not been conscious of meeting one. I would say that true saints are the holy men who are dead and in heaven.'

This brought a smile from Ross. 'I see that you are not willing to commit yourself.'

'Because I have yet to meet perfection. And would I want to? I don't think so.'

'My father was impressed with his talk to you. He said he had found peace, yet this time you were not able to persuade him to return to England and sort out his troubles.'

The shepherd was silent for a moment, then he said softly, 'Any peace your father found here came from the place itself. But there, we shall talk about that later. Now I shall get you something to eat.'

He raised a flat slab of stone in the ground and inside it was lined with thin slabs, forming a square. From it he brought out a billycan of rabbit stew and within minutes the stew was warming over a fire. Ross declared it was one of the most delicious meals he had ever tasted. They had goat's milk in their tea and in the mildness of the day, with the sun shining, Ross even forgot the torrential rain and penetrating cold and dampness of the night before.

When they had eaten, they walked among the sheep and Ross watched as Conal tended an ailing animal and took a stone from the hoof of first one sheep who was limping, and then another, saying that sheep had a lot of trouble with their feet.

Ross followed the shepherd along a path that led to a part of the mountainside where a cottage had once stood but was now just a pile of stones.

'A couple once lived there,' Conal said. 'Started their married life in it and had only one child who died. Here is her gravestone.' The piece of stone had broken in two and some words had been carved on it in Gaelic which translated said, *In Memory of Cathy Malone, our only child. Aged six years.* Then underneath were the words, *We loved her.*

Ross, who felt deeply moved said, 'How awful to lose their only child. There's no year on the stone. How old do you think it would be?'

The shepherd raised shoulders. 'As old as human grief.' He crossed himself and murmured a prayer, then they walked on.

The shepherd had a wealth of wisdom to impart. In the evening he talked of having travelled around Ireland before he went to the monastery.

'I felt I must get some mental picture of my country in my mind before shutting myself away. Wherever I went I found beauty. There was a magnificence in the Bay of Moher, where waves crashed against the cliffs sending spumes of spray rising to such a height that when the sun touched them diamonds were dancing in its midst. There was great beauty in ruined abbeys and castles, their misshapen edifices transfigured by coverings of ivy in different shades of green. I saw fathomless tarns that looked dark and menacing during the day but which became works of art in flame and gold at sunset. In crevices of rock in a barren place I found rare orchids; one time I walked along a road that led from a deserted village where work had been unavailable, and found the hedges alive with pink rhododendrons and white bells of fucshias with red centres, the bells swinging gently in the breeze.'

'What made you come to Connemara when you left the monastary?'

'During my early travels I saw the blue mountains of Connemara and loved the place in spite of finding only rough territory at first. Then one evening, after three days of heavy rain, I saw in the valley hundreds of small pools silvered by moonlight and I became conscious of the silence. It was all around me, resonating. It reached inside me, touching my very soul. A great calmness came over me and I knew I was ready to take holy orders.

'And when you returned here did you find that calmness returning to you?'

'Not at first. It was the animals that drew my attention to it. They would be restless, bleating, wandering about. Then the night sky would close in and they would be still, listening to the silence. Afterwards, they would all settle. I listened and the silence wrapped itself around me. I knew a wonderful feeling of peace.'

Ross asked the question that he had asked the day before of the man who lived alone: didn't he ever feel lonely?

'How can one be lonely? There is so much movement – fleecy clouds moving slowly, busy clouds scudding along, storm clouds gathering, grumbling and rumbling before the storm breaks and the rain comes. Sometimes the rain will be gentle and caress your skin; other times it is angry and will strike you with whiplash force. But afterwards it is sorry and calls the sun out and the mountains are alive with colour.'

When Ross asked him if he had left the monastery because he had lost his faith in God the shepherd looked at him in surprise.

'How could one not believe in Him? You have only

186

to think of the makings of man and to look at the heavens to know there is a Supreme Being.'

When Ross asked him why, with so much faith, he had left the monastery, the shepherd replied quietly, 'There were dedicated men in the monastery, good-living men, but even they had ambition, although it would never be admitted. I was told of the evils of men. I wanted to live among them so I could understand why they were evil. I had actually to experience the true beauty outside before experiencing the bad. Soon I shall be ready to go into the real world.'

The two men covered many subjects that evening and in the early hours of the morning Ross told Conal of his experience with Rosin Dannet and Alicia Sylvain.

'They are both withholding a part of themselves. Rosin is away travelling in her pony trap when I'm with Alicia. They may be the same person. It is too coincidental, for my liking.'

'Study their hands. Identical twins can seem alike, but more often than not their hands vary. Look for the length and shape of fingers and for the shape of nails. If the hands of the young ladies are different then they are two different people, but if the hands are alike then it could be that it is one young lady playing two parts. In either case there will be trouble.'

When Ross queried why, the shepherd inclined his head. 'You mentioned being in love and talked about marriage. If they are twins you would find it difficult to choose. If you did then you would always be torturing yourself, wondering whether you would have been happier had you married the other one.'

'And if Rosin and Alicia are one, what then?'

'Then you will have been deceived. On the other hand, the lady might have a very good reason for playing two parts. The decision could only come from you.'

187

With his mind so full of all that had been said, Ross was sure he would never sleep that night. He thought that it would be useless to attempt to follow his father now, and that he must see Rosin and Alicia and solve the mystery of their identity, and after that he remembered no more.

15

Ross woke to a glorious sunrise, as he had done the day before, and although he gave a little shiver at the freshness of the chill morning air he had a wonderful feeling of wellbeing. In spite of this, however, there was a sudden longing in him to be back with the family, to talk about his experiences and about his father; especially about his father, feeling he had failed in his task of persuading him to return to England.

The shepherd was already up and walking among his flock, and Ross, noticing his gentleness and the way he talked to the animals, wondered how he would fare in the world away from the mountains.

Conal turned before Ross reached him and raised a hand. 'Good morning, Mr Ferris. I trust you slept well.'

'Splendidly. And I'm sorry I shall have to leave.'

'So soon. What a shame, I enjoyed your company. Come, I shall make you some breakfast.'

It was mid-morning before Ross left – with a promise from the shepherd that when he came to England he would look him up. Ross had a feeling of having known the man all his life.

He had not notified his aunt of his imminent arrival at Killorglin, and was glad when he found her alone. It was an emotional meeting, Eileen being full of remorse for having treated his father so badly.

'I did a terrible thing, Ross, not taking into account that he was not quite himself. Now you say that he's on his way to India.'

'As far as I know. I decided not to attempt to follow

him. He's a strong-minded man and I felt sure I would never have been able to persuade him to come back to London. I felt guilty too, Aunt Eileen, aware that I had never really understood him. Even now I don't know whether he was brutal towards Mother or whether, as he said, her bruises were self-inflicted.'

Eileen gave a sigh. 'There's something I have to tell you about that and there's also something else you should know. While you were away –'

The room door was suddenly flung open and Tara rushed in.

'Oh, Mama, William told us that cousin Ross was back. Oh, Ross, there you are.' Running across the room, she flung herself at him. 'Why didn't you let us know you were coming? We would have met you. Is Uncle Addison with you?'

Her mother said, 'Tara, for heaven's sake! Stop smothering Ross.'

Fiona and Ashling came in and although they were not as effusive in their greeting as their sister, their pleasure at having him back touched Ross.

Over dinner he told them about his visit to the west of Ireland and they listened absorbed when he described his meeting with Conal.

'What a lovely man he sounds,' said Ashling. 'I would very much like to meet him.'

It was not until later in the evening as first one and then another of the family questioned him that Ross realized just how much information the shepherd had imparted.

It was getting on for midnight when their mother insisted the girls go to bed, and, as Patrick and Brendan were leaving early the following morning to go to a cattle auction, they went up at the same time.

Alone with Ross, Eileen told him that his father had told her about his mother's ruse to get attention, but that she had refused to believe there was any truth in it. Now, however, having thought it over while he had been away, she remembered something.

'It was during one of the summers we all spent at Three Gables. Your mother had gone upstairs to have her afternoon nap and for once I decided to do the same. Other than Maura and your father I was the only other one in the house and I was in a semi-dose when I heard shouting. It was your parents quarrelling. Your father had been away overnight and your mother was accusing him of having slept with another woman, which he denied. Then I heard a moaning and a thumping and I got up and went and listened at their bedroom door. Then I heard your father shout, "Stop it, you fool", followed by more words that I couldn't make out. Your mother was sobbing and I went in and saw your father with the clothes brush in his hand. I snatched it from him and flung it across the room and screamed to him to get out. Although he was angry he told me quietly that he had never touched her. I screamed at him again to get out and he left. Your mother was in a terrible state, sobbing and saying he had hurt her wrist. The following day her back and her wrist were badly bruised. I wanted to get a doctor, but she begged me not to.'

Eileen was silent for a while then went on, 'Yesterday I lay down in the afternoon and I fell asleep. I don't know if I had been dreaming, but I woke to hear your father's voice saying, "Stop it, you fool. Give me that brush." All those years ago – and I heard the words repeated in my mind. I'm sure now that your mother's wrist had been bruised because he had been trying to wrest the brush from her to stop her doing any more damage to herself. Oh, Ross, how I've hated him all these years.'

Tears brimmed in his aunt's eyes and Ross put his arm around her and said gently, 'I hated him too.'

When Eileen was calmer she said, 'There's something else I have to tell you. Mrs McKnott called early yesterday morning to tell me that Tara had been to see her, wanting to know whether you were in love with Rosin.'

Ross's heart missed a beat. 'What on earth possessed her to do such a thing?'

'Jealousy, according to Mrs McKnott. Tara told her in no uncertain terms that you belonged to her and that no one else would ever get you.'

'Was Rosin there at the time?'

'She was staying there but was out when Tara called. Mrs McKnott had sympathy for Tara, saying it was a terrible heart-pulling thing to be in love and be possessive. She thought I ought to have a talk with Tara, but I think it would be better if you spoke to her. In spite of her possessiveness towards you she has always respected any advice you gave her.' Eileen looked at Ross appealingly. 'Am I being punished through my daughter for all the bad things I've done?'

'If you are then the God you worship on Sundays is not the same one that Conal the shepherd respects. He says He forgives people their sins because He knows that every one of us is capable of making a mistake.'

Eileen gave another sigh. 'I think it would have been better if He had made us all nicer people.'

'But what a dull old world it would be.' The dryness in Ross's words brought a brief smile to Eileen's lips.

She got up. 'Now I shall go to bed.' She touched Ross's hand. 'We can have another talk in the morning. It's so good to have you back.'

Ross found it impossible to go to sleep that night. Tara's behaviour was worrying him. There was something unnatural about her action. Tara was now nineteen and should know better than to threaten another young woman. He would certainly have to talk to her the next morning.

Ross rose early next morning and went into the garden. The forlorn figure of Tara was sitting on a wooden bench. She looked up as he approached, then stood and rubbed the palms of her hand over the skirt of her blue dress.

'Good morning, cousin Ross.' Her voice was barely audible.

'Good morning. What got you up so early?'

'I had a nightmare. I woke Mama shouting. She made me come downstairs and told me she knew the reason for it. I did something dreadful.' Her voice wavered but although she was on the verge of tears Ross did not spare her.

'I know you did and for two pins I would have packed my bag and left because I felt I didn't want to see you again.'

'Cousin Ross!' Her dismay hurt him. 'Please, please, don't do this to me. I love you, and that is why I did what I did.'

'Sit down,' he said sternly, 'and don't you dare start weeping because you won't get any sympathy from me. Who the devil do you think you are, going to Mrs McKnott's and threatening Miss Dannet who has never done you any harm?'

'I'm sorry, very sorry, I didn't mean to say what I did. The words just came out, I couldn't help it.' Her eyes were brimming with tears, which only served to harden Ross.

'Don't talk such rubbish, Tara. You are nineteen, a woman, carefully brought up, educated. It's time you started behaving like a woman, not a spoilt child.' She sat silent, head bowed and he went on, 'I'm very fond of Miss Dannet and I will not have you malign her in any way.'

'She's a gypsy,' Tara replied in a low voice. 'I thought she might have put a spell on you.'

'Oh, Tara, for heaven's sake grow up. In the first

place Rosin is not a gypsy, and even if she were it has nothing to do with you who I choose to marry.'

'Marry?' Tara's head shot up. 'You can't mean it. She's not your type of person.'

Ross felt a little shocked at the desolation in his cousin's eyes, but he continued relentlessly, 'Let me inform you that Rosin has more common sense in her little finger than you have in your whole brain.'

At this she jumped up and would have been away had he not thundered, 'Sit down! I'm not quite finished.' She sat down again, her head bowed. 'You might think I'm being harsh with you, but I will not have anyone interfering in my personal life. You could have driven Rosin away had she been there and heard your jealous tirade, deciding she was not going to be mixed up with *your* type of person. Yes, Tara, your type.' He spoke more gently now. 'A harridan is a despised person and that is what you must have sounded like, raving to Mrs McKnott that I belonged to you and no one else would get me. Any man worth his salt would rebel at a woman who wanted to possess him.'

'I can only say I'm sorry,' she whispered. 'I had no idea I had behaved so badly. I won't ever do such a thing again.'

Ross, remembering Tara's vivacity, her fun, her joy in living, began to think he had said enough and when he put his finger under her chin and saw big tears running slowly down her cheeks he relented and, putting his arm around her, drew her to him.

'You know how fond I am of you, Tara. I might have sounded cruel but it's for your own good.'

She searched his face with tear-filled eyes and said piteously, 'You would never stay away because of what I did?'

'No, I promise.' He pulled a handkerchief from his pocket and wiped away the tears. 'And now we had better go in for breakfast.'

She begged a few more minutes until she had pulled herself together and he had a feeling that she had matured a little for the talk and thought if circumstances had been different he could perhaps have loved her in the way she wanted. They went back to the house and Eileen, looking from one to the other, gave a nod of approval.

Fiona and Ashling chatted over breakfast, but Tara sat silent, not sulking, just looking as if all her vivacity had been drained from her. If Ross spoke to her she answered, but avoided looking at him.

Then Fiona said lightly, 'So what is planned for today? Shall we all go a-wandering and have a picnic lunch? You can tell us more about your adventures in the mountains.'

Ross, who wanted to see Rosin, prevaricated. 'I have to see to some business after breakfast, but I may be free later to go "a-wandering", as you call it. If you all want to go out early, leave a message where you are likely to be and I can follow on.'

Ashling, buttering toast, said, 'How long are you staying, cousin Ross?'

Aware of Tara's intent gaze on him he waved the question aside. 'I'm not sure yet. I shall have to see how long my business takes.'

'How long do you think?' It was not like Ashling to be persistent and Ross asked why it was so important to know.

'I'll tell you why,' declared Fiona. 'Because we're going to a party on Saturday evening and she hasn't got a partner yet. None of us has, so if you are available then we shall have to draw lots.'

Ross grinned. 'I'm flattered, but suppose I tell you that I already have an engagement with a young lady for Saturday evening.' His intention had been just to tease them but when he saw the pain in Tara's eyes, he regretted his words.

When Ross left to go to Queenie McKnott's cottage, Eileen walked to the end of the garden with him, asking him to try to explain to Rosin that Tara was not really a mean person.

Rosin was alone in the cottage when he arrived and his heart was thumping when she invited him in. Queenie was taking food to a neighbour who was ill.

Rosin looked different but Ross was unable to fathom why. He kept trying to get a look at her hands and it was almost as if she knew and was keeping them hidden. She made tea and asked if he had enjoyed his journey to Connemara. It seemed to Ross then that her eyes were a deeper amber. Or was it that the morning had clouded over a little and the room was darker?

He told her something of his meeting the shepherd. When she raised the mug of tea to her lips with both hands he saw that she had long, slender fingers and that her nails were oval. He would have said they were not the nails of a working girl, but Rosin's work need not be hard on her hands. Now what he wanted to see were the hands of Alicia.

He drew his gaze away from Rosin's hands to find her studying him. She said, 'That is why I enjoy travelling the countryside – because one meets such interesting people. I met two sisters out walking once when I was looking for a house where I was to give a reading. They were delightful women, with a lovely sense of humour. We got talking and they told me they were not married but did know two brothers who had asked for their hands. Their brother refused to give his consent, saying they were stupid even to think of marriage at their age. They were both in their early thirties and were astonished when I told them that they would soon be married. There are some people I can read when I meet them. That type, however, are rare. I asked if I could meet their brother and they were very reluctant, saying I would not be welcome, but I managed to persuade them. The brother stormed and raved, how dare they bring a visitor to the house. I suggested he calm down as I had something important to say to him. He told me to get it said and leave.

'Finding I could read him as I had his sisters, I told him if he did not allow them to marry, the Lord would punish him severely for his misdemeanour. He went pale and sank onto a chair.'

'And what was the misdemeanour?'

'I didn't know then, but I found out later that he had been a priest and had been unfrocked for assaulting a young girl. He did allow his sisters to marry, then went to live with a relative.'

'How satisfying it must be to do such splendid work.'

He knew he had spoken in the light way of a non-believer and Rosin put down her mug and said quietly, 'You can scoff, Mr Ferris, but you might not have done had you seen those two sisters happily married.' She got up. 'And now, if you will excuse me, I have some jobs to do.'

Feeling appalled at the attitude he had taken over her story he apologized. 'Forgive me. I wasn't really scoffing. It's just that I haven't met anyone who has your gift.'

'It's not a gift I wish to have.' She appeared to relax. 'Will you walk with me this afternoon?'

She hesitated. 'I can't, I have certain things planned.'

Ross suggested a walk that evening instead. She agreed and it was arranged he would call for her at five o'clock.

He took his leave then, not wanting to give her a chance to change her mind.

Eileen and the girls were delighted to see him back so soon and started to prepare for their picnic. While they were busy who should call but Liam and Dermot McLane. Mr Colhoun had told them of Ross's visit and as they had business to do in Killorglin they had decided to call and see if Ross had returned.

Within minutes there was so much talk it was as if a big party were in progress. Tara was not her usual vivacious self, but she was brighter than she had been earlier.

Fiona had claimed the attention of the brothers by telling them of Ross's adventures in the mountains and of his meeting with the shepherd. Dermot was the only one who did not agree with the shepherd leaving the monastery and a heated discussion began with the others disagreeing with him.

The afternoon was sunny when they set out and the sky a cloudless blue. Soon, however, the sun went in and clouds began to gather. There were groans. Was the weather going to change? Should they seek some shelter? There was a big, disused open hay shed about a hundred yards away and although part of the roof had collapsed the other part was still intact. One or two big drops of rain fell and the party made in the direction of the shed.

Grey clouds gathered momentum so that the patches of blue sky were soon obliterated. Within seconds it was deluging down. They had drawn to the back of the shed, all in good spirits, laughing about their picnic, which was a risk so early in the year anyway, when some shouting came from behind the shed. The next moment a man and girl came rushing in, both laughing. Then realizing there were other people there the man said, 'I hope you don't mind our sharing your shelter.'

There were cries of, 'Of course not,' with Liam adding, 'The more the merrier.'

Ross, however, was staring at the girl, who was rubbing her hair with a man's handkerchief and still chuckling. She threw her hair back and then she was staring at Ross.

He said, 'Welcome, Miss Dannet,' and the coldness

198

in his voice, reflected the chill that had invaded his body.

Rosin had never shared laughter like this with him. He felt as though he had been betrayed.

16

Liam said, 'Well, Ross, aren't you going to introduce us to your friend and her companion?'

After Rosin had introduced her escort as Mr Davidson, Ross introduced her to the others, then stood, anger rising in him at having been put in such a position. The others, apart from Tara, chatted to the couple about the suddenly traitorous weather. Tara was obviously weighing up the situation and, perhaps having decided that Rosin was no longer a threat to her, joined in the talk.

The rain had soaked Rosin's dress under her shawl and the close-fitting bodice emphasized her dainty curvaceous figure. He was about to remove his jacket to drape around her shoulders when her escort forestalled him. She gave him a loving glance over her shoulder and Ross had to clench his fists to control his jealousy. Never once had she hinted that there was someone else in her life. Nor had Queenie known of him. Well, that ended his obsession with the mysterious pedlar girl. He wanted nothing more to do with her.

But even as Ross thought it he knew he would meet her that evening as arranged.

The rain stopped as suddenly as it had started and within seconds a watery sun was peeping from behind clouds. Liam gave a cheer and declared they could still have their picnic after all.

'And sit on the wet grass?' Eileen queried.

'No need for that,' said the smiling Mr Davidson. 'If you wait I can bring a tarpaulin from the carriage. It's just beyond the spinney. The head gardener forecast heavy showers. I would have enjoyed picnicking with you and I am sure that Miss Dannet would have done so too. She must, however, get out of her wet clothes.' He had addressed the last sentence to Ross who agreed as graciously as he could.

Rosin murmured it was nice to have met them all then, and, smiling at Ross, said in a clear voice, 'I shall see you this evening as arranged, Mr Ferris.'

This was so unexpected that it was seconds before he replied.

'Yes – of course. Six o'clock.'

There was a sudden silence. Then everyone was talking at once. A servant arrived with the tarpaulin and a message from Mr Davidson to say to keep it, that it might come in useful some other time. When the man had gone and Eileen was asked who Mr Davidson was she shook her head.

'I have no idea. I haven't seen him before. Guessing, I would say he was a visitor to the district.'

Liam began to muse about Rosin. 'Strange, I've never met her before, and yet she seems oddy familiar.'

Ross, to change the subject, suggested they spread the tarpaulin on the floor of the shed for their picnic as the sky was still overcast.

Eileen and the girls were against it, the shed was not exactly picnic scenery, but as Dermot pointed out, neither were grey skies and pouring rain. Eileen then suggested that they return home and picnic in the summer house, but it was settled they would stay where they were, with Liam suggesting laughingly that they put it down to experience.

The picnic turned out to be a success owing to the bantering of Liam and Dermot and the fact that there was another heavy shower, making the old shed and the tarpaulin seem their saviours. When they left, the sun was shining again and the young ones were in a merry mood and ran on ahead. Ross and his aunt followed,

Eileen saying, 'Rosin was a very different girl to the one you described. I could see you were upset.'

Ross stopped suddenly and turned to her. 'A different girl? Yes. Therein could lie the answer. Is she Rosin or Alicia? Are they playing a game with me? That has to be it. The girl in the shed was not Rosin. This evening I shall know and, if I'm right,' he added grimly, 'they'll regret their silly games!'

Eileen laid a hand on his arm. 'Don't jump so quickly to conclusions, Ross. If they are two different girls then there's a good reason for the subterfuge. I don't know what but no two girls would do such a thing for fun, especially Rosin, whom you describe as being withdrawn.'

'But then Alicia is also secretive, only more complicated. There was a mystery about her too, only a different kind from Rosin. It was a seedy, underhand thing.' Ross pushed his fingers through his hair. 'I wish the Devil 1 had never met either girl. I've been unsettled ever since.'

'Now that's not fair,' Eileen protested. 'Other things were upsetting your life, first losing your money and then your father's involvement with the share market. We still don't know if he's guilty of fraud.'

'And at the moment, Aunt Eileen, I don't give a tinker's cuss whether he is or not. He's caused nothing but trouble in my life.'

'Or was it your mother who caused the trouble?' Eileen asked quietly. 'I think perhaps there's a great deal happened that we might never know.'

Although one part of Ross wanted to get the mystery of Rosin solved, the other part fought shy of it. He had left the shepherd in Connemara with a wonderful feeling of peace and here he was all churned up inside by two people who, he felt, were making a fool of him.

Liam and Dermot were still there when he left to see Rosin and he stood their teasing, knowing it was something he would have done himself had the positions been reversed.

Tara had joined in the fun since returning home but when he was ready to leave he was aware of her quietness and of her watching his every move.

It was Queenie who came to the door to greet him. She was beaming all over her face when she told him that Rosin was ready and waiting. He felt a great warmth steal over him for this big, ungainly woman and felt sorry that he would eventually have to tell her that Rosin had been cheating on them both.

Or need he tell her?

Rosin got up when he came in and the wind was taken out of his sails when she greeted him smiling. She was the Rosin of that afternoon. He gave her a bow.

'Good evening, Miss Dannet. I trust you did not get another soaking this afternoon?'

'No, I was able to shelter from further showers.'

Queenie looked from one to the other, then said to Rosin, 'When did you get soaked?'

'When I went to read the cups for Mrs Gideon and her sister. Their nephew was visiting and offered to take me for a picnic.'

'We met in a shed,' Ross explained, 'where my family and friends were sheltering from a sudden downpour.'

Queenie looked affronted and asked Rosin why she had not mentioned it and Rosin replied pertly, 'Because, dear Mrs McKnott, you would have been asking what my companion was like, how long I had known him and did I think we might get married.'

'I would not!' protested Queenie, 'because I'm hoping you'll marry —' She stopped abruptly, then added lamely, 'Someone nice.' She glanced quickly at Ross then away.

'Mr Davidson is nice,' declared Rosin. 'He's also very attractive and charming.'

Ross knew then for certain that this was the girl in the shed. Not Rosin, but Alicia. Rosin had never acted coyly . . . Alicia had.

'Shall we go,' he asked, 'and enjoy the pleasant evening?'

'Yes, I'll get my coat.'

Queenie came to the door with them and suggested they walk up Broom Hill, adding, 'It's a stiff climb but a lovely walk.'

Ross did not want to walk, he wanted to sit down and talk, but for Queenie's benefit, who was still waving to them, he cupped Alicia's elbow and directed her to the field from where a narrow winding path led up the hill.

Then he stopped at a stile and said, 'I would like to have a talk with you, that is, if you don't object.'

'No, of course not, why should I?'

'Because although I know that Rosin enjoys walking, I don't know if you do, Alicia.'

He spread his handkerchief on the stile for her and when she was seated she looked up smiling. 'You called me Alicia. Have you a special lady friend of that name?'

'Shall we stop playing games?' He sat down beside her.

'I know you are not Rosin. She is a withdrawn person, does not smile very often and is not coquettish.'

'You surprise me. I thought I was being very coquettish that first day we met at the Puck Fair. I liked you on sight.'

Ross, recalling the day, could see Rosin, twirling round from one customer to another, smiling as she displayed her tray of wares. She was a pedlar girl trying to interest her customers but quite definitely was not trying to sell herself. Ross picked up her right hand. 'You are obviously identical twins, but your hands are not alike. Your fingers are shorter than Rosin's and your nails are squarish while hers are oval.'

Alicia snatched her hand away. 'You are being quite ridiculous.'

'I do know it was you who came in distress that night in London and told my friend and myself that a man had photographed you naked in bed with another man.'

At this Alicia's shoulders sagged. 'All right, I admit it. But I don't want to talk about it. I came last night unexpectedly. Rosin was cross with me.' She got up. 'I'll take you to her. She can explain. She's in a cottage belonging to a friend who's away.'

'Tell me one thing,' Ross said, as they walked away, 'how did you get Mrs McKnott to accept you as Rosin? Although you are very much alike in looks you have different ways. And you were living with her. I would say she's a very discerning woman.'

'No, please don't ask me any more. I hate my life.'

The cottage nestled at the foot of the hill but out of sight of the main road. Alicia gave a tap on the door, opened it and called, 'I've brought a visitor, an unwelcome one, but don't blame me.'

Rosin, who had been sitting at the table having a meal, stood up and stared at Ross for a moment then looked at her sister and said in a hurt way, 'How could you do this, Alicia? You promised you would never tell anyone.'

Ross said softly, 'It's all right, I won't give your secret away.'

Alicia pulled out a chair. 'Sit down. I'll leave Rosin to tell you the whole miserable story. I can't bear to hear it.'

'Please stay,' Rosin begged, but Alicia in turn begged to be excused, saying that her sister was a much stronger person.

Rosin sighed and said to Ross. 'I'll pour you a cup of tea. It's a long story and I really don't know where to start. From our birth, I suppose.'

'Take your time, I'm in no hurry. May I say that I regret now having forced you to reveal your secrets?'

'No, this could not have gone on. I was beginning to feel like a criminal. The two people I hated to live out a lie to were Mrs McKnott and yourself. I love and respect you both. I can say that because I shall be going out of your lives after the story is told.'

So she loved him. He felt suddenly elated until he remembered how his pulses had raced that afternoon at seeing Alicia's curvaceous figure in the rain-soaked dress.

Rosin continued, 'Our mother was a music-hall artiste. According to what we have been told, she was not only very attractive but was a splendid mimic and dancer. She had many admirers from the upper classes but fell in love with only one man, an earl's son, who set her up in a small but beautiful house. He seemingly adored her and when she became pregnant, wanted to marry her. But his father was furious and took his son abroad, where he died months later.' At this point Rosin's voice faltered and it was a few moments before she could continue. 'Our mother lived only to see us born.' She swallowed hard. 'Alicia was adopted and I went to foster parents. They lived for the Church and although I was fed and clothed and educated they knew nothing about love. When I was sixteen I was sent into service and they emigrated to America to join a religious group.'

'Why didn't they take you with them?'

'I don't think they really wanted me. I believe they felt it was a duty and it would get them into heaven. I only heard from them twice after they left and I was seventeen before I learned that I had a twin sister, and this was by sheer chance. Cook had sent me to get some raspberries from the garden and one of the gardener's sons was picking them for me when I noticed a girl crouching behind some bushes. She put a finger to her lips, then was staring at me. There was the sound of a voice calling, "Alicia", and she ran from behind the bushes laughing. The boy, Joe, said, "You ain't 'alf like that young lady. You're the dead spit on her." He laughed. "I mean you would be if you was dressed like 'er."

'I thought no more about it. She was class. I was a skivvy. But the next day a lady came to see me and asked me questions. I could only tell her about my foster parents and how they had emigrated and after writing down their name and address she left. I did venture to ask Cook what it could be about, but she simply said it was probably one of those nosy parker do-gooders who wanted to know if I got enough to eat, and I accepted it.

'Then about two weeks later, while I was hanging out clothes in the garden, the girl appeared again. She kept behind some bushes and told me to go on with what I was doing, and then she told me she thought I was her twin sister and that I might be coming to live with her. Joe got me excited, saying that things like this did happen, but when two months went by and I hadn't heard any more I presumed that the girl had been fantasizing.'

'Then one day, right of out of the blue I was told by Cook that I was to pack my bag. I was going to live in the home of a titled lady and be companion to a young lady my own age. I won't go into all the details of my bewilderment at first when I had no idea what-soever of what it was all about, but I will mention the elderly lady whose house I went to. She gave me a kiss and a hug, something I had never known before. I cried.'

'And who was she?'

'Lady Sylvain, the mother of my mother's lover. I was bathed and clothed, I met my sister, Alicia, who was wild with joy. I ate with her, and Alicia and I were taught by a very solemn and elderly tutor. My sister loved to hear about my work as a skivvy and I enjoyed knowing there was a different world where people were rich. The one thing I didn't share with Alicia, however, were the times when she was taken out socializing, Lady Sylvain explaining that she had only known of one child being born and would have to delve more deeply into my birth.'

'How did Lady Sylvain treat you otherwise?'

'She was a very kind, gentle person but, according to Alicia, was dominated by a niece, who had hoped to be her aunt's beneficiary when the old lady died. She resented Alicia being brought into the family and would certainly not accept me as Alicia's twin, even though it was difficult to tell us apart if we happened to be dressed alike.' A smile touched her lips. 'Because of this Alicia suddenly decided one day that we would have some fun and change places from time to time. We started to imitate each other's little mannerisms and voice inflections and discovered that we were both excellent mimics.'

'So what happened then?'

'When we felt we were as perfect as we could be, I took Alicia's place and went socializing with Lady Sylvain. I was terribly nervous at first but Lady Sylvain was such a lovely person I soon relaxed and everything went off perfectly.'

Rosin's expression suddenly changed, became solemn. 'Three months later Lady Sylvain became ill and died. Both Alicia and I were bereft.' She was silent for a moment, then went on, 'The following evening Lady Kereslake told me a job had been found for me as an underhousemaid in a big house in Middlesex and that I would be taken there.'

'And how did Alicia take that news?'

'She stormed and raved and stamped her feet and was told that if she didn't calm down I would be sent abroad and she would never see me again. That calmed her and the two of us plotted how to write to one another so our letters would not be intercepted.'

'You've had quite a complicated life,' Ross said gently, to which Rosin replied that that was only the beginning of it.

'I could not have been sent to a more miserable house. There was not a smile from anyone and I was determined to run away. Then one day a young girl came to the kitchen and offered to tell fortunes. The cook told her to get out, she didn't want any fortune-tellers telling lies to the servants. The girl said, "Lies is it I tell? Well let me tell you that the kitchen maid who went home because her mother was ill won't come back because she has had a fall and broken her leg." No sooner had this been told than a young lad came to say that his sister had fallen down some stone steps and was laid up with a broken leg.'

Rosin smiled. 'I can still see the utter astonishment on that cook's face. It ended up with the girl taking the job of skivvy and telling the fortunes of all the staff free. She was Irish and had run away from home because her father beat her. Her name was Bernadette, and she and I took to each other at once. She confessed to me that she had heard the news of the young skivvy's fall and had come straight to the house as she wanted a job. She was, however, very proficient at fortune-telling and eventually taught me how to read palms and tea leaves and tell the tarot cards. She could have made the house a more lively place had it been allowed, but Cook was always on to one or the other of us for talking and Bernadette said to me one day that she wanted to go back to Ireland and asked me if I would go with her.

'I was tempted. Then, when Bernadette told me we could earn a living selling cheap jewellery at fairs and telling fortunes, I became really interested and felt I wanted to leave that very day. Bernadette told me she would not be going home but staying with a friend. She did promise she would find someone I would like to lodge with. It was dear Mrs McKnott.'

Ross said, puzzled, 'But where does Alicia come into all this?'

'Well, when I told her what I was planning to do she said that she wanted to break away from Lady Kereslake but was held there by the money. Then she had this plan that we could exchange our life styles and no one would know. It all sounded foolish to me but Alicia persisted and even managed to come to Middlesex, while Lady Kereslake was away, to arrange it all. She was excited, she was also very persuasive, but I think what finally made me accept the plan was the fact of being able to have some freedom. It was heaven for me to do exactly as I pleased. I've taken a long time to tell you all this, you must be getting a little weary.'

'Weary? I'm fascinated. What happened to Bernadette?'

An impish look came into Rosin's eyes. 'Now that is a story in itself. On our first trip to Ireland she met a young man and they fell in love. Six weeks later they married and she is now expecting their baby. They are just so happy. She says that I was responsible. I slipped on the deck, bumped into her and she fell. Then this young man rushed over and picked her up.'

'And I saw you at the Puck Fair and fell in love with you.'

Rosin sobered. 'You also fell in love with Alicia.'

'It was the likeness. Alicia has a different nature to you.' He reached for her hand and said softy, 'It's you I love, Rosin.'

She drew her hand away. 'I do love you, but there it must end. I don't want to get married. No, that is not the truth. I do, I want a home and children, but you come from a good family. I am a bastard.' He heard the pain in her voice as she uttered these words.

'Rosin, whatever happened is not your fault. You were accepted by your father's mother.'

'No.' She spoke harshly. 'She only accepted Alicia. I was never her social equal. I was always the kitchen maid really.'

'You are the girl I love,' said Ross. 'I don't want anyone else.'

'Alicia is in love with you.'

'No.' He spoke harshly. 'She was looking at Mr Davidson with love.'

'With coyness. She wanted to make you jealous. She told me so. She came unexpectedly. I was not expecting her.'

'I don't like coy women, Rosin. I'm in love with you and you have admitted loving me.'

'Only because I'm ending all this exchanging of our life styles. It spelled adventure at first, now it's gone stale on me. I've seen too much poverty, too much misery. I shall stay in Ireland and continue going to fairs and telling fortunes. With the money I get I can manage to help a poor family here and there.'

'Will Alicia except that? Incidentally, is she able to tell fortunes too?'

'Yes, she was quick to learn. We are so alike in many ways and unalike in others. She longs to be married and have children and she is in love with you.'

'But I am no longer attracted to her.' He took Rosin's hands in his then, drawing her to her feet, put his arms around her and said softly, 'And I want you.'

He bent his head to kiss her and when his lips moved sensually over hers, she gave a small gasp and responded with passion. Ross, sweeping her up in his arms, carried her to the sofa and, laying her down, began to undo the buttons of her dress. His heart was pounding and when he slid a hand inside her bodice and cupped the warm flesh of her breast he could feel the wild beating of her heart. She gave a little moan of pleasure but when he moved his hand further down she gripped his wrist and made an attempt to sit up.

He was over her now, trying to slip the dress from her shoulders. She made an effort to push him away. 'No, it's wrong.'

'I love you, Rosin. I want you, need you.'

'No! I'm a bastard and I don't want to bring another one into the world.' Her voice was suddenly harsh.

'You won't, we'll get married.'

'My father wanted to marry my mother.' There was a weariness about her now and aware of all the hurt she had suffered, he got up, all passion gone.

Rosin sat up and swinging her legs to the floor made an attempt to fasten the buttons on her dress. Her hands were shaking so much that Ross took over, saying gently, 'Let me try. I'm sorry I let myself get carried away. I've wanted you for so long.'

'You wanted both of us. I was the one available . . . and willing.' She looked at him, her eyes full of pain. 'I'm sorry I responded. I was at fault for leading you on.' Her voice had lowered. 'I love you, but I had to control my feelings.'

'We'll get married, Rosin.' He spoke with firmness. 'As soon as possible.'

She shook her head. 'No, it wouldn't work. You are in a different class.'

'Forget class. It means nothing.'

'Oh, but it does. Alicia was accepted in our grand-mother's house. Lady Sylvain took me into her home too, but I was kept in the background. She was kind but could not get over her class instinct. I only know that I feel a nonentity.'

'Not to me, Rosin,' he said quickly. 'We will get married. No, don't shake your head. I'm determined on it. We shall live in Ireland if you wish and I can help you help the poor.'

She gave a sad little smile. 'We can talk about it again, but deep down I know it wouldn't work. Your business is in London, you enjoy the life there, you have many friends.'

'The family I love live here, Rosin. I would be quite happy to live a simple life. I felt I wanted nothing more when I was in the mountains.'

'That was in the mountains and for how many days? Two, three? You would need to be there a year at least to know whether you could live the life. This is spring. You have no knowledge of the winters, the blizzards, the ice so thick on pools even a hammer won't break it. There is such a lot to discuss. Leave it for now. We can talk about it again.'

Although Ross tried to persuade her to thrash out the situation there and then, she was adamant that they would talk another time and he teased her, saying he would have to beware or he would be having a wife who wanted to wear the trousers.

She laughed at this and told him she hated women who tried to rule the roost and added if she did marry she would be quite happy to be a wifely wife.

That night after everyone else had gone to bed, Ross told Eileen the whole story.

It was Eileen's opinion that Rosin was the sensible one for wanting to discuss the situation again.

'You know her attitude and she may not be comfortable living your way of life, Ross. And it's no use saying you would live here and lead her kind of life. You are a businessman, it's something you've revelled in. Think things over very carefully.'

'My mind is made up and I'm quite sure when I see her in the morning the answer will be yes.'

But when Ross called the next morning at Queenie's cottage he was met with the news that Rosin had left.

'For good,' Queenie said, her eyes red rimmed. 'She left you a note.'

Dear Ross, it said,
Forgive me for leaving like this. I just couldn't bear to tell you face to face that I couldn't marry you. I love you and always will, but I know that it wouldn't work. I would always be unhappy feeling that I was bringing you down to a lower level. Marry someone in your own class, Ross.
I wish you every happiness. Please, please, don't make any attempt to follow me. I would not change my mind. Rosin.

Ross said at once that he would go after her, but after two weeks' search and remembering that Conal had said that if a person was determined to hide away in Ireland they could live and die there without anyone knowing, he decided to return to Killorglin.

He arrived feeling depressed and was met by Eileen, who, with tear-filled eyes, said without preamble, 'I have some awful news. Your father seduced Tara and she could be pregnant.'

17

It was seconds before Ross took in what his aunt had said and he stood staring at her. 'I don't believe it. Tara's lying. My father might be a rogue as far as business is concerned but he would not touch his own niece. I know it.'

'I ordered her to swear on the Bible and she did so. She would not lie with her rosary in one hand and the other on the Bible. Oh, Ross, what am I going to do?' Eileen sank into one armchair and Ross into the other.

'I don't know, Aunt Eileen, I just don't know. No wonder he wanted to get away. He'll be out of the country by now.' Anger suddenly flared in Ross, 'And it's a good job he is because I would have killed him and would have had no compunction in doing so! He's betrayed the trust of all of us.'

'Tara was partly to blame,' his aunt said in a low voice. 'And yet, I told her if she went to see him again I would send her to live with her Great-Aunt Henrietta and that should have been warning enough. She hates her.'

'What did happen?'

'According to Tara she felt sorry for her uncle because he looked so sad. She kissed him on the cheek when she was about to leave and he put his arms around her and began to cry.'

'To cry? My father, never!'

'Tara said his tears were genuine, he sobbed and because he was so unhappy she put her arms around him. One thing led to another.'

Ross felt only impatience with Tara. She had been kissed by plenty of young men, she had boasted about it.

He said, 'You suggested she could be pregnant.'

'Well the . . . the monthly cycle was due two days after and . . . it hasn't happened.'

'But surely it could be delayed because of what had happened? Isn't there something that women take?'

'We have used hot baths and some old-fashioned remedies that could bring on the . . . We can only wait and see. I should never have blurted this out to you, but there's no one else I can talk to.'

Ross lowered his hands. 'You did right. I just still can't accept that my father . . . But there, as you say, Tara wouldn't lie about it. We can only pray that nature will take its course. I should be getting back to London. In fact I had been thinking about leaving tomorrow, but I'll stay a few more days.'

His aunt urged him to make plans to go home, saying that Tara was under strain trying to behave normally and if Ross was there it would be a bigger strain knowing that his father was responsible.

She concluded, 'I shall let you know one way or another.'

Ross was silent for a while then said, 'Aunt Eileen, if it is bad news then I shall marry Tara.'

'You will not. I won't have two lives ruined. You love Rosin.'

'That is over. I'm very fond of Tara, as you know. My father has ruined her life. It's the least I can do.'

Eileen refused to accept such a sacrifice. 'You have a life to lead. I refuse to let you be a hero.'

'Aunt Eileen,' he said softly, 'all of you here are my family. I love you all, it will be no sacrifice. I only ask that Tara is not told unless there is no other way.'

Eileen's voice broke as she promised, and they clung to one another, both knowing that the shared secret would make them even closer, a bond that would last until the end of their days.

Ross planned to leave the next morning and knew

when he saw the misery underlying Tara's forced brightness, and his aunt's effort to appear normal, that he would not regret his offer should it be required.

He had a big sendoff at the station, promised to return again soon and prayed, at the same time that there would be no urgent need for him to return.

He had told himself he would be firm in forgetting about Rosin, but this did nothing to ease the ache of losing her, and during the first part of the journey he reproached himself for his behaviour. If only he had contained his emotions, led up to making love with gentle words and caresses, instead of rushing like a gauche youth to take her. It had been a question of what *he* wanted, *he* needed. How stupid he had been. Fool, fool!

Although later on in the journey he began to wonder if he had been too ready to suggest marrying Tara as Rosin might change her mind, he knew deep down that this was something she would not do. She had a great strength of will, a positive streak that one could not change, which she needed to get her through all the traumas in her life.

John Davies was at the station to meet Ross, and the grip of his friend's hand and his smile of welcome lifted Ross from despair. Returning the firm handclasp he said, 'It's good to see you, John, good to be back.'

'A satisfying visit?' John queried.

'On the contrary, but there, I shall tell you all about it later. How's business here? I saw in the papers that the Querifold shares had shot up fifty per cent.'

They talked business until they were home and sitting down to a meal. Then Ross gave his friend an account of his visit to Ireland and the search for his father in the mountains.

'So, he's gone abroad,' said John. 'I wonder why? It was announced today that fraud has been proved with Fray and Hulton, but your father is not involved.'

They discussed it for some time. Then, when John asked about Ross's family, Ross told the whole story of clearing up the mystery of Rosin and Alicia, of Rosin leaving, and finally of Tara's trouble.

John pushed his plate aside and said, 'Good God. I can't believe your father would stoop so low. In fact I refuse to believe it.'

Ross repeated what his aunt had told him about Tara swearing on the Bible and John shook his head. 'That might be so, but I do think you are carrying loyalty to your father too far.'

'It's not out of loyalty to my father,' Ross said quietly. 'It's mainly for the sake of Aunt Eileen and Uncle Patrick who are very close to me. I know what I shall be taking on if I have to marry Tara.'

John leaned forward. 'Marriage is for life, Ross. It could be hell being married to the wrong woman. It really is foolish to love one girl and marry someone else.'

'I've known Tara since she was a child. I've always been fond of her – could have loved her if she hadn't done so many stupid things, but with a baby to care for I think she might mature.'

John sighed. 'Well, here's to it.' He raised his glass.

'Let us drink to something else. I may not *have* to get married, as the saying goes. If it has to be marriage we'll go to Gretna Green, get it over quickly, so that we might avoid the whispers of a possible shotgun wedding.'

John set down his glass. 'But, Ross, there are no quick marriages today at Gretna for those living outside Scotland.'

'Oh Lord, I was wanting to create romance, a runaway marriage, without all the delay of banns having to be called.'

'You could speed things up by applying for a special licence. And you would still have the romance if you

218

went to Gretna and were wed there. In Scotland you can be married in a house, so long as the person marrying you is qualified to do so. Apply for the licence tomorrow and write to Eileen explaining your plan. Then you would be prepared to leave at once should the marriage be needed.'

John then explained that he had a friend in Gretna who would be more than willing to have them stay with her. 'Her name is Miss MacDougal. You would both like her.'

Ross said, 'All this planning gives me a feeling of foreboding that it's going to be needed.

John dismissed it. 'Better to be prepared than have no plan.'

As it turned out, Ross's feeling of foreboding was right. A few days later he returned home from business to find Tara perched on the edge of a chair in his sitting room, her dark blue eyes looking huge in a paper-white face.

'Tara!' he exclaimed. 'Is your mother with you?'

'No,' she replied in a strangled voice. 'I came on my own. Mama was away for the day and Fiona and Ashling were visiting friends. I left a note for Mama to say where I was going.'

Ross pushed his fingers through his hair in a distracted way. 'What am I to do with you? I shall have to send a telegram and let them know you are here. Why did you come?'

'I knew I was pregnant and when I told Mama she said . . .' Tara looked at the floor, 'that you had offered to marry me.' Her voice was now little above a whisper.

'Tara, look at me,' he demanded. 'As if things were not bad enough as they stood, you had to come here and cause masses more trouble and expect me to −'

She raised her head and there was now a pleading in her eyes.

'I wanted to ease the shame for Mama and Papa. I

thought if we . . . if we could run away to Gretna Green and get married, it would make it, well, so it wouldn't seem like a forced marriage.'

He eyed her suspiciously. 'Who told you about Gretna Green?'

'Girls talked about it at school. We thought it very romantic.' She got up and knelt in front of him. 'I'm not treating this lightly, Ross. I'm very grateful indeed that you offered to marry me. But if you've changed your mind, I'll understand.'

'I said I would marry you and I shall keep my word.' He could hear his own voice, without warmth and knew how much he had been hoping that she wouldn't need to get married.

'I know I did wrong,' she said, 'but I don't want the baby to suffer for my sin. I'll do my best to be a good wife and mother, I really will.' Two big tears hung on her lashes, then slid slowly down her cheeks. 'I promise.'

Ross relented. He pulled out a handkerchief and handed it to her. 'Here, dry your eyes. We'll have a long talk later. At the moment you need some rest.' He put an arm around her and led her to a sofa. 'Now you lie down there and I'll send a telegram and let your parents know you are safe.'

'You don't hate me?'

How could he, with that look of pleading in her eyes? He drew the back of his fingers lightly over her cheek. 'No, Tara, I don't hate you. There, lie down, I'll get a rug.'

When he came back with it she was asleep. He tucked the rug gently around her, then bent to kiss her on the brow. His whole life would be changed from now on but at least it would not be dull. He went to send the telegram.

When John arrived home he was full of praise for Tara's initiative in coming over to go to Gretna Green.

'The sooner you are married the less speculation there will be. Also think of the delay in calling banns and all there would have had to be done – invitations to be sent out, wedding outfits to be made, catering to be arranged, a hundred and one things. Lucky you to avoid all this. You go to Gretna Green, spend a few days honeymooning and come home with a welcome awaiting.'

When the two of them sat down for a drink. John brought up the question of accommodation for when they returned. The sharing of the house would be all right at first, but every bride wanted her own home, especially when the baby arrived.

Ross looked grim. 'That is for the future. At the moment I have enough to contend with making arrangements for going to Gretna Green and may God forgive me, but I wish it was all over.'

Tara awoke not long after this and they were having a meal with John when a telegram came: *Relieved to know Tara is safe. Go ahead with plans. We send our good wishes. Letter follows. Love and kisses.*

Ross handed it to Tara and her relief was evident. She had been picking at her food until then. Now she started to eat and there was a hint of her usual vivacity as the evening wore on. She talked about Fiona and Ashling, saying how disappointed they would be at not being bridesmaids and Ross said drily, 'You have a choice. A church wedding or Gretna Green.'

Obviously aware of his manner, she said, 'Ross, I'm sorry. It's Gretna, of course.'

Later, after Tara had gone to bed, John said to Ross, 'Tara seems determined to try and make it a good marriage and I hope that you will too. You offered to marry her but there were odd times this evening when you made it sound as if you were doing her a favour.'

Ross looked at him shocked. 'It was unintentional, I assure you. Mind you, there was one time when it

221

suddenly struck me that I would not be having a son or daughter, but a little brother or sister. It seems ludicrous somehow.'

'Think of the child as a son or daughter,' John said gently, 'or you will live a tormented life.'

The next morning John was up early. He saw to train times to Gretna and got the tickets. Ross and Tara packed and were ready to leave at ten o'clock. Tara was quiet, so was Ross. As John had said, marriage was for life and it was Rosin he ached for.

They boarded the train with John's good wishes and Ross, aware that Tara was on the verge of tears, made an effort to be gentle with her.

At one part of the journey they had a carriage to themselves and Tara ventured to say, 'Ross, there's still time to change your mind if you wish.'

An angry retort rose to his lips at the fact they were on their way, but he managed to calm down. 'If I had wanted to change my mind, Tara, I would have done so before now.'

'Yes, of course. A thousand thoughts are running through my mind and I'm having difficulty in trying to sort them out.'

She had the look of a bewildered child and Ross suddenly felt sorry for her. He leaned forward and took her hands in his. 'The next few months are going to be difficult for both of us, Tara, but if you are disturbed about anything, even a small thing, tell me about it and we can talk it over.'

'Yes, I will, because I get confused about certain things.'

'Such as?'

She twisted a fine lace-edged handkerchief between her fingers. 'You were talking about getting married to . . . to Rosin and then you suddenly offer to marry me. Had you suddenly fallen out of love with her and decided to marry me because of pity?'

'No, to be honest I was angry with you. I was sorry for your parents who I knew would be so terribly hurt, especially your mother who was always on to you to do the right thing.'

'So it wasn't because you loved me just a little bit?'

Ross gave a small sigh of despair. 'Tara, you know perfectly well that I'm fond of all of you three girls. Don't expect any more from me at this stage. Being married to you might bring love. I hope it will. Marriage is for life. I don't want you to mention Rosin at any time. That is over.'

'You won't have any worries on that score,' she said firmly. She gave a sudden impish grin. 'I'm going to surprise you and make you the best of wives.'

'Good, I shall look forward to it.'

This lifted the atmosphere and Ross made an effort to try to share Tara's pleasure in the journey. By the time they arrived at Gretna, however, even Tara was beginning to feel weary. Miss MacDougal was at the station to meet them and they went by carriage to her cottage. Both Ross and Tara took to the spinster on sight. She was a gentle person who explained they would stay with her that evening, but the marriage would take place in the Ceremony Room at the Gretna Hall Hotel at eleven-thirty the next morning. Afterwards there would be a wedding breakfast, with a few friends of hers invited so that it would make it more a family affair.

'All this was suggested by Mr Davies,' she said, 'but he does stress that if there are any changes you wish to make then please do so. Incidentally, you may wish to spend your wedding night at my cottage. It's very quiet and I shall be staying overnight with my sister and her husband.'

Tara said she thought it a wonderful idea and when she looked at Ross for his opinion he agreed too. After all, it was Tara's day.

The large cottage had a comfortably furnished living room with a kitchen adjoining, two bedrooms upstairs, one large one with a big double bed with chintz cover and curtains to match, and a smaller room with two single beds in it and not much else.

Miss MacDougal said that Mr Ferris could sleep in the large bedroom that night while she and Tara could share the smaller one. 'And I laid the supper ready,' she smiled.

Tara and Ross were both too tired to do justice to the meal. Tara was beginning to look drained and when Miss MacDougal suggested they have an early night they both agreed.

As tired as Tara was, however, once she was in bed she thought of the following evening when she would be sharing a bed with Ross and excited tremors went through her body.

Ross had no such feelings. He felt annoyed that John had made arrangements for a wedding breakfast. It had nothing to do with him. Ross wanted the wedding to be over and done with, not prolonged. Rosin came into his mind, but he could not recall the short passionate scene in the cottage at the foot of the hill. It was all vague. His eyelids drooped. He drifted into sleep.

Miss MacDougal roused him the next morning, saying she had left a cup of tea and hot water for washing, outside the door. When he glanced bleary-eyed at his gold hunter on the side table he was astonished to find it was after nine o'clock.

He took time shaving, not wanting any cuts on his chin on his wedding day. He was still not ready when Tara knocked to say that breakfast was ready, and he felt bad-tempered.

It was the smell of bacon cooking that made him realize he was hungry. When he did go downstairs he was not allowed in at once and he heard giggling and

224

someone rushing around. When Miss MacDougal unlocked the door she was smiling all over her face.

'Sorry, Mr Ferris, it was women's business that kept you out. I shall put the breakfast on the table.'

Tara said brightly, 'Good morning, Ross. I trust you slept well.'

'Yes, thank you. And you?'

'Splendid.'

There was porridge with bacon and eggs and toast to follow. This time both prospective bride and groom did justice to the meal, which Tara said surprised her as she had expected to feel jittery.

'I should imagine that will come later, at the ceremony,' declared Miss MacDougal, adding, 'I say it only to prepare you. It's what other brides have told me.'

There was a note of sadness in her voice and Tara wondered if she had ever been a prospective bride and something had happened to prevent the marriage.

They sat talking until the grandfather clock chiming made them realize it would soon be time for the carriage to take them to the hotel.

Tara gave a shaky laugh. 'And now I am feeling jittery.'

'You'll be all right,' Ross said and realized by the hurt look on Tara's face that his tone had been cold. He put his arms round her. 'Don't worry, Tara. You'll make a lovely bride.' He would liked to have told her he loved her but he couldn't bring himself to say it. He kissed her gently and she smiled and whispered, 'Thank you, Ross.'

Then Miss MacDougal was calling that the carriage was here and they put on their coats. Tara had said she would change her dress at the hotel.

At the hotel, relatives of Miss MacDougal were waiting. They were friendly people and Ross was left in their company while Miss MacDougal took Tara to change her dress.

It was then Ross learned that Tara would be wearing the wedding dress that Miss MacDougal would have worn had her fiancé not been killed by a runaway horse the day before they were due to be married. Miss MacDougal's niece told him that her aunt would not have suggested Tara's wearing the dress had not Tara said she only wished she could have worn a dress for her wedding that she had not worn before.

When Tara came out wearing the dress, Ross got up, held out his hands to her and said softly, 'You look beautiful, my love.'

She did. The dress was simple – white muslin with a full skirt edged with lace, sleeves full at the top and tight at the wrist, a high neck pinned with a silver brooch inset with pearls. A ring of white silk daisies on her hair completed the outfit.

But it was the ethereal look on Tara's face that moved him.

The next moment the door burst open and a voice was saying, 'Tara, oh, Tara.'

Tara turned swiftly. 'Mama! I don't believe it.'

Then mother and daughter were clasped in one another's arms, both weeping, both trying to talk together, Tara saying it was the most wonderful thing that could have happened and Eileen saying, 'Oh, my darling, I didn't think we were going to get here on time.'

It was then that John walked in and Ross, who had been thinking badly of him the night before, went over and pumped his hand, saying, 'Well, this certainly is a surprise.' He looked about him. 'Where is the rest of the family?'

'There are just the two of us, I'm afraid. It's a long story. We'll tell you later.'

Ross was hardly aware of the actual ceremony and said afterwards that he couldn't remember saying, the words, 'I will.'

'Oh, you said them,' replied a radiant Tara. 'You can't get out of it. There are witnesses.' There was laughter and Ross knew then that John had done the right thing in making all the arrangements, although it was not until after the reception that he learned the whole story from Eileen.

The wedding breakfast itself went off splendidly, and Ross, although he had not worked out a speech, managed to convey the affection he had always had for Tara and her sisters and how Tara had suddenly become very special, which, although not in the right context, was certainly true.

When Ross put his hand over Tara's to cut the cake it came to him for the first time that he was now a married man with a wife to care for and, in a few months' time, a child too. His responsibilities suddenly seemed a burden. Tara was beautiful, she was loving, but she didn't seem to know the meaning of responsibility. He caught sight of his aunt watching him, her expression anxious, as though aware of his thoughts and, realizing the strain she must be under having to keep the guilty secret, he gave her a warm smile, trying to reassure that all would be well. She returned his smile looking suddenly relieved.

After the reception Eileen explained to Ross why she and John had turned up unexpectedly.

'John telegrammed to say you were getting married at Gretna Green and everyone was excited, the girls especially. They were just about on their bended knees to come and Patrick was getting to the state when he thought we should all go. But, knowing you would be getting married by special licence and they would guess why, I couldn't let them come. John then telegrammed again to say he had decided to go to the wedding and would I like to travel with him? I was aching to see you both and, knowing how much it would mean to Tara, I decided to tell Patrick the truth. He was horrified at first. Then, realizing what you were doing, he said I must go to Scotland, but that I was not to tell another soul. In the end I concocted a tale of a friend who was moving to England whom I wanted to see before she left. Oh, Ross, the lies I have told in my life. But I'm just so pleased I've seen you both and Tara was delighted.'

Later, Tara was tearful as her mother departed, but she said to Ross, 'I couldn't have been happier had I had the biggest wedding in the world.'

'I'm glad,' Ross said softly, then added, 'I think it's time to leave.'

When they arrived at the cottage, fires were burning brightly.

Ross was determined to make it a proper honeymoon night for Tara, but all he could think of was how different it all would have been had he married Rosin.

Tara went up to bed first. He had told her he would follow a few minutes later. Oh God, he thought, what a fiasco. Never in all his affairs of the heart had he not been ready, very ready, to make love.

Knowing that Tara must be undressed and in bed he could put it off no longer. He had intended to go into the smaller bedroom to undress but as he was passing the door of the big bedroom he saw that it was ajar. He pushed the door a little wider, then drew a quick breath as he saw one of the most beautiful and sensual scenes he had ever witnessed.

Tara was standing in front of a long mirror, her back to him, hands cupping her small pointed breasts. Ross had never seen such perfection. She seemed taller than he had imagined, narrow-waisted, with small firm buttocks and long shapely legs, the skin delicately tinted in the soft glow of candlelight.

She gave a small sigh, then picking up her nightdress was about to pull it over her head when Ross said softly, 'Don't.'

228

Startled, she spun round holding the nightdress in front of her. He went up to her and made to take it from her but she clung to it.

'Tara, you are just so beautiful. I want to go on looking at you.' She let the nightdress fall to the floor but crossed her arms over her breasts, her gaze searching his.

'If only you loved me. I don't mean making love to me as a duty, I mean, well . . .'

'I think I've fallen in love with you, Tara. I want to take care of you. Is that what you mean?'

She nodded and he could see the glistening of tears in her eyes.

He picked her up and put her between the sheets. He saw her shiver and he smiled and said, 'Give me time to get undressed and I'll have you warm in seconds.'

When he was beside her she gave a shaky laugh and put her arms around his neck. 'You are warm, sir.' She traced a finger around his ear, then around his mouth, and he had a sudden feeling of unease at her confidence.

This was forgotten, however, as her fingers explored his body sending his blood pounding and pulse racing. Desire made him rough and she moaned with pleasure, exciting him still further.

When he took her she raised herself to him and, to his joy, they climaxed together. It was when the vibrations had died away that he found himself worrying. He had been lying with his arm around her. Now he withdrew it.

'What is it,' she asked alarmed. 'Did I do something wrong?'

He turned his head. 'No, you did everything right, that is what is bothering me. I had imagined myself teaching you how to respond to love-making, but of course I had forgotten you were not a virgin.'

The moment the words were out he regretted them.

She eased herself up in bed and he could see the pain in her eyes as she said in a low voice, 'I've loved you for years, Ross. All that I did seemed natural to me. The other was . . . different.'

She threw back the bedclothes and slid to the floor. Then picking up her nightdress she put it on. She was starting to gather her clothes together when Ross got out of bed and, dragging on his dressing gown, said, 'Wait. Where are you going?'

'To the other bedroom.'

He felt suddenly choked. The simplicity of the white cambric nightdress with its tiny pink and blue bows gave her the innocence of a child.

He said, 'Tara, I'm sorry.'

'I'm sorry too because it was an unforgivable thing to say. You brought me down to the level of a street woman.' Her voice broke.

'No, such a thing never occurred to me.'

'Oh, but it did or you would never have said what you did.'

'Come back to bed.'

'I couldn't. I shall sleep in the other bedroom. To-morrow I shall make arrangements to return home.'

Ross, who felt he had humbled himself enough, said wearily, 'All right, go home if that is what you want. But I shall sleep next door. Get back to bed.' With that he left, slamming the door behind him.

He cursed as he stubbed his toe against a chair. Cursed that he had offered to marry her. What a fiasco. He waited until his eyes were used to the darkness, then looked around for a candle. He found one but had not had time to light it when the door opened and a small voice said, 'Ross, are you awake?'

'Of course I'm awake,' he snapped. 'I can't even find matches.'

'Ross, I'm sorry. Come back to bed. I don't want to

go home. I want to be with you. We are man and wife.'

He didn't want to give in, otherwise she would expect it every time they had words but on the other hand, remembering their lovemaking and hearing the contrition in her voice, he said, 'I shall come on one condition, that all this between us will be forgotten and never brought up again.'

'I've forgotten already,' she said, a smile in her voice. 'What was it all about?'

He swept her up in his arms and carried her back to the other bed. He laid his cheek to hers and said softly, 'I love you.'

'And I love you, love you, love you. What are you going to teach me now?'

'Wait and see, witch.' He threw off his dressing gown, got in beside her and nipped out the candle.

18

When Ross awoke the next morning he knew that many men would give their eyeteeth for such a passionate wife, and yet he felt that something was lacking.

Tara was not forward, she had not made an advance towards him during the night and had been gentle and loving with him afterwards. She had talked sweet words to him when he was exhausted and drifting into sleep, and when he was awake later and wanted her she responded at once.

Was it because Rosin had come into his mind during the night and he had imagined her being a little withdrawn and this is what he would have preferred? No. He shook his head. There would be no satisfaction in making love to a woman if she did not respond. He remembered a man he knew once telling him that making love to his wife had become a duty because she expected it and an ordeal because she had lain wooden. And yet, he had added, he could not take a mistress because he would feel so terribly guilty.

Ross glanced at Tara, who was curled up against him, and felt a tenderness for her sweep over him. She was someone who needed to be loved.

Tara yawned and stretched, then opened her eyes.

Ross said, 'Good morning, Mrs Ferris,' and a slow smile spread over her face.

'Oh, doesn't it sound lovely? I like being a married lady.'

'And I like being a married man.'

'I'm glad,' she said softly. The next moment she was sitting up listening, clutching the sheet to her. 'Someone is downstairs.'

'Probably Miss MacDougal come to see if we've behaved ourselves.'

Tara giggled. 'Perhaps she's going to bring our breakfast up.'

Ross said in alarm, 'I hope not.' He grabbed his dressing gown, and shrugged himself into it. 'And you had better put something on too.'

'If it is your wish, sire,' she said demurely.

'It isn't.' He pulled the sheet away and drew a quick breath. 'Tara . . .'

There were voices under the window. A woman laughed. 'Well, who can blame them, just wedded.'

'I've lit a fire for them. There's a bit of a nip in the air. I'll come back in a wee while and make their breakfast.'

Tara whispered, 'Miss MacDougal,' and, sliding out of bed, put on her negligée.

Ross picked up his watch from the bedside table, then exclaimed, 'Heavens above! It's half-past ten! I thought it would be about six o'clock.'

'Did you? We did cover a lot of ground through the night,' she teased.

Ross pulled her to him. 'Temptress!' She was looking up at him, lips parted, her look telling him of her love. Desire flamed in him but he put her firmly from him. 'No, we must be washed and dressed and downstairs when our dear landlady returns.' He chucked Tara under the chin. 'Think of all the nights we have to make love.'

She gave an impish grin. 'And waste the days?'

He kissed her lightly. 'We shall be going sightseeing but I'm sure there will be many little secret dells where we can indulge in a kiss or two.'

'Oh, I do love you, Mr Ferris,' she breathed.

Her negligée had fallen open revealing the perfection of her lovely pointed breasts. Her very stance was sensual. Breathing raggedly he laid her on the sheepskin rug and took her there.

233

Afterwards, with eyes closed, she murmured in a dreamy voice, 'I never knew that marriage could be like this.'

Ross groaned. 'At this rate I shall be worn out in a couple of months.'

She rolled partly onto him and put a leg over his. 'Not you, my lovely strong master.'

The touch of her flesh on his had sent his pulse racing again. He lifted her away. 'On your feet, wench. The party is over ... for the time being, at any rate.'

Tara laughed. 'You shall beg for my favours the next time, sir.'

She was about to turn away and he caught her arm and swung her to face him. 'Remember this, Tara, I do not beg favours of anyone and certainly *not* my wife.'

'Ross, I was jesting.' She was wide-eyed, her expression one of dismay. Turning away from him she picked up her clothes and went behind the small bamboo screen to get dressed.

Although he knew how hurt she was he could not bring himself to say he was sorry.

The arrival of Miss MacDougal healed the breach. There was a knock on the door and she said, 'I heard you were up. I'll leave hot water outside then I'll start on the breakfast.'

'Thanks, Miss MacDougal. We won't be long.'

Ross was in the middle of shaving when Tara appeared.

She said, 'I hope I'm forgiven, otherwise it will be very awkward for Miss MacDougal, who will think I've denied you conjugal rights.'

Ross had to laugh. 'Why on earth should she think such a thing?'

'Well, I read a novel once where a bridal couple were staying at a seaside resort and they never spoke a word after their wedding night and the landlady said to her sister, "I wouldn't be surprised if the bride denied

234

her husband his conjugal rights. She's such a primsy madam." '

'I wouldn't describe you as a primsy madam, but I could tell Miss MacDougal how many times we made love last night.'

She looked at him shocked. 'Ross, you wouldn't!' Then realizing he was teasing, she began to laugh and said she liked being married, it was such fun.

They had decided to spend their honeymoon travelling around the countryside, staying overnight at different places, and over breakfast, they asked Miss MacDougal what she would recommend. She gave them the names of so many places to visit that Ross said though they had planned a week's honeymoon it looked like being nearer a month before they would be leaving. They decided to start with the famous blacksmith's shop.

The blacksmith's shop was a long low building with grey stone walls that Ross judged to be nearly three feet thick. Although Tara felt she would have liked to have been married at the anvil for the novelty of talking about it she was glad she had been married at the hotel. At least she had a feeling of being in church. Would she have done so had she been married at a blacksmith's anvil? And she would still be able to say that Ross had romantically whisked her off to get married at Gretna Green. How all her friends would envy her.

During the following week they made love in a humble cottage, in a noisy inn, in the best of hotels and once on a bed of bracken where sheep and trees were more plentiful than people, and only the moon was out to see them. Tara remembered the beauty of the silvered grass and how she had cried with happiness.

They walked on the white sands at Anan, watched men fishing and visited the cattle market, they saw children swimming in big rocks pools that would be full at high tide and empty when the tide went out.

One afternoon Tara developed a headache and, feeling sick, she went to lie down. Ross tucked her in and said he would go for a walk.

As he walked by a stream, moving against the flow, it seemed to him that he was going against the flow of their lives. He cared for Tara, felt tender towards her, but was not in love with her in spite of their passionate lovemaking. Something he had found with Rosin was lacking in Tara, yet it was impossible for him to define what it could be. He thought of his Aunt Eileen who was still in love with the charmer Preston Rafferty, who had once robbed her of all her jewellery. How could one answer that?

Ross stopped a moment, watching the water tumbling over stones, running over smooth pebbles, then rushing to squeeze between two stones only inches apart, and he realized more than ever how like life the stream was. There would be turmoil but there would be the smooth parts. There was an impatience in the flow but a joyousness too and he would have to accept all the different facets of life.

He had promised to accept the baby as his own and he must never go back on his word or taunt Tara with her sin.

By the time he went back to the hotel he felt ready to go back to England but how could he put this to Tara?

As it turned out, he didn't need to, for she said with a wan smile, 'I feel much better, my headache's gone, but I think I feel a little homesick.'

He took her in his arms and rocked her, 'And so do I, my love.'

'Oh, Ross, how wonderful that we think alike. That surely must be true love, don't you think?'

Not wanting to disillusion her, he kissed her.

They decided they would go to Ireland, spend a few days with Tara's family, then to London and live in Ross's rooms until they could find a suitable house. Telegrams were sent to Ireland and London stating their plans.

Ross ordered champagne at dinner that evening and guests at other tables in the hotel, having been told they were on their honeymoon, toasted them.

Tara's eyes were shining as she said softly, 'Could any bride and groom wish for more?'

Ross, who wanted nothing more than to be in London and back to business, had to force a smile.

There was a crowd waiting to greet them when they arrived at Killorglin, including his Uncle Edward, which surprised Ross.

'There you are, dear boy,' said Edward, face beaming as he slapped Ross's back. 'Aren't you the sly one, running off to Gretna with my lovely niece without so much as a hint of romance. I think I might follow suit and persuade my fiancée to run away to Scotland.'

'Your fiancée? Oh, you've reached that stage, have you?' Ross smiled. 'May I ask the lady's name?'

'That is a secret for the moment. Here are your other two lovely cousins to welcome you.'

Fiona and Ashling gave him loving and laughing greetings, reminding him that each was now a sister-in-law as well as a cousin. Then Eileen was there, dragging him away to help Tara open all the gifts that had arrived for them and the ones that had been brought by relatives and friends.

There were uncles, aunts, cousins, every one of the girls longing for a Gretna marriage – how romantic, how terribly exciting. Tara thrived on all of this and by the end of the evening was sparkling, while Ross felt like a washed-out rag.

He said to his uncle, 'Don't think you'll escape all the fuss by going to Gretna. This is the second celebration and I know we shall have the same to face when we meet John Davies. He won't let us escape a gathering.'

'What are you moaning for, dear boy? You are young and your bride is younger still.' He gave a mischievous grin. 'Or, is that the trouble? Let me tell you that the time to worry is when she goes off to bed early every night pleading a headache.'

Patrick came up laughing, saying, 'Edward, you are incorrigible. Here is Ross, a week married, and you put dreadful thoughts into his head. Ross, take no notice of him, his best days are over.'

'Not so,' declared Ross. 'Uncle tells me that he is going to persuade his fiancée to go to Gretna. How's that?'

'I'll believe it when I meet her.'

'You will. Just you wait, you'll get a surprise and she's not after my money, she has plenty in her own right.'

Patrick chuckled. 'How old is she? In her seventies?'

Edward just grinned. 'Wait and see.'

Ross, wanting oblivion that evening, had too much to drink and roused to find his two uncles undressing him. The next time he woke it was to find Tara with tea poured for him.

'Come along, darling, drink this, I'm sure you must be dry.'

He groaned, turned on to his other side and pulled the clothes over his head. He was vaguely aware of Tara arguing with her mother who said, 'Tara, do not try to alter Ross. He'll be better left alone.'

To give Tara her due, when he did get up she was gentle with him and accepted that it was one of those nights that a wife has to live with. He could not help wondering how long that attitude would last.

He and Eileen had a talk late one night and to her questioning he was honest about his feelings towards Tara, concluding, 'I do think we can make a success of our marriage. You did, and I think you will understand how I feel.'

'Yes, I do, Ross. It's an awful situation to be in, but I'm sure you will fare better than I, because you are a stronger person. You will be firm with Tara. If Patrick had been firmer with me I don't think I would have allowed my feelings for Preston Rafferty to dominate my life at times. Tara needs moulding. Being married is a novelty to her at the moment, being pregnant is a novelty. She will drool over the baby at first but she won't like to be tied to looking after it. She's always seeking excitement. She is the weakest of our children. Try to give her as much love as you can, Ross.'

He promised he would.

The following day they returned to London and Tara, who had wept when she left her family, was brimming over with excitement when John met them and told them there was a crowd at home waiting to greet them.

All the office staff were there, some of John's relatives and a few special business friends of both of them.

At the end of that evening Ross groaned and declared he did not want any more celebratory parties for the next twelve months. To which Tara replied, as she snuggled into him, 'The next one should be in a few months' time, darling.'

He tensed and she moved away, saying in a sullen way, 'You told me you would accept the baby and bring it up as your own. It's not going to be very pleasant if every time I mention it you're going to get upset.'

Ross, furious, drew himself up in the bed. 'Tara, listen to me and listen carefully. I am fathering my own father's child. Not the best of situations to be in. I married you to save your parents embarrassment. You are totally without shame and I can tell you now if you speak in that sullen way again, we will live separate lives and you can bring the baby up on your own.'

'Ross!' The shock in her voice was enough for some of his anger to evaporate, but he did not give in to her. 'Your parents might tolerate your sulkiness, but I won't. Is that understood?

'Yes.' Her voice was little above a whisper. 'I'm sorry.'

'Good.' He lay down and turned on to his side.

After a moment she said, 'Ross, please don't turn away from me. I can't bear it. I love you. I won't ever mention the baby again.'

He shot up. 'Oh, for heaven's sake, stop being a martyr. I didn't tell you not to mention the baby again, I told you I won't put up with your sullen attitude.'

'But I didn't know I was being sullen. I didn't mean to be. I'll try not to be in future, I promise.'

When he made no answer she turned on to her side and he guessed she was crying. He let her cry for a moment. She knew all right when she was in a mood. She would have to break the habit.

He lay down again and said, 'I shall do my best to treat the baby as my own when it arrives and be a good father to it but you have to compromise too, and not get into petty moods.'

'Tell me when I am,' she pleaded. 'I'm not aware of it. Mama says that Papa spoils me and he says that Mama spoils me. I don't want to be a nasty person.'

She ended on a sob and he forced himself to say, 'It's only some times when you act in this way.'

Tara moved closer to him, but although he wanted to take her in his arms and comfort her he found it impossible.

Looking at him from a dark corner of the room was Rosin, a solemn expression on her small oval face. Oh God, was he never to be free of her?

The following morning no one would have guessed there had been any upset between Ross and Tara. Tara was bright, chatting about how much she was looking forward to going shopping with John Davies's sister-in-law Catherine and her daughter Marianne.

Ross was pleased that Tara would have company, being anxious to get back to business.

When Ross told her he would give her some money she said, 'Oh, that is all right. Papa gave me some, saying it was for falderals and that I was not to get any big ideas and start looking for fur coats as you would be having the expense of setting up a home for us. Where are we going to live, Ross?'

'Here for the time being. We shall have to look around for somewhere suitable to rent.'

Tara assured him she was quite all right here for the time being. She got on splendidly with Mrs Fox, who had promised to teach her to cook. Not that she would need to cook, she added, when they had their own house and staff.

It brought Ross down to earth and he wondered if he should tell her there and then that he was not a rich man, or wait until a more convenient time. He settled for a more convenient time.

He wanted to leave with John for the office and Mrs Fox assured him that his lovely wife would be all right in her care until Mr Davies's sister-in-law came to call for her.

Ross said to John when they went to get a cab, 'Who would have thought that the tight-lipped Mrs Fox would have been delighted to take Tara under her wing?'

'Thwarted motherhood. She told me once that she had longed for children, but sadly her husband had died quite young. By the way, Ross, a friend of mine who is going to America on business is wanting to let his mews cottage furnished. The rent will be minimal if he can find someone who will take care of his antiques. I did mention you to him, knowing that Tara wants to have a place of her own.'

'Sounds interesting. How long will your friend be away?'

'A year at least.' John smiled. 'It's not that I want to be rid of you, in fact I shall miss you, miss our talks.'

'So shall I. But having burned my boats, however, I shall have to adjust. I think the mews cottage would be the answer to my prayers.'

It was a pleasure to Ross to get into the swim again and when he came home that evening with John, he felt almost surprised when Tara greeted him.

'We've had a lovely day,' she said, 'Oh, I love London, the shops are wonderful. I must show you what I've bought.'

'Later, Tara. John and I have some unfinished business to discuss. It will only take a few minutes.'

Ross saw John shaking his head and then noticing that all the joy had gone from Tara's face he said quickly, 'Or I suppose we could discuss it later.'

'Of course,' John said smiling. 'We have all evening.'

Ross put his arm around Tara. 'Now then, what have you bought?'

'Come into the sitting room.'

She was all vivacity again and as Ross was shown lace collars, a flimsy scarf and lace edged handkerchiefs, he stifled a sigh. Was this to be his life in the future? No enjoying a drink with John as they discussed the day's business, no slipping out to the club, meeting friends. Then he thought no, he must start as he meant to go on. It was the wife who would have to adjust. He was the head of the house.

For the time being they had agreed that they would all dine together to make it easier for Mrs Fox, unless, of course, John was having guests, and over the meal they discussed the mews cottage with Tara. She was as animated as a child at Christmas.

'A mews cottage with antiques in it? Wait until I tell

the family. How wonderful. When do we move in? Oh, we'll be able to have dinner parties.'

Ross gave John a quick glance, then said quietly, 'The rooms are quite small, Tara.'

She laughed. 'Big enough to seat six or eight people, surely? I can't wait to act as hostess. Then I shall feel well and truly married. How many bedrooms are there? Mama and Fiona and Ashling could come and stay with us for a holiday. Oh, we could have such a wonderful time. We could go shopping together. We would go to the theatre.' Tara prattled on; Ross wondered how he was going to endure it.

It was the nights in bed with Tara that made his life bearable. He had only to see her naked for him to know a wild passion and she never failed to respond to it. Afterwards she would curl up beside him like a kitten and then he felt a deep tenderness for her and could forget her little irritating ways.

There were times when it worried him that she seemed so experienced, but she swore that it was nature and Ross's experience that made her mould to his ways. He had known many women but not one had ever aroused him to the heights that Tara had done.

She never mentioned the baby, nor did he, but at times he was conscious that some mornings she looked a little pale.

It was two weeks after having been told about the mews cottage that John said he had the keys to view. In those two weeks Tara had spent most of her time with Catherine and her daughter. Ross liked them. Catherine was a very down-to-earth woman and Marianne, although slightly younger than Tara, seemed much more mature. She actually seemed to mother her and Tara took notice of all she had to say.

When they first went into the cottage Tara was absolutely entranced by it. It was luxuriously furnished – deep-pile carpets and rugs, silk velvet curtains, beautiful Sheraton furniture, brocade-covered sofa and chairs. There were oil paintings on the walls, silver cutlery and dishes, crystal ware.

There were two bedrooms, both elegantly furnished, and a bathroom.

Viewing these set Tara making complaints. They really needed another bedroom at least. If her mother and sisters came there were not enough rooms and the bathroom really was very small. Then when they went back downstairs she remarked that the dining table was very small, certainly not big enough to entertain eight or more people.

Ross had been getting more and more annoyed by the minute but had not complained because John was there, but when Tara said, 'I think I must ask Catherine and Marianne to come and see the cottage and get their advice,' he snapped, 'They are not paying the rent, I am. We shall find a house with more rooms but don't expect the luxury of the cottage. Come along, let's go.'

A look of panic came over Tara's face. 'Oh, I do like it here, Ross. I love the furniture and – and everything, it's just that –'

'Yes, I know, not enough rooms.' He felt wooden.

John held up a hand. 'If you take my advice I suggest you think about it. The rent is reasonable. I could store some of the furniture for you. Take the dining room, for instance. You won't need a sofa and armchairs in there, you have some in the sitting room. You won't need such a big sideboard. I can speak to Charles about these things. Two cupboards in the bathroom are not necessary. I feel many small adjustments could be made.'

'Oh, John, you're wonderful,' Tara enthused. She turned to Ross. 'I think they're excellent suggestions, don't you?'

'We shall have to talk about it. I'm certainly not rushing into the transaction, then having you being miserable.'

Ross was aware at that moment of sounding sulky like Tara.

'I won't be, Ross, I know it. I do like it. We can discuss it. There may be more ideas we can use to make improvements. Don't you think so?'

The desperate appeal in her voice made him relent.

'Yes, I do think so.' He managed a smile. 'We shall pick John's brains and if you want female opinions, we shall ask Catherine and Marianne.'

Her relief and gratitude were reward for having given in.

On the Saturday morning they went again to the cottage with Catherine and Marianne, who made further suggestions for improving space.

They had all finished lunch at John's and Mrs Fox had brought in the coffee when the front door bell rang.

John said, 'It could be my friend Charles. I told him to call and we can discuss moving furniture around.'

It was not Charles, however.

'Ross, dear boy.'

'Uncle Edward! What a surprise.'

'And I am not alone. Meet your future aunt.' Edward held out a hand. 'Come along, darling, meet all these lovely people.'

The gaze of all was on the woman who walked in looking shy. Ross found himself gripping the edge of the table.

No. Not Rosin. It couldn't be.

Then the visitor smiled and Ross felt weak with relief. Not Rosin, but Alicia. Thank God.

19

After the first relief of knowing it was not Rosin with his Uncle Edward Ross felt a rising anger. How had Alicia got her claws into him, because this must certainly have been her aim.

Edward happily introduced his fiancée. John was outwardly as courteous as always, but Ross was aware of a faint disapproval in his eyes.

Edward turned to Ross, giving him a broad grin.

'So, Ross, and what do you think of my future bride-to-be? Isn't she beautiful?'

Ross, poker-faced, said to Alicia, 'And how are you, Miss Sylvain? It seems only days ago since we met you in Ireland with your gentleman friend.'

'You know one another?' Edward looked like a schoolboy, who has been deflated by having his special surprise ruined.

'We met in Dublin last year,' declared Alicia. 'Ross and his party had been invited to a ball by some friends of my aunt. It was tremendous fun, wasn't it?' She touched Ross on the hand.

He had made up his mind he wanted nothing to do with her, but her touch sent a quiver through his body and he was glad when John drew attention away from him by asking Edward and Alicia to be seated and he would pour drinks.

Edward thanked him, but refused. It was really just a brief call. He had regained his equilibrium and was his own charming self.

Tara, to Ross's annoyance, begged them to stay for a while, but Edward, in a confiding manner said, 'There's nothing I would like better, my dear, but Lady

Kereslake does not like Alicia to be out of her sight for long. To be honest, we are playing truant.'

Alicia laughed. 'I'm afraid your uncle is inclined to exaggerate a little. He is the one who wants me all to himself.' She linked her arm through his and, leaning against him, looked up at him in an adoring way. 'But I would not want him to be otherwise.'

Her sickly, coy manner made Ross wonder why he had ever wanted her.

As they were preparing to leave, Edward promised Ross he would call again soon.

Alicia said, 'I am trying to persuade Edward to come and stay at the Savoy for a few days, but he says he has business to attend to.' She pouted. 'Should one's fiancé put business before his loved one?'

Edward assured her earnestly that this was not the case, but before any further discussion could take place, Ross said, 'Well, Uncle, I shall look forward to another visit soon. There are some things I want to ask you, just to satisfy my curiosity.'

After they had gone there was a short silence, then Tara gave a long drawn out, 'W-ell. What will Uncle Edward get up to next? Now it's a prospective bride young enough to be his daughter.'

'His granddaughter more like,' Ross retorted.

John smiled. 'Good luck to him, I say. If Miss Sylvain makes him happy, why not? As he said, the young lady is not after his money. She has plenty of her own.'

Catherine, who had been looking from one to the other during this said, 'I can understand an older man marrying someone much younger than himself, but I cannot accept a young girl marrying a man so much older, not when she has money and could have a choice of suitors.'

Later, when Catherine and Marianne left, Tara went with them, 'for women's talk'.

Ross said to John, 'Thank goodness. I needed some

man talk. I feel so furious with Alicia Sylvain. She made complete fools of us that evening she came seeking help.'

John looked thoughtful. 'I would say that she's a very mixed-up young lady. You do realize, of course, that she's in love with you?'

'With me?' Ross gave a derisive laugh. 'With herself, you mean. She doesn't give a tinker's cuss for anyone.'

'She's in love with you, Ross. I've lived a little longer than you and can read the signs. She's a very unhappy young lady. She lost you to Tara, but when she met Edward and found out the relationship between you, she saw a way to see you again.'

'I still say I am not on her list of favourite people.'

'Then why did she mention she was trying to persuade Edward to stay at the Savoy for a few days, if it was not to let you know that she would be having tea in the lounge at four o'clock where you used to meet her?'

Ross gave him a bow. 'I applaud your deduction, sir. Perhaps in your wisdom you can tell me if my wife was a little suspicious of the strong comments I made about Miss Alicia Sylvain?'

John smiled. 'To misquote Shakespeare in *Hamlet*, The *gentleman* doth protest too much, methinks.'

'Oh, so I could be in trouble.'

'Maybe not. Tara was thoughtful as she watched you. She was probably thinking how best to cope with the situation. Don't belittle females, Ross, they're much cleverer than men at dealing with relationships.'

Ross was half annoyed, not sure that he wanted John to notice more about Tara than he had himself. Then, remembering all the help John had given him over the years, he said, 'It seems I still have a great deal to learn about life.'

John gave a wry smile. 'You know a lot more about life now than I knew when I was your age.'

'Hark at him!' Ross appealed to the room. 'To hear

him talk anyone would think he was in his dotage.' He paused then added soberly, 'Do you think Edward and Alicia will marry?'

'Difficult to tell. You seem to consider Rosin to be a complex character but I would say she's a very straightforward person. She could see the snags in getting married and for your sake she went right out of your life. Not so with Alicia. She wants you and she'll do her best to get you one way or another.'

'That is ridiculous. It takes two to make that possible and I am no longer the least bit interested in her.'

But as Ross said it he knew he would have to go to the Savoy the next day and see if Alicia was there waiting.

She was, and greeted him smiling. 'I wondered if you would get my hidden message. I did hope so. Do sit down.'

When he sat down she put her hand on his but he withdrew it.

'I'm not here to stay, Alicia, but simply to explain there won't be any more such meetings. You are betrothed to my uncle.'

'I had to do it. Don't you see, it was the only way I could get close to you.' She spoke earnestly, but Ross was not impressed.

'As I remember, you had no difficulty in contacting me when you actually came to the house late to tell a wild story of two men coming to your bedroom.'

'That was not a story. It happened.' A waiter brought him tea and cakes and Alicia begged Ross in a low voice to accept them. When the waiter left she said, 'I gave the order when I saw you come in. I have to talk to you, Ross. You and Mr Davies are the only ones I've ever been able to talk to.'

'Strange,' he said wryly, 'I didn't notice that you had any difficulty talking to your gentlemen friend the day of the picnic.'

'It was to have been a picnic, no more, no less. We didn't even have the picnic.' She poured his tea, but he sat back.

'You had plenty of time to talk to me when you took me to see Rosin, but it seemed to me you were in a hurry to get away once we reached the cottage.'

Alicia shook her head slowly. 'You don't understand, do you? Rosin was in love with you, still is, so I couldn't do anything to spoil it. She's my sister and I love her dearly. It was when I knew she had made up her mind to go out of your life in spite of loving you that I decided to try and win you for myself.'

He stared at her. 'I can't believe this. You actually become engaged to my uncle, knowing that I have recently married, and expect to fall into my arms.'

'You are the only man I've ever loved,' she said with a woebegone expression.

'Alicia, you must pull yourself together. This is all quite ridiculous. I haven't been long married, I love my wife.'

'If you did I would go out of your life as Rosin did, but I know you don't love her. I happen to know that you married her because she is pregnant.'

Ross stiffened. 'Whoever told you such a lie is despicable and if I find out who it is he'll regret it.'

'No one told me, I deduced it for myself. You loved Rosin, wanted desperately to marry her. Then suddenly you rush off to Gretna Green to get married. There could only be one reason. You had made her pregnant.'

'I did no such thing. I've loved my cousin for years and she's loved me. Rosin came into my life and it was a different feeling I had for her. When she turned me down I came to my senses and realized how I must have hurt Tara. When I suggested that we go to Gretna to get married she agreed at once and I have certainly not regretted it, nor has she.'

'She might do one day,' Alicia said sadly, 'because I

250

know that the love you have for Rosin is stronger than it is for Tara. I am still Rosin to you. You still love me.'

'You have it all wrong, Alicia. I was attracted to you because you are so like Rosin in looks, but you are totally different in character. You enjoyed the game you played, trying to let me believe that you and Rosin were one and the same person, but Rosin didn't. She gave me up in spite of loving me. You would not have made such a sacrifice. She is the real person, you are the mirror image but the glass has many flaws.'

'You know how to hurt, don't you?' Her expression still held a sadness.

'I'm only trying to get you to understand the truth.'

'And I can only say to you that you will never be rid of me. I want you and I shall have you.'

He got up. 'Then I am sorry for you, Alicia, because that can never be.' He laid money on the table to pay the bill. 'Goodbye.'

Although Ross was satisfied that he now had Alicia out of his system he knew he had to talk the incident over with John, and he went back to the office.

At the end of the story John said, 'I can only suggest, Ross, that you repeat what you've told me to Tara.' And when Ross began to protest he held up a hand. 'Alicia has proved to be a dangerous person. She made us feel sorry for her when she told us the story of the men coming to her room. She made it real. How real would she make a story of lies if she told them to Tara who is so vulnerable? She could ruin your marriage. It must be nipped in the bud right away. We can tell Tara the story together to give credence to the trouble that Alicia could cause.'

At first Ross was reluctant to let Tara know of his involvement with Alicia, pointing out that the poor girl was hardly back from her honeymoon, but when John asked if there was a time when it would seem right to tell her he gave in. They would talk to Tara that evening.

They waited until after dinner when Ross said that he and John had something to explain to her.

She looked alarmed. 'Is it about the mews cottage? Has the owner changed his mind? I really do like it, Ross, it was just that it is a little small and –'

Ross assured her it had nothing to do with houses, then went on to tell her about his meeting with Alicia, adding, 'I told you I would never bring up her name, but it's necessary after what has happened today. And, as John has been involved with part of the story, we shall tell you between us all that has happened.'

Tara listened intently, looking from one to the other without interrupting once. When Ross had concluded, she looked near to tears. 'Oh, dear. I had no idea there was all this turmoil going on in your life. I'm sorry that I –'

'Tara,' Ross took her hands in his, 'you would have known nothing about this had John and I not thought that Alicia might tell lies about me to turn you against me.'

'I would never do that.' She was indignant. 'I love you and always have.'

John said quietly, 'Alicia is clever, she has a way with her. I believed her story and I am a hard-headed businessman.'

'You are not a bit hard-headed,' she protested. 'You are one of the nicest people I know. I won't speak to Alicia if she calls.'

'You will speak to her, Tara, and she will talk to you and you will find yourself listening because she is such an excellent actress. What you must not do is believe her.'

'I won't,' she declared stoutly. 'I will never let her in the house, I promise.'

Ross stressed that she must not repeat what she

had been told to anyone, not even Catherine and Marianne.

Tara was hesitant. 'But they won't tell anyone, they're my friends.'

Ross threw up his hands. 'I knew it was wrong to tell her. Tara is used to sharing secrets with Fiona and Ashling. She can't keep a secret.'

Tara jumped up. 'I can, if I have to. I just thought –' She burst into tears and it was John who soothed her.

She calmed down then, and Ross took her in his arms and apologized for not believing her. But he was uneasy, wondering if she would keep her promise not to mention to Edward about Alicia, her excuse being that he was family and had a right to know.

Everything went smoothly during the next month. John's friend Charles Kent had been delighted that Ross and Tara were taking over the cottage and was more than willing to allow John to store the larger pieces of furniture in his home.

'All I wanted,' he said, 'was to have people who would love and care for the cottage. I've been so happy there, and only business would make me desert it for a time.'

'What a lovely man he is,' Tara had said dreamily. 'He spoke of the cottage as if it were a person.'

When everything was to Tara's liking in the cottage she did her first entertaining, with Mrs Fox doing the cooking. John, his brother, Catherine and Marianne were invited, also Charles Kent, who was due to leave for America the following day. Tara was in her element and Ross agreed with John that she had never looked lovelier.

The only thing that marred the evening for Ross was the attention she gave to Charles. He made allowances at first because Tara was a naturally affectionate person, but when she was sitting beside him on the settee and she was inclined to snuggle up to him a little he made the excuse to get Charles away from her by suggesting they go upstairs to see some papers he had found in a secret drawer in a small cabinet.

Ross had not thought them important, nor did Charles at first, then he found a slip of paper among them that had him excited.

'Good grief!' Charles exclaimed. 'I can't believe it. We did trace back two centuries of the family, then came to a dead end. This piece goes back even further.' He examined the cabinet. 'I've always looked for secret drawers, but this one eluded me. Why?'

'It was a chance thing with me. I had dropped a cuff link, which went under the cabinet, and when I put my hand underneath I heard a click. I must have touched some mechanism because one of the top drawers seemed to move. But there was nothing to indicate a secret drawer. I moved my hand underneath the cabinet again, I even emptied the drawers and turned it upside down and examined it thoroughly, but nothing happened. I put everything back and had almost forgotten about it when I noticed that one very small raised piece in the centre of a knob was different to the others. Ah, I thought, this is it. But it wasn't. There was something slightly different in every knob and it took hours pressing various ones in turn before I found the code that opened a small drawer at the back of the top one.'

'Amazing! So ingenious. How clever of you.' Charles laughed his delight. 'What is the code?'

'I'll show you. I had to write it down.'

Ross read the combination out, and Charles was pressing the knobs when a breathless voice behind them said, 'What is going on?'

Tara . . . Ross stifled a groan. Now everyone would know. Charles turned to her grinning.

'Your husband has found a secret drawer.'

'A secret drawer?' Tara's eyes were wide. 'Ross! And you never told me.'

'I only discovered the code last night,' he answered shortly. 'And please don't spread the news around.'

'Why not? This is exciting.' She turned to Charles. 'Can't I tell the others?'

Charles looked at her fondly. 'I don't see why not. No hoard of gold or diamonds are involved.'

She touched his hand, smiled and was away running downstairs.

'You have a beautiful wife,' Charles said.

And you are a handsome man, Ross thought, and I am jealous.

Because Charles would be in his late thirties and due to go abroad for a year, Ross had not thought of him as a threat but, realizing just how much Tara was taken with him and how Charles was drawn to her, he could see trouble in the future. Tara would have to be watched carefully. She blossomed on attention.

Before the two men could go downstairs the guests were trooping up to see the miracle secret drawer and within seconds the bedroom was alive with excitement.

Later, when Ross was preparing for bed, he said drily, 'Well, no one could say that your first party was not a success.'

Tara, who had just taken off her negligée spun round, the negligée held above her. 'Oh, wasn't it wonderful? I wanted it to go on and on!'

The outline of the still beautiful figure in the flimsy nightdress made Ross catch hold of her and say in a ragged voice, 'Tara, don't you ever make eyes at another man.'

All the joy went from her. 'I don't, Ross. It's only you I want.'

'But you were making eyes at Charles Kent this evening. You were always touching him.'

'I was not. I was happy, enjoying everything, now you've spoilt it all.' She pulled away from him, dropped her negligée and got into bed.

Ross got in beside her and tried to take her in his arms but she turned onto her side.

'You are always hateful to me about other men, making out that I flirt with them. Charles Kent is like a brother to me. I'm fond of him.' Her voice broke. 'I miss Brendan, who was always teasing me. I know I did wrong about the – the baby, but even God forgives sinners.'

'Tara, it's because I love you that I get upset if you make a fuss of any other man.'

'If you loved me I don't think I would mind being scolded. But you don't.' Her voice was muffled. 'You still love Rosin and you can't get over the fact that she wouldn't marry you. Your pride was hurt and so you take it out on me.'

'That's not true.'

'It is.' Tara rolled onto her back. 'Why won't you admit it? If I had touched Brendan on the hand or the arm would you have objected?'

'Of course not because he is your brother, but Charles Kent is not. What's more, he's a very attractive man, with, I should imagine, an eye for a pretty face.'

Tara drew herself up. 'Well, that is where you are wrong.' She spoke quietly. 'Six months ago Charles's wife gave birth to a stillborn son and his wife died too. When I touched Charles it was my way of showing sympathy. I felt heartbroken for him. Catherine said he adored his wife.'

'I'm sorry. I didn't know. I'm surprised that John didn't mention it.'

'I only learned about it when a friend of Catherine's told her, but the friend said that Charles didn't want it known generally. He tries to put a brave face on it.'

'I'm sorry, Tara.' He paused then reached out a hand. 'Shall we start again?'

'No, I want to go home. I miss the family.'

Ross thought, Oh Lord, what have I started. He was tempted to say, all right, go home, then thought better of it.

He said, 'It's very easy, Tara, to rush back to the bosom of your family for comfort, but have you thought of how your mother will feel? Just think of all the subterfuge used to make our runaway marriage seem one of romance. And I can tell you now, if you go back home you don't come back here. That is the end. I've done all I am going to do.' Ross turned his back on her and pulled the cover over his shoulders. There was silence. He thought that Tara might be crying, but he did not relent.

Tara was worried. She did want to see her family. She ached to see them, but had not intended that there would be a rift in her marriage. She was simply following what Catherine had advised when speaking to her and Marianne about husbands.

'Men never admit to being wrong. Stand up for yourself, don't give in every time if you have words otherwise you'll just be a slave.'

Tara liked Ross to be masterful, but she knew what Catherine meant. He had just dismissed her as if she were a servant girl instead of his wife. She had not intended to stay long at home, just pay them a visit. Was that too much to ask? It was not as if he would have to fend for himself. Mrs Fox would look after him. He and John could dine together. They always enjoyed discussing business. In fact, there were times when they seemed to forget she was there. But she had never complained. Well, perhaps a little, but in a teasing sort of way.

For a moment Tara had an overwhelming longing to cuddle up to Ross and say she was sorry, but remembering Catherine saying that men never admitted to being in the wrong she steeled herself. If she gave in to him now she would always be giving in. What was more, he could be quite nasty at times and treat her as if she were a child. No, she would wait and see what the morning would bring.

Ross was puzzled. It was unlike Tara to hold a grudge. Had he been too harsh in saying that if she went home to see her family she could stay there? But if he was easy-going with her she would always be wanting to run home every time they had a disagreement. He could see now that they would never be compatible. Although he delighted in her response to his lovemaking it took more than that to make a successful marriage. She was too young in her outlook. Ashling was two years younger and had so much more common sense.

But then it was not Ashling he had married. No one had forced him to marry Tara so he must face up to his responsibilities. In a few months' time he would be a father. It was strange but he was looking forward to it, even though the child was not his. How Tara would react to motherhood he had no idea. He could only hope she would mature later.

Tomorrow he would have a serious talk with her, explain that if they were to make a success of their marriage they must pull together. He might even suggest having Ashling or Fiona over for a holiday. And their mother if Tara wished. And with that magnanimous thought, he settled for sleep.

Usually when he first roused in the morning he reached for Tara, not always with a view to lovemaking, but just to draw her to him. This morning, however, the bed was empty. He was suddenly wide awake. Had she foolishly kept her word and left to go to Ireland?

To his relief nothing seemed to have been disturbed

in the wardrobe. He put on his dressing gown and went downstairs.

Mrs Fox's niece, Jane, a quiet but pleasant girl, came to cook and do the housework. To Ross's query she said that Mrs Ferris had gone for a walk and asked if she should cook his breakfast. He told her yes and, wondering, went back upstairs to wash and dress.

Had Tara gone to Catherine's house to unload her troubles? No, although she might do and say foolish things at times he was sure she would not gossip to anyone about their married life.

He had started on his breakfast when she arrived breathless.

'Morning, darling. Did you wonder where I was? I awoke early and it was so lovely and fresh I decided to go for a walk. My cheeks are tingling.' She took off her cloak and threw it over a chair back. 'And now I'm famished.'

When he made no reply she said, 'You didn't mind my going out like that, did you?'

Aware of the worry underlying all the bright chatter, he made an effort to match hers to heal the breach of the night before.

'No, of course not, as you didn't wake me up and ask me to go with you.'

She laughed and there was relief in it. 'I wouldn't have dared. You are a sleepyhead, like Brendan.'

Now that she had mentioned a member of the family he said, 'Look, Tara, I've been thinking. Would you like your mother and the girls to come over for a holiday?'

'Oh, do you think they would? It would be lovely to see them.' Her eyes suddenly clouded. 'We wouldn't have room to put them up.'

'I thought of that. I could sleep at John's house for the time they were here.'

'No.' She spoke sharply. 'I don't think it's right for husband and wife to be parted so soon after marriage.'

He smiled, teasing her. 'Last night you were going to leave me and go back to Ireland.'

'I was upset. You know I wouldn't have left you.' Her eyes were full of love. 'I mustn't let myself get so bad-tempered again.'

'I was as bad, Tara. We must have a quiet talk this evening. There's a guesthouse quite close where your mother and the girls could stay.'

'Oh, Ross, you're so good to me. I love you so much. I shall write home at once.'

From posting the letter she was in a fever of impatience, wanting a reply before the letter had even had a chance to get there. When the reply did arrive Ross had to take the envelope from her fumbling fingers, slit it open and hand it to her. She pulled out the letter, hastily scanned it then, radiant, flung her arms around Ross's neck.

'They're coming, they're coming! Isn't that wonderful? Oh, Ross, I can hardly wait.' She drew away. 'We must go to the guesthouse you mentioned and book rooms. Shall we go now?'

'Tara, my love, calm down. I was so sure your mother and the girls would come I've already booked accommodation.'

'But you didn't know when they would be coming.'

'Guessing, I presumed they would travel on Saturday.'

'And you're right, aren't you clever! I must go and tell Catherine and Marianne.'

Eileen and the girls arrived in the evening, laden with goodies and even Ross got caught up in all the talk and excitement of the occasion. John was there to share in the festivities.

It was not until the next day that Ross had the chance of spending some time alone with Eileen. This was when John was going to collect his brother, James, Catherine and Marianne, and took Tara and her sisters with him. They were all to meet at John's house for lunch.

Eileen, looking so young, said gently, 'So, Ross, how are things going with my very excitable daughter? I know you say when you write that you are getting on splendidly, but now you can tell me the truth.'

'There have been ups and down, as there would be in any marriage, but considering the situation I can honestly say it's working.'

'Tara is very lovable but so volatile.'

'She does have quiet times now. This was after I told her that her moods would reflect on the child.' Ross grinned. 'It's something I must have heard. It seems to have worked. She was getting so excited I worried about it.'

Eileen smiled a sad little smile. 'You are going to make a good father.' She suddenly leaned forward. 'Ross, tell me, have you ever regretted making the decision?'

He pursed his lips. 'If I'm honest, yes, when we've had a few words, but it is not many times and the thought hasn't lasted long. Tara is a loving person and that is important.'

Then Eileen said, 'Queenie McKnott called early one morning last week.'

Ross's heart began to thud. 'To tell you about Rosin?'

'Yes. I wasn't sure whether it was right to tell you but she wanted you to know. Rosin is in Connemara.'

He stared at her. 'Why there?'

'She apparently wanted to meet a shepherd. Did you talk to her about the man Conal?'

'Yes, I did, but I never expected she would go there.' He got up and moved restlessly about the room.

'You still love her?' Eileen said softly.

He stood looking out of the window for a moment then turned slowly. 'Yes, but that won't interfere with my marriage.' He came across and stood in front of her. 'I've learnt from you, Aunt Eileen. You are still in love with Preston Rafferty, yet you have never let it spoil your marriage.'

She twined her fingers and pressed her palms together. 'I made that vow when he left me.' Then she looked up and her eyes were luminous with tears. 'I've often wondered, Ross, how many women go through married life loving someone else.'

'And how many men,' he said quietly.

'Men are more fickle than woman. They go on having affairs.'

'Not all. Tell me, if Preston Rafferty were to ask you to go and live with him and was serious about it, would you go?'

She shook her head slowly. 'No, that is something I would never have done. Not only did I have obligations, but if I am honest, I think this love I have is strengthened by the fact that Preston is unattainable. A woman is a dreamer, it colours her life, a life that can be very drab at times.'

'If Patrick were to tell you that he was in love with another woman and wanted to go and live with her, would you accept it?'

'I'm fairly certain he wouldn't.'

'Why? I noticed he seemed to be very popular with women at the ball in Dublin.'

'No, he was being polite, I'm sure of it.'

'Don't you believe it.'

Eileen looked suddenly alarmed. 'What are you trying to tell me, that Patrick does have a woman in his life?'

'Why not? He has every right to, hasn't he? I think I shall always love Rosin, but I'm married and I love Tara in a different way. I'm glad now that Queenie wanted me to know about her visit to Conal.'

They ate at John's house that lunchtime. Mrs Fox excelled herself with a cold collation and the conversation proved to be worthwhile. Ross, who had thought once or twice that Tara was too wrapped up in what Catherine had to say, realized that the older woman was constantly giving her little snippets of advice and she was taking notice.

For instance, when Tara was having a little grumble about a friend who visited the Davies's, saying she didn't like the way the woman stared at her as though she were unimportant, Catherine said gently, 'Mrs Gascoigne is going blind. She's a very kind person and was doing her best to appear interested in what you were saying.'

To this Tara had replied earnestly, 'Oh, I do apologize. I must learn not to speak on impulse.'

Ross knew he would be more willing in the future to accept Tara's quotes of 'Catherine says . . .'

The following afternoon he had a chance of a long talk with Fiona and Ashling when both Eileen and Tara developed headaches and had to lie down.

The subject at first was Tara, with Fiona saying, without any malice, 'I thought our Tara would be less stupid now she's married, but she still hasn't grown up, has she? She says such childish things.'

Ashling said quietly, 'But would we want Tara to change? She loves everybody and she'll do a good turn if she can.'

'Loves everybody?' Fiona scoffed. 'She wasn't being very loving yesterday afternoon about Mrs Davies's friend who was blind, was she? I know it wasn't for our ears, but I was glad Mrs Davies spoke to her about it. Tara was so self-important in not wanting anyone to look down on her.'

Ashling protested at this. 'Now, Fiona, be fair. Tara thought she was being stared at. Would you like it?'

Fiona grinned. 'Men are always staring at me. I don't object.'

'Trust you to switch things.' Ashling's smile was indulgent.

Ross made enquiries about their love lives. Fiona shrugged. 'I'm not looking for marriage. I want a career. Actually, I have almost got the parents round to my way of thinking. I've been doing some accountancy for Papa. He admitted I was employable. But of course, I do not want to work at home. I need to spread my wings. I want to come to London. Any offers, cousin Ross?'

'I'm afraid I don't know of any openings for a young lady. Why don't you enquire while you are here?'

'Mmm, I might do that.'

He turned to Ashling. 'And what is your aim?'

Before she had a chance to reply, Fiona said, 'A husband, a home and masses of children, the more the merrier.'

'That is for the future,' Ashling replied quietly. 'At the moment I too want a career and, I might add, have already had the offer of two posts.'

Fiona sat up. 'You didn't tell me.'

'No, I have only just had the offers and I haven't made up my mind what to do. Mrs Davies said she knew of two women who were wanting educated nannies for their children.'

Fiona groaned. 'Oh, no, not a nanny.'

'Why not?' said Ross. 'Ashling loves children.'

They all went for a walk and when they came back, Eileen and Tara were up, both feeling better for their rest.

Fiona said, 'I can understand Mama needing a rest, but –' She looked Tara up and down then said in her forthright way, 'You're not pregnant, are you?'

Eileen looked shocked. 'Fiona, how can you be so coarse?'

Tara said, 'Take no notice, Mama. Fiona wants to belong to this new generation of young people who think it's very clever to say things that are apt to shock their elders. Marriage is not on their agenda, or at least they try to give that impression, and babies, according to them, are just items to be strangled at birth.'

For a moment Fiona was silent then she said, 'I must applaud your discernment, Tara. A while ago I spoke of you as not having grown up. You have. Perhaps London life has taught you something. But I would disagree about our attitude towards babies. I don't think anyone in our group has a desire to strangle babies.' She paused, then added with a wry smile. 'Only men.'

'How sad,' Tara said. 'I feel sorry for you.'

At that moment Ross felt proud of his young bride.

20

The family had been home about two weeks when Tara began to complain one evening that the cottage was really too small and they ought to be thinking about looking for somewhere larger.

When Ross asked why this had suddenly cropped up she shrugged.

'We will need a larger house when the baby comes so why not now?'

'That is not for months and we agreed we would wait. No, Tara, we are not moving. The cottage is perfect for our needs.'

'Do I not have a say?' she demanded. 'I am the one who is a prisoner in the cottage, not you.'

'How can you be a prisoner when you spend most of your days at Catherine's house? Who has been putting this idea into your head?'

'No one. I do have a mind of my own, don't I?'

Her aggressive manner had Ross worried. Was this all to do with pregnancy?

He said, 'I must ask Catherine to go with you to see the doctor.'

Tara protested that she didn't need to see the doctor. She was quite well. It was his attitude that she objected to, ordering her about as if she were a slave.

Ross decided to let it run, see what happened and if Tara continued to be awkward he would ask Catherine's advice.

Tara seemed to settle down for a few days, then she started again, this time grumbling because he never took her to theatres. Other men took their wives, why was she so neglected? Was he ashamed to be seen with her in public?

Ross explained patiently that the time for going to the theatre was in the autumn, rather than summer evenings and then asked her who had been suggesting she was neglected.

'There you go again,' she snapped, 'suggesting that I'm feeble-minded. I *can* think for myself.'

It was John who brought this problem to a head when he came back to the office after lunch the following day saying, 'Catherine wants to know if Tara is all right, says she hasn't seen her for days.'

Ross felt a coldness stealing over him. 'Tara gave me the impression she was seeing Catherine and Marianne as usual. She has actually talked about them, giving me little snippets of news. Why should she lie? Who is she seeing that I don't know about? Whoever it is has been dropping the poison.'

The two men stood staring at one another for a moment then John said grimly, 'Alicia?'

'No.' Ross shook his head. 'No, I can't believe that.'

'You better believe it and put an end to it. Alicia is a menace. You'll have to find out where Tara meets her. Why not try the Savoy . . . at four o'clock?' John spoke quietly.

Ross stopped and turned. 'I'm sure Alicia wouldn't want to meet Tara there. She would want to keep their meeting place a secret.'

'Hazarding a guess, I would say she wants you to find them together so she can show you the power she has over you. It would be her way of revenge for you rejecting her.'

Ross jumped up, jaw outthrust. 'Well, Miss Alicia Sylvain will soon find she has trouble coming to her. I shall be at the Savoy at four and if Tara is not there with her I shall get it out of her where she has been.'

'If she is there with Tara you must maintain an icy

calm, letting her know that she won't get away with her plan,' said John.

This drew a wry smile from Ross. 'And we thought that Alicia had behaved dramatically.'

'Drama is something that Alicia thrives on. She will probably show surprise when she sees you and will swear it's the first time she's spoken to Tara since you all last met.'

When Ross went into the lounge of the Savoy and saw Alicia and Tara at a table together, Alicia talking earnestly, he wondered if John had had dealings with Alicia before, especially when she looked up when he went up to the table and said happily, 'Why, Ross, what a surprise. What are you doing here?'

Tara, looking alarmed, had jumped to her feet. 'Ross. I – I met Alicia and she –'

'Would you mind leaving us for a few minutes, Tara? I want to have a few words with Alicia. There's a settee over there.'

She glanced at Alicia who gave her a nod. Tara dropped her napkin on the table and left, with Alicia saying reprovingly to Ross, 'You really do treat your poor wife like a child and she's such a darling.'

'She was until you came along and put ideas into her head.'

Alicia pulled out a chair and invited him to sit down. He did, not wanting to draw attention to himself, but said right away in a low voice, 'You are to stop seeing Tara at once, or else –'

She eyed him in an amused way. 'Or else what, dear Ross?'

'Or else I shall use means to get rid of you and I am not being melodramatic, as you were when you described your little bedroom scene.'

She sobered quickly and said earnestly, 'That was not a melodrama. It actually happened.'

'Well, whether it did or not is of no importance to

me, but Tara is. I will not allow her to turn into a liar to further your ends. Do you honestly think that turning my wife against me would make me turn to you?' He got up. 'I'm leaving, but remember what I said. I mean it.'

He left the table without looking back. Tara was already on her feet. She glanced at Alicia, but Ross cupped her elbow and hurried her away. No word was spoken until they were outside, then Tara stopped and looked entreatingly at Ross.

'You must let me explain.'

'You can explain all you like when we get home, but don't expect any sympathy from me. You've behaved as despicably as Alicia.' Ross nodded to the commissionaire, who hailed a cab.

No sooner were they in the cottage than Tara began to complain that his silence was making her feel ill.

He eyed her steadily. 'Really. I would have thought that going against my wishes and telling deliberate lies would have had that effect on you, but no, you never turned a hair when you told me of conversations you had had with Catherine and Marianne.'

'I had to do it. Alicia made me.'

'Rubbish. You didn't have to do anything Alicia told you. You wanted to be with her, you enjoyed it, enjoyed flinging your weight around, enjoyed nagging.'

'I didn't, Ross. I like you to be master.' There was a pleading in her voice. 'I didn't want to behave the way I did. Alicia has a sort of influence. I just had to do as she told me.'

'Tara, stop it, for God's sake. You're a married woman, not a child. Later in the year you'll be a mother. I had no idea until now how much you must have been indulged at home. Utterly spoilt. Even Ashling makes excuses for you.'

'So you don't want me living with you any more.' There was a piteous note in her voice.

'I'm married to you!' he shouted. 'I have responsibilities. I'm forced to look after you. I would like to wash my hands of you and get some peace, but I can't.'

She sank onto the settee and there was the look in her eyes of a child who has been punished for something she didn't do. At that moment Ross remembered how he and John Davies had treated everything Alicia had told them as gospel and they were men of the world. Tara had been cushioned against life. His anger died. He sat down beside her and took her hands in his.

'I want us to lead a normal married life together. I don't want these upsets, but you must pull your weight. There must be no more lies. You were happy with Catherine and Marianne, they have missed you.'

'I've missed them,' she said in a low voice. 'They are like family to me. It was Alicia. I won't have any more to do with her, I give you my word.' She looked up at him, pain in her eyes. 'I love only you, Ross. Please don't stop loving me.'

'That depends entirely on you, Tara.'

The rift was finally healed in bed that night and afterwards Ross saw that he spent more time with Tara. Through James and Catherine they led a busier social life, went to theatres, were invited out and Tara blossomed under the constant attention she received.

Tara carried her pregnancy well. The day that she quickened she was so excited she would have had anyone available to feel the child kicking. It was on a Sunday and she kept saying to Ross, 'Oh, come quickly, feel him kicking.'

He teased her saying that it could be a girl, but Tara would not have it. It was definitely a boy and she started to choose a name.

Until that moment the child had been vaguely there and Ross had accepted it as someone who was eventually going to be a part of his life. It was not until he had felt the movements of the baby, however, that he realized it was a flesh and blood creature that would grow and come to depend on him. It was a big responsibility. Who would it resemble? He hoped Tara. If it took after his father it could become a thorn in his flesh.

Eileen wrote regularly giving news and wanting it, and each member of the family sent the occasional letter. Brendan had postponed his marriage saying he was waiting so that Tara and Ross would be able to attend the wedding. Fiona told Tara in her letter that she was sure that Brendan wanted to try to end his engagement and added it was not his fiancée that was the trouble but her mother who was so terribly possessive. Fiona also said that she had been half promised an office job in Killorglin, but she still wanted to work in London.

Ashling's last letter said she hadn't taken a job as a nanny because she was hoping she could be nanny to Tara's baby.

Tara, of course, was delighted about this. To have her own sister there would be heaven. She so missed them all.

Ross, knowing that Eileen would want to live in the house when she came to be with Tara for the birth, and also accepting that Ashling would have to live in if she were going to be nanny to the child, decided to look for a larger house and was lucky enough to find a suitable one to rent in the street next to Catherine's family. Both Catherine and Marianne were delighted and offered to do all they could to help with the move.

When Tara knew about the house she was thrilled. They could have more scope for entertaining, have more people for dinners. This was not on Ross's agenda, but he went along with Tara, knowing it was important to her.

Catherine told him not to worry. That wouldn't be

for some time. Tara would not be doing any entertaining before the birth of their child and would not feel like it for some time afterwards.

Ross liked Catherine, she was very down-to-earth. She had had five children, but only Marianne was at home. They were both very fond of Tara.

When Tara was six months pregnant, Ross had a letter from Eileen to say that Edward was back in London. Alicia had broken the engagement and he had gone abroad, broken-hearted, to hide his wounds. She had added, 'Edward, *heartbroken*?'

Ross smiled to himself. She too knew him. Later, he wondered about Alicia. Who was she involved with now?

And, of course, thinking about Alicia brought Rosin to his mind. Although he never allowed himself to dwell on her, there was still a regret that she had gone out of his life. Had she met Conal in Connemara? If so, how strange life was. Who would have thought when he first met Rosin that they would both seek an unknown shepherd in a remote spot, he in an effort to trace his father and she to . . . to what? Find herself?

As Ross reminisced over his short stay in the mountains he realized how easy it would be to cut oneself off from the rest of the world. But how long could he have stayed without having a challenge to face? How long could he have stayed without needing affection?

In this mood he reflected on his future life with Tara. She had been more settled since the upset with Alicia, was always eager to please him and yet she had never made demands on him. Her loving, generous ways held her close to him. The real testing time would be after the birth of the child. Although she never complained about being worried about the actual birth he knew deep down she was afraid and also knew she was worried that when she got nearer her time that he would hate her misshapen body.

'I'll be fat and ugly,' she wailed one night, 'and you'll not love me any more.'

He took her in his arms. 'How could I not love you? Motherhood is a beautiful thing.'

She searched his face. 'But will you love him?'

He teased her. 'I love her more and more every day.' He drew his fingertips over her cheek and added, seriously, 'Son or daughter, I will love this child as if he or she were my own. I can give you my word on that.'

The day for moving into the larger house turned out to be easier than they had thought because curtains had been hung beforehand, carpets had been laid and the furniture they had bought had been delivered. Even then, they had collected quite a few items and, in spite of Tara's complaining about the cottage being too small, she wept when they left. Ross told her that with the new tenants the cottage would be well cared for, but Tara shed tears several times during that day, not wanting the cottage to feel deserted.

From then on she had weepy spells and when she had reached the middle of her eighth month and was constantly upset at what she called her distorted figure, Ross wrote and asked Eileen if she could come over early to be with Tara, who kept getting more and more depressed. Eileen sent a telegram to say she would be with them the following day.

Tara cried for an hour when she knew her mother would be coming.

Ross had spoken to the doctor about Tara's state but he smiled and told him to take it in his stride. He should feel glad that his wife didn't have a desire to eat bacon with every meal, or pounds of peaches or chew cucumbers. 'She's a strong, healthy young lady. Stop worrying.'

When Eileen arrived Tara fell sobbing into her arms. 'Oh, Mama, I'm sure I'm going to die.'

'Of course you're not, my love. You are going to be

fine,' her mother soothed her. 'The doctor told Ross you are doing splendidly.'

'I hate him, he's old and doddery. And I hate the midwife too. She's bad-tempered, keeps telling me I'll hurt the baby with all my crying.'

'So you will.' Eileen spoke firmly. 'This weeping must stop. The poor little mite must be very unhappy.'

Tara gave a hiccupping sob. 'But how can it? It's not born.'

'I told you when you are carrying a baby how it can be upset if you eat the wrong food or get angry.'

'Oh, I must have forgotten. But I still don't want the doctor or the midwife to examine me,' she added stubbornly.

'You have to be examined to find if the baby is in the right position. I shall telephone the doctor in the morning and no, Tara, it's no use protesting. This is one time when you won't get your own way. A child's life is involved. You must face up to your responsibilities.'

Later when Tara said she was tired and was going to bed, her mother went up with her. She was away a long time and when she came down Ross said, 'Everything all right?'

'Yes. Tara had some pains, they seemed like labour pains, but they've gone, thank goodness.' She gave a wry smile. 'The last thing we want is a premature baby, isn't it? If it arrives at the right time it will be a month early, so far as the outside world is concerned. I'll take a look at her again in a few minutes.'

She was down again soon, saying, 'She's sleeping. It was possibly a bout of indigestion. I suffered terribly from it with all the children. I remember one day when I was out shopping, I –' She stopped suddenly and began to laugh. 'Don't worry, I'm not going to bore you with tales of my pregnancy. Oh, did I tell you I had a letter from home this afternoon?'

They talked until quite late, Ross and Eileen taking

turns to look in on Tara, who was still fast asleep when they went up to bed.

Eileen had been sleeping with Tara since she had arrived and Ross, who had been banished to a spare room, looked in on Tara before he went to bed. She looked so young, so angelic, he felt a rush of tenderness for her sweep over him as he thought of all the pain she would have to suffer. He prayed she would not have to endure a long confinement. He kissed her gently on the brow and went to the loneliness of his single bed, longing for the time when Tara would be with him again, curled up lovingly against him, always responsive to his demands. How could he have been impatient with her constant weepy moods?

Ross found himself recalling the comment made by a great-aunt when he was quite young: 'If God had decreed that men should bear babes, the world would be poorly populated.' He had not understood it at the time. Now, smiling to himself, he agreed.

He was roused from a deep sleep by Eileen shaking him and saying urgently, 'Ross, Tara is in labour. Will you send someone for the midwife and call the doctor and let him know that the pains are coming every fifteen minutes. We can let the nurse know later.'

Ross, who was wide awake in seconds, was up and putting on his dressing gown.

'Is Tara all right?'

'Yes, I'll go back to her.'

He heard Tara shouting, 'Mama, Mama!' and Eileen went running.

Ross's heart began to pound. He ran downstairs to telephone the doctor. The woman who took the call said the doctor would be there as soon as possible. He then called Jane, who was living in since they had moved, told her to get dressed and go for the midwife. He gave her the money for a cab then hurried upstairs to get dressed.

After that Ross paced the floor, not quite knowing what to do. Then he thought, tea ... Women always needed tea in a crisis. He had prepared a tray when the door bell rang. It was Jane with the midwife. Jane took her upstairs. Seconds later the doctor arrived, all amiability.

'So what is all the fuss about? You men are all the same. Your wife could be a long time yet.' He asked if the midwife had come and when told yes, he said cheerfully, 'Lead the way.' When they went upstairs Eileen was on the landing.

'I'm glad you came, Doctor. Mrs Ferris is having pains every five minutes.'

Ross whispered that he had made tea, but Eileen said later. She went into the room with the doctor and Ross felt utterly useless. The door opened and Eileen looked out. 'Ross, will you ask Jane to put plenty of water on to heat?'

Ross had never felt so neglected in all his life. All these people in the house and he had no idea what was happening. He became desperate for someone to talk to and was relieved when Eileen came down.

Before he could ask about Tara she said, 'Everything is going all right.'

She looked worried and Ross said, 'Tell me the truth. Are there any complications?'

'No. According to the doctor the baby should be here soon.'

'But you *are* worried,' Ross persisted.

'What mother wouldn't be,' she replied lightly.

Even with the room door closed, Ross could hear moans and shouts coming from above and he said, 'This is the first child and will definitely be the last.'

'That's what all father's-to-be say. A friend's husband said it and they had a child every year for ten years running. Stop worrying. Tara hasn't been long in labour. She's young and strong.'

There was more moaning, then two screams. Eileen and Ross stood motionless, listening. Then there came a shriek and Eileen said she would go up and try to find out what was happening.

She was away five minutes. It seemed like fifty to Ross. She was tearful but smiling when she returned announcing, 'Ross, you have a daughter.'

Ross found himself thinking, no, not a daughter but a half-sister.

'I only had a glimpse of her,' Eileen went on. 'She's small but quite lovely.'

'Is Tara all right?'

'Yes, weepy and sleepy.'

It was the doctor who came down to congratulate him. 'You have a beautiful daughter, Mr Ferris. Don't be disappointed your first-born isn't a boy. I had three girls before my son arrived and they are all my pride and joy.'

'She's not . . . deformed in any way, is she?'

'Of course not. Why should she be?'

'Well, I thought coming a month early . . .'

The doctor gripped his shoulder and laughed. 'You've miscounted, Mr Ferris. This child has gone her full time. She's adorable.'

Eileen said quickly, 'A drink, Doctor Mellor? Whisky, brandy?'

'Well now, I'll have a wee drappie of whisky to wet the babbie's head, as one of my Scottish colleagues would say.'

Ross, who had been standing frozen, seeing that his aunt's hand was shaking as she picked up the decanter of whisky said, 'Here, allow me. Sorry, Doctor, I'm forgetting my manners.'

He poured whisky for all of them, a stiff one for the doctor, who congratulated Ross again and swallowed the drink at one go.

He put the glass down, smacked his lips then said, 'I shall look in later. Your wife is in good hands.'

After Ross had seen the doctor to the door he came back slowly into the room. Eileen was standing, the drink untouched in her hand, a look of anguish in her eyes. Neither spoke for a moment, then she put the glass down and said, 'I can't believe it, Ross. Tell me he was talking about some other baby.'

'I wish I could,' he replied, his expression grim. 'But why? Why should Tara lie? She must have known she would be found out when the baby was born.'

'I imagine she was hoping for a miscarriage. She talked a lot about miscarriages, but I put it down to the position she was in. Had she been taking something to try and get rid of it? What a mess it all is. How could she have blamed your father when he was innocent?'

'Who *is* the father? That's what I want to know,' Ross said grimly. 'I agreed to marry her and accept the child as my own to make up for the shame of my father. Now I'm landed with some other man's bastard and I can't stomach it, Aunt Eileen. I won't and that is definite.'

'I don't think that anyone would expect you to.' She sank into a chair. 'Holy Mother of God, was there ever such a situation? How are we going to overcome it?'

A silence followed that seemed to go on and on . . .

21

Eileen broke the lengthy silence. 'A new baby is a reason for celebration. I could perhaps manage to put on an act, but it would be impossible for you. I think it would be wise if you went to stay with John. I can always say you had been called away on urgent business.'

Ross shook his head. 'I have to face Tara sometime.'

'But she has to be kept quiet for a while.'

'I shall have to put on an act too. I'll do it for your sake, Aunt Eileen. We'll get over this trauma as we've overcome others.'

The nurse, all starch and bossiness, came to tell Ross he could come to see his wife and child but warned it would only be for a few minutes. She made no mention of Eileen coming too so Ross held out his hand to her, saying, 'Come along, Grandmama, meet your first grandchild.'

She gave a faint smile and took his hand. When they went into the bedroom the nurse warned Ross again, 'Only a few minutes. We can't have the mother upset.' To Tara she added, 'Now don't get excited or your milk will curdle.'

Tara, who was propped up with extra pillows and had the shawl-wrapped bundle in her arms wore an anxious expression as she apologized to Ross that the baby was not a boy. He leaned over and lightly kissed her brow. 'The important thing is that both you and the baby are all right.' He was aware that his voice lacked warmth and, knowing that Tara was aware of it too, he touched the shawl and added, 'So this is the newcomer to the world?'

He had no wish to see the baby, knowing he would hate it, but forced himself to look when Tara undid the shawl so he could see the child better. Ross had never seen a newly born baby but had heard fathers describe them as red-faced bundles who didn't resemble anyone. He intended to give the child a quick look and let Eileen come forward, but he found himself caught by the expression on the small face. The baby yawned, then screwed up her eyes and, putting a tiny first to her mouth, began a vigorous sucking. Then, as though feeling cheated she let out a cry. Tara shushed her, the crying stopped and the eyes opened. They were a deep blue and seemed to be studying Ross with interest. She had a lot of dark hair, which curled damply.

It was then he felt a great tenderness for the child and when she suddenly burped he laughed aloud and asked if he could hold her.

The nurse handed the baby to him, saying in the voice one would use to a child, 'Now just be careful. A baby is a fragile creature.'

'Look at her nails,' he breathed. 'So perfectly formed.' He then marvelled at the baby's strength as she gripped his finger and from that moment he felt she had claimed him as her own. He said to Eileen, 'I'm sure you'll want to hold her?'

The nurse intervened. 'Another time, madam. The baby is not something to be tossed about from one to the other. She's hardly come into the world and needs her mother. She must learn to suckle.'

'Do as nurse tells you,' Tara said with mock severity and there was a closeness between the three of them that had not been there when Ross and Eileen came in.

Downstairs Ross and Eileen looked helplessly at one another, then Ross said, 'Honestly, that wretched nurse made me feel like a five-year-old.

What am I to do, Aunt Eileen? I felt quite a strong love for the baby. She is not to blame for any of this, but I feel I could not live with Tara as man and wife again. It's the lies, the deception.'

'I know, but I never dreamed of such a thing. I was away for a week the month before . . . but who was the man who seduced her? The girls haven't mentioned anyone Tara showed interest in and Ashling would have noticed, even if Fiona hadn't. I feel at my wits' end, Ross. I ache that Tara should do such a thing.'

'I know and I'm sorry this has had to happen. I'll go to the office. I need to be doing something.'

Ross did not go to the office. He walked along the Embankment hoping, now he was away from the house, to find a solution to his problems. But there were too many distractions, the busy river, the noise, the people. What he needed was the peace of the mountains in Ireland, the silence, the communion with the shepherd, who would understand his needs. And yet he knew it was not the answer. The peace had to come from inside him.

And how could that be achieved with a wife who had lied in her teeth, who had been willing to scar his father's reputation to win a husband and a father for her child?

God, what a life he had built up for himself, married to a woman who obviously had a hunger for men. There was no other name for it. Well, he was not going to be a fool to satisfy that hunger. But even as he thought it, he could feel her warm body curled up beside him and he groaned, knowing there was going to be no easy way to make a break. There was a caring in Tara, a need to be loved, petted. Was that her fault? Hadn't the shepherd being constantly stressing how important it was in life to be tolerant of the faults in others?

Although Ross stayed out for a long time walking, he could find no peace. He took a cab home.

Eileen said quietly when he came in, 'You look all in. You went out without having anything to eat. Catherine is upstairs. Tara asked for her. She said she wanted her to see the baby, but I think it was because she sensed my animosity towards her and felt the need for a mother figure.' Her voice broke. 'I did try not to show my real feelings.'

It was Eileen's pain that gave strength to Ross. 'We'll have to try and get back to some normality,' he said. 'If we work together I think we'll manage. When Tara is up and about we shall all have a talk.'

Catherine came down smiling. 'I've been ordered out by your battle-axe of a nurse. I am apparently exciting the patient. Oh, Ross, congratulations. What a lovely baby. I could eat her. Tara says you don't have a name for her yet because she was so sure it was going to be a boy.'

'That's right. Tara did mention one time that if the baby *was* a girl –' He smiled. 'I think she thought this an impossibility – she quite liked the name Jacinta.'

'Oh, I do. It has a nice rhythm. Ja-cinta.'

Eileen said she liked it too and Ross stored it in his mind as a talking point when next he saw Tara.

Tara slept most of the day and it was early evening before Ross and Eileen had any conversation with her. The nurse immediately gave orders that the baby was not to be disturbed and Ross told her they had no intention of disturbing the child, then asked if she would kindly leave them alone for a while. Looking affronted she informed him that *she* was in charge and he said quitely, 'No, Nurse Blane. This is my house, I am in charge. Now please leave us. I ask for ten minutes, not a second less.'

She stormed out. Tara laughed.

'Oh, Ross, you were splendid. I've been wanting to

shout at her several times. The only reason I didn't was because she's so caring with Jacinta.'

'Oh, you've decided on the name for her?' Eileen said smiling. 'I like it.'

'It depends on what Ross thinks.'

'I too like it,' he said. She was looking at him lovingly and he got up. 'I must go and say hello to her.'

He looked down at the sleeping child, her tiny fist was cupped under her chin, as though contemplating something, and he felt like weeping. She had not chosen her parents. Was she to be brought up by two people in conflict with one another? He remembered his own parents, how he had first become aware that all was not well between them and how he had come to hate his father, thinking he was hurting his mother. Yet if truth were told, his mother was to blame for the rift.

What of this tiny mite? Tara was caring and loving. Would he be blamed if they lived a separate existence? He found himself thinking of boys he had met at boarding school whose parents had no love to give them and how they had cried themselves to sleep at night, having been torn away from a caring nanny, who had given them the only affection they had ever known.

A door banged somewhere and the baby jumped, startled. Ross settled her and whispered, 'There, there, you're all right, I'll look after you.' And he knew then that there could be no breach in the marriage no matter how hard it would be to accept Tara's behaviour.

The healing started when he went back to the bed and said gently to his wife, 'Nothing must hurt our child.'

She searched his face. 'No, I promise to care for her. I give you my word.' There was a tremor in her voice. 'Thanks, Ross, I don't deserve you.'

When they came downstairs. Ross explained to Eileen his thoughts when looking at the baby and added, 'Now I find myself wondering what sort of childhood Alicia had and what went wrong in her life.'

This did not turn Ross into a wonderfully caring and loving husband. Many times he had to control his temper when Tara, who was so smug about their relationship, would whisper to him, 'I can't wait, darling, to be in your arms again and making love. How long must we wait? Do ask the doctor.'

'He told me three months.'

'*Three* months?' Tara's eyes were wide in disbelief. 'That means not until the end of January. You must have misunderstood him.'

'I did not misunderstand him, Tara. He explained to me why this was important to you.'

'I think he's talking rubbish. I remember a wife of one of Papa's workers having a baby and barely ten months later she had another.'

'And how many more babies did she have?'

After a moment's hesitation Tara said in a low voice. 'None. She died when the second baby was a few months old. I had forgotten.'

Although Tara had objected to being denied any lovemaking for three months, she was quite content to stay in bed to recuperate and be fussed over by visitors.

'It's doctor's orders,' she would announce happily.

One day Catherine said in a wry voice, 'It amazes me that mothers in poor families are up the same day they have a baby and look after their families, but those with money are cosseted and can spend a month in bed after giving birth.'

'Poor people don't have a choice,' Tara declared. 'We do, and I want to look after my body.'

'I defied my doctor and was up a week after confinement with each of my five children and I never ailed anything.'

Tara said with a lift of her head, 'Ross insists I follow doctor's orders. He really cares about me.'

'That's very nice for you.' Catherine got up to leave.

Ross was patient with Tara preening herself in her role of invalid, but exploded when he learned that the baby had been sick a lot because Tara had been guzzling chocolates secretly. The doctor, the nurse and Eileen had told her to have an occasional one and keep the rest for when she was up and about but Tara had ignored this.

'Self! That's all you think about,' Ross stormed at her. 'Your greed could have killed the baby and you say you're sorry! No, don't waste your tears. They don't impress me one bit.'

Eileen was angry too at her daughter's behaviour and said, 'I think it's time for our talk with Tara. She must pull herself together. She's into her third week of recovery. We'll talk to her tomorrow when she's up and our dragon of a nurse is taking the air. Then, I must start thinking of going back home.'

Ross knew he was going to miss Eileen terribly. Ashling was going to come as nanny to the baby and Eileen promised she would be back again with the rest of the family for the christening of Jacinta.

The following afternoon, Tara was downstairs and settled in front of a glowing fire, 'I do like these interludes. Mama, will you get me some more novels from the library when you are out?'

This was when Eileen decided to get down to some home truths.

'I'm planning to go home, Tara, and Ross and I want to have a talk with you. This should have been done after you gave birth, but we waited to give you time for recovery.'

Tara, looking a little annoyed, said to Ross, 'I'm still not fit and I don't think the doctor would approve of this.'

Ross drew up a chair and sat facing her. 'This has nothing to do with the doctor, and seeing you were well enough to stuff yourself with several boxes of chocolates, we both feel you are well enough to listen to what we have to say. In the first place, Tara, you knew you were pregnant a month before you accused my father of seducing you. And as if that wasn't bad enough, you swore on the Bible, with your rosary in your hand, that he was the one responsible.'

She looked frantically from one to the other. 'I had to, don't you see. It was impossible to tell Mama and Papa.'

'We had to know eventually,' Eileen said.

'Yes, but –'

'There are no buts in this story. What we want to know now is who did seduce you.'

'I can't tell you.' Tara lowered her head. 'And it wouldn't do any good.'

'Oh, but it would.' Ross spoke firmly. 'I want to know whose child I'm fathering. And, please, no more stupid nonsense. We've waited long enough.'

'I don't feel well,' Tara wailed.

'If you collapse we'll call the doctor,' said her mother, then added grimly, 'but if we do, he'll be told the reason, so make up your mind.'

Tara's body went slack. 'I don't even know the young man's name. We met at a party. I had had one or two drinks and he took me outside because I felt sick. And then, then he – made love to me.'

'Don't talk to me about love,' Ross taunted. 'You haven't the faintest idea of the meaning of it.'

'Oh, but I do.' There was pain in her voice. 'I've loved you from the time I was small. I worshipped you. As I grew up I ached for you, I never knew that one could suffer so much pain in the name of love. At times I wanted to kill myself. Then, this night of the party when my head was all swimmy and this man – fondled

286

me. I —' She burst into tears but neither Ross or Eileen made a move to comfort her.

Tara wiped her eyes and looked from one to the other. 'He couldn't have married me because he already had a wife. I didn't know that until afterwards. I didn't mean to be bad,' she pleaded. 'I know I shall be punished for telling a lie with my hand on the Bible, but that won't be until I die and then I'll probably be too old to care.'

Eileen glanced at Ross momentarily and a smile touched her lips. Then she said, speaking briskly, 'Age won't stop you suffering the flames of hell. And remember this, Tara. You are a mother now, with responsibilities. If you won't learn to speak the truth do try, for heaven's sake, at least to teach Jacinta to speak it.'

'Oh, I will. After all, I have a lot to make up for, haven't I?' She spoke so earnestly, Ross found himself relenting a little. After all, he had not exactly led a blameless life himself.

Eileen told Tara then, more gently, that she would have to go home, but would be back again with the family for the christening and reminded her she would have to be churched beforehand.

Tara looked tearful for a moment, but when her mother added that Ashling would be coming to be nanny to the baby, she was bright and smiling again.

Actually, Eileen stayed until Ashling did arrive, so that Tara would not be without one of her close family with her, and for that Ross was glad. Although he had accepted that they would try to live a normal life again, there were times when it angered him that Tara had deceived him. Yet he would not be without the baby. He marvelled that he could love another man's child, and a stranger's at that. And who better than Ashling to take charge of Jacinta?

What he was longing for now was to be rid of the

wretched nurse who laid down the law about rules that ought not to be broken.

As it turned out it was Nurse Blane who had to relinquish her post, having to take care of her father who had had a stroke.

Tara said after she had gone, 'Do you know, Ross, I feel really sorry for the woman. You only saw the bossy side of her, I saw her when she thought she was alone with Jacinta and was all silly baby talk, like a young mother. Catherine knew of the family. Nurse Blane spent her earlier years caring for a crippled sister. When the sister died she went in for nursing and had just done her training when her mother became bed-ridden. After she died she went out nursing. Now she's back at home caring for her father.'

Ashling, who had come in while Tara was talking, sighed. 'The poor woman. We don't know the lives of other people, do we?'

Ross, thinking of the lives of Tara and himself, thought no, and it was perhaps better that they didn't.

He missed his aunt and was pleased that Ashling was there. Although the two sisters spent all day together, Tara was still going to bed early so he and Ashling would have a walk together in the evening and Ashling would talk of the baby's antics and of the family. She was in her element caring for the baby and said she thought she would like to train as a maternity nurse. Ross teased her, said that the trouble would be that all the babies under her care would be spoilt to death.

She denied this saying, 'Nurse Blane was very implicit with her instructions and Tara and I are following them strictly. We can now distinguish from a hunger or a pain cry to know when it's just because Jacinta wants to be picked up for a bit of petting, bless her.' Ross came to realize how caring for the baby had brought the two sisters very close.

She told him how Fiona, for all her talk of wanting

a career, had met someone whom she was sure she was in love with. 'I like him, he's a quiet, thoughtful man and he's always talking about Fiona, what an intelligent young lady she is and how he enjoys discussions with her. They seldom agree but I know that Fiona enjoys them too. She says they're a challenge.'

'And what challenge do you enjoy?' Ross teased. 'It's time that you were finding the right man and settling down.'

She gave him a quick glance, then said lightly, 'I shall be the spinster in the family. There always has to be one daughter who doesn't marry so she can look after her parents when they are old.'

Ross laughed. 'I can't imagine either of them growing old and I'm quite sure your mother will be finding a husband for you soon if you don't start making up your own mind.'

'To set your mind at rest I had better admit that I have the choice of three men who want to marry me, but haven't yet made up my mind which one I like best.'

'Well, I can say with confidence that whichever one you choose will be a lucky man indeed for he'll not only get a loving wife, but a caring mother for his children who will run his home excellently.'

She went quiet after that and Ross wondered if the three suitors were a figment of her imagination, she not wanting him to know that there were no men in her life.

The weeks went by and although there were times when Ross wondered how long he could go without making love to Tara, there were other times when she made up to him so that he drew away from her, the unknown man in her life there, tormenting him.

The baby came to be very much a part of Ross's life. He would always be home in time to see her being bathed. Tara shied away from bathing her, saying she was so afraid she would drop her. One time, at Ashling's insistence, she did try and she was so nervous that the baby, obviously conscious of it, gave little shivers and the tiny hands went up as though trying to find something to cling to.

'Oh, take her, Ashling, please,' Tara begged, near to tears.

Ashling's handling of the baby was so different and once the infant was in the water, legs kicked and hands twisted and turned as she was held firmly and water scooped over her.

'Oh, you are so good with her,' Tara said, 'and doesn't she love her bath? I'll try again when she's a little older.'

Always when Jacinta was in her night clothes Ross would hold her and think there could not be a greater pleasure than holding a newly bathed baby, so sweet smelling, damp curls touching his face. In time he never thought of her as belonging to anyone else.

Tara fed her for a time, then said she thought she would put her on a bottle. She wanted a social life, she was tired of being at home all the while.

Catherine suggested she had a wet nurse and recommended a woman she knew whose baby had died and would be glad to nurse another child, but Tara would not hear of it. The woman might become too possessive of Jacinta and she was not going to have that.

Ashling, who was all for the wet nursing, said, 'You should consider what is best for the baby. The woman has plenty of milk.' But Tara was adamant. Jacinta would be bottle-fed.

And because Tara wanted to go socializing and to entertain, she went to be churched the following Sunday. That done she said she now felt she was out of prison and could enjoy herself.

The first night they dined out, Tara was all loving with Ross and begged him to come back to her bed.

He refused, saying they must follow the doctor's orders, but knew if he had wanted to make love to her he might have broken the ruling. The trouble was that Tara had flirted with John and two of the other men in the company and he felt she had cheapened herself.

He put her away from him. 'Another time. I know this was your first night out since Jacinta was born, but I felt you were a little too free with your favours. And anyway, it might be wise to follow doctor's orders and wait until the end of January as planned.'

'Very well,' she said, huffily. 'If that is your wish.'

The following morning she came into his bedroom as usual to call him, teased him with kisses and ran out when he sat up. Damn her, he thought, emotions aroused, but in spite of finding it difficult to work for wanting to make love to her, he did not approach her that night or many another night, determined to show her that he had the will power and was the master.

When December came in, Tara suggested they should arrange to have Jacinta christened and ask the family to spend Christmas with them. Ross agreed, and Tara wrote.

By return letter Eileen said they would be overjoyed to visit and asked if they would wait until then to decorate the house so that they would all be involved in the Christmas festivities.

The girls were in their element and arranged that Catherine would come and look after the baby while they went shopping to buy decorations and presents.

They came back in a cab, laden, and Ross, caught up in their excitement, lifted Tara off her feet, swung her around, then said a little sheepishly as he put her down, 'It made me think of my childhood and the excitement of Father Christmas arriving.'

Tara whispered against his cheek, 'I hope he might visit me this evening,' and his heart began a wild beating.

The house was silent when he went to their room. It was moonlit and Tara was standing waiting for him, clad only in a flimsy negligée and when he stopped she slipped the gown off and let it fall to the floor.

Ross was back to their wedding night, only then he had seen her naked in candlelight. She held out her arms to him and he went to her, his breathing ragged, saying, 'Oh, Tara, I love you, I've wanted you, ached for you,' and everything was forgotten as he picked her up and put her on the bed.

The following evening Tara said she would like to have a try at bathing the baby and was jubilant when she bathèd, dried, powdered her, put on her nappy and nightclothes with Jacinta seeming quite content and blowing bubbles.

'I did it, Ross,' she exclaimed. 'Oh, I'm so pleased.'

He dropped a kiss on her cheek. 'Keep up the good work, my love, then Ashling can have an evening off for a change.'

'Yes,' said Tara doubtfully, then, seeing Ross eyeing her, she said brightly, 'Yes, of course. That is only fair.'

Tara was more often than not missing at Jacinta's bathtime but Ashling said not to worry, she enjoyed bathing the baby and there was no place she wanted to go.

As it neared Christmas the weather became colder and farmers prophesied snow. How lovely, said the people who would not be affected by icy roads and pavements or have to work out of doors.

Eileen, Patrick, Brendan and Fiona arrived on the eighteenth to be in time for the baby's christening, which was to be on the twenty-first. They arrived in a snowstorm and from then on for Tara it was a lovely madhouse, everyone talking, friends calling, decorations being hung, the Christmas tree being trimmed with tinsel and bright baubles, which delighted Jacinta every time she was held out to see it. If it had not been for Ashling's firmness the baby would have been thoroughly spoilt. Even Brendan insisted on holding his lovely niece, saying that he supposed he would have to be holding his own children one of these days.

Ross worried about the baby being taken out for the christening in such cold weather, but Eileen assured him she would be well wrapped up, the church would be heated and water in the font warm.

The wind had dropped by next morning, the sun was shining, sparkling the snow that was crisp underfoot. The carriages were waiting to take them to church. Patrick, Brendan and John were to be godfathers and Eileen, Fiona, Ashling and Catherine, godmothers.

Jacinta was wide awake and looking about her as though with interest. She was as good as gold and never even made a murmur when the priest put the water over her head and gave her name as Jacinta Maura Siobhain, the latter names being after Ross's mother and Patrick's mother.

Other friends who had been in the church came back to the house for the celebration and it was a lively afternoon. Afterwards the family settled in the cosiness of the room, the firelight playing on the walls of the darkening room.

Eileen said, sleepily, 'I shall remember this Christmas, if only for the christening and the snow. How lovely it all looked when we came out, birds sitting on the white branches, as though waiting for us, and the robin waiting on the steps. Did you see it?'

Patrick teased her and said she was seeing everything through a lovely champagne haze.

Eileen smiled at Tara. 'Your father thinks I've had too much to drink, but I've only had one glass of champagne. I'm happy, very happy. It's been a lovely day and I'm sure we are going to have a wonderful

Christmas and that next year is going to be the best year we've ever known.'

There was a chorus of 'Hear, Hear!'

But Ross gave a shiver as though someone had walked over his grave ... And wondered why.

22

Eileen had been right when she said it was going to be a wonderful Christmas. Weeks later when Ross looked back on his life he thought of it as one of the best times in his life. Tara had been sweet and loving, and seemed more contented than she had ever been.

That was why he was unprepared for the change in her. She started to grumble that she hardly had any social life and he looked at her in astonishment. 'Tara, we went to the theatre on Monday. We were out to dinner on Tuesday, we had friends here last night. Quite frankly I thought you would be pleased to have a night in tonight. I know that I am looking forward to it.'

'If I'm honest, it's my family I'm missing.' She was sulky.

'It's only weeks ago since they were here. You have Ashling with you. You're married now. You have a baby, you can't go rushing back to Ireland every time you feel a little homesick.'

She looked tearful. 'You don't understand, you were never close to your parents.'

'I was close to my mother,' he said quietly.

'Yes, but you didn't have sisters or brothers. I know that I only have one brother, but I really do miss him. He's a tease, he's fun. All your friends are older.'

This was true, but as well as having Ashling, Tara saw Catherine and Marianne most days. And Tara often had long chats with Jane, who was a sensible girl and educated.

'Look, why don't you wait a while until the weather is better? I'll go with you and we can take Jacinta.'

She became agitated. 'No, no, we can't take the baby. It could be a rough crossing. And anyway, I want to go now and I want to go alone. I am a married woman and don't need a chaperone. I thought that Ashling would –'

'Would look after Jacinta? Is that fair?'

'She is a nanny. It's what she wanted.'

Ross thought of all the pleasure he had had with his aunt and uncle and family, and said, 'Well, if you are set on going, but I really would much rather someone was travelling with you.'

'Why? Don't you trust me? Anyone would think I was five years old! I'm tired of being treated like a child.'

'Then stop acting like one,' he said quietly.

'I'm sorry. I know I behave badly.'

Ross drew her to him. 'All right, you write to your mother and ask if it's convenient for you to come.'

The letter was sent and a reply came from Eileen saying Brendan would come over so he can travel back with her.

Tara threw the letter down. 'I don't want him! I'm a married woman. I travelled alone when I came to London when you and I were going to Gretna.'

Ross said, 'Yes, and I vowed I would never let you travel alone again. I wrote to your mother and told her if she would come over, stay a few days and travel back with you, I would pay her fare both ways. It seems she's sent Brendan instead.'

At this Tara flounced out and did not return for an hour. Then her manner was aloof and Ross wondered why she was so upset.

He was in bed that night and recalled Charles Kent, who was back for a holiday, saying he was going to pay a quick visit to Ireland before returning to the States and, remembering what a fuss Tara had made of him, wondered if she had been planning to travel on the same boat.

Suddenly he felt as though someone had stuck a knife in his guts.

The next morning Tara was still in a mood and he suggested it might be a good idea if she put a smile on her face for when her brother arrived. He was expected that day.

She said, 'He's someone I could do without.'

Ross caught hold of her arm and turned her to face him. 'I think we had better get a certain matter settled before your brother arrives full of goodwill. Why were you so anxious to travel alone to Ireland? Who were you planning to meet on board the boat?'

Her colour drained away, then flooded her cheeks. 'What are you insinuating?'

'Charles has been home and is planning to go to Ireland for a short visit this weekend, and I'm suggesting that you might have wanted to travel with him.'

He knew by the scared look in her eyes that he had been right and felt sick. There was a loud rat-tat at the front door and Ross, wanting to get out of the room, went to answer it.

'Surprise, surprise,' called Brendan, a broad smile on his face. 'I've brought a visitor.'

Ross found himself staring at another beaming face. Then he gave a laugh. 'I don't believe it. Conal! Where have you come from?'

'From the mountains. I told you I would visit you when I came to London and here I am but . . . much earlier than I expected. I met your brother-in-law on the crossing.'

Tara was suddenly there, embracing Brendan, then, full of smiles too, waited to be introduced to the shepherd.

'Well, come on in,' Ross exclaimed. 'Leave your luggage in the hall. I'll get Jane to make you a meal.'

No, they said, they had eaten, but Brendan suggested that a cup of tea would be very welcome. They went into the sitting room and Ashling followed them in with the baby. Brendan greeted her joyfully and after he had introduced her to Conal, the two men made a fuss of Jacinta, with Conal asking if he could hold her.

'Let her hold your finger,' said Ashling. 'She has such a strong grip.'

Brendan was suitably surprised. Conal handled the baby with expertise as though he had a family of his own, while Jacinta eyed both men in turn, as solemn as an owl. Her expression delighted them and Ross informed them he was sure she was weighing them up.

'And no doubt found us wanting,' Brendan declared with a grin. 'She's nearly asleep.'

Ashling took the baby upstairs to have a nap and when she came down again Tara was holding court, praising Conal for keeping Ross so interested during his visit to the mountains.

The shepherd replied quietly, 'But *your* husband is a most interesting man, Mrs Ferris. I was inspired by him. I had heard a great deal about London, but your husband brought it to life for me. Most people talk of the beautiful architecture, he did too, but he also spoke of the slums. I want to know every aspect of the city.'

He talked about Ireland, places he had visited on his travels and Tara said there was one place she would like especially to visit and asked if he had ever done the pilgrimage to Croagh Patrick.

'Ireland's Holy Mountain,' he said. 'That I have, once when I was alone and the next time on Pilgrimage Day. Each was a wondrous experience. The first time I climbed it the day was misty and a fine drizzle soaked me to the skin. It grieved me because I wanted to see the glorious view from the summit that I had been told about, but even the path ahead was blocked out. There are few experiences more uncanny than climbing a mountain in a mist. I had a terrible fear that I would step off into eternity. Then I thought, this is a Holy

Mountain from whence all demons have been banished and, as I thought it, the mist cleared and above me I saw a little Mass chapel. To build it, many, many seven-pound bags of cement had been left at the foot of the mountains and pilgrims had carried them to the summit as acts of devotion.'

Tara said, 'Is it true that some people walk barefooted up the mountain?'

'Indeed it is, and some pilgrims have been known to go part of the way on their knees.'

'Did you go right up to the shrine?' Brendan asked.

'I did, both times, but the first time impressed me the more. The shrine is smaller than I had imagined. There was a strange atmosphere, and I felt as though it was the most wonderful place I had ever knelt at and prayed. I remembered the story, told by medieval monks, that it was from this height that St Patrick flung his bell away, only to have it returned to him; and at each sound from the bell the toads and the adders fled from Ireland.'

'And did you believe it?' Brendan asked.

Conal looked at him in surprise. 'Of course.' The grandfather clock began to chime, and he got up. 'I must go. It's been wonderful to meet you all.'

They all begged him to stay a little longer, with Tara insisting that he at least have lunch with them. He agreed, but said he must leave afterwards, he was staying with friends in Poplar. Ross and Brendan said they would take him there.

Tara suggested that Conal come for dinner one evening before she went to Ireland and it was settled he would come on the Tuesday while Brendan was with them.

It was not until Ross and Brendan came back from taking Conal to Poplar that Brendan told the girls their mother had been ill with bronchitis.

'She did want to come,' he said, 'would have liked

nothing better, but it was impossible. She is, however, on the mend and is so looking forward to seeing you.

So far as Tara was concerned her mother might not have been mentioned. All she was interested in was finding out more about Conal. Was he planning to settle in London, or was this only a visit? Did he have a family?

Ashling said, 'Forgive me for interrupting but I would like to know more about Mama. How did she come to get bronchitis and is she confined to bed?'

Brendan said it started with a cold. She had sat up one night with Mrs McGowan, one of their tenants who was ill, and the old lady insisted on having the window open in spite of its being a cold, damp night. 'But there,' he added, 'Mother is improving every day and is up for most of the time.'

Tara was thoughtful for a moment, then looked up. 'I'm not sure whether it would be wise to go home now. I don't want to pick up her cold germ and pass it on to Jacinta.'

'Mother will be better by then. She has no fever or cough even now. Actually, she did ask the doctor about this and he was sure there would be no risk.'

Tara was still looking doubtful when Ross said coldly, 'Your mother would be the last person to allow you to take any risks.'

Although the incident of Charles Kent having gone to Ireland at the weekend still rankled with Ross, he decided to make no more mention of it because of Brendan being there. At bedtime, however, Tara brought it up as she was undressing.

'Well,' she said, 'isn't it time to get your grievance off your mind?'

'And what would that be?' He reached for his dressing gown.

'You know perfectly well what I mean. Your accusa-

300

tion that I had arranged to travel on the steamer to Ireland with Charles Kent.'

'Well, hadn't you? I didn't mean that Charles knew you arranged it, simply that you thought it would be nice to travel with him.'

'Oh, you did, did you?' She glared at him. 'I never guessed that you could be so despicable.'

The contempt in her voice inflamed him. 'And I never guessed that you could be so despicable as to palm another man's child on to me.'

'Oh, well, if you are going to bring that up every time we have words!' She sat on the stool at the dressing table and, swivelling round to face the mirror, picked up the hairbrush and began to brush her hair with vigorous strokes.

'Don't you think I have a right to retaliate when you describe me as being despicable?' Ross stormed. 'You had a ready-made husband, you had a mews cottage, which wasn't big enough for you to do your entertaining, and you not only grumbled that you were being neglected by not being taken to the theatre, but were conniving against me with Alicia Sylvain. Well, I've had enough of playing the loving husband and father!' He brought a suitcase from a cupboard and began bringing his clothes from the press.

Tara said, 'Ross,' in a scared voice. 'I'm sorry. I – I get a bit uppity now and again, but I don't really mean it. I can't help it.'

He threw a suit onto the bed. 'I'm sick to death of hearing you say you don't mean it, that you can't help it. You do mean it and you're vicious with it. I'm not taking any more.'

'Ross, please, please, don't leave us. I'll try and not say stupid things.'

It was the word 'us' that got to him. He would miss Jacinta. He brought another suit out of the wardrobe, stood with it for a moment, then threw it on to the bed too. It was no use, he couldn't go on in this way, Tara not only hankering after travelling with Charles Kent, but now wanting to cancel going to Ireland because of meeting Conal. Always having to have a change, never satisfied. What did it make him? He was an appendage in her life, nothing more.

He packed the case and was starting to get dressed when he caught sight of her and felt a sudden ache. Big tears were sliding slowly down her cheeks and she looked like a lost soul.

He said, 'Get into bed, Tara. I'll sleep next door. I need to be alone to think. I'll decide what to do tomorrow.'

'Yes,' she said, 'I'll understand if you don't want to stay.'

If it had been said with any self-pity he would have walked out but she had spoken in a matter of fact way.

She climbed onto the bed, he automatically pulled down the covers and when she slid into the bed he pulled them over her.

'We'll talk tomorrow, Tara.'

She nodded but when he went into the next room all he could see were two large sea-blue eyes brimming with tears, looking at him over the sheet, and he felt a tug at his heartstrings.

Fifteen minutes later he climbed into bed beside her. The pillow was wet with her tears and she gave little hiccupping sobs as she apologized for being such a dreadful wife. He soothed her as he might have done Jacinta.

'There, there, everything is all right.

It was an agony to stop himself from making love to her.

The next morning Brendan said to Tara, 'Are you all right, sis? You look a bit peaky. Not sickening for something, are you?'

'I hope not.' She laughed. To Ross it sounded forced.

302

'I think it was all the excitement of seeing you and meeting Conal. You must admit he's quite an extraordinary man.'

'So he is to be sure,' Brendan teased. 'I thought I knew a lot about Ireland, but after hearing Conal I realize how little I do know.' To Ross he said, 'Can I come to the docks with you today?'

'Yes, of course. I'd be delighted. John was saying I must bring you along.'

When the two men had left Ashling said bluntly to Tara, 'So what was all the trouble last night between you and Ross? I've never known him sound so angry.'

She told Ashling about having wanted to travel on the steamer to Ireland with Charles Kent, and then half deciding not to go back with Brendan.

Ashling said she thought that Ross had every right to be angry. 'You don't deserve him. He's loving, generous, he adores Jacinta and you start laying the law down about what *you* want. You've been spoilt, Tara, and it's time you started to spoil him for a change.'

'Or perhaps you would like to spoil him,' Tara snapped. 'I've noticed the way you look at him at times, all loving.'

'That's it,' declared Ashling. 'You can get another nanny to look after Jacinta. You've made just one too many of your snide remarks about my only having eyes for Ross.'

'Ashling!' Tara's eyes were wide with alarm. 'You can't mean it. The three of us have always been making asides about liking one another's men friends, but they've never caused any ill feeling.'

'I agree, but the remarks you've made to me recently are quite different. Less than two weeks after I arrived you were letting me know that Ross was your property. Oh, you spoke very lightly, but the warning was there in your eyes. Your eyes have always given you away, Tara.'

Tara lowered her gaze. 'You're right. But how do I overcome my jealousy? Ross tells me it's no use saying I can't help it because I can. But I *can't*, Ashling, I really can't.' She spoke in an impassioned way. 'It's there inside me. I must have been born with these nasty little traits. Don't leave me, Ashling, please. I need you. Jacinta needs you. You make a much better mother than I do.'

'Now that's nonsense.'

'No, it isn't. I couldn't tell anyone else this, but I'm still afraid of holding Jacinta, afraid I'll drop her, then what would I do if I hurt her? I worry all the time about it.'

Ashling felt a lump come into her throat. She went over and put her arms around her sister. 'Oh, Tara, what am I going to do with you? You are your own worst enemy. Stop thinking in this way. You know how Conal was talking about mind over matter? Well, this is what you must do. I'll let you deal with Jacinta more until you get confident. You love her, I know that.'

'I adore her.' There were now tears in Tara's eyes and Ashling, near to tears herself, said, 'You must start bathing her. We'll work together and put everything right.'

The next morning Tara laughed with delight when she managed to bath Jacinta without any trouble.

'I've done it, Ashling. I must tell Ross. I'm not going home with Brendan, not because of wanting to see Conal while he's here, but because I've become a proper mother at last.'

Ross was duly told about Tara bathing the baby and he said to Ashling later, 'I get so cross with her at times, sometimes she's all woman and other times a child.'

Ashling tried not to feel envious of her sister who had a husband who could forgive her all her sudden changes of mood.

The next morning when it was the baby's bathtime, Tara was missing. She had remembered she had promised to call on Catherine early. The story was so garbled Ashling gave up trying to sort it out. The following morning at Jacinta's bathtime Tara had a headache. She really did have to lie down. Ashling just sighed.

Catherine, James and Marianne had also been invited for dinner on Tuesday, and Tara was none too pleased when they and Ashling seemed to come in for a great deal of attention from Conal. It stemmed from music, all of them being lovers of opera. Several times Tara tried to change the subject, but they were not deterred. And after the evening was over and she found that Conal was going to spend the following two weeks visiting missions in the East End, she decided, after all, to go to Ireland with Brendan.

It was planned they would leave on Thursday and that Marianne would come to stay with Ashling for company, but when Tara realized how well Ross, Ashling and Marianne got on, she changed her mind again about going to Ireland, saying that on second thoughts her mother might still be able to pass on germs and she could not take any risks with the baby.

Brendan suggested that Ashling might like a break and come home with him but before she had a chance to reply Tara was in a panic, begging her not to leave, the baby needed her, she couldn't deal with her as Ashling could.

Ashling, who had been undecided when Brendan mentioned her going home with him, said to Tara, 'Very well, I shall stay, but from now on, Tara, you are going to share looking after Jacinta. And I mean it. I could be ill sometime and you would have to take over.'

'Oh, I will, I definitely will. I'm looking forward to it, once Brendan has gone.'

The following morning, after Brendan had gone, Tara bathed Jacinta and, in spite of being nervous, was jubilant later that she had succeeded. It did not make her want to do it every morning, however, and she would have wriggled out of it had not Ashling been adamant that she must continue on odd mornings to bath the child in case of an emergency.

A letter came from Eileen to say how disappointed she was that Tara had not come for a visit, but went on to add that Brendan and Celina's wedding was to go ahead so they were to get prepared to come to Ireland in about two months' time. She said that she was almost back to normal after her bout of illness and was so looking forward to all the family being together again.

When she had read the letter, Tara sat daydreaming for a while, then she said, staring out of the window, 'I think that Charles Kent would make a lovely husband. He travels, is always moving around. He's been all over America.'

'Perhaps because he's grieving over the loss of his wife and child and can't settle.' said Ashling.

Tara, unheeding, went on. 'And there is Conal. He will be going all over trying to find how he can help other people.'

'Yes, Tara, *poverty-stricken* people, living in slums! Do you remember how you used to screw up your face when Mama sent us with food and clothes for the workers who were unable to work any more?'

Tara raised her shoulders. 'They were smelly.'

'It was the smell of infirmity, Tara, old age. When will you learn? When will you start being thankful for what you have in life, a wonderful husband, a beautiful child? Why are you always reaching for the moon, which is unattainable? Grow up, grow up!'

Tara looked across at her. 'Don't think because you lead an ordinary life that I should do the same.'

Ashling leaned forward and said quietly, 'It might interest you to know that I have been offered one of the kinds of lives that you thought might be interesting. Conal has written to ask me if I would like to work with him.' She got up. 'I'll let you know what I decide.' She walked to the door.

'You can't do this to me,' Tara shouted. 'I need you. Jacinta needs you.'

Ashling went out, closing the door quietly behind her.

Tara sat back in the chair, misery overwhelming her. *She* wanted to work with Conal. Her sister had cheated her.

23

Tara realized that Ashling had not been cheating her. She was single and free. But Tara felt hurt that her sister had not confided in her. She was about to go upstairs and find out more about her plans when Ashling came in looking contrite.

'Sorry, Tara, for being so abrupt with you about Conal. But you see I envy you having Ross and Jacinta. You should be a close little family and instead you grumble.'

'I know it's wrong, but sometimes I feel caged.' She paused. 'If you work with Conal what would you be doing?'

'Travelling around, helping the poor, I suppose.'

'Why didn't you tell me he was writing to you? We've always shared everything.'

Ashling sighed. 'I didn't tell you because I knew you would be upset if I were to take him up on his offer.'

There was a silence between them, then Tara looked up. 'I feel bitter at Conal's behaviour. We gave him hospitality and he tries to steal you from us. He, who preaches religion, is a schemer.'

'No, Tara, he did not try to steal me from you. He suggested I talk it over with you both. Also he does not preach anything. All he's trying to do is to ease the lot of poverty-stricken families.'

'And no doubt you've talked it over with Ross, telling him how unhappy you are, living with me who is always grumbling.'

'You are the only one I've discussed it with. Unfortunately, you are only interested in yourself. We all have our dreams, Tara.'

'I know. I daydream, but I do love Ross and Jacinta. If I were to die, Ashling, would you marry Ross and look after them both?'

'Stop talking like that.' Ashling spoke sharply. 'It's morbid.'

'Young people as well as old die. It's not an impossibility.'

'I won't discuss it. It doesn't even bear thinking about and I would advise you to put thoughts like that out of your mind. It can cause depression very quickly.'

'I'm not being morbid. It's something I must know. Just say yes or no. I can't bear the thought that some stranger would look after Jacinta if I were to die.'

'All right, yes, I would look after the baby, but now can we talk about more pleasant subjects?'

'Ashling, you're not really thinking of going to work with Conal, are you?' There was a pleading in Tara's voice.

'I don't know, I really don't. When I think of leaving Jacinta it hurts. On the other hand I shall have to leave her sometime. I want to make a life for myself.'

'Would you marry Conal if he asked you?'

Ashling gave an impatient sigh. 'Tara, it never even occurred to me and I don't suppose it did to him. The subject is closed.' She got up. 'Don't forget that Catherine and Marianne will be here soon.'

Ashling, usually so clear thinking, found her thoughts in turmoil. When her sister had mentioned dying, the thought had flashed across her mind that she would be there to look after Ross. Holy Mother of God, what sort of person was she becoming? Should she go home?

But going home, she decided, would not bring her peace of mind. She would be leaving Ross whom she loved and, worse still, leaving Jacinta who had become a part of her life.

Tara's head began to ache. She often had headaches nowadays, which had first started when she knew she was pregnant. What a shock it had been. It was a pity that the young man who seduced her had been married. He would have made quite a nice husband. She frowned, trying to think of his name, but it eluded her. Had she ever known it? She just couldn't remember.

Ross kept wondering that evening what had happened between Tara and Ashling. Their laughter seemed forced. Also, when Jacinta was ready for bed, Tara had gone up with Ashling to see the baby into her cot, which was unusual.

Later, when he had Ashling on her own and asked if something was wrong, she was silent for a moment before replying, 'I told Tara today that Conal has asked me to help him with his work.'

Ross could not have looked more astonished if she had told him that Jacinta had started to talk.

'Work with Conal? You are not going, of course.'

'Why shouldn't I? I have no ties.'

'No, but – well, I thought that you liked looking after the baby.'

'I do. It's just that, like Tara, I need a change now and then.'

'Tara is woolly-minded, bless her, and will always be needing a change. You are so sensible, Ashling.'

'In other words, I'm plain and I'm likely to be a spinster.' There was a bitter note in her voice and she felt ashamed.

'You are not plain, Ashling,' Ross said softly. 'Conal was greatly taken with you, thought you had a wonderful personality and said you were one of the most sensible people he had ever met. I am not saying don't go, even though I know we shall all miss you terribly. But I would ask that you give the matter some thought. Don't feel guilty if you don't accept. Conal already has a small army of helpers. He has the power of drawing people to him.'

Ashling had a sudden feeling of disillusionment. Why

310

had she thought that she was important to Conal? As Ross had said, she would just be one of his many workers.

Ross went on, his tone earnest, 'Don't let me put you off, Ashling. There are thousands of people in the world who need help, a friendly hand, need someone to care, need to feel wanted. And really, isn't this so in all walks of life? Yes, even we who live very comfortably and have enough to eat.'

'You're right, Ross.'

Ross had a sudden bereft feeling and was not sure whether it was the thought of perhaps losing Ashling, or whether it was that Tara these days always seemed to want to be with other men.

It was not until the following evening at dinner that Ashling announced she had decided to go to have a talk with Conal.

'I have to,' she said earnestly, 'otherwise I might regret it later in life. I've always had strong leanings to help poor people. This seems to be an opportunity. It's like fate, as it were. If you had not gone into the mountains to find your father, Ross, you would never have met Conal and we would never have known anything about him.'

Tara began to plead, 'Oh, Ashling, you can't leave. We need you. Jacinta needs you, desperately.'

'I shall stay until you can find a suitable nanny.'

'I can't manage without you, Ashling, you know I can't,' Tara wailed. 'I couldn't bath her if you weren't there. Did you see her this morning when I was putting her in the bath? She gave a little gasp and a shiver. Her tiny hands were trembling. I would drop her if you weren't there.'

'Tara, calm down.' Ashling spoke gently. 'You've done very well. It's just a question of holding her firmly. And anyway, I would be back in time to give Jacinta her bath.'

'You must be fair to Ashling,' said Ross. 'We can't keep her tied here. She could meet someone tomorrow, fall in love and want to get married.'

'She's in love with Conal, that's what! She'll leave and she won't come back.' Tara was on the verge of hysteria and Ashling, after a quick glance at Ross, went and put her arms around her.

'It's all right, Tara, I won't go to see Conal. I'll stay and look after Jacinta and you. Come and lie down.'

'I have such a headache.' Tara began to cry. Ross picked her up. 'Come on, my love. Ashling will give you a pill for your headache.'

When Tara was tucked up in bed, Ross and Ashling came downstairs.

Ross said, 'I must get the doctor to look at her. There's something sadly wrong. She's been acting strange for some time.'

Ashling explained that many women suffered from depression after having had a baby. 'It takes some time to get over it. The doctor might suggest a change. She might recover sooner if she went home for a while. She does get terribly homesick.'

Ross shook his head. 'I don't think that's the answer. I feel that Tara needs extra treatment. I'll arrange for her to see a specialist.'

'Then be honest with him,' Ashling said quietly.

'Honest in what way?'

Ashling hesitated a moment then plunged in, 'About the baby. I think it would be important for the specialist to know the tension Tara has been under since she knew she was pregnant. It must have been a very big strain on her emotions.'

'You knew?'

'Yes. Mama told me at Christmas. She was trying to find a reason for Tara's erratic behaviour. Although I had no particular liking for your father, I just could not imagine him seducing his own niece.'

'Rage blinded my judgement when I was first told about it. I refused to see any goodness in him at all. Now I'm beginning to think he had a difficult life with my mother. There are still a lot of things to be cleared up, but they will have to come later. At the moment I feel I have enough to contend with. Tara is a complex person. She never seems to know what she wants.'

'I think that circumstances have a lot to do with it. She's a warm, loving person, generous. She was the first daughter and so was a little spoilt, and, of course, being such a beautiful child, she got used to people making a fuss of her. But although Tara played on her looks she was always the lovely warm-hearted girl that she grew up to be.'

'So what is the reason for this drastic change in her? Surely not just since she was pregnant?'

'I would say it was. She never had any troubles to cope with. It must have been a dreadful shock to her and what would make it worse was being unable to confide in anyone. It must have played havoc with her, having to bottle it all up. This, I would say, is affecting her now.'

Ross smiled. It was a gentle, teasing smile. 'Why should I call a specialist in when I have you?' Then, soberly he added, 'If Tara has to go away, Ashling, would you go with her? I'll engage someone to look after Jacinta. I feel she needs someone close to her, who understands her.'

Ashling hesitated. 'I don't think she would want me with her. I am the enemy at the moment, but there, what is needed is expert medical advice.'

Ross agreed and an appointment was made with a doctor for the following day.

When Tara was told about the interview she was furious and refused to go. Ross, who until then had been very patient with her, lost his temper.

He said, 'Tara, if I have to tie you up and put

you in a cab you are going to Harley Street to see Mr Rowan, so make up your mind how to go, quietly, or –'

She gave in but would not let Ross help her into the cab.

When they returned Tara was quiet and went straight upstairs, Ross following.

He came down alone and said that Tara had gone to bed, then went on, 'When we arrived at Harley Street she was quite passive but after Mr Rowan had examined her and suggested she went to Ireland for a while she became aggressive, told him she was staying at home and no one could persuade her to do otherwise. All she wanted was to be left alone to rest.

'And did the specialist agree?'

'He was most patient with her. He pointed out that she had a husband and child who needed her. Many people who thought they knew their own body were now dead and buried. He then went on to say that a few days in bed would do her no harm, but asked that she would take some medicine he would prescribe for her. When she hesitated he sat looking at her for a while then said quietly, "Mrs Ferris, you are too young and too beautiful to die." '

'So she gave in?'

Ross sighed. 'Yes, but will she carry out his instructions? I think the medicine will calm her, make her sleep. That is, if she takes it. She wouldn't take any while I was in the room. She insisted she be left alone.'

Tara had taken the medicine. She slept all that day and took another dose when Ashling poured it for her. The next morning she poured it herself. And for the next three days she lived in a dreamy world where she was not interested in anything.

On the fourth day she said she wanted to get up. She felt much better. No, she said, there was no longer a need for medicine.

Although she sat about most of the time, she took an interest in the baby and was her own sweet, loving self to Ross.

'Thank heaven she's back to normal again,' he said to Ashling. 'Long may it continue.'

'I hope so. I must say, she's recovered from the depression sooner than I expected.'

When Catherine and Marianne called Tara was full of going to the shops in a few days' time.

'Good,' Catherine said. 'There's nothing wrong with a woman who talks about going on a shopping spree. We'll have a lovely time. When are you planning this big spend?'

'Saturday? No, let us say Monday. I'll get a cab and pick you both up about eleven o'clock.'

Tara was all excitement on Monday morning, telling Ashling they would have lunch out and not to expect her until late afternoon.

Ashling was busy getting the baby ready to take her for a walk in her baby carriage when Tara called upstairs from the hall, 'I'm away, Ashling. Give Jacinta a hug and a kiss for me.'

When Ashling went out onto the landing to tell her to take it easy and not get too tired, the front door was closing.

Half an hour later Catherine phoned to ask if Tara was all right. She had not yet arrived.

And from then on it was all panic.

Ashling phoned Ross who arrived with John. They went to the cab rank and found the man who had picked Tara up. He had taken her to Harrods and left her there. He said she was carrying a suitcase and he asked if he could help her with it but she told him she could manage.

When the men returned Catherine and Marianne, agitated, came in with them.

'Why the suitcase?' Catherine exclaimed. Then, 'Oh,

315

was Harrods just a blind to put us off the track? But where could she be bound for?'

'Conal?' Ashling said suddenly.

Ross shook his head. 'Conal would have brought her back.'

John suggested she might have gone to Ireland. Ross said they would try all venues before getting in touch with the family as it would only start them worrying.

Ross and Ashling went through all of Tara's things to see if they could get the smallest hint of where she might have gone, but drew a blank.

Ashling said, 'Why not telephone Conal? Tara might have gone there, he might be talking to her now. You have the address.'

A woman answered the telephone where Conal was staying. She said he had just left for the mission; she would call him back.

He came to the phone breathless. 'Ross, what a nice surprise. I was going down the street when Mrs Bates called me. How are you?'

When Ross explained why he was phoning, Conal sobered and said that Tara had telephoned him the day before, saying she just wanted to know how he was getting on and if he had plenty of helpers. If not, she was available.

'She was laughing,' he said, 'and I treated it in a jesting way. I told her I had acquired many disciples but one more would not go unnoticed. She then asked me if I meant it and I was not sure how to take it. She had gone suddenly serious. I told her I would call on you both the next day and she said, no, no, she had not been well, but although feeling much better, she was not yet ready for visitors. I accepted it and told her to look after herself. But I must admit it worried me a little. I intended to get in touch with you at the office but it was a hectic day at the mission. Let me know if she returns. If not I'll try and get up a search party.'

When Ross went back to the others he said, 'What on earth possessed Tara to want to work in the East End? She has a home and family to look after.'

'Just change, I should imagine,' Ashling said. 'But I don't think she would go wandering on her own in the East End. She wanted to work with Conal. She thought him an interesting man, which of course he is, and she would no doubt be disappointed that he had plenty of helpers.' She suddenly tensed and when Ross asked what was wrong she said, 'I've just thought of Alicia Sylvain. Do you think that she could be involved in any way?'

Ross's mouth tightened. 'She could be. But where in heaven's name could we look for her? Not the Savoy, I'm sure of that.'

Then Jane came in with an envelope saying, 'This has just been delivered, Mr Ferris.'

Ross glanced at it, then jumped up. 'It's from Tara. Who brought it?' he asked Jane.

'A youth, but he'll be gone by now, sir.'

'Damn.' Ross slit open the envelope. He read the note enclosed then said angrily to Ashling, 'She's making a fool of us. Here, read it.'

Ashling read it out: *'Dear Ross, I'm sorry I had to leave but I couldn't stay any longer. I've left a note entitled To Whom It May Concern, explaining why I had to leave. But it's hidden. You'll have to search for it if you are interested in knowing why I couldn't stay. I love you and Jacinta and everyone, Tara.'* Ashling looked up, her eyes brimming with tears. 'She's sick, Ross, very sick. I can't understand why you are angry.'

He walked over to the window and said in a low voice, 'I know she is and I'm annoyed with myself for being angry.'

John went to him. 'Come along, Ross, sit down. I'll pour you a drink.'

Ross sat down. 'What can we do? Where can we

317

look? *Is* there a note or is it a figment of her imagination?'

John said, 'I think there will be a note somewhere. And I don't think she's mad, just come to the end of her tether. We can start searching the house.'

'There's a hundred places it could be,' Ross protested. 'I wouldn't know where to start. It could be in one of the books in the bookcases and how many books are there? A hundred?'

'If there were five hundred, we would have to go through them,' Ashling said quietly. 'And if you can't be bothered to go through everything then I will. Excuse me, I'll make a start.'

'Ashling —' Ross covered his face with his hands then lowered them. 'Forgive me. I'm worried sick about Tara. I want to know *now* where she is. She's such a helpless sort of person.'

It was decided that the five of them would do a room at a time, each taking a part to search. They started on the attics.

In the middle of the search Jacinta started a whining cry, which was so unusual for her. She was a good baby, who had bursts of crying, but mostly when she was hungry.

Jane offered to look after her but was unable to pacify her. Ashling took over. It sounded to her as though Jacinta was missing her mother. Ashling cuddled her and sang little lullabies and gradually the crying eased to little hiccupping sobs that pulled at Ashling's heartstrings. She held the baby cheek to cheek, patting her back.

'It's all right, my darling, your mother loves you. She will be back soon.'

But would she? Where could she have gone to? Was there some other man in her life that they knew nothing about?

By early evening they had been through the whole house, Ross and John tackling private papers together

318

and all of them having gone through the books and drawn a blank.

They sat down together for dinner in a state of exhaustion. Ashling said, 'I feel it's time to let the family know what has happened. We must, it's only fair. I know they are going to be terribly worried but if we let it go another day in the hope that we find Tara . . . and don't, they are going to be more upset.'

Ross got up, looking pale and distraught, and said he would do it now. He would send a telegram. He had been praying it would not be necessary. He said, 'And if nothing has happened by morning the police will have to be informed, something I had hoped to avoid.'

None of them had an appetite and they were soon sitting down to coffee when they once more went over every minute detail that might give them a lead to solving the mystery. But without success.

At nine o'clock a reply came from Eileen to the telegram that Ross had sent: *Will arrive tomorrow with Brendan.*

This started them talking again and at ten o'clock Catherine and Marianne got up to leave with the promise they would call early the next morning. John said he would see them home, then would come back to stay overnight.

When they had gone, Ashling said, 'I'm glad John is coming back, Ross. You need support, but try not to stay up too late. You'll need all your strength tomorrow to face not only the police but Mama and Brendan. They are bound to be in a state. Something like this is always worse when one is deeply affected by the trouble but has not yet been involved.'

The telephone rang, startling them both. Ross jumped up to go to take the call and in his haste knocked over a chair. Ashling sat tense, hands clasped tightly.

When Ross returned he spread his hands with a gesture of despair. 'It was Conal, wanting to know if we had heard anything. He apologized for ringing so late. He had been giving a talk at the mission. He offered to come over in the morning but I explained about the police and Eileen and Brendan arriving and he said he understood. He made me promise to get in touch with him if we need any extra help. I told him about the note.'

'I think we should tell everyone about it who knows Tara. Some small thing might be mentioned that had not registered with us.'

Ross sighed. 'You could be right. I just don't know. Oh, Ashling, why did Tara leave? Did I fail her in some way?'

'Don't ever reproach yourself, Ross. I think there's a lot we don't know and won't know until we find the note she left.'

John came back and after Ashling had asked that they would not sit up too late, she went up to bed. She walked over to the cot, always feeling a warmth steal into her as she looked at Jacinta, who went to sleep with her fist curled under her chin.

This time Ashling's heart skipped a beat, then began racing.

The cot was empty!

It couldn't be. She flung the covers off one by one, then looked around her as though the baby had escaped and was hiding. She felt encased in ice. She tried to shout but no sound came.

Then suddenly she was running down the stairs. She stumbled and went headlong into the hall. Fortunately, she fell on a rug and when she shouted this time, her voice had come back.

'Ross, Ross, Jacinta's been kidnapped!'

She couldn't find the strength to get to her feet. She was aware of running footsteps then blacked out.

When she came to, she was on a sofa in the drawing room and John was holding smelling salts under her nose. She pushed the bottle away and said, 'Where is Ross?'

'In the hall, telephoning the police. Lie down, Ashling, you've had an awful shock.'

The evening turned out to be like living in a nightmare, the police asking numerous questions, questions that had no answers. It was found that the kidnapper had come in through a ground-floor window and they presumed it was someone who knew where all the baby clothes were kept, for they, too, were gone. But who?

Tara or an accomplice?

24

The next day, the worst part was waiting for Eileen and Brendan to arrive. John had gone to meet them and he had said he would break the news to them about Jacinta.

It was an emotional meeting, with Ross shocked at how pale and thin Eileen was, but she dismissed it. The bronchitis was responsible but she was over it now and just needed time to recover.

She cried when she hugged Ashling, saying she only hoped it was Tara who had come back for Jacinta and in the next breath added, 'But what sort of life would it be for the baby, the mother running away to heaven knows where? Tara must be very sick indeed.'

The police came again to interview Eileen and Brendan, but there was nothing to add to what they already knew.

A number of people telephoned, having heard about the trouble. Ross said wryly, 'Bad news travels fast.'

Ashling said the more people who know about it the more help they could get.

Charles Kent called unexpectedly at the house and asked if he could help in any way. Ross invited him in and asked if he had seen Tara recently.

'Not recently. I've been in Ireland, just got back yesterday. I saw James Davies this morning and he told me all that had happened.'

Eileen said, 'If only we could find the motive for Tara leaving.'

Ashling looked thoughtful, 'There must be reasons behind the words To Whom It May Concern, and why she has hidden the letter.'

Brendan said, 'To Whom It May Concern suggests something legal, a document.'

Charles Kent sat up and repeated, 'A document? This somehow rings a bell in connection with Tara. But what?' He got up and walked around, frowning in concentration. 'I feel that there is something to do with the mews cottage. We were celebrating you and Tara moving in, Ross. But where does the document fit in with Tara?'

Ashling said suddenly, 'Could it be the secret drawer? There were papers in it?'

'Y-yes, but it was to do with my family tree. Oh, just a moment – Tara was most interested in the words, to whom it may concern. She found them fascinating, said that supposing the document had been there for two hundred years, how different the way of life would have been then to what it was now – that people now could learn a lot from mistakes others had made in the past.'

Eileen said quietly. 'There are your reasons, Ashling. She perhaps wrote down the mistakes she had made and put them in the drawer, hoping that in the future people would benefit from them.'

Brendan queried, 'But if Tara was expecting people to read her confession in centuries to come why did she leave a note to Ross to say that the note she had left was hidden?'

'And how did she get into the cottage?' Ross asked. 'I believe the young couple who live there were away.'

'They were, still are, but Tara had a key. She was always saying she must remember to let me have it.' He paused and looked at Ross. 'Would you care to come with me and take a look in the drawer? The Simpsons gave me free access to the cottage.'

'Yes, I would.'

The letter was there. Charles handed it to Ross and left him so he could read it alone. There were two closely written pages, the outpourings of a woman bearing her soul.

It was headed, 'To whom It May Concern.'

Today I left my husband and baby, both of whom I love very much, in the hope I can find the reason why I behave the way I do. I am also cutting myself off from my very dear family who have always been so kind and loving to me.

I am writing my faults down in the hope that if I find the answer to my problems it may help other people in future years to avoid making the same mistakes.

My name is Tara Ferris. I have a brother who is the eldest and the only son. I am the eldest of three daughters.

From being a child I have been told I am beautiful. Perhaps this was a mistake. I grew up expecting everyone to give me special treatment. My mother, very sensibly, disciplined me as she did my brother and sisters, but I resented it. I sulked.

Although I loved my sisters I was jealous when they had praise for something good they had done. I have a cousin Ross, who I loved from being small. I claimed him as my own.

When I grew up and became pregnant I lied and said that Ross's father was the one responsible. Ross married me to save my family and myself from shame. I lied on the Bible, with my rosary in my hand. It was a terrible thing to do. Why did God make me wicked? I didn't want to lie. I just couldn't help it. I do a lot of bad things that just happen and no one will believe it when I say I can't help doing them. I can't bath my baby regularly because I'm terrified I will let her fall, and no one will believe me when I say I can't help feeling this way. I adore her and can't bear the thought that I might hurt her.

I long to be liked. I enjoy being with interesting men. I love my husband, he's a good and generous man, but I like to be with other men too. I would like to go away and

*help Conal with the poor people. I would like to go travelling
with Charles Kent when he goes abroad. I know it's wrong
but I can't help it.*

*I've wanted for nothing in my life and I think this is
perhaps the reason I am having to suffer, for taking
everything and giving nothing in return. I do want to know
a different kind of life. Now I have decided I must leave
my lovely husband and baby and try and do a penance to
rid me of the wretched faults I have.*

*I know that the Devil is always waiting to pounce on
sinners, but perhaps God will help me. He should. He
made me the way I am.*

*If I manage to cast out the evil in me I shall return and
write my experiences. I pray that this will be soon. I am
aching now to feel my husband's arms around me and to
hold my baby to me and feel her soft skin against my face,
to see her smile and punch my chin with her tiny fist to
let me know that she loves me too.*

*Please God, be kind to me. Give me strength on my
pilgrimage.*

Ross lowered the letter. If only he had known, had
understood her torment. He must find her, bring her
back, allay her fears, help her wounds to heal.

He sat for some time, then when he was calmer, he
went downstairs to find Charles. He told him briefly
the contents of the letter, missing out the part about
the baby being illegitimate.

Charles was full of concern. 'Tara is such a warm,
loving person. She's such good company and is so
effervescent. How tragic that she had kept all these
fears bottled up. The thing is, where can she be?'

Ross got up. 'I must go. The family will be waiting
to know if there is a letter.'

Not wanting to reveal all the contents of the letter,
Ross explained that some of it was personal to him but
told them of Tara's thoughts. Eileen and Ashling wept.

The main question was where to start searching.

Ross suggested asking Conal's help. He had people working for him in the poor areas of London. He felt it was where Tara could be. He would take a photograph of her to Conal.

Conal and his helpers, however, who now numbered about forty, had not seen her, but then, as John said, anyone could hide in the warren of streets and tenements for months without being noticed.

The police reported several false alarms and Eileen was near despair when she had a letter from Cook saying that Patrick was not well, he had a dreadful cough.

'We must go home,' Eileen wailed. 'Brendan will have to take over Patrick's work. Oh, Ross, I hate to leave not knowing anything about Tara.'

Ashling told her mother she would let her know the moment there was any news.

Eileen looked from her daughter to Ross and felt worried. Ashling had not only taken over the routine of the house, but Ross too. She had known for a long time that Ashling was in love with him, but had not worried, knowing how sensible her youngest offspring was. But now Ross was vulnerable, his emotions taut. He wasn't sleeping. Twice, aware that someone was downstairs, Eileen had come down and found him moving around restlessly. If Ashling were to come down and offer comfort, goodness knows what it could lead to.

Ashling, guessing her thoughts, said, 'Mama, Ross is married to Tara and loves her. I love him too, yes, but I'm not likely to cause any more trouble than we have already.'

'No, of course not.' But Eileen still felt worried.

With her mother and Brendan gone, Ashling felt at a loose end. Ross, who had not been to the office since Tara had disappeared, had now gone back. Ashling

326

decided to go to see Conal, find out how his work was progressing and if there had been any sightings of Tara and the baby.

She had expected the mission to be in a well-populated poor area but it turned out to be in a quiet street. The mission itself, however, was not quiet. When she opened the door that led into the hall a wave of voices blasted her eardrums. Well-dressed women mingled with the poorer people. A well spoken young woman asked if she could help. She had to raise her voice to make herself heard. Ashling shouted back that she wanted to speak to Conal.

The woman took her by the arm and led her to a small room at the back where it was a little quieter. 'If you give me your name I'll tell him you are here.'

Ashling did so and added, 'Say I only want a quick word with him.'

The woman nodded and went outside.

Curious, Ashling opened the door that led into the hall. She saw that a long table must have held food. Several women were clearing away empty plates. Some children started to chase around the hall, but were immediately stopped by their mothers and scolded. Several babies were crying, but were being shushed. There was quite a good proportion of men and she thought they were probably out of work.

A voice behind her said, 'Miss McCoy!' and Ashling swung round to see Conal, his arms outstretched towards her, his face full of pleasure. 'I trust you've come to tell me that your sister has been found.'

'Unfortunately no. I was hoping that you might have heard something.'

'No.' His expression sobered. 'But come over to the shed where we won't be interrupted.'

The shed held a large old table, and chairs were placed around it. Part of the table held papers and files. Conal said, 'This serves as my office and committee room.' He pulled out two chairs. 'Do sit down, Miss McCoy.'

'Please call me Ashling.'

She told him about the letter and how the baby had been taken from her cot and he looked so sorrowful it made her want to cry.

'Your sister was so full of life, one can't imagine all this unhappiness locked inside her. Pray God it will soon be released and she will be back to normal again. Many people are on the lookout for Mrs Ferris. Her photograph is on the board in the hall. I shall tell them about baby Jacinta.'

Ashling said, 'I was surprised at how many helpers you have.'

'They are splendid, Ashling. Many of them are wealthy people, but none has a superior air. I turned down the offers of help from people who do charity work for their own satisfaction, people who want recognition for the money and the time they give.'

Conal talked about his work and his expression reminded her of her mother once describing the children, when they were small and bathed and ready for bed, as having an angel shine. Conal, as he talked about the people he helped, acquired a spiritual inward beauty.

'It's so rewarding, Ashling. When I opened the mission people came in dribs and drabs and they were withdrawn, defeated. I gave talks, asked them to talk to one another. But the ice was eventually broken at the suggestion of one of the helpers that we offer food and cocoa. They flocked in. But what pleased me was that then they came to hear me speak without any food being offered. There was communication among them. They unburdened themselves of their troubles. One woman, who had a bruised face, told me, "My husband bashes me about, but since coming to hear you speak, he does say he's sorry afterwards." She smiled a twisted smile and said, "It's a start, guv."'

'Our helpers collected clothing for them. Initially I made it plain that if I found out any clothes had gone to the pawnshop for money to buy drink they would be barred from receiving anything else. It seems to have worked in most cases. What I want now is better accommodation for them. Some are living in hovels, or in tenements with stinking drains, rooms overridden with cockroaches and bugs tormenting them.'

Ashling winced. 'You really have your work cut out.'

'But it's so worthwhile. I said to one of my colleagues last week that I regretted the years I had spent in the monastery and he told me no, that without those years, I would not have known how to approach these people. And do you know, Ashling, he was right. I can see now they were valuable years.'

His soul seemed to be shining through.

Ashling got up to go. No, he said, she must come into the hall with him and he would introduce her to some of his helpers and the people who needed help.

Ashling had to admit that the helpers were most pleasant, asking if she was coming join them. She told them not at the present, but might later.

The poorer people did nothing but praise Conal. 'A saint, 'e is,' said one woman. 'Can't do enough for us folk. Sat up wiv Mrs Blake's 'usband night afore last, and the old man said there were angels singin' near, and 'e were better the next mornin'. Got the gift, 'as Conal. I could kneel to 'im and so could a lot more who worship 'im, miss.'

A small child in her mother's arms held out her arms to Ashling and she took her and laid her cheek to the little girl's.

The mother said to Ashling, 'You must be Irish, miss. Brindy won't go to anyone who isn't.'

Conal said softly in an Irish brogue, 'She is, an' all, Mrs McNulty, and isn't that strange now?'

Ashling left with the promise to come again soon.

Conal walked to the main road with her, where there was a cab rank, and clasped her hand in his.

'It's been so good to see you, Ashling. Rest assured that many people are looking for Tara and the baby. If we hear of only a fleeting sighting I shall let you know at once.'

He helped her into the cab and she waved to him until the cab had turned a curve in the road, and she was sure that she would always see Conal as she left him that day, in his cream linen robe, a look of tenderness in his dark eyes.

On the drive back, Ashling had many things to think about. There had been quite a lot of helpers in the mission, but there was room for many, many more. When Tara and Jacinta were back safely at home, should she offer her services?

The question pulled at her. Tara would need help. Ross would need help too. And she needed to be close to Jacinta. It was a force inside her. It was all right to say that sacrifices had to be made where love was concerned, but it was not going to be easy. The rest of the day was going to be long waiting for him to come home. If only she could have had news of Tara and the baby to take away his awful look of strain.

When she got back Jane said, 'A young lady called, Miss McCoy. She asked for you or Mr Ferris.'

Ashling pulled off her gloves. 'Did she give her name?'

'Yes, Miss Rosin Dannet. She said she would call again later.'

Ashling felt as though the room was spinning around her, then it steadied.

Rosin . . . whom Ross truly loved.

25

Why had Rosin come back? Obviously she must have heard about Tara leaving Ross, but this was no reason why she should turn up now. Was she under the impression that Tara had left him for good? If so, it was not fair. He did love Tara, even though it was different to the love he had for Rosin. What was more, he had a child, whom he really adored.

Ashling was in a fever of impatience. Why didn't Rosin come back? She would have liked to have had a talk with her before Ross came home, find out her real reason for calling. Rosin was supposed to be very different from her wily double, Alicia Sylvain, but that was only Ross's opinion, and men were more gullible than women.

When Ashling asked Jane if she was sure that Miss Dannet had said she would come back later, Jane said, 'I'm positive, Miss Ashling. I couldn't tell her what time you would be back because I didn't know, but I did tell her that Mr Ferris was usually home by six o'clock, unless he said otherwise.'

The time dragged and Ashling, who was not prone to headaches, started to develop one about five minutes before Ross was due home. When she heard his key in the lock she jumped up and stood tense. She heard the door close and before Ross would have had time to hang up his hat and coat there was a gentle rat-tat on the front door.

Her heart began a fast beating. Rosin?

He spoke her name and there was surprise and loving in the saying of it. Then, softly, 'I can't believe it. Do come in.'

331

Ashling heard her say, in a low voice. 'I had to come and see you about Tara.'

'I'm glad you did,' he said. Then he called, 'Ashling?'

'Yes.' She came into the hall.

Ross introduced them. Rosin, the *real* Rosin, not her twin pretending to be her, strongly resembled Alicia Sylvain but this girl had a more reserved manner.

Ashling said, 'Come into the drawing room, Miss Dannet. I'm sorry I was out when you called earlier, I'll order some tea.'

'Not for me, thank you. It's an awkward time to call under the circumstances.' She turned to Ross. 'I came feeling I may be of some help. You see, I saw Tara some days ago. I came to stay with my sister and we were out shopping when I noticed her on the other side of the road. She kept looking up and down as though waiting for someone and every now and then glancing at her fob watch. I drew Alicia's attention to her and said, "Whoever she's waiting for is obviously late." '

'Where was she waiting?'

'Outside Harrods. There was a suitcase beside her. As Alicia and I were looking, a man came hurrying up. He spoke to her and hailed a passing cab and they both got in.'

When Ross asked if she could describe the man she said, 'He was good-looking, quite well dressed, tall and slenderly built. When I said to Alicia that I wondered who the man was, she snapped at me to mind my own business, that it had nothing to do with me. This was true, but somehow I felt there was something wrong about the incident. Then this morning, when I saw the news placards saying that Tara and the baby have been missing for days, I recalled the incident. I came to tell you and when I found that neither you nor Miss McCoy were in I decided to try and find the cabby who had picked them up.'

'That was very resourseful of you,' Ross exclaimed.

332

'The cabby had a distinctive birthmark on his right cheek. I found him eventually and, after offering him a tip, he gave me the address where he had taken your wife and her companion. This is it.' Rosin handed him a piece of paper.

He read it then said, 'Well! I can't thank you enough. Not many people would have thought of such a thing.'

Ashling tried desperately not to feel jealous of the way he looked at Rosin in her dark green velvet caped coat and matching hat. She was not beautiful like Tara, but she had a presence, and she found herself applauding her for her observation and determination to follow up Tara and her companion's whereabouts.

Ross got up. 'I must go to this address.'

Ashling suggested he should go to the police. It would be unwise to go to this place on his own, not knowing the situation, but he refused to listen. It would just be wasting time, and seeing the police might cause them to flee somewhere else.

To Rosin, he said, 'Do you want to wait until I come back, or can I take you to your sister?'

'I would have liked to wait but my sister doesn't know I'm out. I can find my own way back. May I telephone you later this evening?'

'Of course. I must go. Ashling, will you see that Rosin gets a cab?'

Ashling agreed, pleased that she might have the chance of a few words with Rosin.

When he had gone Ashling said, 'Ross has spoken of you often, Miss Dannet. We met your sister in Ireland while we were sheltering from a storm. Ross thought it was you.'

Rosin spoke ruefully: 'All that changing places is finished. We should never have started it.'

Ashling, guessing she did not want to pursue this subject, asked if she still told fortunes, then, sensing her reluctance to talk about this either, said quickly, 'Not that I want you to tell me my fortune. I don't want to know what the future holds.'

'How wise. Neither do I. One then loses that excitement of wondering what is going to happen next.'

'Yes, but Ross says that you enjoy telling other people what is going to happen.'

'If they are pleasurable things, not otherwise. I tried to read the cards to find out about Mrs Ferris and the baby, but the cards seemed all muddled, which means there is no settled plan at the moment.' She got up. 'I really must go.'

'Are you staying on in London?'

'No, my sister kept pestering me to start our changing places again and I came to convince her that it's definitely finished. She's a very persistent person, also rather a restless one.'

Ashling, reluctant to let her go, asked her if she still stayed with Mrs McKnott in Ireland.

'Yes.' Rosin's expression softened. 'She's been a good friend to me. It was always like going home when I desperately needed a rest.' Rosin glanced at the grandfather clock, then said again she must go.

Ashling said she would walk round to the cab rank with her and when Rosin told her there was no need she said, 'I want to. It's been good talking to you. Until now you were just a name. Ross is very fond of you. He was always talking about you.'

As Ashling spoke the words she realized just how much she liked this girl, and on an impulse said, 'I would be so pleased if we could meet again.'

'And I would enjoy a talk with you, Miss McCoy.'

Ashling felt a warm little glow. It was arranged that Rosin would call the following afternoon.

Ross was away ages and when he did return he looked distraught.

'What's happened?' Ashling asked in alarm.

He dropped into an armchair. 'A great deal, none of

334

it good, I'm sorry to say. I've just come from the police station. Give me a few moments to pull myself together.'

Ashling poured him a brandy. He tossed it back, then after squaring his shoulders began: 'The address Rosin gave me was a guesthouse near the docks where Tara had booked in, telling the owner, Mrs Harris, she would not be staying long as she was soon sailing to America.'

'America?' Ashling exclaimed.

'Yes, but we don't know if this is true. Then a man arrived, whom she said was her brother. They went to her room where they apparently started to quarrel, the man saying he would not hand over the baby until he got the money.'

Ashling's hand went to her throat. 'Oh, no.'

'Apparently the man left but returned a short time later, the baby in his arms. Then Mrs Harris heard Tara shouting, "I'll give you my jewellery but not my wedding ring!" Mrs Harris said she thought then it was time to interfere and she went into the room and demanded to know what was going on. She saw that the baby was on the bed and the man was trying to pull the ring from Tara's finger and she hurried out onto the landing and shouted to her husband to call the police. The man then came out, brushed past her and rushed down the stairs.'

'Not with Jacinta, I hope?'

'No, Tara had her in her arms and by then she was in a near hysterical state. In spite of it, she begged Mrs Harris not to bring the police, saying she could handle the situation. Mrs Harris told her that her husband was out, and she had used the ruse to scare the man. She said she would go and make Tara a cup of tea. But when Mrs Harris took the tea up, Tara and the baby had gone.'

'Oh, Ross, no!'

'That is not the end. Shortly after Tara had gone, a young lady turned up on the doorstep asking for her, and judging by Mrs Harris's description of her, it was Alicia. When Mrs Harris explained what had happened Alicia fled to the end of the street, got into a cab and was away.'

'Holy Mary,' Ashling murmured weakly.

After a silence Ross said, 'I then went to the police. They were annoyed that I had not gone to them right away. The man who was wanting to trade Jacinta for money or jewellery is well known to the police. He steals babies, then offers to sell them back to the parents. They, of course, pay up, but they don't get their child back. He snatches it, has a cab waiting, and eventually he sells the children to childless couples abroad.'

Ashling suddenly felt sick. 'Do you think that Alicia was involved in this terrible thing?'

'I don't know. The police say a woman accomplice was involved who gave the man information. But although Alicia is a mixed-up person, I just can't imagine her stooping so low.'

'Do you think that Tara was going to go to America?'

'The police got in touch with the only passenger ship companies and Tara's name was not on any lists, nor has there been any woman travelling alone with a tiny baby. I can only hope –'

The telephone rang and Ross hurried into the hall. Ashling got up and followed slowly, not knowing what to expect.

She heard Ross say, 'Oh, thank God,' and her spirits lifted.

When Ross hung up the receiver and turned to her his eyes were filled with tears. Ashling said, 'Tara and Jacinta have been found?'

He shook his head. 'No, only Jacinta. She was left at a police station with our address pinned to her shawl. Someone is bringing her to us.'

Ashling burst into tears then and Ross held her, smoothing a hand over her hair.

'It's something to get the baby back. They might find Tara soon. All we can do is hope.'

While they were waiting Rosin telephoned to say that Alicia had gone, leaving a letter she would like them to see. She would be over right away. She arrived before the police.

She had not noticed Alicia's note at first, she told them. It wasn't until she went into the bedroom and saw the chaos that she realized something was terribly wrong.

'Clothes were strewn all over the place. Two suitcases were missing. It wasn't until I went back into the living room that I saw the note, which simply said, *Had to go away. Won't be back. A.* Then I saw a baby's rattle. I started seaching for clues and found this letter in the wastepaper basket.'

The letter had been screwed up. It began.

My darling Garren, Please be careful with the baby. I'm enclosing a key for the front door and a plan of house. Will be seeing you soon and showing you how much I love you. I shall leave here on

The letter ended there and they were pouring over it when the police arrived. Rosin begged Ross and Ashling not to mention it until they had sorted something out, and they agreed.

A police sergeant came in with a woman in a navy costume carrying Jacinta. Ashling held out her arms saying she was the baby's nanny. The woman said smiling, 'You have a delightful charge. She hasn't been the least bit of trouble. She's just started to suck her fist vigorously so I presume she's hungry.'

Ashling took Jacinta to Ross and he held her close for a moment before handing her back. He introduced Rosin as a family friend.

The sergeant said. 'Well sir, I just wanted to discuss one or two things.'

Jacinta give a little whimper and Ashling excused herself to make the baby a feed. But no sooner had she reached the door than Jane was there with the bottle all ready and asking if she could give it to the child. Ashling, near to tears, handed her over.

The sergeant talked first about Garren Hunter, the man who snatched the baby.

'He's a lady-killer, who gets information from women who make friends with the mothers of young babies. Has your wife made any new women friends lately?'

Ashling, who was sitting next to Rosin on a sofa, was aware of her tensing. She glanced at her and Rosin shook her head.

Ross was saying, 'No, she hasn't mentioned anyone and I'm sure she would have done. And the friends we have are above suspicion. Have you had any hint of where my wife might be?'

'Not yet, but we hope to. She can't be very far away. According to Mrs Harris she looked worn out. We think she'll be hiding somewhere, resting. My men are doing a door-to-door enquiry in the vicinity.'

'And the kidnapper?'

'We are on his trail. We've been after him for some time. He's gone underground, but it won't be long before he surfaces again. He likes to be in circulation, coining in money. If there's anything you or Miss McCoy or your friends can think of that might help us in the search for your wife, do let us know.'

'I most certainly shall, sergeant, and thanks for all you and your people have done. I'm truly grateful to get Jacinta back.'

When they had gone he looked at Rosin and said with a frown, 'I think it was wrong to keep news of Alicia from them. She's involved with this Garren Hunter who's a well-known criminal.'

'But Alicia wouldn't be mixed up in selling babies,' Rosin pleaded. 'She said in the letter she had started that she didn't want Jacinta hurt. If nothing happens by tomorrow I'll go to the police.'

Ashling said gently, 'Tomorrow may be too late.'

'Yes.' Rosin's shoulders sagged. 'Perhaps I've been foolish. I'll go now and explain that I wanted to protect my sister. I won't mention that I had already told you about the letter. No,' she held up a hand as Ross began to protest, 'it's my responsibility. I was being too loyal to Alicia when she certainly doesn't deserve it.'

Ross went to the police station with her.

When they returned Rosin said, 'Well, I must say they were very lenient with me, scolding me for withholding the letter, but in the next breath telling me they were very pleased indeed to have the information. I only hope it will lead them to that wretched criminal who charmed Alicia into helping him steal Jacinta.'

Ashling, who had been doing a lot of thinking while they had been away, suggested they may be wronging Alicia. 'She had obviously come back into Tara's life, but supposing that Tara had decided to run away and Alicia encouraged her. Perhaps they had planned to find adventure together, go to America.' She paused. 'On the other hand I can't understand Tara leaving Jacinta.'

'I can,' Ross said grimly. 'Alicia is a most persuasive person, an excellent actress. She fooled John and me. She would coax Tara into believing it was best for the baby.'

Ashling told them that this is what had been in her mind, adding, 'But Alicia had reckoned without Tara's deep love for the baby and she refused to go, wherever they had planned, without her.'

'And this is where the wretched Garren Hunter must have come into it,' Rosin declared. 'Perhaps Alicia mentioned the problem of the baby and he suggested getting into the house and stealing her, but without Alicia knowing anything about his filthy trade. I do exonerate her from that.'

'I don't,' Ross replied, tight-lipped.

Days went by without any word and the only one unaffected by the disappointment was Jacinta, who thrived on the attention she was getting. A crib had been brought into the drawing room so that she was in sight during the day. Every time Rosin called she made straight for Jacinta, just to stand looking at her, if she was asleep or to talk to her softly if she was awake.

One day she said to Ashling, 'I shall miss Jacinta very much when I return to Ireland,' and there was an ache in her voice.

Ashling, who had welcomed Rosin's company, felt dismayed. 'Do you have to go?'

'I will have to soon. I couldn't afford the rent for the rooms for many more weeks.'

After hesitating for a moment, Ashling said, 'I'm sure Ross would be pleased if you moved in here.'

Rosin looked horrified. 'I couldn't, Ashling. Not under the circumstances. I feel guilty every time I call. Just suppose that Tara was found and I was here. It would be enough to make her run away again.'

'Would you be willing to stay with Catherine? I'm sure she would be very pleased to have you. Both she and Marianne like you.'

'I like them but they are Tara's friends.'

Ashling, as a last resort, asked if Rosin would accept the money for the rent. As a loan, she added, having realized how very independent Rosin was.

Rosin thanked her, but said no, it would be better if she left. 'I can't stay, Ashling,' she said. 'Seeing Ross, even for a short time when I call is an agony to me. I can cope when I'm away from him, but being near . . .' Her voice broke and Ashling got up to comfort her, thinking how strange life was, comforting someone who was also in love with Ross.

Rosin left before Ross came home from business.

When Ross returned he asked immediately about Rosin, and Ashling, not wanting to tell him the truth, said she had arranged to meet a friend. Later she mentioned that Rosin would be returning to Ireland soon and she grieved for him when she saw the pain in his eyes.

Then Conal called with news of Tara. A couple at a meeting had seen a woman who they were sure was Tara by the description and the photograph. She had hurried out of a house, then ran to board a horse bus. When they called at the house she had just left, the woman who opened the door said that Tara had asked the day before if she could be put up for the one night. She had eaten very little breakfast, had paid the bill and left.

'I went to the house,' he said, 'and judging by the description of the couple and of the woman it had certainly been Mrs Ferris who had stayed there. Now we have people searching other districts and can only pray that she will be found.'

This at least gave some hope. It was now two weeks since Tara had disappeared.

Catherine asked Ross and Ashling to dinner for the following Wednesday, saying she had asked Charles Kent, who would be returning to America that Saturday, and Conal was invited too. She thought it would be nice for them all to get together.

Ross said, 'Ashling and I don't want to be away from the house together so why don't you all come here?'

Catherine agreed on one condition — that she provided all the food and came to help Jane to cook it. This was laughingly accepted.

Rosin was invited and when she hesitated, Ashling coaxed her by mentioning that Conal would be there.

Coupling them together at the dinner table turned out to be a great success and by the end of the meal Ashling heard Rosin promise to call at the mission the following day.

When the guests had gone Ashling said to Ross, 'Well, I think everything went quite well, don't you?'

'Why did you do it?' he asked, in a hurt tone. 'Why did you put them together? You know how I feel about Rosin and I get so little chance of a talk with her.'

'I put her with Conal because I knew they have a lot in common. Also because at times your affection for Rosin shows and you are a married man with a wife who is missing.' Ashling spoke gently.

He flushed. 'Yes, you're right, of course.'

'I've discovered that she's a very lonely person, Ross, and I don't think she's had much love in her life, not that she has said as much. I hope she and Conal will get into correspondence. Conal was singing her praises this evening.'

'He was singing yours a while back.' It was said without any malice.

'Do you know what I think, Ross? I feel sure that Conal, deep down, is also lonely in spite of all his good work and the people who surround him and treat him as a god. Every man and woman needs a very special person to love and to be loved by.'

'And who is the special person in your life, Ashling?' he asked softly.

'I don't think he has appeared yet. I'm still of the opinion that I'm spinster material.'

'Don't belittle yourself, Ashling. You would make a perfect wife and mother. I don't know anyone more fitted for both roles than you.'

Ashling, who found herself on the verge of tears, jumped up and said lightly, 'Thank you, sir, for your kind words. And now, I must go to bed.'

Ross got up too. 'Ashling, thank you for bringing me

to my senses. I shall always have a love for Rosin. I love Tara, but in a totally different way. Foolishly I let myself be carried away this evening. I ache terribly at times for Tara, wondering where on earth she can be and how's she's faring. Pray God, that she will soon be back with us again.'

Ashling's pillow was wet with tears that night. She wept because of the hopeless love she had for Ross, and for her lost sister and for the baby who was without her mother. She also thought that some of her tears could be for Conal who was missing something in his life while he tried to make better those of others.

Early the following morning the police arrived with the news that Garren Hunter and Alicia Sylvain were bound for America on a cargo boat. The kidnapper was wanted for taking part in a jewellery robbery the day before he sailed and that both he and Alicia would be arrested when they arrived in New York.

'And my wife?' Ross asked anxiously. 'Is there any news of her?'

'Not yet, sir,' replied the sergeant, 'but we do have leads and hope to give you positive news soon.'

26

After the police had gone Ross and Ashling stood silent, looking at one another for a moment, then Ross said, 'I feel as if I'm in the middle of a nightmare.'

Ashling nodded. 'The trouble is that there's no waking up and finding that everything is back to normal.'

Later that day Rosin telephoned to ask if she might come over and Ross said, 'Yes, of course, we wondered if you had heard the news.'

'Yes, there is a piece in the newspaper.'

She arrived outwardly calm but condemning Alicia for her stupidity. 'I know she likes to be adventurous, but leaving for America with this criminal is going beyond the realms of decency. She's always talking about being free, now she'll be facing a prison sentence. It'll be torture to her.'

'It might bring her to her senses,' Ross said, his tone bitter. 'We could have lost Jacinta forever because of her so-called adventurous spirit.' Then this expression softened. 'Have you planned what to do, Rosin?'

'Yes. I'm staying until I find out what is happening. A companion to an elderly lady is ill and I'm taking her place until she's well again. Conal told me about her. The lady is a supporter of the mission and I can have afternoons to help there if I wish. I want to; they do such good work.'

Ashling, noticing Ross's disapproval, said quickly, 'That's splendid, Rosin. Perhaps I can come along one afternoon and we can find time for a chat.'

'I would like that.' Rosin's sudden smile seemed to dispel the gloom that had been hanging over them since hearing the news of Alicia and the kidnapper.

Ashling and her mother had exchanged letters regularly since Eileen had returned to Ireland and Eileen kept saying she felt she ought to come over again to help search for Tara, but Patrick was against it, saying she should reserve her strength for when Tara was home and would need her. This mention of 'reserving her strength' gave Ashling the impression that her mother had after all not fully recovered from her illness and she longed to go home and see them all. As this was impossible at the moment, she wrote to Fiona asking her for the truth.

By return came a reply saying she was not to worry. Their mother was not ill, it was only their father's caring for her and wanting her there all the time.

To be truthful, she wrote, *it was the worry of Tara that made Papa ill. Brendan is doing most of the work. They've postponed the wedding again, feeling it's not fair to have anything celebratory while Tara is missing.*

And now I must tell you my secret. Niall and I are unofficially engaged to be married. Don't breath a word of it to anyone. I no longer crave for a career. I want a home and children. Strange, isn't it, how one can change? I so enjoyed hearing from you. Write again when you can.

Your loving sister, Fiona.

Ashling lowered the letter and sat back. So Fiona was to marry, she who had been so determined to have a career. And where will I end up, Ashling asked herself, being spinster aunt to my brother and sisters' children?

Two weeks later Ross heard from the police that Garren Hunter and Alicia were not on the cargo boat when it docked in New York.

The sergeant said, 'The captain denied all knowledge of them and we can only presume that the couple had been transferred to some other boat before reaching the harbour and disappeared among the flotsam and jetsam of thieves in the area.'

'A dreadful thought,' said Rosin, with tears in her eyes, 'that Alicia should end up being a fugitive from the police.'

Later, Ross said to Ashling, 'With the money from the robbery she and her criminal lover will probably be living it up.' And with fists clenched added, 'I feel I could kill them for what they did to Tara.'

The grief and pain in his voice tore Ashling apart. If only she could give him some hope, could give him comfort.

The baby was his solace. He would sit nursing her and repeat nursery rhymes and began to know which ones were her favourites. If he sing-songed, 'Mary, Mary, Quite Contrary', she would look solemn, but if it was, 'Hey, Diddle Diddle', she would kick, and blow bubbles, and her fists would flail as if she could see it all happening. Then Ross would chuckle and holding him to her would tell her she was his darling girl and he didn't know what he would do without her. These were the times when Ashling cried inwardly for him.

Twice a week she and Catherine would walk to the mission, pushing the baby in her perambulator, where Jacinta became a favourite with the people. One afternoon they helped to serve the food with Rosin, and the other afternoon listened to Conal talking to the people. There was never any preaching, it was always advice offered in a roundabout way, and Ashling was impressed with his spiritual goodness.

Ashling had thought that Conal spoke to Rosin in a special way but soon realized it was a way he had with everyone. To him they were all God's children and were treated equally.

Ashling would invite Rosin to small social gatherings where they had a game of whist, or a musical evening.

Sometimes Conal came to these too, but Ashling began to notice that they always seemed to make him sad.

When she mentioned it to him he said, 'Music reminds me of Ireland, the sound of the wind, the sea, the storms. I miss it, Ashling. I long to go back, but there's too much work to be done here.'

She said, 'Why don't you go back for a short holiday? No one could deny you that.' Then on impulse added, 'If you were to go you could accompany Rosin. She'd like to go back but I don't think she wants to travel on her own. She does need a change.'

'I would be delighted to accompany her.' There was a glow about him and this time it was not a spiritual one. He said he thought it could be arranged. He must not get big-headed and think that the mission would not run satisfactorily without him. There were many qualified people who could take over.

But when Ross knew what Ashling had suggested about Rosin he was furious.

'Who gave you permission to rule her life?' he demanded. 'Were you jealous that she was getting too much attention from Conal? Or did you want her out of my way?'

Ashling, deeply hurt, said quietly, 'You may not have noticed that Rosin has not been looking well lately. She's been working too hard. She not only has a job as companion to the old lady who supports the mission, and cooking and caring for people belonging to it, but is knitting and repairing clothes in what some might say was her sleeping time. Catherine mentioned yesterday how poorly Rosin looked. So have several more people. I suggest that you don't condemn unless you know the truth.'

She made to move away and Ross caught hold of her arm.

'Ashling, I'm sorry. I don't know what I'm doing or

347

saying most of the time with worrying over Tara. But
then you are worrying as much as I am. Forgive me.'

She was fighting back tears and was unable to answer.
He put an arm around her. 'Come and sit down and
we'll have a talk.' She shook her head but he sat down
and drew her down beside him. 'Look, why don't you
go with Conal and Rosin? You need a rest too. You
need to see your parents.'

'I don't want to leave Jacinta.'

'There are others who will look after her. I had a
letter from your mother today, asking my advice. I
intended to tell you later. She says she's longing to talk
to someone about Tara, but Patrick has become possessive and doesn't want to be left.'

'It's not like Papa.'

'The doctor apparently says he's suffering from delayed shock over Tara. In a way he's lost two daughters.
Your mother suggests that if you go for a visit it might
help him to recover.'

Ashling was silent for a moment then, thinking how
wonderful it would be to see the family. She said, 'Yes,
I would love to go but only if Catherine will take charge
of Jacinta and also if you promise to send a telegram
if you get any news of Tara.'

'I promise.' He kissed her gently on the lips and gave
her a hug. 'I'll ask Catherine to come round.'

With the kiss, unbidden thoughts came to her mind.
If only things had been different. Then she dismissed
them and concentrated on the knowledge that she was
going home. Oh, what heaven.

When Rosin knew that she too was also going to
Ireland, her laughter was so infectious that Ashling
could understand more than ever how Ross had fallen
in love with her.

A telegram was sent home and by return came one
from Eileen saying: *Everyone overjoyed. Conal and Rosin must
stay overnight.*

It was a happy threesome who left for Ireland the following morning. The biggest pull for Ashling was in leaving Jacinta but she knew she was in good hands with Catherine, who was going to come round every day. Catherine told her she was not to worry, she would also take care of Ross.

Ross had seen them off at the station and had put on a bright manner, saying to Ashling, 'Just forget everything here and enjoy your holiday. If you want to stay longer than the week I'm sure that Catherine would oblige.'

'No,' Ashling said firmly, 'I couldn't bear to be parted from Jacinta longer than that.'

'And what about me?' he asked lightly, looking from Ashling to Rosin.

They chorused, 'Of course, you too.' Then Conal was saying his goodbye and promising to look after his 'charges'.

It was a joyous meeting in Dublin with Eileen, Fiona, Brendan, and Liam and Dermot McLane, the brothers happening to be there for their firms.

Conal and Rosin were introduced and although Rosin was a little shy, the others were talking as if they had known each other for years.

Ashling was delighted to see her mother looking so well and when she told her so Eileen said, 'I feel very well indeed, but be prepared to see a change in your father. The doctor says that all he's suffering from now is martyrdom. We are hoping that having you here and being able to talk about Tara will lift him out of his melancholic state. We must try and get him back to work. His tenants come to see him and commiserate with him and he revels in it. And, as you know, this is not like him.'

Patrick wept when he saw Ashling and she cried too. But he showed an interest in Conal. So this was the shepherd he had heard so much about. How good it was to meet him. He made room for him on the sofa where he was sitting. Eileen raised her eyebrows at Ashling and crossed her fingers.

After they had had a meal they talked about Tara, Ashling telling the story. Conal, talked about problems in life that beset us all and such was his way of handling it that Patrick said he could now understand Tara and could no longer condemn her for leaving her husband and child.

He spread his hands. 'But where is she? If only we knew.'

Conal said, 'I think she made up her mind to know a different way of life and will not come back until she has found the answers.'

Dermot said, 'Tara always distanced herself from the poorer classes yet she was always asking questions about them, wanting to know how they existed on such low wages.'

Both Fiona and Ashling said she had not talked to them on this subject but Liam upheld Dermot, saying that they often had arguments with her, because she was apt to blame the poor for living in such conditions.

It was a new angle on the missing Tara and caused a lot of discussion, with Eileen saying it proved how you could live with someone for years and not know them.

'For all one's life,' Patrick said, and Ashling noticed colour rush to her mother's cheeks.

Fiona was the only one whose sympathies were not with her sister. 'To me,' she said, 'Tara has behaved selfishly. She lived well, was never denied anything, married the man she wanted, then suddenly leaves him and her child.'

Conal said, 'Dare we judge anyone when we have not had a particular person's experience? How do we know how we ourselves would act under such circumstances?'

'But for all we know,' Fiona said, 'she might be with this criminal and Alicia living well in America.'

Conal shook his head. 'No. She's in England, I'm positive of it. Tara will return when she is ready.'

It was Eileen who changed the subject by saying to Rosin, 'I made a point of letting Mrs McKnott know that you were coming and she was overjoyed.'

Rosin smiled. 'And I am looking forward to seeing her.'

Later Eileen said to Ashling, 'Well, what a change in your Papa. And did you see the way that Liam and Dermot were eyeing you and Rosin?'

'I saw them eyeing Rosin. I felt they were both smitten.'

'Both have been smitten with you for a long time, but you've never given them any encouragement.' Before Ashling could remark on this, Eileen went on, 'How about you and Conal going with Rosin in the morning to see Queenie McKnott? I mentioned it to her and she said she would be delighted to see you.'

Ashling pointed out that Conal wanted to go to his beloved mountains and Eileen gave her a broad smile. 'He will, but I persuaded him to stay another day.'

When they set off the next morning to visit Queenie, Ashling saw the beauty of the countryside. With the autumn the cotton grass had turned a beautiful red. Mists drifted so that sometimes the mountains were lost in it, then as it moved she would catch glimpses of purple and pink heather and the autumnal rusts and gold of trees and foliage.

Queenie, who was waiting at the cottage door, greeted them with a beaming smile.

'Well, now, isn't this really special, having Rosin back, and seeing you all and meeting Mr Conal. Come away in. I've made cocoa, it's on the hob.'

She pulled out chairs. 'Sit you down. I'll pour it.'

When she handed the cup of cocoa to Conal she

351

said, 'I feel I should dip me skirt to you, sir, You being a holy man an' all.'

Conal smiled, 'I'm just a shepherd, ma'am, helping the poor.'

'Our Lord was a shepherd and He helped the poor.'

'He had power. I need money.'

'Love and kindness is what poor folk need.'

Rosin said, 'Love and kindness alone won't feed them. Tell me, Queenie, did your family come over from Australia?'

'Indeed they did and we had a wonderful time.' Queenie paused. 'I see what you mean. It cost a lot of money. Mind you, they worked hard to save it.'

'Yes, but the money helped them to make a decision. They could have spent it differently, but they came because they loved you.'

Queenie nodded, and suddenly flicked a tear from her eye. 'I hadn't thought about it that way.' She changed the subject by telling Rosin she had been painting her pony cart while she had been away and suggested she should take a look at it later.

Rosin got up. 'I'll have a look at it now. Ashling, would you like to see it?'

'Yes, I would.' She guessed that Rosin was on the verge of tears. They went to a shed where they saw the pony cart. It had been painted a bright red, the edges done in emerald green and on the sides was painted the name Rosin in black.

'It's a little gaudy,' Rosin said. 'But –' Her voice broke. She was silent for a moment then looked at Ashling with appeal. 'What do I do? Queenie's so kind. I know she'll be hoping I'll be here to stay. I'm torn. I feel I'm doing something worthwhile working with Conal and the short times I see Ross means so much to me, although I know I can't see him when Tara returns. Help me, Ashling.'

'You can perhaps promise to come to Queenie for

occasional visits. After all, when you were in Ireland you were away for spells.'

'Yes, but Alicia took my place.' She sighed. 'I'll have to come to a decision.'

When they went in, Queenie said, 'Did you like your pony cart, Rosin?'

'Yes, I did. My customers will recognize it at once when I . . . when I come back in the spring. Thanks so much, Queenie. You're so good to me.'

'Well, as I told you once,' she said gruffly, 'to me, you're kin. Drink your cocoa, it'll be getting cold.'

They stayed until midday. As they left, Queenie said to Conal, 'May the Lord keep you in His hand and never close His fist too tight on you.'

'Bless you both,' he said, his smile including Rosin.

When Conal and Ashling were walking back over the fields he said, 'What a splendid lady Mrs McKnott is. I find myself wanting to stay in Ireland longer.'

'Why don't you? You have the mission under way.'

'There are many things to be done. I ought never to have left, but my mountains called me and I hadn't the will to resist. I'm a weakling, Ashling.'

'That is nonsense. I see the hand of the Deity in this. You need the rest, otherwise you wouldn't be able to help anyone. Stay until you are refreshed. The demands of some people can completely drain one. Now do as you're told.'

'Yes, ma'am,' Conal replied, a twinkle in his eyes.

Eileen, of course, wanted to know about their visit and although Conal had been praising Queenie on their way home it was Rosin who came in for his praises now.

'I have the greatest respect for her,' he said. 'She wants to stay in Ireland but denies herself this pleasure and works hard at the mission. She's very popular with the people and I hear of all the extra little things she does for them.

Patrick, who was looking a great deal better, started trying to persuade Conal to stay for at least another day, but he shook his head.

'I must see my mountains, see my old friends, my flock of sheep. They knew me and I knew every one. I'll be here again to travel back with Ashling and Rosin. That's a promise.'

After Conal had gone, Patrick said, 'Be he shepherd or holy man he put new life into me. I think I'll start work tomorrow.'

The following morning Patrick did go to the office with Brendan and Eileen and Ashling got down to a heart-to-heart talk about Tara.

Eileen said, with a note of desperation, 'I would have liked to have had a session with the runes to try and find out if Tara is alive, but Maeve is abroad and Fiona won't read them. She says it's better not to know, which seemed somehow like a death knell to me.'

'You mustn't think like that, Mama. Do you remember Conal saying he's sure she'll return home when she's ready? He either has some knowledge of her whereabouts or something spiritual tells him so.'

'I hope you're right,' was Eileen's fervent reply.

Twice that week they went to see Queenie and Rosin, and Ashling was surprised at how much better Rosin looked. Rosin was included in an invitation to dine with Liam and Dermot and, as Eileen said afterwards, it would be difficult to say which girl had the most attention from the two bachelors.

By the end of the week Ashling was longing to see Jacinta again and, if she was honest with herself, Ross too.

Conal was at the docks to meet her and Rosin, looking bright and smiling when he greeted them. 'I'm sure you will both have plenty to tell me,' he said, 'and I shall probably bore you with all the talk of my sheep.'

Rosin and Ashling laughed, pleased to see him again. It was good to know someone like Conal, holy man, philosopher and shepherd, who had a lovely sense of humour. But for all of them, the worry about Tara mixed with their happiness at returning to London.

27

For Ashling it was a joyous homecoming, not only being back with Jacinta again but being aware of Ross's pleasure at having her back. 'How we've missed you,' he said softly.

As Ashling took the baby from him, Catherine echoed this.

'Thanks, Catherine, for everything,' Ashling said softly, holding the baby close. 'I enjoyed my holiday but it's lovely to be back again. I missed you all.'

Catherine put on her hat and coat. 'Marianne and I are going now, and will let you and Ross talk about family news. We'll see you tomorrow.'

Ashling thanked her and Marianne again. She noticed that Jacinta's eyelids were drooping and also that her cheeks had plumped out.

'You're so beautiful,' she murmured. 'If only your mama could see you.'

Ashling told Ross everything they had done and talked about. What Ross picked out in the telling was everyone's interest in Conal.

He said, 'And Rosin is greatly impressed with him too, isn't she?' He spoke quietly, but Ashling was aware of the hurt in his voice.

'No more than anyone else. And, of course, we didn't see very much of Conal. He spent the majority of the week in the mountains.' She paused then said, 'I really ought not to say this, but Rosin told me that she had to stay away from you because loving you so much upset her to be with you.'

'Oh God, what a mess.' He buried his hands in his face for a moment then looked up. 'But I give you my word, if Tara came back I would put all thoughts of Rosin out of mind.'

'It's easy to say, Ross.'

'I had to put Rosin from my mind and give my love to Tara when we married. Tara was happy at first.'

'Ross, I'm sorry, forgive me. I know you made her happy. It's just that things are so complicated. I'm fond of you and I'm fond of Rosin and I hate for either of you to be hurt.'

'I know. I missed you, Ashling. I've been used to you being here when I came home and that was the worst part of the day for me. The house seemed so empty.' He smiled suddenly. 'You must get married. You are depriving some man of a very caring wife.'

'One of these days,' she replied lightly, trying to ignore the ache of there being no Ross in her life. 'Now I think I'll go up. I can hardly keep my eyes open.'

There was a knock on the front door.

Ross groaned. 'Oh, no, who could be calling at this hour?'

He went to see who it was. Seconds later he was calling to Ashling in an urgent voice to come and help him. She ran into the hall, saw the limp form of a woman in his arms, then hurried forward, her heart thudding like mad.

Ross whispered, 'Tara' in an anguished way, then more strongly, 'Will you call the doctor, Ashling?'

Ashling was suddenly calm and ice cold. She made the telephone call, took a blanket from a chest, then went into the drawing room where Ross had laid Tara on a sofa and was chafing her hands.

She was about to put the blanket over her when she froze. Tara was just skin and bone, a skeleton, her eyes sunken in their sockets. Oh, Mother of God. She laid the blanket over her, saying, 'The doctor's coming right away,'

When Ross looked up at her she thought she would

never forget his sheet-white face and expression of devastation.

Soon the doctor was calling from the hall. Ashling had told Jane he was to come straight in.

He started to examine Tara, and before he had finished she was coming round. Her eyes opened.

She whispered. 'I had to come home . . . Jacinta?'

Ross took her hands in his. 'She's fine, Tara. We're glad you've come home. We've been so worried about you. We love you, we need you. Jacinta needs you.'

Her eyes closed. The doctor drew Ross aside.

'She's very low but I think she'll recover. I want some hot-water bottles around her, the bottles just warm. Will you see to those while I slip back home? I want to make up some special medicine. I won't be long.'

Jane and Ashling saw to filling the bottles while Ross stayed with Tara.

When the doctor returned he said, 'A nurse will be here soon. She's efficient and very caring. Now, shall we get Mrs Ferris up to bed? Lift her gently, she's very frail.'

Tara's frailty shocked Ashling when she and Jane started to undress her. It seemed impossible that she had managed to get home. Her clothes were shabby but clean.

By the time Tara was in her nightdress Nurse Grey was there, a middle-aged woman with a sympathetic manner. The doctor said he would stay and Ross, Ashling and Jane went downstairs. Jane went to make tea for them all.

Ross and Ashling were silent for a while as they sipped their tea, then Ross said, 'Where has Tara been? How has she been living? How did she get here?'

'She's so emaciated, but the doctor seems hopeful that she'll recover.'

'Yes, and that gives me hope. Doctor Waring never minces words.' Ross put down his cup and, getting up, began to walk around the room. 'Why did I get annoyed with her at times, instead of seeing that she was ill?'

'You aren't to blame, Ross. We can all be wise after the event. Now we must nurse her back to health. Her one thought was for the baby and that's good. She has a reason for living.'

They discussed whether they ought to send a telegram to Eileen and Patrick now or wait until the morning. Ashling suggested that if they knew now, they could get the earliest possible boat. Ross agreed and went to send the telegram.

It was a long night. Ross and Ashling took turns catnapping. At five o'clock the doctor told them that Tara had taken a turn for the better.

'I'm going home to have a nap,' he said. 'I'll be back again about seven-thirty. Go to your beds. Mrs Ferris is in good hands. Don't go in, you may disturb her.'

Ross saw him to the door and when he came back he said, 'Thank God Tara's over the worst. I really thought we were going to lose her. The doctor told me not to expect a quick recovery. She is not to be questioned until he gives his permission.'

It was three days before anyone was allowed to speak to her. Even Eileen and Patrick were allowed in only to take a peep at her. Tara was still sleeping. Both of them came back downstairs terribly upset at the way she looked.

Ross and Ashling, who had also only been allowed a glimpse of Tara, were able to assure them that there was an improvement in her since she had turned up on the doorstep. There was now a little colour in her cheeks.

The doctor explained that to be in this emaciated state, she must have been living under terrible conditions, and speaking to her might bring her experiences to the surface before she was ready and cause her great distress.

Ashling, remembering how Tara had mentioned Jacinta, asked if the baby should be there when they did speak to her.

'She can be there in the background, but you must wait until she asks for her. She may have temporarily forgotten her. Yes, I know it sounds unbelievable, but this sort of thing does happen.'

Eileen was impatient at the delay and wanted Ross to seek the advice of a specialist, but Patrick said Doctor Waring talked sense and they must wait for the outcome.

On the third morning the doctor told Ross that he could speak to Tara, but only for a short time.

'She's still a little hazy but did sound rational when she asked where you were. So far she has not asked for Jacinta, but your aunt could be in the room with the baby in case she does.'

Tara was looking far from normal but there was an interest in her eyes when Ross went over to the bed. He laid a hand on hers and said gently, 'How do you feel, Tara?'

'A little better.' It was a whisper. 'Who is – looking after you?'

'A lot of people, but of course I missed you terribly.'

She frowned, closed her eyes a moment, then opened them. 'Jacinta?'

'She's here, and your mother.'

Eileen came over with the baby and Ross stepped back. Tara tried to raise her arms and couldn't, and Eileen held the baby close to her saying gently, 'I'll hold her. Tomorrow you will be able to.'

Tara turned her cheek to the baby and Eileen put Jacinta's cheek to hers. Then the baby, sleepy, gave a huge yawn and a faint smile touched Tara's pale lips as tears welled up and ran slowly down her face.

The nurse came up and whispered, 'No more now.'

When they were outside the doctor said, 'She cried. That was good. It relieved tension. She has a long way to go but that is a start.'

Her recovery was slow but there came a day when she was up for the first time, a day when Jacinta heard the clip-clop of a horse in the crescent and tried to imitate it with her tongue. When everyone laughed, she began to chuckle. Tara was holding her and her eyes were shining as she hugged her, saying, 'Thank God I managed to get back.'

She was still frail-looking and was unable to say much, but a week later, when there was a big improvement in her she said, 'Very soon now I shall tell you what happened.'

Ross said gently, 'There's plenty of time for that,' but she lifted her head.

'I won't be properly well until I've told you. It's like a weight pressing on my chest.'

The story took Tara three evenings to tell, the telling exhausting her, but she was determined. She started where she had met Alicia while out shopping. And, keeping the meetings secret because Alicia was talking about a big adventure and planning to go to America, they met a number of times.

'I got more and more caught up in the idea,' Tara said, 'and decided I would go with her. I had expected to take the baby with me, but Alicia told me it was impossible and said I was being selfish to even contemplate it. Jacinta could die during the voyage.'

Tara explained that Alicia had a very persuasive way and she decided to leave the baby with Ross and Ashling. No sooner had she left the house, however, than she began to fret for Jacinta, so much so that she refused to go without her. In the end Alicia gave in and told her she knew a man who would steal the baby, adding that he would want money for doing so. Tara agreed and this was when the trouble started. She shuddered.

'He not only took the money but tried to force my wedding ring from my finger.'

Ross explained that they knew about this, but not what had followed when she ran away from the house with the baby.

'It was a nightmare. I hid in an empty building but Alicia found me. I was exhausted. She took me to a small hotel where she said we would stay for the night, then she would take me back home the next day. In the night I roused to hear raised voices, one a man's voice, but I was so exhausted I went to sleep again. The next morning Alicia had gone, so had my jewellery. I knew then that the man who had stolen Jacinta for me was the culprit. I also knew I was unable to keep the baby.'

'Why didn't you come home?' Eileen asked.

'Because —' Tara paused. 'It's difficult to explain.' For one thing I was ashamed at the way I had behaved, but also I didn't feel I was me. I suppose I was ill even then. I left the hotel and started to walk aimlessly, not quite knowing what to do for the best. My head felt as though it was full of cotton wool. One day I came to a park and sat on a bench, the baby clutched to me. She was asleep and I must have gone to sleep because when I woke my suitcase and my money from my handbag had gone.'

'Oh, that was dreadful,' Ashling declared. 'You should have gone to the police and reported it.'

'I did eventually go the police, but not to report I had been robbed. I must have been crying because a woman came up and asked if I needed help. I told her I hadn't any money and my baby needed her bottle. She took me home, borrowed a bottle and a feed from a neighbour and she fed Jacinta without asking any more questions.

'The house was poorly furnished and I saw that her cheek was bruised. Later, she told me she couldn't let me stay longer than about six o'clock because her husband would be home and he wouldn't have visitors in the house. She said he was not a nice man and I guessed he had done the bruising to her face.'

Tara was silent for a while, then she said, 'I told her that I had left home, but that I wanted Jacinta returned to be looked after. It was she who suggested I leave the baby at the police station. She found me a cardboard box, some pieces of blanket and after wrapping Jacinta up carefully in her shawl and pinning the address on it, we went to the police station. The woman kept the man at the desk talking and when no one was looking I left the box on a bench and walked out. I felt then that my heart was breaking.'

Tara could not say any more that evening. It was the following evening when she completed the story.

She began by saying, 'I'll never forget the kindness of that woman. I never knew her name. She cried with me, having lost two young children recently. She had two older ones who were at school. She told me that she knew of a woman whose husband had left her and who took in washing and could do with some help. Did I think I could manage the work? I told her yes.'

'Oh, Tara, you didn't,' Eileen said. 'You were ill.'

'I had to try. The reason for leaving home was to find out how other people lived and find myself.'

Ross said, his expression grim, 'And how did you manage?'

'I didn't,' Tara replied in a flat tone. 'I discovered that the young girls she hired to do the washing ended up as prostitutes.'

They all sat up at this and Ashling said, 'You mean that the woman who helped you sent you there?'

'No, it was the neighbour of the washerwoman who

ran the brothel. Then I heard that the police knew what the house was being used for and I left at once.'

'And where did you go from there?' Eileen asked, distressed.

'I can only say I went from place to place, each more poverty-stricken than the last. I learned how poor people live, and I also learned about kindness – how rich people would turn their backs on me when I was forced to beg for money to survive when the poor would share their last crust with me. I once slept on bare boards on a freezing night with a piece of sacking for a cover and cockroaches crawled over me during the night. Another time I was flea-ridden. I stole once when I hadn't had anything to eat for two days, just a drink of water a tramp gave me. I could go on and on. I spent a day or two days with a family who were criminals, even the children, but when I became ill it was they who looked after me, who gave me clothes, who even saw that I had a bath. Yes, I lived and I learnt and I'll never despise poor people again.'

'How did you manage to get home, Tara?' Ross asked.

'I wanted to die in my own home if I had to. I wanted to see everyone again and I desperately needed to see Jacinta. I became really ill in the house of the criminals. They nursed me, fed me. Then, when I began to recover, two of the men were arrested and because I didn't want to be recognized I left. I hadn't any money so I had to walk at first. I begged on the way and got enough money to travel at times on a bus. Then I got lost. I don't know how I did get here in the end. I only know that the Lord was good to me and I didn't deserve it.

'That is my story,' she concluded, 'and no one I'm sure could learn any more about humanity than I did. I really did grow up.'

There was a silence. Then Ross got up and, drawing

her up, held her close, saying, 'I love you, Tara. We all love you and we're glad you came back to us.'

Eileen and Patrick stayed another two weeks and in that time Tara gained strength and would chat quite happily about everyday things when friends called, but there were times when she would sit silent, gazing into space and, guessing where her thoughts were, they all would be silent too.

Then came the day when Eileen and Patrick said they must return home and asked Tara if she would like to come with them for a while.

She shook her head and smiled. 'No, I have a lot of lost time to make up with Ross and Jacinta. Perhaps in the spring we can come for a visit. Say the first week in March?'

'That would be splendid,' Eileen declared. 'There are so many people who haven't seen the baby. It will be something to look forward to.'

Life settled down after Eileen and Patrick had gone. Tara bathed Jacinta every morning and no one could have handled her in a more expert way. She nursed her, crooned to her, told her nursery rhymes and laughed at the way Jacinta chuckled when she quoted 'Hey, Diddle Diddle'.

Although Ashling accepted there was a big change in Tara and that she was much more adult, she felt there was something else different about her too, but was not sure what it could be. Ashling discussed it with Catherine and although Catherine said she had not noticed anything herself, she suggested asking Conal to dinner. He was very good with people who had been ill.

Tara was sat next to Conal and although she had lost her former animation she and Conal talked, but mostly about the mission it seemed.

Since Tara had come home, Ashling had not been to the mission and had not see Rosin.

When she spoke to Conal about her, he said, 'She's quite well, such a worker, one of our best. She sent her best wishes and hopes to see you soon. I think she worries about Alicia. She hasn't heard anything.'

Ashling took the opportunity to ask him his opinion of Tara's condition. He frowned.

'Unfortunately, she's seen some very dark sides of life, probably more than she admits to, and it will take a long time for them to fade. I feel I would like to help, but it might not be wise at this stage.'

'Help in what way? I know I can speak for us all when I say that any help would be welcomed. I feel at times that there is something strange about her.'

'People speak of me as a healer. I simply talk to them in an effort to soothe the mind. Some people benefit from a talk, others don't.'

Ashling said she would speak to Ross about it.

Ross was very much against it, pointing out that although Conal was a most interesting man and was able to help people in many ways, Tara had an excellent doctor who, one could say, had brought her back to life. Look at her now, the same loving Tara they had known.

Ashling said no more and tried not to worry that her sister was in some way different, and now that Tara had almost taken over the care of Jacinta, she started going to the mission with Catherine.

Rosin's welcome was touching. Normally, not a demonstrative person, she put her arms around Ashling and said, a break in her voice, 'You've no idea how pleased I am to see you. All the people are nice here, but I don't feel I can confide my worries to them.' She smiled suddenly. 'Oh, dear, that isn't very complimentary, is it, that I want to see you so you can share my troubles?'

'I am complimented,' Ashling said gently. 'Isn't that what friends are for?' She looked around her. 'Catherine is busy. Where can we go to have a talk?'

Rosin said that Conal was out, they could use his shed and when they were seated she thanked Ashling for coming to the mission.

'I longed to call to see you, but couldn't, of course, with Tara being home. I'm so glad she's recovered. What a terrible time she has had. Ross must have been so relieved to have her home.'

'He is and it was good to see him losing his gaunt look as Tara improved.'

Rosin was silent for a moment, then she looked up, an anguish in her eyes. 'I must leave here, Ashling. That is what I wanted to discuss with you. Conal is thinking of starting a mission in Ireland and he's more or less persuaded me to help. He'll divide his time between the two missions. It will probably be in the poorer part of Dublin. It's not settled yet. He says he'll be able to find plenty of helpers and also knows of an excellent man who will take charge when Conal is in London.'

'Rosin, are you sure you are doing the right thing?'

'I have to leave here. Ross is too close to me. I haven't the will power to dismiss him from my mind. But I can cope when he's not near. I did before. And I would be able to visit Queenie. I miss her and she misses me. There is also the misery while I'm here of not knowing what has happened to Alicia. I know she's behaved very badly, but she was so kind to me, so generous, when we first knew we were sisters. I do feel if I go away I can forget, at least some of the time.'

Ashling said, 'Deep down I had hoped that you and Conal might get together. I know he's very fond of you.'

'I'm fond of him. He did ask me to marry him, but I couldn't. Not loving Ross the way I do. It wouldn't be fair.'

Ashling told her they were all going home in the first week of March and suggested they could perhaps meet.

Rosin declared it would be wonderful, and it would be nice to spend some time with Queenie. She would tell Conal she wanted to be away then.

The days went by with Tara devoted to Jacinta and Ross, and no one could say they had ever met a happier family.

Rosin was more settled. Conal had been to Ireland and found a suitable hall and when she told him she would like to spend the first week in March with Queenie he had said he would go at the same time and sort out a number of things that had to be discussed about the mission. His friend, who turned out to a saintly-looking middle-aged man, whom Rosin liked on sight and whom the people at the mission had taken to their hearts, was going to be in charge while they were away.

On top of this Rosin had a note from Alicia. She simply said she was as happy as she would ever be and Rosin was not to worry. There was no address. Some-one would post it from a foreign port so the place where they were would never be known. The postmark was Buenos Aires. It was signed *Much love*.

'That was all,' Rosin said. 'But it settled me. I had been thinking of her rotting in some jail. I know she's behaved stupidly, but who am I to judge her life?' She suddenly smiled. 'I feel I can now look forward to going to Ireland and Queenie is overjoyed that I shall be there.'

Ashling would have looked forward to the visit more if only she could have fathomed Tara's mind. Outward-ly she was living a normal life, but she was aware at times of her being in 'dark places' as Conal called them. And it worried her.

28

The day Ross, Tara, Ashling and Jacinta travelled to Ireland, the weather was warm, the sun shone and the sea was calm. The family were there to meet them and the party spirit began, with everyone talking at once.

At home, friends who arrived positively drooled over Jacinta and she gave one of her best performances. There was a demand to hold her and Tara had to be firm so that the baby would not get overexcited.

'Isn't she gorgeous?' Fiona said in a voice of envy. 'I must get married soon so I can have a baby.'

Brendan laughed. 'And this is my sister who said marriage wasn't important, she wanted a career.'

His father said, 'Ah, well, it's a woman's privilege to change her mind.'

Presents had come for Jacinta, and Ashling was delighted to see Tara as excited as they had been as children, opening the baby's presents of clothes and toys. Jacinta rattled rattles and chewed on the ear of a teddy bear as she patiently allowed her mother to try bonnets on her and also held dresses up to her to see how they looked. They went to Mass and after breakfast visited Patrick's tenants with gifts of food, and sweets for the children. The elderly and sick were especially delighted to see Jacinta.

When they had been home a few days, they had a celebration lunch, Fiona and her young man, Niall, having officially announced their engagement, with both parents' approval.

Fiona and Niall had arranged to spend the rest of the day with his family, and left after lunch. When

Ashling, having decided to call on Queenie and Rosin, announced she was going for a walk, she was surprised when Patrick and Brendan offered to go with her.

Eileen teased Patrick saying, 'Off you go then, you young ones, and leave the older ones to have a rest.'

The day was sharp but the air fresh. They set off for Queenie's cottage and on the way Brendan told Ashling that he and his fiancée, Celina, were parting. Brendan shook his head sadly. 'It's the parents, Ashling. They are much too possessive and they're mean people, cold. Being with the family today helped me to accept Celina's decision. We are a close, loving family, each offering help if needed. We laugh, tease, we're happy in one another's company. There's no laughter in Celina's house and the whole family are the same. We would be expected to go when they invited us and I just couldn't see my children playing happily there. They have grandchildren and they sit like wooden puppets, not daring to speak one word unless they are spoken to.'

'But, Brendan, have you thought of Celina? You're committing her to a life of misery. She loves you. Put up with the family for her sake. You'll have your own home when you marry.'

'She wants to be a nun, Ashling, has done so, apparently, since she was a child. She's been indoctrinated by her parents. They've never liked me, and I had to beg them to give their consent to the marriage.'

'Well, I think it very sad.'

Patrick said, 'To be fair I don't think that Celina is making a sacrifice if being a nun is what she has wanted all her life.'

Brendan shook his head. 'I have accepted it so let's not talk about unhappy things today.'

Patrick suddenly stopped and said in a reverent tone, 'Just look at that view. Isn't it impressive?' They had turned a bend in the road and the distant mountains were capped with snow, the afternoon sun giving them a glory. 'I've been this way many times,' he went on, 'but I can't say I've ever seen them looking so beautiful.'

Ashling said softly, 'It's because it's Sunday.'

Brendan said, 'It's because of the clarity of the air. I can't remember seeing them look so near.'

Patrick glanced at Ashling and smiled. 'Not exactly the romantic, my son, is he?'

Queenie and Rosin's pleasure at seeing them all made the visit worthwhile.

'What a treat,' Queenie declared. 'It's like having a visit from Santa Claus. I'll make some tea and cut you some cake.'

Although they all tried to refuse as they had not long finished their meal, Queenie insisted that the Lord would not be very pleased if they didn't accept her hospitality.

Rosin, who seemed a little shy at first, asked about the baby, then enquired about the health of Mrs Ferris and before long they had talked about the beauty of the snow-capped mountains, the price of cattle, and Queenie, Brendan and Patrick began on agricultural affairs, giving Ashling a chance to ask Rosin about Conal.

Rosin said, 'He's coming tomorrow. I was hoping you would be here.'

'I shall be. I want to know more about the mission.'

'We talked about it during the crossing and it appears that everything is more or less settled. Ashling, how is Mrs Ferris? Is she getting better after her ordeal?'

'She's made a wonderful recovery and I think it's brought Ross and Tara very close.'

'I'm so glad.' Rosin lowered her voice. 'I always felt so guilty about loving Ross. But how does one not love someone?'

'How indeed?' Ashling said quietly, thinking that

soon she would have to make a decision to leave Ross and Tara. But how was she going to bear leaving Jacinta? The baby had become her life. Without her it would seem so empty.

Ashling was brought into the conversation of the others when Brendan said, 'Ashling, what was the name of the man Ross was telling us about who left all his horses, his cattle and his house to a tramp because he wanted to wander the world?'

'Miller, was it? No, Mel something. Meldrum, that was it.'

'A tramp,' Queenie said softly. 'Now wasn't that kind of him.'

Brendan laughed. 'The tramp didn't want it. He said he liked to go where he pleased and in the end Meldrum left everything to his neighbours and went off with the tramp.'

'Well, would you believe it.' Queenie eyed Brendan solemnly. 'And was the gentleman any happier?'

'Ross said he was told so, but we don't know if it's true, do we?'

'Probably not. We never really know the inner minds of people. And why should we? It's private.'

Patrick got up. 'On that note we must leave. I'm sorry, very sorry. I had intended just to go for a short walk. Ashling guided us here and I'm so glad she did, Mrs McKnott. You and Miss Dannet must come and visit us. Ashling will arrange it.'

Queenie tried to protest that she was not the visiting kind, but Patrick refused to accept it, and was about to say more when Brendan interrupted.

'Well, would you believe it, it's snowing and they're big flakes.'

Queenie walked to the window, then said softly, 'Could there be a more beautiful sight, the purity of the whole countryside unblemished by animal hoof or footstep?'

Brendan laughed, saying it wouldn't be when they had walked over it. Ashling gave him a nudge and shook her head. He looked contrite for a moment then said, 'Oh, Mrs McKnott, I think I can show you something that might interest you.' He brought an envelope from his inside pocket. 'I met a scientist who had drawn designs of snowflakes that had been greatly magnified. I brought them to show the family, then forgot about them.' Brendan spread them on the table and Queenie lit the lamp so they could all see them.

There was silence for a moment, then Queenie said, a note of awe in her voice, 'I can't believe that all these amazing designs are snowflakes.'

Ashling, studying the delicacy of the various patterns, found herself thinking of Ross describing the drawings in the Book of Kells as 'a tracing of angels', and felt a reverence she had never experienced before.

Queenie said to Brendan, 'Thank you for showing them to us, Mr McCoy. I shall always remember your visit every time I look at the snow.'

Patrick and Brendan promised to call again sometime.

'Mrs McKnott is an interesting woman and, although a simple soul, seems to have had some education,' said Brendan.

Ashling repeated what Rosin had told her about Queenie's background and described her life with her awful husband, which had Brendan saying how different her life might have been had she had an intelligent husband.

'But that couldn't happen,' Ashling protested. 'Fate decided she had the man she married. Nothing could change that.'

Both men disagreed, Brendan holding the opinion that a few words could change a person's life and Patrick said, 'Your mother almost decided on the eve of our wedding that she didn't want to get married, and it was only because her parents were furious with her for causing so much upset that she gave in.' He smiled. 'Mind you, she said it was only pre-wedding nerves.'

'No, Papa, you have it all wrong. What her parents said had nothing to do with it. It was ordained from birth that you would both marry.'

This started a discussion that lasted until they arrived home, which led to the others joining in, Ross and Eileen agreeing with Ashling that fate shaped one's life, Eileen stressing that Fiona had been set on a career until fate stepped in and she met Niall and fell in love.

Patrick said patiently, 'That was coincidence, Eileen.'

'It wasn't. Both had been going to different parties and at the last minute changed their minds and went to a dance to which both had been invited. That was not coincidence.'

It was all light-hearted but Ashling wished she could have told them how Ross was in love with Rosin and would possibly have married her had not Tara let a stranger make love to her and become pregnant. And if Ross's father had not got into trouble through business and sought sanctuary with Eileen and Patrick, Tara would never have been able to say that her uncle had seduced her. Ross married her to save the family shame and little Jacinta became his daughter. All this, she was sure, had been mapped out many years before. There was such a strong pattern to it. There was no way anyone could claim that it was all coincidence.

When Ashling was in bed that night she wondered what fate had mapped out for her. To be a spinster? Well, there was one thing certain, nothing could change the path of fate.

Overnight there had been a heavy fall of snow and Ashling awoke the next morning to a sun-filled room and rooftops with the sparkle of diamonds. Hearing the sound of snow being shovelled she got up and went to the window that overlooked the back garden. Ross and

Brendan, with a shovel each, were clearing the paths and using the piled up snow to make a snowman.

Ashling washed and dressed quickly and went downstairs. Tara now had Jacinta's cot in her and Ross's bedroom and had brought her down with them. Tara, who was in the breakfast room, Jacinta in her arms, turned as Ashling came in.

'This little imp has been awake since six o'clock, demanding that I get up. She's excited watching Ross and Brendan clearing the snow. They've already cleared the front path and half the street. It makes me feel exhausted.'

Jacinta, moving up and down, held out her arms and Ashling took her saying, 'Well, and this will be the first snowman you've seen, my darling. Does your papa know you are watching him?'

Tara said, 'No, I didn't want to distract him from —'

There was a sudden silence, then with a sigh she slumped to the floor. For a split second Ashling stood paralysed. Then, putting Jacinta in her crib, she rushed to the window and knocked on it.

Both men looked up, grinning. Then, as Ashling shouted and frantically beckoned, they dropped their shovels and came running.

Ashling, her heart thudding, dropped to the floor and raised Tara. Her face and lips were colourless. Ross came bursting in, saw Tara and shouted to Brendan to call the doctor. He strode to the drinks cabinet, poured out some brandy, then, taking Tara from Ashling, put the glass to her lips.

She moved her head and whispered, 'Kiss me, Ross.' Then, 'Jacinta . . . want to hold her.'

Ashling ran to get the baby. Tara was unable to hold her and Ross put Tara's arm around her and placed Jacinta's cheek to hers.

The doctor arrived, handed Jacinta to Ashling and began to examine Tara.

Ashling saw him shake his head then, as though from a distance she heard him say, 'I'm sorry, Mr Ferris. I'm afraid your wife has gone.'

It was Eileen's anguished cry that brought life to Ashling's limbs. There was a feeling of suspended belief.

Ross just stood saying, 'It can't be . . . It's impossible.' Then Patrick was there trying to comfort him. Brendan brought brandy but Ross wouldn't touch it. The doctor pulled out a chair and insisted that Ross sit down.

Ross stared at him. 'How? Tara was so well.'

'On the face of it, yes, Mr Ferris. But she was a sick woman. Her body had suffered a great deal. She put up a brave fight, wanting you both to enjoy life while you could. I saw her only two days ago. She left a letter with me for you, but asked that you would not read it until after the funeral.

'Oh God.' Ross covered his face. 'If only I had known.'

'She didn't want you to know,' the doctor said gently. 'She did not want sympathy for what she called her second mistake.'

Ashling wondered afterwards how they ever got through that first day. She felt she hated snow because there was such misery, then she realized it was one of the last things Tara had seen, the beauty of the morning, the sun sparkling on the snow, Ross and Brendan making a snowman to please Jacinta. The baby had been solemn all that day.

Fiona and Niall were called back as soon as they could come. There were Catherine and John to tell too, and a message to be sent to Queenie and Rosin. Eileen, who had all but collapsed at first, had became a tower of strength, organizing everything. And when Ross declared she was doing too much she said, 'I'm not doing enough,' and he understood.

Conal called that afternoon, to offer his condolences and sympathies from Queenie and Rosin. Rosin sent Ashling a note to say she would be at the funeral, but would stay in the background. They were all so shocked. Conal could only stay minutes, but somehow they all felt soothed afterwards.

News got around and there were so many callers that the day soon passed.

Fiona and Niall arrived late. Fiona, greatly distressed and unable to stop crying, was full of remorse for not having been nicer to Tara in their younger days. Niall, a quiet young man, got her to understand that her sister would never have borne her any malice, for, by what he had been told, she was not that kind of person.

Ross was so quiet, so withdrawn, that Ashling ached for him. Sometimes if someone was holding Jacinta he would take her back and sit just holding her close, as if she was all he had left, and when Ashling was thinking how strange it was that he was loving a stranger's child, it came to her suddenly that this was what fate was all about. Jacinta had been destined to come into the world to console him when Tara had died.

It seemed to Ashling then that it was all related to the Book of Kells. The beautiful patterns in life, then the black on the white lines . . . a tracing of angels. She mentioned it to Ross.

'How strange,' he said. 'I was thinking about the Book of Kells last night in bed. There must be an affinity between us. Sometime we must go together to Trinity College.'

The following day Eileen broached the subject of Ashling staying at home with her and Patrick when Ross returned home. Ross was a widower now, and people would frown on Ashling living in the house alone with him.

'So what happens to Jacinta?' Ashling demanded. 'Do I just walk out and leave her with only her father to look after her?'

'Now just calm down, Ashling. I was going to suggest that we keep Jacinta here with us.'

'Ross wouldn't part with her. He loves her, she's his life now, the baby is all he has.'

'If he wants to keep Jacinta with him then he will have to employ an elderly nanny.'

'He could employ a housekeeper,' Ashling retorted. 'Then I would be chaperoned, if that is what you want. But let me tell you that Ross would never harm a hair of my head. He has too much respect for me.'

Eileen said gently, 'I want what is best for Ross and Jacinta and for you, Ashling. We have to be sensible. I know that you love Ross and I don't want any harm to come to you. Love causes many problems. Ross needs to be loved, like Tara. It would save a lot of problems if he agrees to let us care for the baby until he can sort out his life. He's in a state of shock at the moment. John is going to suggest that he stays at his house for a time when he returns to London. I think it's a good idea. Ross can come and visit us and be with Jacinta.' When Ashling made no reply, Eileen went on, 'Imagine if you stayed and Ross came home in the evening in a depressed state and didn't want to talk. What could you do? Make idle conversation that he wouldn't want? If he stayed with John, they would go home together and would always have business to discuss. John entertains business friends. Would Ross want to entertain alone? Which is the best picture to help Ross over Tara's death?'

Ashling gave a deep sigh. 'You are right, of course. I'll accept Ross's decision.'

Ross decided to go and live with John for a while. He said to Ashling, 'I just hate to be without Jacinta but I have to do what is best for her welfare. I am only glad that you will be with her, Ashling. Without you there with her I don't think I would have agreed to losing her. She's known you since birth and I've noticed that she will only allow someone else to take her for a while, then she holds out her arms to you. The only other person she snuggled into was Tara. I'll come to Ireland as often as I can.'

The snow soon melted and became slush and when Ashling saw the snowman dissolving she felt she was crying inside. Only days ago Tara had stood with Jacinta in her arms watching the snowman being built. How did one cope with the death of a loved sister?

There was no sun on the day of the funeral but the day was dry with only remnants of snow left. Wreaths arrived from early morning and later the house was full of mourners. Conal was at another funeral and Ross missed his support.

There were several carriages for the mourners, but when the cortège left there must have been nearly fifty people following on foot. Ashling had had no idea that Tara had been so well known. The ache in her throat was appalling and she wished she could shed tears to relieve it, but there was no relief.

The family had their emotions under control, but Ross's suffering showed in his drawn face and pain-filled eyes.

Tara had once said when she was young that she thought it awful that all blinds and curtains were drawn when there was a death in a family, that it seemed to be shutting people in with their misery, whereas the one who had died was going to be with God in heaven, and that should be an honour. Ashling had hated living in the darkened house and drew the curtains immediately they returned from the cemetery. And Jacinta, who had been as solemn as a judge, beamed around at everyone and chuckled.

'Poor darling,' Eileen said, 'It's a good job she doesn't understand that she is motherless.'

'I shouldn't think she will for long,' Fiona said. Although she spoke in a low voice there was a touch of venom in it. 'No doubt her papa will marry that gypsy girl.'

Eileen and Ashling looked at her aghast. Eileen said, 'I just don't believe it. How could you say such a thing when your sister is hardly in her grave.'

Fiona coloured but she shrugged her shoulders. 'Well, he was in love with her, I simply presumed –'

'*Presumed*?' Eileen moved closer. 'I only ask that you stay out of my sight for the rest of the day. I'm ashamed that you are my daughter.' She pushed past Fiona and went out of the room.

Fiona watched her go then turned to Ashling. 'Why all the fuss?'

'Do you really have to ask? I don't want you to come near me today either. I feel sorry for Niall. He's getting a very cold-hearted, vicious woman for a wife. Heaven help him.' Ashling made to move away and Fiona caught her arm.

'What's wrong? We've always been able to have our say without all this rejection.'

'This gets worse by the minute,' Ashling said, shaking her head. 'I can hardly believe it. Ross is suffering from shock. He loved Tara, they were a loving couple. She's dead and you are not really bothered. All you can think of is sullying Ross's name. You were always saying that Tara had never grown up. It's you who've never grown up and it's certainly time you did.'

Many people talked in low voices of other funerals they had attended and of ailments the dead people had suffered from. Others discussed business and the present state of it. Ashling helped to take plates of sandwiches and cakes around, and wondered if the majority had had anything to eat before they left home. She longed

380

for them all to leave and yet, when they *had* all gone, there seemed to be a terrible emptiness. Was it because the time had come to read Tara's letter?

They were all seated around the fire in the drawing room in silence when Ross came in with it. He looked around them all, then said in a low voice, 'A letter to me was enclosed but it is personal. The other one is to go into the secret drawer at the mews cottage.'

He still looked drained, but there was purpose in him that had not been there since Tara had died.

He began by saying, 'Tara wanted you all to know the contents so that you would understand her reason for leaving and perhaps learn from her mistakes. She said she hoped her experiences might help other people in another generation too.'

He opened the letter, scanned the beginning then read:

I hoped to conclude 'To Whom It May Concern' after my experience of living with poverty-stricken people, getting to know their problems and to understand my own motivations in life. God gave me the opportunity of returning to my family and for that I shall be eternally grateful.

I made many, many mistakes, the first being leaving my lovely husband and baby. I know now I should have talked this over with him and enlisted his help. I left with some money to start me off, hoping to get some kind of work where I would learn how the poorer people lived, but my money was stolen from me. By then, my baby had been stolen from home for me because I felt I couldn't live without her.

I very quickly realized how stupied and selfish I had been. I left my baby at a police station to be returned home.

People who lived in utter squalor were kind to me, but nothing could take away the awful degradation of living with rats running around, cockroaches crawling over me, being bitten by fleas who invaded every part of my body, been bitten by bugs who dropped on me from ceilings while I tried to sleep. And there were the smells, overflowing sewers, some overflowing into houses, babies with no more than a vest on them lying in it. Children left on their own all day because their parents had to go out to work, some women earning no more than a few pence. One woman had had eight miscarriages and went to work the day she had had the last one.

I didn't know that such utter misery existed in the world, didn't know that people just existed without hope.

I became ill and was nursed back to health by criminals. When I felt that I had not long to live I came back home, almost crawling the last half-mile. And it was then I learnt that my one big sin was selfishness. Always had been, but I would not acknowledge it.

My family were wonderful to me and I lapped up all their love and attention. I tended to my baby, not wanting anyone to hold her. I wanted all the love I could get and I gave, in my own way, having come to realize that to love and to be given love is the most important and wonderful thing in life. But because I was selfish I didn't tell my family everything about how dreadful the lives of poverty-stricken people could be. I didn't want their attention to be taken from me.

Lately, I have written numerous letters to well-known people to plead with them to help these desperate people and now I ask my family and friends that they will do all they can to help the poor and sick.

God bless you all. Tara Ferris.

In the silence that followed, every one in the room was unashamedly crying.

Fiona was the first to speak. She said, a tremor in her voice, 'I must ask forgiveness for my behaviour,' and hurried out. Niall was about to follow her when Eileen indicated that she would go.

The silence continued and Ross was about to speak

when Eileen came in with Fiona, who murmured an apology.

Ross said, 'I think we will all feel a little guilty at the revelations of Tara, but we do know that this was not Tara's intention. She wanted us to help and we will. As this has been an upsetting day I suggest it's something that can be discussed tomorrow.

They all agreed.

29

It was not that everyone was bright the following morning, but the awful feeling of gloom had gone and they were able to discuss Tara and her project without anyone dissolving into tears.

Although Tara had said she had written to well-known people for help, no list was found of any names. In the end Ashling suggested they get in touch with Conal at the mission in Dublin and enlist his help.

His visit was rewarding. He said that wealthy people already helping at the mission would speak to Members of Parliament and get things started, but warned there could be long delays before anything would get under way.

A journalist friend of Conal wrote a rousing article on the disgrace of people dying of starvation, of babies dying at birth because of their mothers' malnutrition, and of sewage seeping into houses where families were having to sleep on floors with only sacks or old clothes to cover them.

Money came in straight away after this and Conal suggested a body of responsible people to handle the project.

The day came when Eileen told Ross that they must make arrangements about Jacinta.

He looked up startled. 'Yes, of course.' He turned to Ashling. 'And you will be staying here too, Ashling . . . Forgive me. I think I must have been living in a fool's paradise, trying to persuade myself that I'm waiting for Tara to come home.' His shoulders sagged.

Ross was desperate to keep in touch with Jacinta and he said he would pay a visit every month.

It was when Ross and Eileen were alone that she said, 'I have a secret I promised never to tell you, but you have a misconception of someone you know and I feel that it's all wrong. I'm between the Devil and the deep blue sea.'

'It's about my parents, isn't it?'

Eileen looked at him startled. 'Y-yes.'

'And you want to tell me that Addison Ferris is not my father?'

Her expression was suddenly bleak. 'Oh, Ross, I'm sorry I've started all this.'

'I had to be told. I've wondered for a long time why Addison began to hate me after treating me decently when I was young.' He paused. 'And John Davies is my father.'

Eileen's eyes went wide. 'I wasn't going to tell you that. I simply felt I had to tell you the truth about Addison to ease my conscience. I lied so terribly about him because I never wanted to put your mother in a bad light. I loved her so much. Addison never knew for certain that you weren't his son until your mother confessed that you were John's child. I think you would be seven or eight. And it was then he became stern towards you, sometimes brutal. But to give him his due, he never told a soul about your mother's sin.' She paused, then went on, 'The family has a terrible record – myself, your mother, Tara. And because of our sins the innocent suffer.'

'John has been a good father figure to me. He taught me many things, got me started in business. Tara knew sorrow, but she also knew love. Something she said to me when she returned home after her awful experience seems more poignant now. She said, "If one knows happiness, knows love, even for a short time in one's life, it's worth having been born." '

'Oh, Ross.' His aunt's eyes filled with tears. 'It's taken my poor dead daughter to make me actually realize what I've passed over all these years. An appreciation of Patrick's love, his goodness, his loyalty. He must have known of my affair, but never once hinted at it. I think my worst sin has been in longing to be with a man who robbed me.'

'That's behind you, Aunt Eileen. You've been a good wife, a good mother. I think the Lord will allow us our dreams if we don't go beyond that.'

'From now on, there will be no more dreams,' she said grimly. 'I can I assure you of that.'

Ross returned to London, Tara's death and Eileen's words heavy on his mind.

When he saw John he said quietly, 'I don't think it would be wise at this stage to call you Father, but I want you to know that I know.'

For a moment John was emotional, then he gripped Ross's shoulder.

'I'm glad you know, Ross. Who told you, your aunt?'

Ross repeated the conversation and John nodded.

'I was always angry with your father because your mother and I were going to be married. He was endowed with a great deal of charm and your mother was a little weak. She admitted it herself. But that part of our life is over.' He smiled. 'It's like branching out into a new one.'

When Ross was next going to Ireland to spend a long weekend and Eileen asked John if he would like to come too, he agreed at once, which, as Ashling said, would make it easier for Ross to leave Jacinta and have company going back home.

Ashling began to feel a great peace at home. Yellow and purple crocuses were everywhere and buds were opening on trees and in hedges, in beautiful shades of green. To Ashling it was as though they were telling her that a different kind of life was beginning and although she would not see Ross for a month she had Jacinta to love and care for. She did not look any further than that. She would go one step at a time.

Jacinta was made a fuss of and was always lively. Fiona insisted that Niall hold Jacinta so he would get used to handling a baby and when she began to explain how to hold her he said, smiling, 'I know how to handle babies,' and proceeded to show how competent he was.

One morning Eileen decided she would take Jacinta out in her perambulator, giving Ashling the opportuninty to go to see Queenie and find out news of Rosin.

Queenie held her tight and talked about the tragedy of Tara.

Ashling asked about Rosin, and Queenie said, 'She seems to like being at the mission. She likes working with Conal. What a clever man he is. Sometimes, however, she's looked very sad and I think she worries about her sister.'

Ashling thought her sadness could be because of Ross.

Queenie always had plenty to talk about and when Ashling said she would bring Jacinta one morning, she was overjoyed. She would have to start making Jacinta a little woolly lamb, which had Ashling thinking on her way home that Queenie would have revelled in having grandchildren near her.

Ashling realized she had come to depend on seeing Ross regularly. She also realized how much Tara and Fiona had been a part of her life at home. They had done everything together. Now Fiona was seldom in, and not once asked Ashling if she wanted to go with her. And yet they had made up the rift there had been between them, with Fiona begging forgiveness for being so thoughtless.

The first week was the worst. Then Ashling settled down to a routine and the times she enjoyed the most were taking Jacinta to visit the tenants where there were other children and to see Queenie. Queenie knitted Jacinta a curly white lamb from wool she had spun herself and it became the baby's favourite toy, cuddling it to her and crooning to it in her own way.

Then Liam and Dermot were in Killorglin for a week and they spent nearly every evening with the family, both making a fuss of Ashling and pretending to be jealous of the other getting more attention from her.

Ross wrote twice a week and ended each letter saying that he missed Jacinta and Ashling. John wrote saying that Ross was coping and they were not to worry.

Ashling always wrote by return to Ross, knowing how much her letters would mean to him, being without the baby, always telling him something that would make him smile.

A highlight of that first month since Ross went home was a visit from Rosin and Conal, who thought they would have a break.

'Rosin has worked fourteen hours at a stretch this past week,' Conal said with an affectionate smile. 'Such a worker. The people love and admire her for her dedication.'

Rosin dismissed this. 'It's Conal who is to be admired. He's tireless. I just don't know how he keeps up the pace. Some nights he doesn't even go to bed.'

Patrick said, 'Well, I must say you both seem to thrive on it. But then the Lord is on your side.'

Later, Ashling and Rosin managed to get a little time on their own and the first thing that Rosin asked was, 'How is Ross? I would have liked to have written to him, but thought it best not to.'

'I think it's been hard for him, but I feel he's recovering a little. He'll be here on Friday evening.'

'Friday? Oh, I wonder if I could persuade Conal to stay an extra day. I would like to see Ross.'

'And I'm sure he would be pleased to see you, Rosin.'

Ashling was aware of a flatness in her voice and she added, brightly. 'I'll have to have a talk with him.'

Rosin shook her head. 'No, on second thoughts let things take their course. I never want to upset any of Conal's plans. He manages to do all the things he does because of discipline. He's a wonderful man. It's an honour to work with him. He's staying with a friend in Killorglin and I'm going to stay with Queenie. Do you know, I miss her. I think of her now as a mother.'

'I'm glad,' Ashling said softly. 'She thinks of you as a daughter. She'll be thrilled to see you.'

When Rosin and Conal had gone, Eileen looked thoughtful. 'I can't weigh Rosin up. Is she in love with Conal?'

'I think she's in love with all that he does for the poor. It could be hero worship. I'm sure she's still in love with Ross. The moment we were alone she asked after him.'

Eileen said nothing more and Ashling tried to weigh up the situation. She had seen an affection for Rosin in Conal's eyes and affection or adoration for him in Rosin's eyes. Then she had felt hopeful that they might get together, but then when Rosin had asked about Ross there had been a tenderness in her voice.

Ashling thought she would know how Ross felt when he and John came on Friday and Ross was told about Rosin's visit.

But she found it impossible to get his reaction as Eileen mentioned Rosin's visit while he was playing with Jacinta.

'How is she?' he asked. 'Enjoying her work?' The next moment he was laughing and saying, 'Jacinta Ferris, your tiny nails need cutting. You are drawing blood on my cheek in your effort to show me how pleased you are to see me again.'

That weekend Ashling and Ross were never alone, not even for five minutes. If they were not being

389

whipped off to have dinner with friends of the family, Eileen was entertaining or Ross was out with Patrick and Brendan, discussing agriculture.

When he and John were ready to leave on the Sunday evening, Ross put his hands on Ashling's shoulders and said softly, 'We haven't had much time for a talk, Ashling. Next time I shall come a day earlier and we can spend it together.' He kissed her on the cheek and added in a low voice, 'I still miss you.'

Ross did not get a day longer on his next visit. He had been caught up in business. And it was the same next time and the next until Ashling came to the conclusion that he was deliberately trying to avoid any close contact with her because he would be marrying Rosin eventually and Ashling would be losing Jacinta. The thought was heart-breaking.

When she mentioned it to her mother, Eileen said, 'I like Rosin, but I don't think she would be right for Ross. She's wrapped up in her work at the mission. On the other hand, if she really loves him I'm sure she would make the sacrifice. And she does love Jacinta.'

Then one day they had a very unexpected visit from Charles Kent, which caused quite a stir of excitement.

'I'm being treated like royalty,' he laughed. 'You are too kind. I had some business in Cork and thought it would be nice to call and see you all.'

He was asked to stay the night, and accepted.

Charles was a most interesting man who talked about America and how it was a more open society. The people were less reserved than the English. One could meet another traveller and he would be a friend within minutes.

The different way of life generally intrigued not only Fiona but Ashling.

Fiona was already there in her mind's eye, working as a stenographer, and she said to Ashling, 'We could both go. You could get a job as a nanny.'

390

And when her mother said, 'And where does Niall fit into all this?' she replied, 'He would have to get a job there too.'

This was when her father stepped in. 'Just a moment, Fiona, just a moment. There are immigration laws. They don't let everyone into the country.'

Fiona dismissed this. There were ways and means, she said, and would have taken over the conversation had not Eileen cast a despairing glance at her husband, and he asked Charles about other aspects of the country, not allowing Fiona other than a few words here and there.

Fiona had been invited to a card game at Niall's house but wanted to cancel and bring Niall home. Her father said, 'No, Fiona, you have an obligation. I insist you go.'

She left reluctantly, and when Eileen apologized for her daughter's enthusiasm Charles smiled and said, 'Fiona is what is known as a go-getter over there and would probably have no difficulty in finding an excellent position.'

Brendan had been away for the day and when he came in later he was as enthusiastic as Fiona about emigrating.

Ashling, although enjoying the evening, had said very little and when she and her mother left the men to have a talk over their drinks Eileen said, 'What a charming person Charles is. He has a lovely courteous manner and such a beautiful voice. There's music in it.'

Ashling, remembering how Tara had been very taken with Charles, said, 'I could imagine it would be very easy to fall in love with him.'

Eileen gave her a quick look. 'Don't say that you would be wanting to go rushing off to America?'

'No, interesting as it was hearing about it, I'm afraid I'm a stay-at-home. When Ross marries, which I should imagine he will eventually, I shall try and get another nannying job.'

Eileen was silent for a moment, then she said gently, 'You need a home and children of your own, Ashling, and I don't think you would have any difficulty in finding yourself a nice man. Charles never took his eyes off you all evening.'

'Now, Mama, don't start trying to marry me off. I'm quite happy as I am.'

'Are you, my love?'

Ashling made no answer.

Charles was leaving early the next morning and when after breakfast he was ready to leave, he said, 'I'm going back to America for a month. Then I shall be back to settle down. When I do return I hope I can reciprocate your wonderful hospitality when you are in London.'

Patrick said, 'We have thoroughly enjoyed your company, Mr Kent, and we shall look forward to seeing you again when we visit Ross in six or seven weeks' time.'

Eileen gave him a questioning look, but did not say anything until they were waving Charles away in the carriage when she said, 'I didn't know that any arrangement had been made to visit Ross.'

'It hasn't, but it will be made. I should imagine by then that Ross will have had time to find out whether he's still interested in Miss Dannet and, if so, I shall see that Ashling gets to meet our Mr Kent quite often. He's a fine fellow and very comfortably off and he certainly had eyes for Ashling.'

Ashling said, annoyed, 'Papa, when I marry, *if* I marry, I shall certainly choose my own husband. There will be no arranged marriage for me.'

She was about to storm off when Fiona arrived home, breathless, wanting to know if Charles was still here.

Patrick happily told her that she had missed him by two minutes and Fiona was furious.

'I wanted to come home but Niall insisted I stay as usual. I think he was jealous. He has no ambition to go to America. I shall go alone.'

'Why not?' Patrick said, and cupping Ashling's elbow he led her away saying, 'I fear we are going to hear a lot about America if I don't put my foot down.'

'Both feet,' Eileen said behind them in a tight voice.

Ashling did a lot of thinking during the next few days, having been aware that Charles Kent had been watching her quite a lot. He was a very attractive man, very charming, and she knew he loved children. He was a man it would be easy to love. But, even if he were genuinely attracted towards her, would she want marriage on that basis? Her love went very deep for Ross. But then so did Rosin's and it was Rosin that he wanted.

A few days later she was in the garden taking out some weeds when she heard firm footsteps behind her. She turned and stared in astonishment as she saw Ross striding towards her.

Her heart began to thud at his grim expression. She took a few steps.

'Ross, what's happened?'

'I'll tell you what's happened. You didn't tell me you were thinking of marrying Charles Kent.'

'Marrying him? Who told you that?'

'Fiona. I had a letter from her.'

Ashling's lips tightened. 'Oh, she did, did she? Well, she won't be able to write letters for a long time when I'm finished with her. She should have her fingers cut off!' She stormed away and Ross ran after her.

'Ashling, calm down.' He caught her by the arm but she pulled away and ran on.

Fiona, who was on the lawn, turned at seeing her, then backed away as Ashling reached out for her.

'You miserable lying wretch. I'll cut off your fingers.'

She grabbed her arm and began pulling her towards the house. Eileen came running and Ross caught hold of Ashling and drew her to him. She collapsed against him and burst into tears.

Eileen, although not knowing exactly what had happened, started pushing Fiona towards the house saying, 'For once you've gone too far. You can go to America and good riddance to you!'

Ross put his arm around Ashling and walked her towards a seat. 'Now then,' he said gently. 'Let us sit down and talk this over.'

Ashling, having calmed down, wiped her eyes. 'Fiona lied when she told you that I was marrying Charles Kent. He never even hinted at such a thing. He was at Cork, thought he would call on us and stayed overnight. The talk was mostly about America.'

'But why should Fiona lie to me about such a thing? She had nothing to gain. Not unless she wanted to hurt me for some reason. I had told her in my last letter that I wanted to marry you.'

Ashling looked up. 'Marry me? But I thought that Rosin . . .'

'Rosin and I had a long talk about ten days ago. I knew when you had been away for a few months that it was you I wanted, Ashling. I could cope without Rosin, but I knew I would never manage without you. Rosin told me then that Conal had asked her to marry him and now she could give him his answer. She was extremely fond of him she said and they would work splendidly together. It was the kind of life she wanted and would not want any other.' Ross paused, then went on, speaking softly, 'Will you marry me, Ashling? It won't be for a while but I ache to know.'

All Ashling could think of was how unromantic it was. Ross had rushed here because he thought another man wanted to marry her and she had been in a rage with Fiona.

She said, 'Are you sure you want to marry me? I was threatening to cut off my sister's fingers.'

A smile played about his lips. 'I've wanted to strangle a number of people in my life. We would make a good pair.'

Ashling found it impossible to respond.

Eileen came up. 'Look, why don't you two go for a walk while I get Fiona sorted out. She doesn't seem to think she's done any wrong. But then, she never does. Why don't you go and see Queenie? She would love to see you both.'

Ross looked at Ashling. 'Would you like to?'

She got up. 'I don't mind. Do you want to take Jacinta?'

Eileen said quickly, 'She's having her morning nap. It would be a shame to disturb her. You go off on your own. I'm sure you'll have plenty to talk about. I'll see you later.'

Ashling and Ross left the garden and, crossing the road, opened the field gate. Neither spoke.

As they neared the stream Ross said, 'I remember when I was a boy an elderly woman saying she hated streams, they were always so querulous. I didn't know what the word meant. I asked my mother and she said it meant complaining, peevish. I told her I didn't think that streams were at all complaining, they were joyous and she explained gently that the old lady was not a happy person, that she had had a lot of trouble in her life, so nothing seemed very bright to her. Then my mother added, "Always try to see beauty in nature, Ross, in streams and rivers and waterfalls", and so I have tried to.' They stopped at the stream and Ross said, 'Just look at it.'

The water rushed over the stones, leapt over obstacles, splashed into a pool and, brimming over, ran happily on.

What was he trying to tell her? That she was like the old woman, miserable? She had been grumbling to herself that his proposal of marriage had not been very romantic, but hadn't he come all this way to tell her he loved her and that he wanted to marry her? She was the unromantic one for not realizing this. Romance should be in the soul. Hadn't someone once said that two people could find romance in a cow byre if they truly loved one another?

She turned to him and said softly, 'I love you, Ross, have done since I was a child. At the moment I cannot think of anything more wonderful than being your wife and mother to Jacinta.'

'Ashling...' His strong arms wrapped around her and she could feel his heart pounding. His kisses were gentle at first, then as they became more passionate she could hear music ... and knew it was the singing of the stream.

A beautiful, romantic sound.